Dark Variant

Broken Heavens, Book one

Richard Canning

To Georgina

Contents

Chapter One

K asper held the scope over his eyes. It sensed the warmth of his skin and tightened, gripping his face and pressing firmly against his cheeks. He let go and its lens painted the world with vivid colours. Satisfied, he leaned forward and looked out of the window.

Far below, he saw people heading home from the city centre. The lens followed them along the wide, grey street, humming as it painted each person red then moving on to the next. After three red figures, the lens settled on someone heading against the flow, back towards the city centre. It hummed for a second, chirped twice, then painted the figure green.

"Got her," said Kasper.

Leon sat a few feet away from Kasper, out of sight of the window, with his back against an empty filing cabinet. Rows of desks sat around him in disarray. Their drawers lay smashed on the floor, leaving dark, oblong mouths yawning over their spewed contents.

Street art and vulgar slogans competed for space across every upright surface in the deserted office. The whole place summed up the state of decline across the city—a sad sight for people who had once worked here, but now an ideal watch point for Leon and Kasper.

"We have you on the scope," said Leon, whispering into his cupped hand.

The local troopers had the traffic in this district restricted. Nobody should fly past at this height. Even if a trooper came this way, their engines were loud, so Leon and Kasper could take cover before it even came close.

Kasper pushed the window to one side and felt the breeze on his face. He tugged on the tension strap of his harness. Satisfied, he stepped out of the window, planted both feet on the outside wall, and leant forward. Looking down, he saw the green-lit figure pass directly below him.

"Tell her to slow down. She'll be early," said Kasper.

"Slow down. You'll arrive early," said Leon.

The green figure slowed. Kasper looked ahead of it to the open-fronted kiosk. It squatted at the base of two tall, dark buildings, like a glowing, multi-coloured toy dropped at the feet of a parent.

He could see the owner serving his first customer: a man, overweight, likely obese. He lingered, enjoying a chat with the owner while another customer waited a short distance behind him.

"He's open. We're on," said Kasper.

Leon reached into his backpack and pulled out a short, solid tube with two buttons at the top. He pressed the first button, and a tiny blue light came on beside it. He stretched out his arm and handed to the tube to Kasper.

"RDP," he said.

"Thanks. Tell Alis we're ready," said Kasper.

He watched the green figure continue towards the kiosk. She got almost to within range of the lights, then stopped. "What's she doing? Ask her why she's stopped."

Far below him, Alis squatted, unslung her pack, and rummaged through it. Her hair fell from her shoulders, covering her face.

"You think I'm doing this with other people around?" she said.

"It is a kiosk. Customers are inevitable," said Leon.

"OK, but I'm waiting," she said. "It's too risky with two. I'm not getting caught and I don't want to hurt them."

Kasper watched her squat motionless in the street. She was taking too long. People would notice a woman crouching like that. She needed to keep walking. "Tell her she needs to get moving. If she stays like that someone might think she's a stray dog and shoot her."

At street level, Alis grinned. "Funny. Hilarious."

The customer turned and walked away from the kiosk. Kasper felt adrenaline tickle his fingers. Alis got to her feet, shouldered the bag, and walked as casually as she could into the bright, multi-coloured pool of light.

The owner muttered goodbye to his customer, then nodded in her direction.

"Contact. They are talking," said Leon.

Kasper saw Alis's hand drift slowly towards her right trouser pocket. "Put it on speaker."

A green light flashed on the wall behind the owner. The man froze. His voice crackled through Leon's wrist.

"Say that again," said the owner.

Kasper's stomach dropped. "Voice ID. Tell her to shut up and do it quick!"

"Alis, do not speak again," Leon said into his hand, "You have to be fast now."

Kasper pressed the second button on the dark tube. An orange light flashed beside the blue one. On the ground, Alis said nothing.

The owner's voice came over loud clear. "What was that? I didn't catch it. Speak up."

"Now," said Kasper.

"Go. Do it now," said Leon.

The owner insisted. "If you had nothing to hide, you'd answer me."

Kasper's scope picked up a tiny flash as something flew across the space between Alis and the kiosk. Alis threw herself to the ground. The owner lurched for the exit. Kasper hit the last button on the RDP.

A loud crack came from inside the kiosk. The outline of the little building quivered for a moment, then its lights fizzed and popped like fireworks, plunging it into darkness.

Kasper watched Alis slide cat-like over the counter, pull out her tablet, then slam it onto the reader beside the till. He guessed she'd choose a pouch of sweet-teasers. Next, she just had to enter a massive overpayment, claim the change and run.

The scope showed her green silhouette leaning down and checking on the owner. He'd be fine, thought Kasper. He'd wake soon with nothing but severe nausea and an urgent claim for his insurance company.

She slid back over the counter and disappeared into the gathering darkness. Above the silent kiosk, the hum of a District Trooper's skiff filled the air.

Kasper and Leon scrambled towards the stairs. Traces of the RDP signal still hung in the air, and the skiff could trace it straight to their window in the ruined building. They cleared each flight of stairs in quick leaps, hitting the ground floor at full speed and bursting onto the street. They ran three blocks to the west in complete silence, using the shadows of buildings for cover. When they finally stopped, Kasper had to bend double to get his breath back.

Leon's broad frame heaved from the run, but his breathing barely registered the effort. "The Trooper has not followed us."

Kasper raised a finger. "Yet. He's not followed us *yet*. Let's go."

Leon pulled up his sleeve. A narrow groove in his arm flashed with tiny lights and complex displays. His large fingers jabbed at it, making multiple lights wink and flash as he worked.

Somewhere above him, a large black object shifted away from the side of the building. Disturbed by the movement, a group of oilbats exploded into a furious mess of flapping wings.

One flew low and Kasper, picking his moment, caught its legs as it passed overhead. "Watch this."

Leon shook his head. "There is no time. We have to go."

Kasper laughed and nodded at the large object making its way down the wall. "We've got a minute. You get ready to go."

He gripped the oilbat's scaled ankles and lifted his legs off the ground. His weight pulled them both down for a moment, then the creature pulsed its wings harder, lifting Kasper and carrying him through the air. He pulled down hard on the bat's left ankle. To his delight, it banked left. But the bat was small, and it struggled with his weight. He let go and watched the bat fly off into the night.

The black object floated down and settled gracefully on the street. A door slid open on either side to reveal the blue-green glow of a cockpit. Leon climbed inside, shaking his head at Kasper's stunt.

Kasper slid into his seat inside Leon's Humming Bird. The memory gel moulded around his waist and held him tight as the doors shot home. Electronic lights bounced off their faces, and a thin steel tube snaked out towards Leon's stomach.

"Ready for transit," said the craft loudly.

"What are you doing?" said Kasper, looking nervously up at the sky through the tinted glass, "You didn't think to mute that stupid voice?"

"I never do," mumbled Leon, jabbing at his wrist, "There. Done. No more sounds."

Kasper let out a dramatic sigh. "First Alis with the voice ID, now you with the foghorn. I'm amazed we're not cuffed to a trooper already!"

Leon waved away the thin steel tube. It retreated obediently, and a rather clumsy looking plastic stick rose from the floor in its place.

"Don't use that. Use your cable," said Kasper, "you're not good enough to out-fly a skiff."

"It feels uncomfortable," said Leon, "and my socket is inflamed from the dust in that office."

Kasper looked sceptical. "Fine. But you'll connect if there's trouble?"

"Yes," said Leon. "I will stay within my limits."

"You've said that before," said Kasper. "Sometimes I wonder if you've secretly upgraded those limits."

Leon smiled and urged the craft off the ground. It lifted off smoothly, and Leon eased back on the joystick, taking a slight bank to the right as it climbed.

"Are you supposed to be banking right?" said Kasper.

Leon grunted and moved the joystick a fraction. The ship corrected itself to level flight.

"Great," said Kasper.

A moment later, the bright beam of a Trooper's searchlight swept across them.

"How did that get here so quickly?" said Leon.

"Voice ID gave them a head's-up!" said Kasper.

Leon shifted the stick, and they jumped forwards, climbed for a few seconds, then slammed into the branches of a nearby tree. He wrestled with the joystick, but the little ship stayed wedged in place. The Bird's turbine screamed as he battled to break free. Behind them, the skiff drew closer, pinning them to the branches with its searchlight.

"We're going to get jail time! Use the bioglide!" said Kasper.

Leon didn't answer. He pushed again, and the Bird tore itself free. The momentum shot them straight towards the nearest building. He turned, but the ship's wing screeched like a child as it scraped the metal hoarding. Kasper thought of the Trooper laughing as they bumbled their getaway.

The skiff accelerated to keep pace with them. Lights flashed frantically on the Bird's dashboard.

"He's trying to take control!" said Kasper

That did it for Leon. He dismissed the joystick into the floor, and the bioglide's tube snaked out towards him. He grabbed it, plugged it into his stomach, and sat back.

The craft jolted once, then shot skywards, pressing Kasper into his seat. It hugged the corners and walls of the buildings in the upper flight levels of the city, then dropped its nose and sped down to the lower levels. It met the flow of evening traffic and disappeared among the thousands of other lights and engines. High above them, the skiff continued to probe the gloom of the upper levels.

"That turned out OK," said Leon.

He laughed, a familiar gurgling, wheezy sound that never failed to make Kasper smile.

"Yeah, right," said Kasper. "We were lucky. Screening really is everywhere now. Even those tiny kiosks have voice ID. "

"Makes sense. The RIBs are worried the city will go the same way as Trage," said Leon.

Kasper shifted in his seat to get a better view of the city lights flowing beneath them. "Trage is hundreds of miles away. We've only got the edge of what's hanging over that place. It won't get any worse here."

"Nobody knows for certain," said Leon. "I heard people saying the authorities have sent a message back to the Milky Way, asking the colonies to share their research."

Kasper snorted and shook his head. "They won't know anything. They've done nothing useful for decades, except kill each other for clean water. I don't know why anybody wants to live there."

Leon adjusted the cable attached to his stomach. "Even if they did send a message, it will be several months before a reply arrives. By that time, the wind might have brought the cloud over to us from Trage."

Kasper looked across at his friend. Leon stared straight ahead, his face unreadable as he talked to the craft in silent protocols. The sight reminded Kasper that Leon probably had more in common with the Bird than he did with him. Surrounded by solid machinery, he suddenly felt like the soft flesh inside the shell of an oyster.

"Let it come. Whatever happens, the Bureau's got no right to be checking for ID in the streets like that," he said. "And sod its Rib enforcers, too. They're all on a power trip. Alis better make it back OK, or we'll do more in this city than knock over a kiosk."

Chapter Two

A pale boy, possibly five years old, stepped out of the derelict building. He stared hard at the cuffs buzzing quietly around his wrists. Irvana crouched out of sight on the other side of the street, too far away to see the tears drawing clean lines down his dirty cheeks.

A ragged line of children followed him out of hiding and onto the pavement. Four girls and two boys, all with the filthy, malnourished look of the city's scavenging orphans.

The line of small bodies shuffled towards the open doors of a hovering Containment Wagon. Large, shiny gold lettering on the side of the vehicle spelled out "Registration and Information Bureau - Trage."

Three men ushered the children towards its yawning doorway, each of them with the letters "R.I.B." stamped onto the backs of their flack vests. Irvana saw the bare metal benches waiting inside the vehicle. Large safety clamps hung at intervals above each bench, each one like open jaws, ready to clamp a child in place before the unit sped away to whichever of the state's welfare blocks expected them.

Shouts came from inside the building. The line of children kept moving, heads bowed and eyes on their cuffs. Irvana's eyes scanned the dark windows of the building. Light flashed in a window on the fourth floor. The sound of gunfire split the air.

Adrenaline rushed into her legs. Her mouth went dry and instinct urged her to sprint towards the building. Instead, she swallowed hard and stayed rooted to the spot. She'd seen similar events in similar cities, on similar worlds. The needs of the many must always outweigh the needs of the few, no matter who those few were. If she succeeded in her task, there would be no need for governments to assault any more children.

Two men appeared from the building and shook their heads at the other three. The man closest to the floating Wagon gestured at the children pinned into their seats. The edges of the doorway responded, spiralling inwards until the dim interior lights shrunk to a pinpoint, then winked out. With its human cargo secured, the vehicle glided forward and disappeared quietly down the street.

Irvana tried to remind herself that what she had just seen was further proof of the rot setting into the dying city. It was just research. But the only image in her mind was of a little boy staring dumbfounded at his weeping friends. She blew out the emotion and looked up at the sky.

The vast cloud sat low above the rooftops, slowly gathering its strength and bearing down on Trage like a black mood. Except this cloud wasn't black, it was deep purple, with a swollen centre and thin strands of colour snaking in all directions across the sky.

Its broad surface rippled and rolled as Irvana watched. She studied it carefully, her eyes clicking and whirring as they adjusted her focus. Around the edges of the dark mass, she picked out a narrow curtain of lighter purple. Excitement flared in her stomach. That hadn't been there when she'd checked a few hours ago.

The rate of decay in this city was as scientifically exciting as it was mortally terrifying. On nearby worlds, similar cities were still functioning after several years of infection. But it had arrived above Trage less than six months ago, and already the place was a near-deserted, decaying metropolis.

The cloud was different here, far more powerful and aggressive than the others. She reached behind her and tapped the cylinder strapped to her back. *But so is this*, she thought.

She headed off the main street and into the narrower routes ahead. Progress through the safer parts of the city had been good, but it paid to avoid being out in the open now, as she drew closer to the centre of the city.

Dilapidated buildings stared down at her as she walked. Every so often she passed a shell of a vehicle, stripped of anything valuable by local scavengers. Some people still scraped out an existence even deep within this dark zone.

Shadows lengthened around her as she went, giving the streets more places to hide their hostility. Clanks and thumps echoed around the buildings now and then, but she saw no one. The dark zone stayed silent, its miles of empty streets and buildings forming a mausoleum for the dead hopes of a once vibrant city.

As evening turned to dusk, she stopped, adjusted the settings on her eyes, and watched with satisfaction as the darkness ahead turned as clear as day. Pleased with her modification, she allowed herself a small, private smile.

Ahead of her, a tower rose behind the next block of city buildings. The top of it pierced the menacing bulk of the cloud above. Irvana felt her spirits lift at the sight of her final objective.

A short distance later, she stopped. Roughly a hundred metres away sat a line of broken vehicles, stretching from one side of the street to the other. She couldn't see any lights nearby, so she put it down to a local gang trying to mark out their territory. It might even be a relic from the early riots in the city. She could jump it easily, but first she wanted to be certain there was nothing more to it.

She shrugged her shoulder, and a panel slid back on her wrist. She watched the scan of the barrier building on the display. The outlines of three lightly armed humans appeared at the eastern end of the barricade. She sighed and snapped the scanner shut.

Three would not be a problem, but it troubled her that the barrier sat right here, directly across her path to the tower. She told herself it couldn't be anything more than a coincidence. She'd moved fast through the gloomy streets, picking her path carefully, always avoiding a direct approach to the tower. The chances of an ambush had to be slim to none. Yet, here it sat, a

wall-to-wall blockade with an armed reception committee squatting behind it.

She thought for a moment. *If you're just marking territory, why hide? Gangs that want to keep people out try to show off their strength. They set up patrols, show off their firepower and intimidate anyone they come across. They don't hide. You only hide if you expect someone to arrive at any moment and want to catch or kill them before they know you're there.*

She hadn't seen another soul on the streets for the last few miles. Yet, here were three in one place. This was not good at all. If they expected her, then there would be more of them waiting between here and the tower. She considered retracing her route for a block or two, then trying to skirt around the barrier. Contact base, her training said. If compromised, always contact base. But transmissions in the dark zone were unreliable. The chances of a message reaching back home to the orbiting Salient were almost zero. She was on her own, with only one night to complete her work. She decided not to waste time going around.

She raised her right hand towards the barricade and broke into a sprint. Her palm flipped inwards, fitting snugly against the inside of her forearm. The skin of her arm shifted to flow smoothly over her hand, covering it until, seconds later, it had become part of her forearm. At the same time, the stump of her bent wrist collapsed in the centre, leaving a wide, solid tube jutting from the end of her arm.

She levelled the newly formed barrel at the eastern end of the line, and fired three rapid blasts Each one flew towards the barricade and streaked through empty vehicle windows.

Screams rang out. Tiny projectiles tore into skin and exploded, splitting bone and sending lumps of flesh spiralling into the air.

Irvana dived over the bonnet of a vehicle and cleared the barricade with ease. She dropped to the ground and rolled smoothly into a crouch. The three ruined bodies lay twisted on the ground. She started another scan of the area. It showed no other life-forms nearby.

She stood, then stared down at the bodies. Her skin flowed rapidly around her arm, and her hand reappeared. It snapped back into position, and she flexed her fingers. She knew she should press on, but these corpses had once been alive beneath an atmosphere in an unprecedented rate of decay. Her scientific curiosity won the struggle and, still wary of the chance of another attack, she walked over to inspect the dismembered bodies.

At once, she regretted having blasted them. Her handiwork had made them difficult to examine. The nearest two bodies had opposite ends that were still mostly intact. Between them, she could at least guess what a full body might look like.

She formed a small blade with her hand and cut into the soft flesh of the first corpse. A thin trickle of blood spurted leaked from the incision. She ignored it, but the stench of decaying flesh made her gag. She turned her head and had to swallow hard to avoid throwing up.

Like other victims of the sickness, these people had lived with their own daily deterioration. But the internal organs, though slimy and misshapen, had kept their basic structure. She felt another rush of excitement. It looked as though their bodies had stopped deteriorating some time ago, despite staying under the infected sky.

Ideas of discovering an antidote somewhere in the dark zone flashed across her mind. She continued to prod, poke, and dissect the remains, but found no evidence of more recent physiological breakdown. She grinned to herself in the gloom.

Stopping for this long risked the success of the mission, but it had brought results.

She worked her way to the remaining upper torso and shifted it onto its back. A thick waft of decay hit her full in the face. She pulled away again to avoid vomiting. Recovering, she turned back and looked down. Her stomach jumped. The body had three fully grown arms attached to it.

Each arm finished at oversized hands with long, thick nails on each finger—not quite claws, but enough to inflict more than superficial damage to bare skin. The face looked unremarkable at first, but the longer she looked, the less human it seemed. The bone around the eye sockets looked thicker than normal, pushing the eyes slightly off centre. Below them, bright pink gums stretched tight around overgrown teeth. The result looked more like a child's drawing than the face of a human being.

Irvana's mind raced through her findings. The distorted face looked familiar, but she couldn't place it. She thought back to a study she'd read once, where marsupial creatures evolve to cope with thicker forestation. There was something similar in the changes to these humans. If only she could get an opinion from someone. She tapped at her communicator and tried to send a message. A small red light lit up, stayed bright for a few seconds, then went dark. She cursed the lack of a support drone. Without a comm-link, she had no choice but to cut a sample and discuss it when she got back to her lab.

She held up her hand, and two fingers moulded at once into a sharp point. She gripped the creature's head with her left hand and pushed the point into its lower gum. With a sharp twist, she cracked one of the large teeth. Releasing its head, she reached in and plucked the tooth from its mouth. She grunted her satisfaction and set off towards the tower.

Chapter Three

Kasper knocked a second time. The dull thuds echoed down the corridor and faded into nothing. "She's not there."

"She might still be trying to find a safe way back," said Leon.

"And it's taken her all night? Is she doing it with her eyes shut? No, she's been picked up," said Kasper.

Leon gave a stiff shrug. "We cannot be certain. She might have been forced to avoid a patrol."

Kasper raised both his palms to the ceiling and shook his head. "Come on. She's been out all night. She never does that. I'm telling you, she got ID'd at the kiosk. They've got her."

Leon didn't answer. Kasper turned, and they both walked slowly up the corridor. A steady line of dormitory doors passed by as they went. Some were slid shut, like Alis's room, but others were wide open. Children dangled their legs over the cold metal step and older ones sat inside, their faces lit by handheld screens that hung in the dark like globes.

Leon continued his reasoning. "There's nothing on the troop channels in that district. If they had her, we would have heard by now."

Kasper breathed out a sigh and shook his head once more. "They're closing in on unregistered groups, aren't they? They won't broadcast when they know people can listen in. It just warns the hostels to hide their illegals."

He slapped his hand against his forehead, then jabbed a finger at a panel on Leon's wrist. "The transfer! Check it. If she got caught, it'll be flagged."

Leon's fingers danced over the face of the panel. He stopped, waited a few seconds, then looked up. "No transfer was made."

Kasper's mouth dropped open. It stayed that way for a moment, then he snapped it shut. "She's stolen it. She sent it somewhere else. She's taken our money." He looked up at the ceiling, then back at Leon. "Check her personal account. Can you get into it? I bet it's in there."

Leon went back to work on the screen. His large fingers moved smoothly, pausing every so often before bursting into another flurry of tapping and swiping.

"They checked her ID and she got flagged," said Kasper. "It's all over. They'll find her record, trace every one of our hits, and connect a path right to our front door. She's screwed over the whole hostel."

Leon gave an irritated grunt and shook his head. His fingers stopped moving. "I cannot get into her account, and I cannot see any activity on ours. There is no way I can find that transfer."

Kasper cursed. He stared down the corridor towards Alis's room, as though at any moment she might step out and greet them. "We need to speak to Charnell. Whether she comes back or not, Alis got identity flagged. He needs to know."

They took the wide corridor to their left, heading straight towards the lights of the mess hall. A ragged line of children scuttled out of the hall and down the corridor towards them.

"If we're right, and she's run off with our money, we need to think about how to get it back," said Kasper.

"Maybe we should go out and look for her," said Leon.

"Look for who?" said a voice beside them.

One of the children, a small girl, smiled up at Leon and Kasper. Her blonde hair hung loose to jaw level, with soft clumps sticking out around her ears. Her nightdress had a faded animal picture on the front, and a scruffy-looking doll peered up at them from under her arm.

"Who are you going to look for?" she said.

"Oh nobody," said Kasper, "Nobody in particular,"

"But Leon said you should go outside and look for a lady," said the girl.

At that moment, a woman's voice interrupted them. "Come on Prue, keep up with everyone."

A tired-looking woman appeared and smiled at Kasper. She nodded back towards the mess hall, and looked down at the line of children ahead of her. "There's an induction going on back there. Far too much excitement for this little lot."

Kasper returned the smile. The number of children in the line gave good reason for the woman to be tired. It was a large allocation for a single adult.

"OK," said Prue. "See you in the morning, Kass. See you in the morning, Leon."

"Yep. See you," said Kasper.

The line meandered down the corridor, and he noticed that Prue's hair bobbed as she walked. He thought for a moment about how soft she looked against the solid metal of the corridor walls. He felt a familiar sense of wonder at how all the children in the hostel held the utter belief that their plight was normal.

He stayed quiet for a moment longer until he was sure he couldn't be overheard. "Let's go in. We need to get to Charnell as soon as he's done."

The mess hall was full. Over half the hostel had come to watch the induction. The lack of space, the rising temperature, and the imminent speech by the hostel's steward had turned the room into a steaming human stew.

Kasper and Leon tried to work their way round the room, but soon gave up and instead jostled for space where they stood. The people nearest to them mumbled and muttered as their own space diminished.

"What the hell?" said one, and shouldered Kasper back towards the door. "Watch what you're doing."

Kasper's temper flared, but he suppressed it just as quickly. He didn't want to risk being thrown out. Finally, the familiar voice of Charnell, the hostel's steward, rose above the crowd. The din subsided, and as one, the audience turned to face the far side of the room.

Even when he was hidden from view, Charnell's voice felt so rich and familiar that Kasper could picture how the steward looked while he held the crowd in his spell. From his head to his waist, Charnell looked the same as any other man. But, below the waist, his torso finished abruptly at a broad, shining metal dais.

His upper body sat upright on the dais, like a chef's signature dish presented on a silver platter. He moved through life like this, a half-man gently floating above nothing but space. When Kasper had first met him, he, like everyone else, couldn't help but stare at the impossibility of what he was seeing.

His brain stubbornly refused to accept that there was nothing at all below a perfectly healthy upper body. Charnell had lost his lower body to stop a rot that would have taken his life. So, Kasper had grown to think of the man's dais as a simple line of separation between the life he'd lost and the life he kept.

"...and within these walls lives a proud community. A community of people that believes in the enduring goodness of humankind. We are bound by the bitter touch of the thieving hand of this sickness. We have watched, helpless, as that hand tore down our lives and stole our loved ones away. We know a depth of pain and suffering that no person should have to endure. We know too that, beyond our walls, the tragedy escalates daily. But none suffer more than our children. Orphaned in a time of anarchy, they need our shelter and our guidance. History shall record that we came together as victims and found strength at the end of society as we know it."

Mutters and murmurs of agreement simmered amongst the crowd. Leon tried to move into a better position to see, but two men in front of him refused to give way. Kasper itched for it all to be over.

"This needs to move quicker," he said to Leon, "Troopers might have told the Ribs by now."

Charnell continued addressing his flock. "We know that the State Executive has no answers. It's a sham government. It looks the other way while the welfare blocks here in Nasser become nothing more than prisons. But in our community, we have found a way. We refuse to forsake each other. We are regrouping, reaching out to our fellow humans. Together, we survive. Together, we are proof that we can lose our society, but will not lose our humanity."

This comment drew a passionate response from the crowd. Those nearest to Kasper and Leon shouted in chorus with the others.

"Fuck the Executive!"

"Self-govern!"

"Choose life!"

More voices chimed in, louder than before. More and more followed, spurred on by the shouting, until Charnell finally raised a hand and waved the noise away.

Kasper rose on the tips of his boots and peered over the heads of the crowd. The people behind him cursed and insisted he got out of their way.

"I share your feelings," said Charnell, "But our principles do not stop at these walls around us. When you oppress people, you breed violence. When people have nothing left to lose, they turn to crime. Our hostel stands as a reminder to the Executive there is another way. We don't need registration and we don't need their welfare blocks."

Someone nearby shouted so loud it made Kasper's ear sing for a moment.

"Welfares are prisons!"

Kasper glared at the man and rubbed his ear. Charnell pressed on with the ceremony.

"As we grow in number, our community grows stronger. So, with immense joy, I ask our new brothers and sisters to join us."

Charnell raised both hands to the newcomers standing in front of him. The crowd responded with a cheer.

"Welcome, friends. We are sad to see that the sickness has forced you from your home, as it did to all of us here. But we are glad that you sought us out."

On cue, the group in front of him inclined their heads. People craned their necks to get a better look at the new arrivals, but Kasper took no notice. He knew the ceremony was only a technicality.

The six newcomers were all adults. Residents routinely brought orphaned children here to the community, but these six adult hopefuls would have searched for the hostel themselves. They had no doubt avoided asking people in the street, and had probably watched the street for days before spotting the entrance.

Finally, they would have mustered the courage to approach a resident, asking for an introduction. That would have been the biggest risk. Rejection rates had to be high in the smaller free hostels. It was a simple matter of space. All hopefuls needed a good case to be granted entrance.

Once inside, they would have spent the probationary two days and two nights in the confirmation rooms, where their commitment would have been tested in the selection process. The process was rigorous and they might still be turned away at this point. Although Kasper had never seen it happen.

They were all extremely lucky. Their alternatives were a life in one of the welfares, or dodging registration and scavenging a living in some derelict city neighbourhood.

Kasper was happy with his own choice. Even if he avoided the Ribs, the crime and sickness on the streets would have driven him into a welfare, anyway. Most people either ended up in a welfare or ended up dead.

On the other side of the room, Charnell looked down and smiled at his newcomers. "In welcoming you here, we ask only that you embrace our principles. That you strive always to bring hope to the hopeless and friends to the friendless. Do you now so pledge?"

Having got this far, it was unheard of for anyone to back out. All of them confirmed their pledge at once.

"Excellent," said Charnell, "You may look upon this day as a second chance at life. You are all very welcome among us."

Charnell floated over and shook the hands of each of the newcomers amid cheers and applause from the crowd. Kasper and Leon jostled and buffeted their way through the sea of backs and shoulders as they tried to reach him.

Gaps opened in the crowd as the applause faded. Kasper saw Charnell float towards his offices, then watched as the door slid shut behind him. Two other people headed towards the door, presumably also seeking an audience with the steward.

Kasper looked up at Leon. "Can you make some space?"

Leon responded by gently gripping an armpit of each of the two men in front of him and lifting them off the floor. One was too shocked to speak, but the other kicked and flail at Leon.

"Get off me!" he said. "You can't just grab people, you freak."

Leon ignored the blows and put the men down gently to one side. They complained and shouted abuse but knew better than to tackle Leon any further.

"This place should be for real people, not machines *pretending* to be people!"

Leon ignored them, but the commotion encouraged people to step aside. Kasper grinned and walked swiftly out of the expanding circle, reaching Charnell's door a few seconds ahead of the other two hopefuls. He rapped firmly on the steel and smiled again as green LEDs sprang to life and the door slid to one side.

"Come in," said Charnell from somewhere beyond the threshold.

They entered the large room and nodded to two technicians sitting at consoles, each rendering a picture of the outside world from a myriad of sensory and visual feeds.

Charnell hung towards the centre of the room, looking at detailed holograms that showed the streets around the hostel.

"What can I do for you, Kasper?" said the steward.

Kasper took a breath and looked at the silver dias that marked Charnell's life lost and life gained. "It's about Alis. We have a problem."

"Every day brings more problems," said Charnell. "What is hers?"

"We think she's on the run," said Kasper.

Charnell stared at him for a moment then floated closer. Kasper suddenly found it difficult to look the old steward in the face. "Gone on the run? And why do you think that?"

Leon stepped forward and splayed his hands. "We were out with her earlier and she was due to meet us back here. But she has not returned. We now think she stole money from us."

Charnell smiled, but his eyes stayed cold. "Alis has been a resident of the hostel for nearly a year. Why would she steal and take her chances back out on the streets?"

Kasper glanced at Leon and found his friend looking at him. Leon's head gave a tiny side-to-side movement. Kasper looked back at Charnell. "We're not sure."

Charnell smiled again, but this time it flickered and quickly vanished. He spun around and headed back to the centre of the room, raising his voice as he went. "Knowing Alis, I suspect she has a good reason to run, wouldn't you say?"

The steward bent and waved his hand near a console. Light sprang upwards and formed a wide, flat rectangle in the air.

"I suppose so," said Kasper, "She..."

Kasper's words died on his lips. The rectangle had blurred into focus, revealing the street outside the hostel. At one end sat the familiar sight of the District Trooper's skiff that had chased them earlier that day.

Charnell pointed at it and glared at him. "And what do you suppose about this?" Kasper took a deep breath. Charnell jabbed a finger at the hovering skiff. "That has been drifting around here for over an hour. Perhaps they think Alis is a thief, too?"

Kasper's mouth opened but no sound came out. Charnell sighed. "Why don't you start again? This time leave nothing out."

The steward hovered closer to where Kasper stood. Kasper shut his mouth and said nothing, but he could feel Leon beginning to crack beside him. His big friend was just too honest.

Charnell shifted his attention to Leon, as if he could sense a confession. "If that Trooper decides there's a reason to come in here, it'll be the Ribs that follow them. Process that, Leon. All those frightened people lined up and waiting to be checked. I would guess more than a third of our people are unregistered, wouldn't you? Many of those are children. The Ribs would need to take at least some of them to the welfares, just to keep face. What's the current life expectancy of a child living in a welfare?"

Kasper willed Leon to stay quiet. The steward floated back towards the holograph in the centre of the room. He stopped alongside the image of the skiff and faced them. Two hovering objects, each demanding an answer. Kasper wasn't ready to tell Charnell the full story, but he knew Leon had a strong moral conscience. It was the one thing that made him so human, but was also the only thing that made him unpredictable.

"We think she was flagged by an ID check," said Leon.

Kasper cursed. Charnell looked as though Leon had hit him. "What? How?"

"A night kiosk on the east side," said Leon. "The sensor tripped, but the owner asked for verification, so we do not know if it went any further."

Charnell glared at Kasper. "The east side? Why, of all the districts in Nasser, would you choose to be over on the east side?"

Kasper had a mental library of handy half-truths. Several of his standard excuses flashed through his head. But he knew the old steward was already piecing together the full story without him. There was only one reason to be on the east side after dark. "Scavenging," he said.

Charnell's dais bobbed slightly, but his face didn't change. He held Kasper in his gaze for a full ten seconds before turning to Leon. "You, too? How is it that your processing power fails to keep you out of risky, nonsensical crimes?"

Kasper leapt to Leon's defence. "They're not risky. We're very careful. Leon's on board because we bring an income back into the hostel. It works out well for everyone."

Charnell's face creased in disbelief, and his dais bobbed again. "Not risky?" he jabbed a finger again at the skiff hovering in the street, "Look, of course it's risky! You're knocking people off for cash in a dead part of the city. There's more crime there than anywhere else! You might as well have broadcast your plan to the Troopers before you went!"

Kasper's own temper began to rise. "How could we know they'd start putting voice ID into tiny little night kiosks? Why are they bothering to do that, anyway?"

Charnell dropped his finger and paused, refusing to rise to Kasper's temper. It worked. With nothing to push back against, Kasper cooled down.

Charnell continued. "Thieves steal. Citizens work. I've brought people here with the promise of safety, but you seem to be working hard to put them all at risk."

"They can't prove it was us. We're too good at staying out of their way," said Kasper.

"But not good enough to avoid being ID flagged," said Charnell.

Leon looked down and shuffled his feet. Kasper started to speak, but Charnell held up a hand to stop him. "Tell me, what are the principles we live by in this hostel?"

Kasper looked at Leon. The big man's eyes stayed fixed on the ground. Kasper bit his lip. Charnell pushed them for an answer. "I want to hear you say it out loud. It's what binds us together and keeps us safe."

"Community and Compassion," said Leon.

"Precisely!" said Charnell, "Community and Compassion. When the cloud fades and the sickness ends, it will be us, the free hostels, who will rebuild this city with a clear conscience. We will build by example and practice our values in everything we do. Theft and deceit are the tools of people who do as they please while the world crumbles around them. They are not the acts of good people, and they are not our values."

Kasper smarted at the accusation of not being 'good people'. "Scavenging's the only choice we've got. Insurance pays out, so there's no real harm done. Alis got ID flagged and ran. That could've happened anywhere, anytime."

Charnell looked at the holograph of the skiff. "But it didn't happen anywhere, anytime. It happened while you were doing something illegal." As if on cue, the skiff began to rise and move down the street towards them. "Answer me this: the adults are dying at a faster rate, but every week fewer children are brought here for refuge. Why is that?"

Kasper frowned. "No idea. They're all going to other hostels, maybe?

Charnell threw his hands up in despair, making his dais rock gently back and forth. "It's because the Ribs get to them first. They register them and send them to the welfares. The more they have, the bigger their operation. The bigger their operation, the more influence they have with the executive. The Bureau has its eye on political power, and will crush small hostels that have ambitious ideas. We cannot draw their attention to us."

Charnell let his words hang beside the image of the advancing skiff.

Leon nodded. "You are right. I regret what we've done."

Kasper pulled a face and slowly shook his head at his friend. A small light flashed on the console in front of one of the technicians, causing the man to sit up in his seat.

"Charnell!" said the technician. "Chatter. Front 5, bottom right."

Charnell floated to a nearby console. His hands worked quickly over the surface, and the holograph switched to an empty view of the other side of the block. He waved it away, then waved through two more images until he found the feed from Front 5.

A lone figure stood in the street. Clearly female, she was dressed in a black skinsuit that came over her head and sat tight against her scalp. Beneath its rim, a single holoband sat above her sharp cheekbones, covering her eyes and hiding her expression. She strode confidently towards the hidden hostel doors. The weapon on her hip nodded gently with every step. Kasper's stomach lurched.

Charnell shook his head at the screen. "That Trooper's job was only to keep watch. We now have a Rib coming to see us."

"She might not be coming here exactly," said one of the technicians.

"Could be a random walkthrough in this sector," said the other.

"Turn off the wall," said Charnell.

The technicians hesitated.

"It'll see us," said one.

Charnell's voice dropped. "Turn it off. Show her the doors. If we're open to visitors, we won't look like we need to be searched."

One technician pressed his display, and several lights went out on the console in front of him. Charnell looked at Kasper. "Whether you brought this on us or not, I hope in future you'll think first of your community and not of yourself."

Out in the street, an old brick wall faded out of sight. In its place stood a pair of heavy steel doors with the words "Community and Compassion" embossed across them.

Chapter Four

The tower stood apart from the dark silhouettes of the other buildings. The first building of its size to be built entirely from printed liquid metal, it had cooled and taken its first inhabitants within a single day. Easily the tallest building in the city, it sat on a square cushion of parkland like an arrogant king, lording its height over rows of subservient buildings.

Irvana slowly approached the ruined park at the base of the tower. High above her, the balcony of the celebrated *Risque* restaurant jutted out like a boxer's chin near the summit.

A brief scan showed no signs of life among the park's petrified bushes and powdery grass. She sprinted the short distance across the park and pressed her hands against the base of the tower.

The broad entrance doors gaped open, but even Irvana's modified lenses couldn't penetrate the utter darkness beyond them. She snapped open her scanner and swept the lower floors. Small clusters of figures huddled at various points throughout the structure. Her heart sank. This proved beyond doubt they knew she was coming. Worse, it deepened her anxiety about how they'd found out.

Her work always took her attention, and she never seemed to be around the others long enough to talk about her suspicions. Only recently did she think she had anything that could be worth risking a formal conversation.

She looked down at the comm link on her suit and sighed. Without a drone, she couldn't now send evidence of her suspicion. A flicker of panic danced in her chest. The lack of drones had been a clear sign that someone didn't want her to succeed. She could have gone public with her theory at once, but she lacked evidence. Now she stood frustrated at the foot of her final objective.

She pushed her feelings aside. Whatever was going on, she didn't want to risk delaying the mission. The sooner it was over, the sooner she could find the evidence she needed.

She watched her scan for a few moments. The clusters of figures were on the move. It looked as though they were setting up a line of defence on the second floor. She sighed again and looked around the park. Somehow, they knew she had reached the door.

Fighting her way through every level of the tower was still likely to result in a win for her, but it was a risk and would waste valuable time. There was also the risk of damaging her equipment. That would be a disaster.

She pushed one hand into a pocket and pulled out her diviner. She gripped the small, shiny box and her other hand flipped the lid open. The thick gel inside flashed and pulsed like a beating heart. It was worth checking, but the diviner confirmed what she already knew. The true centre of the cloud still hung directly above the tower. She now had to reach the top.

She flipped the diviner shut and stowed it in her pocket. Eyeing the walls in front of her, she flipped her hands onto her forearms. Her skin shifted and blurred for a few moments until a narrow T-shape appeared at the end of both arms.

Two short tubes protruded above and behind each of them, like a pair of small telescopes. She stretched one hand out in front of her and two bright beams sprang from the tubes, scattering the darkness and almost blinding her night vision in the split-second it took her eyes to adjust.

The force of the beam pushed gently against her shoulder, and her arm throbbed as the energy scored a neat line into the metal wall. She turned off the beam, reached up, and jammed the T-shape into the crevice. Testing the grip, she pulled her feet off the ground and hung for a moment. Satisfied, she pulled herself up and inserted the other hand higher still.

Releasing the first grip, she cut another line into the surface. This time it stretched several metres high. Hand over hand, she followed her slash and grip routine up the outside of the building.

The dark zone fanned out below her like a skirt, spreading its gloom across the streets until its hem met the lights of the last of the inhabited areas.

Above her, the roof of the tower had two levels. One was the landing pad, the other was the comms and service platform. She planned to set up her convertor on the platform. It was higher and improved the chance of striking the cloud above with full power.

With a last pull, she reached the edge of the roof and halted. Her scanner picked up a line of figures rushing upward through the building. They knew she'd climbed the wall.

She threw a leg over the edge, rolled onto the flat roof, then ran at full speed towards the open entrance to the stairwell. The door was heavy, but she set her shoulder against it and heaved it back into its frame. She reformed the fingers on one hand and felt around the surface for the lock. The door was completely flat.

Cursing, she raised her remaining cutter, taking aim at where the edge of the door met the frame. The bright beam split the gloom of the rooftop, throwing her shadow over the roof edge behind her.

The metal surface glowed in the heat of her cutter, then sagged, closing the gap between the frame and the edge of the door. Aware of the threat coming up the stairs, she moved on, spot-welding more points around the frame as quickly as she could.

She heard the first thud of hands hitting the inside of the door. It held. She stepped away and smiled at the confusion she'd caused.

Then something hit her hard between the shoulders. The force smashed her face and upper body into the steel door. Shock and pain ripped through her. She fell to her knees and rolled. Something else heavy clanged on the metal above her. She pulled herself up and instructed her hands to form weapons. Only her left arm responded. Her right arm hung limp and silent by her side.

Panic flashed in her chest for the second time that night. She saw movement a few feet away and fired multiple blasts at it. The rooftop lit up like daylight. A massive creature leapt smoothly into the shadows. It was at least three times the size of her, all sinew and muscle, with clumps of thick hair across its arms and shoulders.

The creature slid into the shadows and out of sight, so Irvana ran at a diagonal to where it disappeared, strafing the same shadows as she went. For the first time in many years, she felt the chill of fear. The creature hadn't shown up on her scan, but still came close enough to smash her arm to pieces. She had never known anything to do that. Not on any planet.

Three shots lit up the creature's flanks on the far side of the roof. It roared, wheeled round, and zig-zagged towards her. *It's not stupid*, she thought. She took aim with her good arm, trying to block out the trauma of her other hand hanging uselessly at her hip.

She couldn't be sure of killing a moving target she knew nothing about, but she'd sealed the door and had nowhere to run. She had to stop it from moving. If it couldn't move, it couldn't reach her. She blurred her hand into a short barrel and fired. Her tiny missile flew straight at the creature's shins, struck the left one and exploded. The beast howled and stumbled, but found its feet again and kept coming. Fear surged like ice in Irvana's veins.

She fired again, this time landing the explosive straight on the creature's other shin. More howls filled the air, and the creature stumbled again. Still it didn't fall.

She had no time to change her weapon. The beast was so close she could hear its breath rasping as it charged towards her. She raised her barrel and fired multiple shots into its upper legs and midriff. The shots glanced away from its body, streaking left and right into the darkness over the rooftop railings. But on its legs, lumps of flesh burst away from bone. The creature screeched. Its enormous body tumbled and crashed to the ground.

She leapt towards it, aiming another shot through its neck. She fired, then watched in horror as the missile hit its mark, then bounced away, leaving her standing only a few inches from the howling, snarling beast. Distracted, she missed the arm reaching for her leg. A clawed hand gripped her boot and squeezed. She heard the bones in her foot popping before the pain hit her. She screamed and fell on her back, sending the other foot smashing into the creature's face.

Blinded by pain, she rolled and tried to push herself off the ground, but her head span and vomit pushed up in her throat. She slumped and cursed at the pain. She had to get control. If she passed out, she was dead. She rolled frantically, banging her head several times on the hard ground and feeling her useless arm flapping like a scarf.

The creature moaned and snarled at the sight of her rolling away. It reached out and began pulling itself, hand over hand, towards her. The edge of the comms platform appeared, and she crashed into it. Cursing, she heaved herself onto her good elbow and let her barrel drop flat onto the hard ground. The loud clank made her feel good.

The creature's arms tensed and strained as it hauled itself towards her. Despite its injuries, it moved fast. Irvana's arm jolted three times. Three bolts of light streaked towards the beast. Two bounced off its shoulders, but the other one struck home. The nano-charge ripped through the beast's upper torso. Its body split wide open and the thick stench of innards hit her like a tide. She clamped her arm across her stomach and finally threw up.

She spat and coughed until she got her breathing back under control. She grappled with her scanner and shook it into life. *No other life forms around.* But that hadn't helped her a few moments ago. This creature hadn't even registered on her scan. If another one came, she needed to be ready.

She returned her hand to normal and pulled a small silver packet from her suit. Tearing it with her teeth, she raised it to her lips and drank the liquid contents. The pain and nausea dulled. The bones in her foot gently began to shift back towards each other. They wouldn't be perfect for a couple of days, but she could probably walk out of the dark zone within a few hours.

Next, she set her good arm the task of mending the other. It got to work fusing wires and printing new servos deep within the channels of her shoulder. Like her foot, a true repair would take proper attention, but before long she would have an arm that would at least allow her to get off this kill box of a roof. She took a deep breath and hobbled over to what was left of the creature.

Barely anything remained of the eviscerated body, but she could see dark, bony plates protruding from the shoulders and shins. The surface of these was hard and smooth. It made sense that her nano missiles had been deflected.

An examination of the exposed skeleton and hands left her in no doubt that, like the bodies at the barricade, this creature was originally human. The mystery, however, was how it had mutated so dramatically, and how it had evaded her scans.

She tried again to transmit a message, but watched in frustration as the red light blinked its denial. She crossed the rooftop and climbed the steps onto the raised comms platform. Satisfied she was alone, she took a moment to stare out over the edge and marvel at the massive blanket of grey and black angles that made up the decaying dark zone of the city below. She briefly wondered how many other undiscovered phenomena lurked in those shadows.

Her arm completed its repairs, and she felt her hand respond to commands. The relief settled her mind back on the mission. She lifted her pack off her shoulders and laid it carefully on the ground.

Irvana quickly became engrossed in the science of the process she was about to undertake. She opened the pack and removed the small squares and pipes from inside. Arranging them neatly in front of her, she took care to lay them in the correct order and in the same direction.

Next, she removed the large cylinder. Placing it carefully on its end, she began assembling the smaller boxes and pipes around it. After a few minutes, the structure stood roughly level with her waist, and resembled a short pillar standing on a honeycomb.

She waved her hand in a pattern beside the large box. It sprang into life. A blue light slowly spread along the honeycomb of pipes and small chambers. After a few seconds, the pillar shot a solid beam of white light into the night sky.

Irvana adjusted her eyes and watched the beam cut through the purple cloud high above the tower. The space around the contact point glowed. As soon as the cloud receded, she would leave.

She tried once more to send her analysis of the two corpses she'd examined. The red light flashed, and she cursed at it. Frustrated, she sent it several more times. A stubborn series of red flashes answered her.

She gave in and sat down beside the blazing pillar of light, watching the glow gathering pace across the purple sky. The fading adrenaline made her shudder, and she smiled. Now that she'd beaten it, the cloud looked quite beautiful. She traced the edge as it disappeared into the distance, and listened with mild amusement as her eyes clicked and whirred to keep it in focus.

The skyline dipped to meet the horizon, and the railings at the far edge of the rooftop came into view. She stopped. A bright patch of blue light sat just beneath them. It looked like a light on top of one of the nearby buildings, but as she stared at it, she could see it perched on the edge, just beneath the lower rung of the rail.

She shifted position and refocused her eyes to get a better look. As if mirroring her movement, it shifted position, too. A streak of light reached out and wrapped itself around the first rail, then another reached out and attached itself to the top rail. An image flashed into her mind of a sea creature, an octopod. She imagined it squelching and sucking its way towards her, all tentacles and slow movements.

But it didn't make any sound at all. Instead, it silently lifted the rest of its body over the railings and stood on two feet on the open roof. It faced her, one solitary glowing man, burning away the shadows. She felt the adrenaline returning to her fingertips.

The man raised an arm towards the platform. A single, bright bolt flared across the dark space between them. Irvana rolled. But the blast wasn't meant for her. A screech of tearing metal split the air, followed by the sound of the convertor bouncing along the floor of the platform. She twisted her head in time to see it hit the railings, spin off the edge of the rooftop, and drop out of sight. She felt a chill run through her as it disappeared. *Too soon! The cloud hasn't receded.*

She turned back in time to see the blast coming towards her, but with no time to move. Everything in front of her turned into a single bright light. It hit her in the chest, lifting her off the ground and sending her smashing into the railings. Her suit held together, but she struggled to breathe. There seemed to be no space between her chest and her back. She shook her head and tried another breath. A whine sounded from the back of her throat. The breath died, unable to reach her lungs.

The blue man stood and stared from the edge of the comms platform. He looked young, younger than her. Somewhere in her mounting panic, she wondered what made him glow.

Behind him, at the very edge of his circle of light, a small patch of gloom faded away, leaving a doorway to a different world hanging in the fabric of the night. As Irvana passed out, a woman in a green skinsuit stepped through it and onto the rooftop.

Chapter Five

The sound of banging rang out from the main doors of the hostel. Charnell floated down the corridor towards the noise, reassuring the clusters of anxious faces peering out of dorm rooms.

"It's OK. Go back inside," he said at intervals, "Nothing to worry about."

Kasper and Leon followed him to the end of the corridor, then hung back and watched him glide around the last corner towards the main entrance. A loud scraping and clatter signalled the opening of the heavy doors.

"Good afternoon," they heard Charnell say.

Kasper imagined the icy gaze of the Rib woman scrutinising Charnell's unusual appearance.

"Merrick, Registration and Intelligence Bureau," said the woman.

"Yes," said Charnell, "And what can I do for the Bureau, today?"

"Can we talk inside?" said the woman's voice.

Charnell didn't reply, but Kasper heard the door clang home in its frame and felt the spreading sense of dread. Charnell had just let a Rib inside the hostel! How far would he go to prove a point?

Charnell's dais appeared, carrying him up the corridor. Somewhere behind him and out of sight, the Rib woman's boots made a precise metal click with her every step. It confused Kasper's brain to see a floating man but still hear footsteps.

The Rib appeared from around the corner, following Charnell in smooth, confident strides. Her holoband removed any trace of humanity. She might as well be fully machine. As she approached, he flicked his gaze to her sidearm. The black handle bobbed above the rim of the holster, its tiny green hammer light drawing a short arc in the air with every step she took.

The hammer light was steady, meaning the Rib was carrying a fully charged weapon. Kasper felt the acid creep of nerves spreading through his arms and chest, and down to his fingertips. He'd made it his business to stay away from the Bureau and its agents, but he had never thought of them as lethal. Now, as the Rib agent walked past him, he realised they carried enough firepower to blow a hole through both him and Leon, as well as the wall behind them.

Kasper watched Charnell and the Rib reach the end of the corridor and enter the common room. Moments later, several people emerged and hurried away from the room. Intrigued, he and Leon moved up to listen by the door. They stood far enough away to give Charnell privacy, but stayed close enough to eavesdrop.

The woman took a seat on the nearest chair, and Charnell hovered in front of her. His face showed nothing of what he might be thinking.

"Now, what brings you to our hostel?" said Charnell

It seemed the agent had no intention of wasting her words. "An unregistered female was identified, tracked by a Trooper census unit, then lost in this sector. You have plenty of people housed here. We're assuming some are unregistered. How many?"

The woman's tone had the same subtlety as her fully charged weapon. Charnell remained cordial.

"None. They are all registered, as required within the Code of Practice of the Federation of free hostels. There are no unregistered children under this roof."

The woman took a moment to consider what he'd said. She looked down at the split fabric on the arm of her chair and smoothed it with one hand. "I should start again. I probably haven't made myself clear, Mister...?"

Charnell was no fool. He'd invited the Rib inside, but he still had a sworn duty to keep everyone safe. "I am the Steward here."

"Forgive me, Steward, " said the Rib. "I am asking how many of your children have been accounted for by my colleagues at the Registration and Intelligence Bureau."

Kasper watched the slender hand stroking the arm of the chair. It reminded him of an owner stroking a pet. It was a peculiarly human action for something so cold.

"And I am again telling you: none. They don't need to be registered by the Bureau. They're all registered by us, as a free hostel licensed by the Executive," said Charnell.

"Very good," she said. Her hand stopped moving, and she looked Charnell straight in the face. "I'm afraid you seem to be out of touch with certain, ah, recent developments, Steward."

Charnell nodded towards the heavy black holster on the woman's thigh. "I do? Perhaps you're right. I wasn't aware that checking the registration of orphaned children had become so dangerous that the Bureau needed to arm its agents."

The Rib lifted her leg and placed a foot on the edge of a nearby table. The holster's straps held the weapon to her thigh like a spider on its prey. She patted it, and Kasper thought he saw a smile flicker on her lips. "A regrettable but necessary precaution in our changing times."

"You mean an open threat to anyone opposing you," said Charnell, his dais swaying slightly as he spoke.

"Some people get rich by setting up licensed hostels as a cover for trafficking children," she said. "Any free hostel could be a small criminal empire. Those people are reluctant to lose their income. It makes sense for us to carry protection."

Kasper looked over at Leon, but his large friend was too focused on the conversation to return the glance. "She's going to bust the place up."

Leon snapped out of his trance and frowned. "Charnell can handle himself. He's a good diplomat."

"We should still be ready," said Kasper.

Leon turned his head. "Ready for what, exactly? What do you think we can do against a Rib?"

"I've thought about this plenty of times. I can fry her with the RDP, then you get in there and rip out her synaptics. Only the human part stays awake, and that can't walk or signal for help."

Leon shook his head. "You're crazy. Ribs don't roll over so easily."

"OK, how about you take her on, head-to-head? You're the same as her."

"No, I'm not. She's a much bigger deal than me. Just wait. Charnell will get rid of her."

Kasper let it drop but made a quick mental calculation of the time it would take to get back to his room and grab the waiting RDP.

In the common room, Charnell continued. "The Bureau has a political agenda, and the welfares are nothing more than labour camps. Children are commodities in those places. They work until they drop. They sleep like animals in pens while the Bureau peddles fear for its own ends. And as for the adults? Forget it." He stabbed a finger at the floor. "The children in here have a proper home. We don't exploit them or let them suffer. And we don't put them in second place behind the unwavering pursuit of power."

The Rib watched the finger, then shifted her eyes lower to the bobbing dais. This time her thin smile curled up one side of her mouth. She gestured at the floor beneath him. "Why didn't you just buy some legs?"

Charnell's mouth moved to reply, but no words came out. He followed the gesture and looked down, as though seeing his own predicament for the first time. Irritation forced his head back up, and he waved an arm expansively, as if introducing the entire building to his guest. "I use my resources to keep a roof over people's heads, not to worry about my appearance."

The Rib's smile broadened, but the shiny holoband hid her eyes and Kasper couldn't tell whether her face had softened. "I'm sure you're an excellent host. However, the number of orphans is rising exponentially. The Executive Care statute never considered that the sickness would kill far more adults than children. Some members of the Executive are now interpreting the law to mean everyone must register with a single authority."

Charnell's face flushed. "And I suppose those members decided that all on their own, without so much as a small financial incentive from your employers in the Bureau?"

The Rib woman spread her hands. "I do not pretend to know their motivation. I only know their conclusion."

But Charnell didn't need an answer. He raised a finger and wagged it at her as he spoke. "You're manipulating human tragedy. Twisting it to serve your lust for power and profit. You should be ashamed."

The Rib woman rose slowly from her seat. She stood with one foot slightly further back than the other, her hands hanging loosely at her sides. In the doorway, Kasper stiffened and thought again of the RDP.

Her voice was low and steady. "You need to calm yourself, Steward. I'm just here to complete a routine check, that is all."

The dais hummed, and Charnell moved closer to the woman. "The Executive are blind to not see what you are doing."

That smile again. "I will make sure I pass on your opinion. Now, I need to find and register that citizen." She paused. "Do I need to ask again whether the fugitive is here?"

Charnell snorted. "Do I need to say again there are no fugitives here?"

The two of them fell silent. Kasper watched them face off against each other. The Rib cool, capable, and impassive while Charnell struggled to prevent his dais from shifting about as his temper rose. Down the corridor, children shuffled, whispered, and clanked nervously in their dorm rooms.

The Rib removed a wallet-sized metal box from her suit and set it on the table. Her fingers danced on the upper surface for a few seconds before the box glowed orange and projected a holograph of the structure of the hostel.

The 3D image hung a few inches above the upper surface of the box. Tiny red dots sat in small clusters throughout the building.

The Rib flicked the butt of her gun and the green light brightened. "Each of those dots is an unregistered citizen. All living here, inside your hostel."

"Unregistered by the Bureau," said Charnell, "But all registered lawfully by the Federation of Free Hostels."

"Today I need only find one unregistered person," said the Rib.

Out of sight of Charnell, but in full view of Kasper and Leon, she removed her gun smoothly from its holster. Kasper's chest tightened.

The Rib's fingers tightened around the handle. "I will give you the choice, Steward. Which one should I take?"

Charnell folded his arms and hovered defiantly before her. "None."

The red dot closest to the Rib darted away down a corridor, turned right into a second corridor, entered the box-shape of a dorm room and stopped. Both the Rib and Charnell stared at it.

"It seems we have ourselves a winner," said the Rib, "Who is that?"

"It doesn't matter who that is. As I just said, nobody from this community will be registered by the Bureau," said Charnell.

In his dorm room, Kasper grabbed the RDP and raced back up the corridor towards the common room. The red dot once again mapped his movements inside the Rib's holograph.

But the Rib was no longer watching. She had turned her attention back to Charnell. "The free hostels are finished."

"I doubt they will agree," said Charnell.

Kasper sprinted towards the doorway of the common room. The Rib raised her gun level with Charnell's face. The boom of the weapon roared like a chill wind through the hostel.

"Now!" shouted Kasper.

Leon fired the targeting disk at the Rib. Kasper crossed the threshold and hit the button on the RDP. Nothing happened for a moment. Then a scream pierced the air, followed by the loud pop, pop, fizz of exploding electronics.

He skidded to a halt in the centre of the room. In front of him, Charnell's body hung over the side of his dais, one arm hanging to the floor.

The Steward looked shorter, somehow. It took Kasper a moment to realise that there was nothing above his neck. Behind the bobbing dais, a wide stripe of red and black matter painted the floor. Kasper swallowed the rising thickness in his throat.

Leon, squatted beside the twitching form of the Rib woman. "Get over here."

Kasper tore his eyes from the Steward and focused instead on helping his friend. The RDP had knocked out the Rib's circuits, and Leon set about doing the only sensible thing: manually disabling its emergency recovery and repair procedure. If he didn't, these synaptics could send a distress signal for other Ribs to retrieve the body.

"We got her," said Kasper.

"Yes, but we are in serious trouble," said Leon.

"Indeed, you are," said the Rib.

Kasper jumped at the voice.

The Rib's head had come loose and lay beside its body. The holoband had fallen off and, although its eyes stared away from them, it spoke directly to Kasper. "Your precious hostel is finished. Once the Bureau knows what you've done, all this will be gone in an instant."

"You killed our Steward," said Kasper. "You deserved what you got."

The Rib's mouth smiled. "He knew what he was saying. I didn't kill him, he killed himself," she said.

Finishing his work, Leon flipped the hatch shut on the Rib's casing, stood back, and nodded. Kasper reached out and picked up a metal stool from beside the nearest table.

"And do you know what you are saying?" he said. "Do you know that you've killed yourself, too?"

The Rib's mouth formed too late to make a sound. The stool crashed through her skull and clanged on the hard floor. Kasper felt the shock die in his arm, and stared at the fresh mess of blood and bone. He turned away to avoid throwing up.

A few adults and older children shuffled into the room to see what had happened. Gasps turned to wails as they pieced together the scene in front of them. They spread the news, and the corridors echoed with the crying of frightened children.

Chapter Six

Alis quickened her pace. Her stomach still felt twisted from the effects of the portal. She'd never travelled well, and usually tried to empty her stomach a few hours before each journey. But this time she 'hadn't been able to. When you received a summons, they expected you to come at once.

She'd made the jump from Nasser to The Salient within an hour of receiving the call. Now on board, she couldn't decide if she felt nauseous from the journey, the confusion she left behind, or the uncertainty of what she was about to find out.

She walked through The Salient's arrival scans and out into the first of the many courtyard decks she had to cross to reach the morgue. Her nausea ebbed away as she passed through The Salient's attempts to recreate courtyards from older civilisations.

This one looked like an ancient human temple, with actual flames set into niches at intervals along the walls. The next had chrome and glass walls, with soft-seating bags in bright colours dotted around the floor. A reference to the digital age of human history, back before people started to leave Earth. Alis wondered if The Salient had set it up just for her, but decided it just adapted its designs to suit their current galaxy.

She reached the morgue, and a pair of double doors slid silently aside. She stepped into the bright, sterile interior and found her way to a large examination room. Bright lights and instruments coated the walls and ceiling and, in the middle of it all, four solemn-looking people turned and looked at her.

"You're late," said Doron, the thinnest and oldest of the four.

It was a statement, not a question. Alis knew from his tone to stay quiet. Doron turned to the doctor standing beside him, pushed his spectacles higher on his nose, and clasped his hands behind his back. Not for the first time, Alis wondered why he didn't just mod his eyes like everyone else.

"You may continue," he said.

The presence of Vivek, Doron's Chief Technician, came as no surprise. Taller than the humans, his long neck and willowy arms moved constantly as he listened. Alis thought he always looked like he had a continuous, slow rhythm playing in his head. As he was the only alien she had ever met, she had to work hard to imagine any other kind.

The last person she recognised was Millan, her most recent mission director. His broad face gave nothing away, and she creased her brow at him in a silent question. He responded by jerking his head beyond the doctor and towards the centre of the room.

Following his direction, Alis realised they were standing at the base of a wide, transparent examination tube. The tube stretched towards the ceiling and finished roughly a meter above them. The sides had no visible displays or controls, just flawless, smooth glass designed to display its entire contents for analysis.

Inside, suspended directly in its centre, hung a skinsuit of the kind specifically used for on-planet fieldwork. It almost matched the one Alis had on, except this one had several large, rough holes punched through the tough fabric.

Each of the holes had dark stains streaking away from it, as though something had burst through them from the inside. Its sleeves ended in a mess that she couldn't quite make out, and another large, dark stain fanned out from the suit's neck hole.

An alarm rang in her mind. She felt Millan looking at her, gauging her reaction.

"It's Irvana," he said.

She felt her chest tighten. The nerves tingled in her fingertips. She looked back at the suit. No head, no hands, no feet. The body was just a ruined suit. But in the mess at the end of the sleeves, she could see empty fluid channels where Irvana's modified arms had burst open. The link to the person inside made the horror come alive.

The dark stains on the fabric became the dry blood leading back to the torn skin and ruined organs. She felt her breath go shallow. Nausea filled her throat like a snake.

She looked away and set her jaw against the sickness. But the emotion was too fast. Too powerful. She bent double and wretched violently. Tears spilled down her cheeks, and she struggled to claw back her composure.

Millan reached out and placed a hand on her back. Doron broke away from his conversation.

"We all feel the same," said Millan.

But Alis batted his hand away, wiped her mouth on her sleeve, flicked strands of hair from her face, and stared at Doron.

"Why the hell didn't you tell me?" she said.

Doron's narrow features darkened. "How is it that you don't already know? If you've been picking up transmissions as you should, you would have known before the summons was sent."

Alis threw up her hands. "I'm busy. I'm in deep. Nasser's a mono-mega-conurbation on the brink of martial law. I can't sit and read every off-planet signal. You should have told me!"

Doron's eyes widened, the only sign that he'd shifted from tolerance to anger. "I did tell you. It doesn't matter where you are, it is your responsibility to read what we send. Your poor conduct gave you this shock, not mine."

Alis dropped her eyes and tried to control her anger. She knew Doron was right, but it only made her feel worse. The thick snake in her throat lifted its head once more, but she held it down. "How did it happen?"

Doron held her in his eyes for a moment, then nodded to Millan. The man took his cue. "Irvana was sent to Trage, a city on the same planet, and about two hundred kilometres from where you are in Nasser. It has a far higher rate of decay than anything we've seen so far."

Alis nodded, her mind flying back to the hostel in Nasser, where Kasper and Leon had first told her they thought the infection had started in Trage. She felt bad about leaving them. They must think she'd run off with the takings from the kiosk. But a summons was a summons.

"I've heard of it. The infection came from there to my host city," she said.

Millan tightened his lips at the interruption, then nodded and continued. "The cloud there caused a massive dark zone over a six-kilometre radius, in just a few weeks. She went in to tackle it. Same approach as normal, hit it in the centre, right where it hurts most."

Alis waved a hand and nodded. "OK. And what happened?"

Millan sighed. "She never came out. The cloud kept growing, the decay kept spreading. Transmissions wouldn't travel through the zone, so we ended up sending in the droids." He spread a palm towards the tube. "They found her and brought her back."

Alis felt Millan was holding something back. She creased up her face. "And? I could have guessed all of that myself. What else? What really happened?"

Millan flashed a weak smile. "We're all frustrated, Alis, but the truth is-"

Doron cut across him. "We're not sure. The truth is we're not sure. We're dealing with the death of one of our strongest and dearest colleagues, but have little to explain why. No certainty means no security. Hence the urgent summons."

Alis's mouth hung open. They had nothing. An image of Irvana sitting at her desk floated into her mind. Irvana smiled at Alis with her mouth, but not with her eyes. She often smiled like that, as though a part of her was always on guard.

Whenever they spoke and Alis became too light-hearted, or admitted to taking risks in her work, Irvana would place a hand on her shoulder and put her feet firmly back on the ground with some kind of cautionary phrase.

"Our entire operation is mortally fragile, Alis."

Or perhaps:

"There are some that do not have the strength to accept the truth about what faces us."

Or the one that had concerned her the most:

"We are only as safe as the weakest-willed among us. We must be prepared for what they might do."

To begin with, Alis felt the sentiment rather than listening to the words. Irvana had been part of the effort long before Alis arrived, and it sounded like a reminder to take her own work seriously.

But over time, she replayed these words in her head and understood the theme within them. Irvana confided in her more often. On one occasion, she handed Alis one of the diviners and asked her to take it back to Nasser to keep it safe. Alis had questions, but Irvana assured her it wouldn't be missed.

"I made sure nobody will know it's gone. We need to keep this one hidden. If the others are lost, we can no longer target the centre of an infection."

She spoke again of sabotage and the potential for betrayal. For someone to decide the fight was too difficult and choose to save themselves instead, even if it meant putting everyone's lives in danger.

Alis had seen less of Irvana in more recent times, but the woman's words made her cautious. She thought the lurking suspicion gave her an edge, kept her senses keen. Standing here now, she refused to believe that Doron had no ideas at all. He must be holding something back. And Vivek and Millan? Did neither of them have anything to offer?

She imagined Irvana dismissing their pretend ignorance. The thought of her face brought back the cold flood of grief. She clamped her jaw to keep herself under control.

Doron cleared his throat and snapped Alis out of her thoughts. He raised one eyebrow at her. "Are you with us, Alis? We have had more time to come to terms with this, so you may excuse yourself if you wish."

Alis shook the memory and nodded. "I'll stay."

Doron signalled to the doctor, and she continued to explain Irvana's remains, pointing at various parts of the suit as she spoke.

"Injuries sustained are from various points pre- and post-mortem, but all within the last fifteen minutes of her life. Cause of death was decapitation." The doctor's tone neither rose nor fell, as though she'd taken no notice of the emotions simmering in the people around her. Alis faded in and out of the lecture, unable to shake her disbelief, and still battling her emotions. "The fibres of the fabric around the neck hole have fused together. This is consistent with the extremely high temperature generated by a Phase 5 energy weapon fired at close range."

Alis tried to suppress the images rising in her mind. Millan interrupted.

"Phase 5?"

Vivek's treble voice wafted gently across them. "Phase 5 is beyond the capability of the indigenous population. The science simply does not yet exist on the planet."

"An off-planet aggressor?" said Doron.

Vivek's long neck contracted and relaxed, making his head shake. "From the evidence, I cannot comment on the existence or otherwise of a third party. However, the doctor's conclusion proposes an anomaly that requires careful examination."

Doron frowned at him. "Can you be more helpful, Vivek? Phase 5 tech had to arrive on the planet somehow. Isn't it possible the killer was alien to the planet?"

Vivek nodded. "It is possible."

Doron breathed a sigh. "Ok, good. Continue, doctor."

An unseen hand pressed 'play' on the doctor. "At the time of death, the cyborg elements of the body were conducting healing protocols. This is clear from the traces of anaesthesia and lymph salts in the remains of the channels within the subject's arm modifications. The work, however, wasn't finished, and those precise injuries are impossible to isolate, because of the massive post-mortem damage sustained when the body fell from the tower."

Alis's shock was fading. The doctor's stone-cold analysis helped her separate her feelings from the burning questions about how Irvana could be hanging dead in a tube. "You're saying she was killed while up a tower, on a low-risk planet, and was dead before she hit the ground?"

The doctor stopped pointing and gave a brief nod. "In summary, yes."

Alis returned the nod. "Presumably she was on the tower to set up her convertor?"

Doron nodded and looked around the group. "Theories welcome, everyone."

"What do her drones have to say?" said Alis.

Doron clasped his hands behind his back and shook his head. "No drones. They were all assigned elsewhere at the time of the mission."

Alis felt her jaw drop again. "No drones? How did she stay in touch? How did she navigate?"

Millan waved the question away. "It was a silent op. Her own mods and systems were more than enough to get it done,"

"Clearly they weren't," said Alis.

Millan made a pressing motion at her with his hands. It irritated her at once. "OK," he said, "but communication via drones was impossible. Interference is too high. The techs can't work it out."

Vivek wafted a long arm and smiled. "Millan's correct. The zone density has manifested shielding properties, which prevent the successful passage of our transmission protocols."

Alis ignored him. She kept her eyes on Millan. "That doesn't mean a drone was useless, does it? It could have left the dark zone to transmit a message."

Millan breathed out a sigh. "As Doron said, no drones were available."

Alis clenched her teeth. "So why not wait?"

"She didn't want to wait," said Millan.

"So you just let her go in alone?" she said.

"It wasn't just my decision," said Millan.

Doron waved a hand at them both. "Enough. We took the decision together. But one transmission did make it out, although it never arrived here."

"What was it?" said Alis.

Doron frowned at her. "As I said, it never arrived."

It was Millan's turn to frown. "So why did that one work, but none of the others? Are you sure it didn't arrive? Have we checked to see if it's still sitting somewhere, unread?"

Doron nodded. His glasses slipped a fraction down his nose. He unclasped a hand to push them back into place, then quickly returned it. "Nobody found a message, but we did find something unusual in her samples."

He nodded to the doctor, and she headed for the corner of the room. A light flicked on and, for the first time, Alis noticed four deep-sided chairs arranged around an empty plinth. It looked like someone had stolen a statue.

"Take a seat," said the doctor.

Alis moved slowly and was the last of the group to sit. It seemed too soon to be turning her back on Irvana's body. Before the chair finished shaping itself to her body, the doctor placed an object on the plinth. Two lasers lifted it a few inches into the air and slowly rotated it for everyone to see.

She peered at the object. It looked like a yellow-white triangular stone, thick at one end and tapering to a sharp point at the other.

Millan breathed out loudly. "Is that—"

Doron nodded. "A tooth."

"It's from some kind of animal," said Alis.

Doron smiled. "It's not. I'm told it's human."

Her eyebrows shot up. "What?"

Millan stifled a laugh. "It's too big for a human."

The doctor nodded. "That's true, but there is a mutation in its DNA."

Millan stared at the tooth, narrowing his eyes as though accusing it of a crime. "A big tooth isn't really *that* unusual though, is it?" Nobody answered. The doctor looked confused and opened her mouth to answer, but Millan continued. "I mean, I've seen plenty of animals with bigger teeth than that. How sure are we that this didn't come from a large dog?"

The doctor's eyes widened. She ran her finger along the edge of the tooth. "We are certain the DNA is human."

She paused and looked at Doron. He gave the doctor a brief nod. "Go ahead, doctor."

The doctor swallowed. "We also found nano-fractures in the biting plate. When we examined them, we found they contained tiny fragments of human bone."

She handed the tooth to Millan and motioned for him to look, all the while watching it like it was her own child. Millan glanced at it, then handed it to Alis. He sat back and laced his hands behind his head.

Alis turned the tooth over in her hands. She drew the only conclusion possible. It sounded ridiculous, so she waited a moment before saying it out loud. "You mean this person bit someone?"

The doctor's face lit up. She nodded several times. "Correct—except they bit more than one person. The bone traces are from several different skeletons."

Alis imagined large teeth closing on a human arm, then crushing through flesh and bone, severing it completely.

Millan dropped his hands. "Humans don't eat humans."

"Well, they could be doing so now," said Doron. "We don't yet know enough to reject the idea."

The doctor nodded again, seemingly pleased that the conversation had moved back to her own specialism.

Alis held up her hand. "Wait. They've turned to cannibalism after just a few months?"

Doron and the doctor nodded.

Vivek bounced gently in his seat. "We are dealing with an excession event," he said. "The Trage infection is beyond our usual experience. Entirely unknown to us."

Nobody joined the Chief Technician in his enthusiasm. The prospect of the unknown seemed worrying, rather than exciting.

Millan sighed. "Whatever owned that tooth must have been pretty vicious, so I don't see a great mystery here. A few of them threw Irvana off the roof and smashed the convertor in the process. It's not enough to prove a deliberate strategy, is it? It's just an evolution in the dark zones we didn't see coming."

Alis raised a finger. "Ah, no. If she was thrown, how do you explain the burn marks from the weapon?"

Millan shrugged. "OK, so they had guns. Just because they've mutated doesn't mean they can't fire a gun. These things must be at the top of the food chain. They're going to hunt down anyone that threatens them, right?"

Doron frowned, making his small eyes disappear behind his lenses. "That's our conclusion so far. But it would still take large numbers to overwhelm her."

Millan pulled one leg up to rest across the other. "Well then, that's what happened. There were lots of them and they won. Case closed."

Alis pounced. "So why not eat her, then? If they've evolved because they need to feed, why throw a free meal off a roof?"

Millan shrugged. "Fair point. Except she most likely fell when they shot her."

"So why not run down and eat her?"

Millan paused, then threw up his hands. "Who knows? Maybe they turned and ate the ones she'd already killed? Or maybe she's just not very tasty?"

Alis couldn't answer. She had a clear image of Irvana's body falling towards the street. Emotion clogged the back of her throat.

Doron watched her for a moment, then fixed his eyes on Millan. "You can show more respect for a fallen colleague."

Millan nodded and took a deep breath. "Sorry. You're right. I didn't mean to be flippant."

The doctor proposed elements of mutated physiology that might have supplied an advantage over Irvana, or indeed over any of them.

Alis zoned out and looked over at her friend hanging in the glass tube. She thought of Irvana's love of science, and how Doron had failed to save Irvana's home planet. She remembered how Irvana had demanded physical mods and weapons training. Despite her value on the research team, he had granted her wish.

In her new body, she'd launched herself into on-planet fieldwork. She created a "convertor" that had rolled back the cloud on five out of eight planets. Those five planets had, and remained alive and well today. If the populations knew an off-world visitor had arrived and performed such a miracle, they'd have worshipped her as a deity.

"Alis?" said Doron.

Alis snapped back into the room, aware that she'd drifted off into her own head again.

Doron raised his eyebrows. "What do you think?"

She'd missed the discussion, so couldn't continue it. Everyone stared at her, waiting for an answer to a question she hadn't heard. She took a breath and paused before speaking. What the hell, she thought. Irvana's been killed. It's a perfect time to tell them what I think.

"What do I think?" she said. "I think the cloud killed Irvana. It knows it's vulnerable, so it's brought this beast, or beasts, to protect it from harm on the ground. They are its defence."

For a moment, nobody spoke.

Doron's mouth opened a fraction, a frown hiding his eyes. "Its defence?"

Millan snorted. "The cloud did this? You're joking, right? How does a cloud-based infection create gun-waving people with massive teeth?"

Alis glared at him. "I know it sounds unlikely. But it's possible. If the cloud is already altering physiology, why can't it create or control some lifeforms of its own?"

Doron's frown softened and he chuckled. "I agree with you, Alis. It sounds unlikely."

Alis felt her cheeks flush. "Plenty of things that appear impossible are in fact possible. We locate the centre of the cloud with the diviner. We use Irvana's convertor to shrivel it to nothing," she held up one hand, her fingers splayed. "Five times, we've done that. This makes us a serious threat to the cloud as it moves from planet to planet. Now you're telling me it's doing everything faster than before. And on the same planet that killed Irvana, one of our best in the field? We shouldn't dismiss the idea that it's fighting back."

Doron sighed. His thin shoulders rose slowly on the inward breath, then dropped with the expelled air. He looked down at his feet, then back up at Alis. "Let me be clear on what you've just suggested. Our adversary, which we've only ever known as an airborne infection, is currently pumping its poison into this planet's atmosphere with the express intent of eroding it, killing the population, and draining all life from it. This is a tried and tested method that has served it well for years. Now, because we've had a handful of successes, this infection has suddenly become sentient, taken mutated human form, and begun to walk about killing our people."

He opened a hand towards her, and raised his eyebrows. "Am I right so far?"

Alis nodded. "Yes, I'm just saying that—"

Doron waved a hand. "Not only killing our people, but first waiting until those people have climbed to the top of the highest tower in the city, erected a substantial weapon, and almost reversed the whole infection process."

The doctor sat up in her chair, then raised a hand as if requesting permission to speak.

"It might sound unlikely, but—"

Millan cut her off. "It doesn't sound unlikely, it sounds impossible."

The doctor ignored him. "It sounds identical to a defensive response from any type of organism. If you consider the cloud as a body, all bodies have a defence system of some kind. In the human body, these would be the white blood cells. Most other organisms that we know of might release hormones, enzymes, electrical impulses, poisons or similar, all to neutralise a threat and ensure its own survival."

Millan laughed and shook his head. "Sorry, doctor. Are you suggesting that the cloud has created soldiers? Wouldn't these *soldier cells* all be killed on impact when they fell from the sky, or has the cloud also invented jet packs for them?"

Doron held up a hand to halt the exchange. Millan fell silent, and the doctor muttered something about it all being simple biology.

"Well, maybe it didn't need to create soldiers. What if all it did was control the local population and turn them against us," said Alis.

Vivek bounced gently in his chair. "Indeed! It is an excession event, and the rate of human mutation indicates local aggressors are the most likely explanation for cannibalistic activity."

Alis wished Vivek would try harder to support her point. "But why leave her? I still can't see a hungry mutant walking away from a warm body." She shook her head. "Irvana wasn't eaten by mutant humans with massive teeth. She was shot at close range, with a weapon that exceeds the capabilities of the planet. That's what we should be looking at."

Millan stretched his arms above his head. "So, a gang in the dark zone has got some off-world tech to play with. It wouldn't be the first time."

Alis felt her frustration rising. "No local gang could defeat Irvana, could they?"

Millan shrugged. "Is that story more or less likely than sky-soldiers?"

Her frustration tipped over into anger. "How did she get a transmission out moments before she died, then? Isn't that odd? Explain to me how the dark zone suddenly thinned out right when she needed it most."

She was pleased with the question, but Millan's counter came quicker than she'd hoped.

"Radioactive interference isn't constant in dark zones, Alis. Transmissions can be blocked one minute then let through the next."

He turned to Doron and splayed his hands imploringly. "We're wasting time here. We have evidence of significant local mutation, nothing else. The doctor isn't a hundred percent sure the burns are from an energy weapon anyway, right doc?"

The doctor pursed her lips. "I would say our best theory is the fabric was melted by a Phase 5 energy —"

"See?' said Millan, "Still not the high certainty we need. This is an excession event. It could be fatal for us. We need to be focusing on the local population. Pick the low-hanging fruit, as they say."

Doron nodded his agreement. "Until we have evidence to the contrary, I'll ask the techs to focus their probabilities on Millan's theory."

Millan blew out a sigh. "Thank you."

Alis let her mouth hang open, unable to express her disbelief. Doron pointed at her, his finger indicating the discussion had finished. "In the meantime, Alis, I want you to base yourself with us. Go and examine the tower where Irvana's body was found. You might find something on foot that the drones missed from the air."

Alis felt her stomach drop. Having her theory ridiculed was unpleasant, but being told not to return to her fieldwork was intolerable. "I'm in the middle of my on-planet research, Doron. I left Nasser with my contacts wondering where I've gone. If I'm away much longer, they'll be suspicious. I need to get back down there."

Doron raised his eyebrows. "I decide how everyone is deployed, Alis. You're still at an early stage in that city. You can drop back into it later with little being lost."

Alis went to protest again, but Doron held up his hand. "And I suggest that while you're here, you do everything by the book. Check your transmissions. You need to follow due process, OK?"

The last words stung. But she knew Kasper and Leon would have to wait. She gave him a curt nod.

They all took their leave until only Alis remained. Perhaps it was the emotion of finding Irvana, or being made to feel foolish in the conversation, but she felt a million miles away from Doron and Millan.

She walked over to her friend's transparent tomb. Tears welled in her eyes and she gave in to them, letting her grief spill down her cheeks and drip gently from her chin. She shuddered as emotion flowed out of her, then gasped and wiped the tears from her face.

Irvana's words of warning seemed even more relevant now. She wondered what Irvana would do if their positions were reversed. The answer was obvious: she'd do her best to find out what really happened. And she wouldn't trust a soul while she did it.

Chapter Seven

"It just doesn't seem possible," said Alis. She hurried along beside Vivek. It wasn't easy to keep up with him, and she had to take three paces for each of his long strides. "Irvana was clever, fast, skilled, and careful. Basically, she was more capable than most of us. And she gets killed by locals? It doesn't seem right."

Vivek walked as if gliding through water. His head bobbed gently on his long neck and his arms floated around him as if caught in a slow current. Alis could never be certain whether he was gesticulating, or if his hands were simply moving with his overall flow.

"You think every death should be justified?" he said.

She frowned and shook her head. "No. I don't mean it feels morally wrong. I mean the explanation should make more sense."

The image of a blood-stained, melted suit rose in Alis's mind. She screwed up her face, then shook her head to get rid of it. A pair of doors opened ahead, and they passed through to a wide courtyard. On the other side, an identical pair of doors led into the vast, high-sided Mission Store.

Alis realised she didn't have much time left alone with Vivek. "Irvana designed the convertor," she said. "It's the only real weapon we have. She gave everyone hope."

"We were using diviners long before the convertor. They are weapons, too," said Vivek.

Alis looked at him and frowned. His long face continued to stare ahead. "OK, but I mean a weapon that actually fires something and does damage. So I take a diviner into a dark zone and find the centre point of the cloud." She threw up her hands. "Great. What next? We literally had nothing until Irvana invented the convertor."

Vivek's head bobbed sideways more than before. Alis took it as a shake of the head.

"We are all weapons," he said. "Just as we are all the answer. It's a question of finding how everything fits together. The convertor relies on other things falling into place before it becomes effective. It only shows its true purpose when it reaches the right place at the right time. As do we all."

They reached the far side of the courtyard. The doors to the Mission Store slid open to let them pass.

Frustration twisted in Alis's stomach. Someone she admired was dead and now she had to listen to this techno-philosophy from a daydreaming intellectual. "OK, OK. I get it. There's a bigger picture here. All I'm saying is that, of all the people who would have wound up dead in a tube, Irvana is bottom of my list of names. I mean, she's been hell-bent on beating this thing since her home got destroyed. She did it, didn't she? Her convertor turned the tide on five planets. Doron honoured her for it—she's a living legend!"

Alis paused, her own words halting her train of thought. Irvana would achieve nothing further. She was a piece of history. The emotion returned, and she fought to keep it under control.

The facts swirled in her head. Millan's theory was so flawed it was ridiculous. She could see that Trage qualified as an excession event, but that didn't suddenly create Phase 5 technology, nor would it overwhelm someone like Irvana.

The sudden clarity almost made her burst. "How could someone so skilled end up dead on a low-risk mission? Even if those mutants are bigger and better organised! And where'd that Phase 5 weapon come from? Millan's theory on that didn't make any sense."

Vivek stayed silent for a moment, then looked at Alis for the first time since they'd started walking. "I agree."

Alis stopped, leaving Vivek to float on alone for a few paces. She jogged to catch him up. "Hang on. *Now* you agree with me? You mean you think Millan's theory sucks, too?"

"There's something wrong with every theory, Alis. That's why they're called theories and not certainties," he said.

Alis slapped herself on the forehead. "Why did I let myself get sucked in? Of course you're not going to give me a straight answer."

"That said," continued Vivek, "I believe that neither your theory nor Millan's theory are superior in merit."

Alis kept her hand on her forehead. "But you just said you agreed with mine!"

He gave another shake of his long head. "I did not. I said I agree that Irvana's death makes little sense. You have raised a valid objection. I will need to go back and review the data."

The entrance to the resource bay came into view. Alis held out a hand and caught Vivek's wafting arm, bringing him to a stop just short of the doors. She looked him in the eye. "Define an excession event."

Vivek frowned, but played along. "An unprecedented state or condition which is superior to, or greater than that expected."

Alis's face brightened. "Right! Something that's bigger or faster or smarter than we've seen before, or all three. But, doesn't contain anything new, correct?"

Vivek frowned again. "The fact that it is unprecedented defines it as new."

Alis shook her head. "No, that just means it's an updated version of the same thing. An excession event is just the same stuff, but bigger, better, or behaving like never before, isn't it?"

Vivek's frown disappeared and his head bounced gently forwards. "Indeed, Alis. Indeed." Alis hopped onto one foot and snapped her fingers like a child. "Right! So the advanced mutation and rapid decay is the excession event, because it's the same thing as elsewhere, it's just faster, or worse, or whatever. But, the weapon that killed Irvana is something completely new, right? It's not pumped-up normality, it's a whole new, different, separate thing!"

Vivek paused for a moment, then slowly nodded again. "Yes."

Alis whooped and mimed a short jig on the spot.

"But," said Vivek, "there is nothing to suggest that the cause of the excession event did not also introduce the Phase 5 technology."

Alis stopped jigging, but her smile remained. "Exactly! An excession event didn't kill Irvana. It couldn't have. There's nothing in it that magically spawns Phase 5 technology. I believe that someone brought that weapon into the dark zone. And I think they did it specifically to protect the cloud from our attempt to destroy it. That same someone used it to kill Irvana."

Vivek stayed quiet for a moment, then frowned. "There are many more steps required before you can rely on that conclusion." Alis opened her mouth to speak, but this time Vivek wafted a hand decisively in her direction. "I still need to review the data, but continue with your theory, Alis. Alternative perspectives are rarely useless."

Alis smiled. The chief technician's eyes creased slightly to return the sentiment. Then he turned and glided away. Buoyed by the thought that she might be making progress, Alis passed through the doors and into the resource bay.

She arrived at a polished metal table to see several square, greasy packets set out in neat rows. Their shape and colour reminded her of the dirty packets of sweets clutched in the fists of children back at the hostel. A pang of regret at leaving Kasper surprised her.

She let her mind wander down the corridors and into his room. She could see him huddled with Leon in the lamplight, both caught up in plotting their next scheme. He turned and his eyes lit up, just as a wide smile split his face.

A loud hiss brought her back into the room. A Q-droid lowered its claw-hand, laid another packet on the table, then withdrew. Her eye traced the arm back to where it disappeared behind the faceless, round centre of the droid's body.

Twenty other arms of varying thicknesses waved, spat, and shifted around the hovering droid. The base of each one disappeared behind its large, button-like centre. Alis wondered if all the arms would pop off if she pressed it.

This Q-Droid had the look of a Mark 3 about it. It had probably seen better days. Far away to either side, Alis could see several Mark 4s and 5s, even a Mark 6, going about their inventory work amongst the rows of towering racks and lockers. Each one looked much faster and shinier than the one now hovering and hissing in front of her.

"Z-13 payloads," said her Mark 3, "Sizes twelve, eighteen and twenty-four."

"Twenty-fours only," said Alis. She pushed aside the rejected packets and picked up the five that remained, shoving them into her pockets. "I also need a rope charge. The insulated type, though. I'm still holding the thing when it fires up."

The Q-Droid hissed and shifted its arms. "All rope charges must be released at first application of pressure. Not following this protocol will cause lethal or grievous harm to the person or persons in possession of the charge."

"I said insulated," she said.

The droid shifted again, flapping its arms in what could have been mild irritation. "Insulation delays payload by a maximum of 2 seconds. Lethal or grievous harm remains within a probability range of ninety to ninety-five percent."

Alis sighed. "I hear that every time I ask for an insulated rope charge. Just get me one."

The Q-Droid hissed and rotated a few degrees to one side. It hung there for a few moments, as if considering whether to obey the command. Then it rotated its arms and floated to the top of the nearest rack of lockers. Alis thought it looked more like a dozy sea creature than a droid.

The last of its busy limbs slowly disappeared over the top of the lockers. She looked down at the rejected packets in front of her, and considered the droid's response about the rope charge.

The droid was right, of course. Q-Droids knew their munitions' capabilities even better than the techs. But ultimately, they were just droids, with no field experience.

One of Alis's early partners, Ty, had shown her how a properly insulated rope charge could be controlled in the hand and, with practice, become a fast and lethal weapon.

She groaned inwardly at the thought of Ty. Their last mission still clung to her like shame. Trapped by fallen debris, they had found themselves stuck in a small basement, with too little power to call droid support.

Ty'd had the idea of combining their comms boxes to boost the signal. Mesh-suits were designed with the comms boxes sewn into the thigh, but Ty had told her they had a release catch on the inner lining, so they could come off for upgrades. He'd done this before, he'd said. They just had to pull their suits down to reach the catch.

Ty had had no problem with that. He'd unzipped, pulled his suit down, and revealed a bare male torso in decent shape. For Alis, it had felt entirely different. While he'd groped confidently down his thigh to reach the catch, she'd had to bear the embarrassment of unzipping and pulling down her top while she was naked underneath.

The last working light bulb in the cramped room was shining towards them both. If she'd turned away, her body would have hidden the catch in shadow. So, rather than turn her back to Ty, she'd been forced to cover her breasts with one arm and reach into the waistband of her suit with the other hand. Two minutes had felt like an hour.

Ty had connected the boxes to the transmitter and hit the button. The transmitter had flashed once, then exploded in a shower of metal fragments. Alis had turned her head and heard the crack of metal on bone. Ty had gasped, and she'd turned to see him slumped against the wall.

She'd sprayed the wound shut and talked to him to keep him awake. He'd slipped in and out of consciousness, but had managed a thumbs up when the droids arrived to cut them out. She hadn't seen Ty since that mission, so they'd never spoken about it.

The Q-Droid reappeared, like the rescue droid that had cut her free. She thought again of that single lightbulb, and her insides shrivelled from the memory of exposing herself.

Chapter Eight

Charnell kept no maps, and no stored instructions for an evacuation to their safe hostel. Keeping copies would make it too simple for Ribs, Troopers, or anyone else to track their escape. But regular practice meant everyone moved through it like they had done it from birth.

A few hours after the Rib's death, a frightened crowd of hostel residents shuffled into six reconditioned sewer maintenance pods. The doors slid shut and each one shot away, streaking through the sewers of the city.

One sure thing about a sharp decline in population was the sharp decline in the level of sewage. The state had abandoned the pods when it closed large chunks of the sewer system earlier that year.

The hostel's techs had found them a while ago, stripped the interiors, and welded benches to the floors. Where once the pods had sprayed chemicals and welded metal, they were now life-rafts, carrying refugees to safety through a complex, underground labyrinth.

All the children under the age of ten had no choice but to flee. Their chance of survival in the welfares would be slim. Everyone else had to choose between doing the same or taking their chances with the Bureau. Nobody chose the Bureau.

Kasper's backpack sat a few feet away in the storage locker at the rear of his pod. Leon had refused to leave his Humming Bird behind, and instead of joining everyone in the pods, was now trying his best to fly undetected high above the city streets.

Kasper thought of the people who stayed behind, and an image of Charnell's corpse flashed into his mind. It was hanging from the dais, limp and still, like a discarded toy. He felt the sharp bite of grief, and forced it from his mind.

Killing the Rib had been a mistake. Her death removed any hope of support from the Executive. The Bureau would surely wriggle free of their leash now. He looked around at the other residents sitting on the narrow benches. Tears streaked the faces of the children, and every so often one of them took a double intake of breath—a reminder that they'd only recently stopped crying.

Everyone stared at nothing, moving only with the rare bump of the pod. By chance, Prue and her carer had been allocated to Kasper's pod and had sat next to him on the bench. Oblivious to the surrounding chaos, the girl fell asleep on his arm. Her hair fanned out over her cheeks and over one gently curled fist. She had the same colour hair as Alis. The thought of Alis made him worry. Ribs would be at the hostel for a week or more, and he had no way of warning her to stay away. She'd be picked up the moment she set foot in the street.

But how likely was it she'd come back? He wondered where she was right now. *It's not like her to disappear like that*, he thought. Although, he and Leon had only been scavenging with her for just over a year, so how well did he really know her? She was clever and useful in a tight spot, but had never said much about her past or where she came from.

They worked as a team, successful because they trusted each other—so he'd thought until this morning. How could she just take their money and run away? And why now? The kiosk job had been no bigger than any other. He could have understood if it had been a ton of money, but it really 'hadn't been.

He and Leon had sworn to get it all back, but they had no idea how to go about it. They didn't even know where to start looking. Now this mess with the Ribs meant they'd have to keep their heads down. He told himself he'd work out a plan once the death of the Rib blew over.

A ping-ping sound stirred the passengers around him. The pod was approaching its destination.

Niall, a tall, lean youth worker from the hostel, rose in front of Kasper and confirmed the docking instruction on the pod's interface. "We made it, safe and sound."

The pod slowed to a halt, and the door slid back. A crowd of refugees from the pods shuffled along a wide gangway jutting from the sewer wall.

Somewhere beyond them, Kasper heard voices shouting instructions, and the crowd slowly formed into lines. It was then he noticed the two men walking in the opposite direction. The crowd thinned, and he saw the nearest one had the long butt of an automatic rifle under his arm.

Another guard appeared through the mass of people and thrust his head into the door of Kasper's pod. His eyes swept the sorry faces, then he held his wrist up to his mouth. "This one's clear."

Kasper filed out of the pod behind Niall and stood on the thick metal floor of the gangway. Warm, damp air filled his nostrils. Around him, his fellow residents smiled, hugged, and clapped each other on the shoulders. But Kasper didn't smile. Emerging like a rat from the sewers didn't make him feel good.

The guard pointed towards a large open doorway on the far side of the gangway. "Stay together. Head for the door."

Kasper's line moved off, bringing him level with the guard. "Why are you all carrying guns?"

The guard looked surprised for a second, then gave Kasper a wide grin. "To keep you softy asses safe. Now get off the gangway. There's more of you due in a minute."

Kasper's line made its way slowly through the doorway, watched by more of the hostel's guards. Everyone seemed happy to be there. They nodded and chatted to each other as they went, all of them shuffling obediently in neat lines towards their new beginning.

When he reached the entrance, the thickness of the hostel door took Kasper by surprise. It sat wide open, pushed to one side, but it still took him a few steps to go from the threshold on the outside to clear it fully on the inside.

Cables streamed out of the hinges, and a complex display flashed slowly on the inside. It felt good to have a heavy door at his back. It would take an entire army of Ribs to get through a door like that.

Inside, someone without a gun pressed Kasper's dorm number into his hand. Newcomers flooded the wide corridor, roaming about, shouting relieved greetings, guffawing, and relaxing into the bosom of their second home.

This hostel had vast corridors, like train tunnels. Bright lights hung in clusters above him. They nestled among hundreds of cables that snaked across heavy steel joists and disappeared into holes high in the walls. Kasper moved through the crowd and noticed more corridors branching off to the sides, each one bearing a large blue number stencilled onto the wall. He compared the nearest number to the one in his hand and headed for his corridor.

The crowds flowed around him, and he attempted to nod and smile at people he recognised from his own hostel. Some stared back at him, but most people simply looked the other way. After a while, he spotted the pale, wiry figure of Aileen. She had lived in the same corridor as him with twins, both with blonde, fluffy hair. He smiled. She stared at him for a few seconds, then shook her head and pushed past him, the twins trailing obediently behind.

Her reaction confused him for a moment. Then it slowly came together in his mind. The stares, the blank looks, the avoidance tactics, and finally the shake of the head from Aileen. The hostel's residents blamed him for what had happened. Perhaps they even thought it was his fault they were here now.

Confusion turned to disbelief, then quickly gave way to anger. He hadn't forced the Rib to blast Charnell to pieces! What did they expect was going to happen after that? Would the Ribs just disappear? No, the Bureau would still have moved in and sent them all off to the welfares.

Two young men glared at him as he walked past. Kasper clenched his fists and stared them down. Cowards, he thought. Where was their self-respect? The Bureau murdered our Steward. He had stood up and taken down one of theirs in response. And all while they hid, terrified in their rooms. And what happened to them? They got a shiny new home with thick walls and big guns to protect them.

"Kasper!" a voice from up ahead jolted him from his thoughts.

Leon strode towards him, towering over people and barely noticing as they parted like water ahead of him.

Kasper's mood brightened at the sight of his friend. "Welcome to the new asylum."

Leon grinned. "It's all very unusual outside. I saw a Rib in a skiff, riding beside a trooper."

"Arrested?" said Kasper.

"Holding a rifle," said Leon.

Kasper's brow furrowed. "A Rib with a gun, riding with a trooper?"

Leon nodded. "They almost found me, so I jumped a level but caught the Bird on some guttering. I'm going to need a new tail rod."

Kasper shook his head at his friend. "You should just sell it. We could use the money to jump somewhere else."

"Sell it?" said Leon.

"Why not? Do you want to stay here? The whole city's going to hell!"

They talked it over until they reached the door of Kasper's new dorm. He checked the card, then stabbed at the panel. The door slid back, and they stepped inside.

They crossed the threshold and stopped. Two men stood in front of them, both dressed in urban combat mesh-suits. One had his face completely covered by a helmet and mask. The other man, stern-faced and ageing, gave them a brief smile.

"Kasper, is it?" he said.

The man in the mask drew a pistol and pointed it at Leon. Neither Kasper nor Leon took their eyes off the muzzle.

"Who are you?" said Leon.

The stern-faced man raised his hand. Lights glowed along the muzzle of the gun beside him. Leon froze. His face twitched and the veins on his neck stood out like ropes.

Kasper lurched towards Leon. He gripped his friend's shoulder and glared at the two men. "What are you doing? Leave him!"

The man dropped his hand, and the weapon fell silent. Leon let out a soft gasp and dropped to his knees.

Kasper kept a hand on Leon's shoulder. "What was that? What did you do?"

"You are Kasper, are you not?" said the man. "The one who killed the Rib earlier today?"

"I am," said Kasper, feeling less confident than he sounded. "Are you Bureau?"

The man's face wrinkled, and he coughed out a laugh. "No!" he laughed again. "Quite the opposite! My name is Gonderson. I am the Steward here."

Steward or not, Kasper had just had a fresh lesson in why you shouldn't trust people with guns. He jerked his thumb at Leon. "If you're the Steward, why did your man here shoot him? We're supposed to be on the same side!"

Gonderson smiled. "Your friend is a hybrid. The same as the Rib you killed today."

Leon pulled himself upright. "I am not the same."

Gonderson nodded. "A younger and much larger model, yes. But you're still an unstable mix of machine and human, I'm afraid."

Kasper's temper surged. "You had my friend shot because he's part machine?"

Gonderson dismissed the outburst with a flick of his hand. "He's fine. And yes, I did. Being part machine makes him unpredictable."

Kasper inched forward, wary of the weapon in the masked man's hand. "The Rib killed Charnell because the Bureau ordered it, not because it was part machine."

The Steward's smile returned, but this time it came with a dismissive grunt. "You might call him friend, I call him dangerous. Hybrids need to earn our trust, Kasper. We've all had to learn this the hard way." Leon opened his mouth to speak, but another look at the gun kept him silent. Gonderson continued. "I'm impressed. No, we are ALL impressed. Killing a Rib? Only a handful of people have ever dared do it. I can't decide whether it was a very honourable, or very foolish."

He looked at the floor, then up to the ceiling. Kasper noticed the thickness of the man's neck. It was the same thickness as his head. The man grunted again. *He's like a farm animal*, thought Kasper. Like the slow-witted livestock that used to live in the fields outside the city.

"Whichever it is," said Gonderson, "your action has pushed us to the brink of a civil war."

Kasper took a moment to consider that claim. It sounded extreme. He and Leon swapped confused glances. "Civil war? From killing a single Rib?" said Kasper.

"One is all it took to light the fuse," said Gonderson.

"I just wanted the Rib to pay," said Kasper. "I wasn't making some ideological stand against the government."

Gonderson's face softened, and he put a hand on Kasper's shoulder. Leon remained rooted to the spot. "Well, whether you like it or not, people think that is what you intended. Forget why it happened, they won't care about that any more than the Bureau will. The good news is that not everyone thinks civil war is a bad outcome. Including me. I'll introduce you to some of my squad commanders tonight. It might help improve your perspective,"

Kasper eyed the gun gripped firmly in the fist of Gonderson's guard. "Sure."

Gonderson dropped his hand and grinned a wide, toothy smile. His eyes widened to match, but they showed no humour. He gave another grunt and moved off towards the door.

He paused at the threshold and looked back at Kasper. The smile was gone, but his eyes stayed wide. He nodded once and left.

The door slid shut, leaving Kasper and Leon alone in the room. It took Kasper under a second to realise they needed to get out as soon as they could.

Chapter Nine

Alis slid across the car bonnet and planted both feet on the ground on the other side. Behind her, the line of abandoned vehicles stretched bumper to bumper across the street. She guessed it had been a barricade. It wouldn't be unusual. Gangs in dark zones often marked the boundary of their territory with some form of barrier.

She focused her attention on the long bundle of rags that she had seen through the smashed car windows. Something about how it lay neatly on the ground, stretched out but not untidy. She moved towards it, keeping low and listening for any signs of life.

As she drew close, the rough arrangement of draped cloth and ridges slowly took on a familiar shape. She could make out a skull, abdomen, and legs. She carefully pulled the rags clear.

The chest cavity of the corpse yawned up at her, shattered and split by a minor explosion. Above that, dead skin hung like damp paper from its chin.

The lower jaw stuck out several inches further than its companion above. Sharp teeth sat in a ragged line along it. *Also too long to be human. More like an animal*, she thought. She gently pressed a fingertip onto the hard point of an incisor and felt the sharp edge threatening to slice through her finger. As she withdrew it, she noticed a gap in the bottom row of teeth where the other incisor should be sitting. She looked closer.

A fragment of tooth sat in the gap, just beside a thin groove scored into the jawbone. The rest of the jaw had no impact marks or damage, so the groove looked out of place. Her stomach jumped. This could be where Irvana's blade had cut out the tooth the doctor had shown them.

The thought of Irvana crouching here and examining the same body brought back the sadness. She stood and looked at the surrounding desolation. She hated these gloomy streets. They had killed her friend. Doron should just blow the whole place sky high and be done with it.

She set off again at a brisk pace, hugging shadows and slipping in and out of vacant doorways whenever she heard a sound. The busiest part of any dark zone was around the fringes, but here, towards the centre, no good person hung around. Every sound was a threat.

She rounded a corner and finally saw the top of the tower poking above the buildings ahead. Its sheer size gave the illusion of it being quite close, but Alis had, for once, focused on her mission prep. She knew she still had a few streets to go before the buildings fell away to the open park at the tower's base.

The sight of her target gave her a lift. She jogged up the street and hopped over a low pile of rubbish. She heard the crack of a weapon before her boots hit the ground. Caught with her weight moving forward, all she could do was twist her face to one side.

She felt the acid burn of the shot sear a line down her cheek. A fraction to the left and it would have driven a neat hole through her face. Biting back against the shock, she landed, rolled onto the ground, and came up onto her haunches with her arm outstretched.

A spray of bright yellow stars streaked away from her hand, tearing into two figures crouched in the shadow across the street. They fell to the ground suddenly and silently.

For a second, she struggled to drag her eyes away from the fallen bodies. She'd finally come across someone using projectile weapons.

Movement caught her eye. A group of six, maybe eight, figures shambled towards her out of the gloom. One of them raised a long weapon to its shoulder. She turned to find cover and found three more figures blocking the street behind her.

Hemmed in by buildings on either side, she thought fast. Maybe eight behind her and only three in front. She took the path of least resistance. She sprinted towards the three figures.

More yellow flashes burst from her arm. Two bodies staggered, only one fell. She flicked her wrist and the curl of the rope charge blazed like an unfurled snake at her side. Another flick, and it streamed through the gathering dark. It wound tight around the shaggy bulk of the nearest figure. She pulled hard, and the cord sliced through fur, flesh, and bone, scything the creature in two before it could cry out.

Something whistled past her head and ricocheted off the street in front of her. Ignoring it, she sprinted to within just a few strides of the last of the three creatures ahead.

The smell of sweat and rotting meat hit her nostrils. The creature's arm swung high, and something came spinning towards her out of the darkness. She rolled as it sailed past, then aimed for her attacker's head.

For an instant, the shot lit up a freeze frame of a pale, greasy face with large, sharp teeth. Then it struck home, tearing away the creature's head in a spray of dark offal.

She ran around the tumbling corpse, her back crawling with the thought of a bullet catching her between the shoulders. She zig-zagged down the street, then crashed through the first doorway she could find.

Stumbling from the impact, she covered her head with her arms as another shot cracked off the wall beside her. Too late, she realised the floor had missing sections and pitched forwards, hitting it hard as another shot zipped through the air above her.

Pain raged in her knee, and she gasped to catch her breath. She cursed her carelessness, pushed herself up onto her feet, and limped towards the back of the house.

Behind her, the doorway darkened. A throng of figures pressed into the small entrance, each trying to be the first to push their way across the threshold. Framed by the doorway, she finally got a sense of their size.

They were exceptionally large. Much larger than her. She hadn't noticed them making any noise in the street, but now the sounds of snarling and growling filled the narrow hallway.

She slid around a corner and pressed herself against the wall. Her mind went back to the tooth in the lab and the fragments of human bone still embedded in its edge. A chill gripped her stomach. Breathing hard, she took a pebble-sized object from her belt. Flicking two buttons on the side, she heard the hum of electrics, then quickly reviewed her decision.

In a confined space, this was a bad idea. High explosives could bring the building down. The last time she had done that, she'd got stuck in a basement with Ty. *But he's not here,* she thought. *If he was, we'd fight the odds. I'm here on my own.*

She flung the grenade towards the front door. A shot whistled down the corridor, missing her outstretched arm and tearing a hole in the wall beside her. She dived into the nearest room, just as a massive thump rocked the front of the house.

Thick, billowing clouds gushed into the room, covering her in debris and choking her with lumps of dry dust. She lay still and listened as it settled. No more snarling came from the hallway.

She pulled herself to her feet, coughing and spitting the dust from her mouth. Around her, long work surfaces hung from every wall. She could see gaps at irregular intervals, each one filled with exposed, open-mouthed pipework waiting for the looted machinery to return.

This part of the city sat close to the epicentre of the infection. It had been the first to go to ruin. Looters had even ripped the thermo-cooker from its housing in the corner. Something like that was so heavy it must have taken five or six people to steal it.

She shook the dust from her hair, then checked herself for wounds. Other than the bullet wound on her cheek, she only had minor grazes and bruises on her upper body. Looking further down, she spotted a small hole in her mesh-suit and dipped a finger into it. It came out bloody. She sighed and wiped it on her suit.

She gripped her left index finger with her right hand, then pulled it back until it snapped. She shook it once, and with her other hand caught a small tablet that dropped out of the broken joint. Swallowing the tablet whole, she snapped the finger back into place and held her hands out in front of her. The cuts dried in front of her eyes. She pushed a finger through the hole in her mesh-suit. No blood. The meditab was already doing its work. Time to leave.

She picked her way around the debris and approached the rear door. Listening for any sign of life, she slowly opened it and slipped out into the rear garden of the house. Moonlight painted the edges of the adjacent buildings and walls, giving an outline sketch of her surroundings. She took a breath and ran.

A few hours later, she stepped off a mono-beam bullet tram, with the tower only a distant point at the other end of the line. The station nestled like a limpet to the inside of the brand new hill complex where the wealthy remnants of the city's population had paid to be rehoused.

A few people alighted with her—all of them clean, fed, and walking like they had all the time in the universe. As though the killer cloud above their city didn't exist, she thought.

Millan stood up from a nearby bench and smiled. Something about his smile irritated her. Before she could speak, he nodded towards the hole in her mesh-suit. "You look like you've been busy."

Alis looked at his spotless trousers and shirt. "Yeah? You don't."

Millan gave a brief laugh. He summoned a taxi, and it descended swiftly to greet them. They climbed inside, and Alis let the warm gel seats shift and adjust to her shape. The gentle grasp felt like a lover's hand after the battle in the dark zone.

The taxi rose towards the vast, domed roof that held the combined hope of survival for the temporary city beneath it.

"Any luck?" said Millan.

Alis shook her head. "No. I got close, but hit too much resistance."

Millan looked out of the window. "Who did you run into?"

Alis shrugged. "I'm not sure. It's dark in there. Could just have been fat, greedy humans."

"Fat humans tore a hole in your suit? Were they military?"

She shook her head again. "Not sure. They were disgusting, that much I *do* know."

His eyes left the window and returned to her face. "Come on, Alis. That's a graze from a weapon. Try to work with me, here. We need to know what we're facing."

Alis lifted her eyes and returned his stare. "Where was my drone? I always have a drone in the dark zones."

Millan spread his hands. "We still don't have any drones left on this planet. Thanks to the hostility here, they're all just rusting heaps of scrap scattered out there in the darkness."

Alis huffed, looked away for a moment, then turned back to him. "If I had a drone, I'd never have been seen."

Millan sighed. "Quit moaning. It was in your mission brief that you had to go in without a drone." A slight smile curled his lips. "You did *read* your mission brief, didn't you?"

Alis ignored his jibe. "With all our resources, we still can't get a single drone redeployed from somewhere in this entire galaxy?"

He shrugged. "Doron is working on it. Now, stop dodging the question. Tell me what you found in there."

Alis sighed. "At first, it looked like a street gang. I took a few out and left the others behind. I thought that was it. Then suddenly there were loads of them, all very keen on getting their hands on me."

"Mutated?" said Millan.

"Dramatically," he said. "Big and heavy. Some carrying weapons, some covered in fur. All of them hostile."

"Fur?" said Millan. "Where did they find fur in an urban dark zone?"

It was Alis's turn to shrug. "No idea. But I think I found the owner of Irvana's trophy tooth. She'd cut it out of a mouth filled with lots of teeth the same kind of size."

Millan waited a moment, then laughed out loud. The shock made Alis sit back in her seat. "Fur and big teeth?" He laughed again. "Maybe they were bears! Were you carrying any honey? Bears love honey!"

Alis didn't see the joke. The flash of teeth, the exploding skull, the fetid stench, it all came rushing back. The teeth made her think of Irvana's body hanging in a glass tube.

"Cannibals," she said, "They stank of dead meat. There's only one source of meat left in the dark zones."

Millan looked puzzled. "You're actually serious."

Alis felt frustration explode in her chest. "Of course I'm serious!"

He held up a hand, "OK, OK. Take it easy. What size groups were they in?

"Between six and ten, I'd say," said Alis.

Millan looked thoughtful, "Moving in patterns, or random?"

Alis shrugged, "Difficult to tell without watching them for longer, but they couldn't all have been hanging around hoping someone would turn up. They knew I was coming that way."

Again, Millan looked thoughtful. "They were armed, you said. What with?"

"Well, mostly just debris fashioned into a weapon of some sort," said Alis. "There were a few guns, though. But no high energy weapons, if that's what you're getting at."

Millan leaned back, his eyes resting on the ceiling of the taxi. "So, we're no better off than before you went in. Although now we know bears seem to thrive inside a dark zone."

Alis ignored his sarcasm. Then a thought struck her. "You're not interested that they were waiting for me? I think that's a pretty big deal."

Millan kept his eyes on the ceiling. "Why assume they were waiting for you? You might just have hit a part of town where they hang out."

But she had fought her way through an ambush before. They had been waiting for her in there. "You're not listening. They were organised. They must have been watching me. It was a perfect spot for an attack."

Millan's frown returned. "I don't see it. They're all mutated and dying. There are no real leaders, it's just a descent into survival of the fittest."

Alis glared at him. "I am telling you, they were waiting for me."

Millan cocked his head to one side and smiled. "I know. I'm just saying there's still some doubt about it."

She felt her frustration surge and breathed out, trying to regain her calm. "But if I'm right, it means the mission was leaked, and someone in that dark zone is trying to stop us from finding out any more about it."

Millan's smile faded. "Alright, Alis. You're making some serious leaps now. Just calm down."

Alis threw up her hands. "How can I *calm down*? We should spot the biggest risk and check it out, not dismiss it because we might have doubts!"

He took a deep breath. "I didn't say I was dismissing it. I'll include your comments in the mission report to Doron," he smiled again, "as I always do."

Alis turned and looked out of the window, annoyed by Millan's lukewarm response to her theory. She searched her feelings to see if she'd over-reacted. She didn't think she had.

Her eyes scanned the flat tops of the apartment blocks as the taxi approached the last stage of its journey.

Despite her obvious annoyance, Millan didn't let the silence last. "The diviner needs to be off the streets as soon as possible. I'll take it back to the labs and have the Techs secure it."

He opened one hand, palm upwards, towards her. She kept her eyes on the window. "I'm perfectly capable of returning it."

"OK, but you can return it to me, right here," said Millan.

"The protocol is for me to check it in," she said.

Millan's palm closed. "I'm the Mission Director. Handing it to me is as good as checking it in."

She continued looking out of the window. "Technically, I should return it to secure storage, as my name is against the deployment."

Millan's mouth hung open for a moment, then closed slowly. "Fine."

Inside her head, Alis breathed a sigh of relief. She didn't want too many people looking closely at the remaining diviners.

The taxi parked, and the busy mezzanines and terraces of the café district fanned out around them. They got out in silence.

Millan led the way into the crowds and picked a route through clusters of brightly coloured chairs and tables. Evening diners sat, ate, drank, chatted, and laughed in a sea of purchased ignorance.

Alis scowled at the decadence. How could these people indulge themselves while their planet slowly died around them? She felt a familiar contempt for people who thought no further than their own tiny lives.

She followed Millan to the other side of the plaza and had almost cleared the last café when a hostess bot moved to block their path. The bot launched into a passionate presentation of the merits of her café over the others on the plaza.

Millan politely brushed off the bot's repeated invitations to take a seat. He led Alis away from the cafes and into a narrow, well-lit street of terraced dwellings. They passed two closed doors and stopped in front of the third.

Millan knocked once, then raised his fist to knock again, but a voice made it stop in mid-air.

"You must come and try our spiced swirls, sir," said the hostess bot.

Millan's face darkened, and he dropped his hand by his side. "Thank you, but no. Stop following us and go away."

But the bot had decided to chase the sale. "Really sir, it's an excellent menu this evening, and you'd be hard pressed to find anything finer than our Cloud Gammon Risotto."

"I said leave us. Now," said Millan.

The bot opened its mouth to speak, and Millan flicked his wrist. Streetlight flashed along the edge of something metal. The bot's power cord split with a loud, fizzing sound. Alis watched as the bot froze and went dark. The loss of power robbed it of life, reducing it to nothing more than an ornate statue.

Millan folded his weapon out of sight. The sudden violence was out of character, but Alis had to admit that his skill was impressive. He knew precisely where and how to disable the bot. And he had done it in the blink of an eye.

"Have you got something against service bots?" she said.

"No, I just prefer them as piles of junk," said Millan.

The door of the house opened, and they stepped inside. Before it closed fully, she saw the dead bot staring dumbly at them from the street.

"Perhaps leaving a vandalised robot outside the door wasn't such a clever idea?" said Alis.

Millan didn't answer. They stepped into a large, open room. A hovering circle of metal and woven cables hung a few feet above the floor.

A bright skin of shifting blues, greens, and reds covered the centre of the circle. Millan strode towards it, bent his knees, stretched out his arms, and dived straight into the centre. Ripples fanned out as his hands plunged through the skin. In a single motion, his entire body slid out of view, and the surface returned to its gentle, shifting pattern.

Alis waited a few seconds then sprang forwards. Like Millan, she stretched out her arms and let her body slide smoothly through the coloured skin. After the last few ripples died away, the portal, much like the hostess bot, fell dark and silent.

#

Chapter Ten

Leon knocked twice on the steel door of Lab 2. Kasper stared at the entry light. It stayed red. Something bumped his elbow as people pushed past him in the narrow corridor. Nobody turned to apologise.

Every corridor in the hostel seemed choked with a human tide of children, carers, sickly parents, and hostel militia. The latter had the most energy: groups of young people in combat mesh-suits, pushing their way to the freight bays with bright eyes and determined faces.

Leon knocked again.

"Who is it?" came an irritated voice from the other side of the door.

"We are friends of Stefan. He said we could come round for tea," said Leon.

Kasper smiled to himself. Years of scavenging know-how had paid off. Within half an hour of Gonderson leaving, he and Leon had found the whereabouts of the local fixer.

Every hostel had at least one. Fiercely reclusive and proud of their disregard for the law, if you had their trust and the right amount of money, a fixer could give you anything, especially information for the curious and influence for the desperate.

"Is that so?" said the voice. "I'm not certain I've got any tea."

"No problem. Any drink is fine," said Kasper.

They waited. Nothing happened. They'd somehow got the code wrong. Leon raised his hand to knock again. Before he could strike the metal, the red light flicked to green, and the door slid aside.

In front of them stood an elderly woman. One side of her long, wrinkled face sagged lower than the other, as though in a permanent state of melting. Halfway down it, a black glass eyeball sat level with the bridge of her nose. Her head was pale, scarred, and hairless, except for a single bright red topknot.

Kasper took a half step back from the sight in front of him. He clamped his lips together, trapping a curse before it flew out of his mouth.

The black glass ball didn't fit her eye socket well. It looked as though she'd found it somewhere and pushed it into the empty hole. The other eye flicked rapidly from side to side, forced to do double the work to take in her visitors.

Kasper composed himself. Fixers spent their lives weighing deals against suspicion, and the work took its toll on their faces. This one had a face that seemed to prefer suspicion.

"Stefan, eh?" she said. She spoke in a clipped manner that made her sound irritated. sounded. "Come in."

The fixer's living space looked the same as the others he'd seen: a single, large room with dilapidated decor, racks of equipment, and piles of junk lying on long tables and strewn at random on the floor.

The fixer gestured at a clear space in the junk at the end of one of the tables. She tipped two chairs, dropping a few small items onto the floor, then dragged them over.

"How do you keep track of your inventory?" asked Leon.

The fixer ignored the question. She grunted and gestured at the chairs. "Sit down, please."

Kasper and Leon Kasper took their places. They sat bolt upright on the front edge of their seats, trying hard not to offend. Their host squatted next to the table, settling at the same height as her guests, but with only her legs taking her weight.

Kasper marvelled at the simple benefits of cybernetics. The fixer looked directly at him. "What is it you need from me?"

Kasper opened his mouth but didn't speak. He realised that he and Leon hadn't discussed how they were going to run the negotiation.

Awkward seconds went by, then Leon jumped in. "Jump Passes. We need passes, cleared for immediate use."

The fixer's good eye widened and she pulled her head back from the table. "Passes? If I had any jump passes, I'd have used them myself. The city is crumbling. Its days are numbered."

She shuffled in her squat. Kasper knew how to play these games. The shuffle could show an unconscious 'tell'. Either her cyborg legs were getting tired, or she was lying about the passes. And everyone knows machines don't get tired.

He focused on her good eye. "OK, so you don't have any. But let's imagine that you could get your hands on two passes. How could we persuade you to give them to us?"

The fixer's eye shifted as she focused on Kasper's face. Its glossy black partner stayed cold and unmoving. "You couldn't."

Kasper knew these dances could be difficult, and found himself settling into a familiar stride. "If we could exchange them for money, you would have something with which to trade elsewhere."

She gave a wry smile, and her human eye darted back and forth between him and Leon. "Good effort. But I suspect such passes would prove rather expensive for you."

"Of course," said Kasper. "We wouldn't expect you to undervalue your favour."

The fixer gave another smile. "I see you are not new to this."

She shuffled again and placed one skinny, pale hand on the table. Progress thought Kasper. "Flattery is insufficient, I'm afraid. Do you have as much money as you've just implied?"

"Between us, yes," said Kasper, "and I'm willing to bet that with the hostel on lock down, your ability to bestow favours elsewhere is in danger of drying up."

The fixer tilted her head to one side and stared at him. After a moment, she relaxed. "Some passes might have recently come to me. But they were given in return for my favour. Why should I now sell my favour to you?"

Sensing a chance to close the deal, Kasper placed his hand on the table—palm down, mirroring the fixer's own gesture—and chose his words carefully. "If Gonderson has his way, the local business climate is going to get pretty tough all of a sudden. Those passes could be the last thing you sell for quite a while."

The fixer frowned. The action pulled her scarred skin into tight ridges, making her scalp look like cracked ice. She held the frown for an uncomfortable half-minute, then the front of her glass eye slid aside.

Inside the exposed socket, Kasper could see tiny, snake-like cables. Each one moved in a writhing, shining pattern, surrounded by an orange glow. Leon stiffened in his seat. Kasper gave him a smile that made him look more confident than he felt.

The fixer turned her head towards the piles of junk in the room. A similar orange glow rose around a small, square locker bolted to the far wall. She took a moment to study the locker then abruptly slid her eyeball shut. The glow died instantly.

She walked over to the locker, took out a package, and brought it back to the table. As she settled back into her squat, Leon nodded. "Resonance tagging. That is how you keep your inventory."

The fixer ignored him. "These are the only two I have."

She laid a small brown package on the table in front of them. "You're very fortunate."

Kasper eyed the package. "Is that leather? I haven't seen genuine leather for years."

"It is leather," said Leon, "and neither have I."

The fixer ignored them again. "Passes are expensive. And you won't find any others that are ready for immediate use."

She unsnapped a flap on the side of the package and opened it carefully. Inside, a shiny oval box nestled in the main pocket. The ends of two slim cards poked out from a panel on the reverse of the open flap.

She slid them out, read each one, then placed them face up on the table. "As I said. Ready for immediate use."

Kasper scooped them up and squinted at them. "Yep. They're lifers! No expiry."

He held them closer. New names for them both weren't a problem, but they'd have to work on switching the previous owner's picture with their own. He looked at the picture on the first one, then the second, then back to the first.

His stomach dropped. "It's Alis!"

On one card, Alis's name stood out clearly in bold lettering, but on the other it said her name was 'Shoran'. Leon took them from him and stared hard at the pictures.

"It cannot be her. She told us she jumped to the city last year. These are dated two years ago."

Kasper spread his hands. "So, she lied to us. It looks like she's been making a habit of it."

Leon held the passes up towards the fixer. "Where did you get these?"

"You're asking a question to which you already know the answer, hybrid. I received them in return for my favour," she said.

Leon tapped a finger on the picture of Alis. "You mean a favour for her?"

The fixer nodded and held out a hand for him to pass them back. Kasper felt like objecting, but he knew better than to try keeping them. He let Leon hand them over and they both watched as the fixer pushed them back inside the leather flap.

"What did she ask of you?" said Leon.

The fixer gave a slight shake of her head. The topknot shook faster than her head, making it look like a tiny figure dancing on her scalp. "Fixers never discuss a favour. I'm sure you know that already."

Kasper couldn't let the coincidence pass. She'd taken their money and been lying to them since they met. "The woman in those pictures stole our money. We trusted her and she stabbed us in the back. If you know anything about her, we want to know!"

The fixer smiled. "Favours for favours."

"We're just trying to find her," said Leon, "If you have some information, we would not forget your help."

The smile stayed in place. "I said favours for favours."

Kasper couldn't hide his frustration, and only just avoided fully blowing up at the brick wall of a woman in front of him. "Look, we don't have time for this. We need to know where she is. What do you want in return?"

The fixer switched to studying Leon, as if seeing him for the first time. "If our idiot steward brings a war to my door, I will need protection. You, hybrid, will come to this room and provide it for me."

Leon thought for a moment. "And you will tell us what we want to know?"

She nodded. The tiny figure danced again. "You will have one minute in which I will answer whatever questions you ask."

Kasper looked at Leon. The plan was to leave well before Gonderson started a fight, anyway. He raised his eyebrows.

Leon nodded. "Agreed."

Kasper turned to the fixer and opened the questioning. "Where is the owner of these passes?"

"Sitting before you."

He groaned and tried again. "Where is the owner of this box?"

"I do not know."

"What was the favour you gave her?"

"I stored the box you see before you."

"Why?"

"Because she asked."

"What's in it?"

"I do not know."

"What did she say about it?"

"That it was very dear to her, and that I should not part with it for anything."

"So, she's coming back for it?"

"She did not say."

"Do you expect her to return for it?"

"I expect nothing."

"What would happen if you did part with it?"

"I will not."

Kasper thumped the table. "You're not answering! You're just playing with us!"

The fixer smiled and her one good eye lit up in amusement.

Leon cut in. "When was she last here?"

The fixer looked distant for a moment. "Five-hundred and seventy-eight days ago." Kasper tried to put that figure into months. Leon managed it instantly.

He turned to Kasper. "Nineteen months ago. She left this here more than a year and a half before she ran."

Kasper glared at the fixer. "Are you certain it was that long ago?"

She nodded. "My records are always accurate."

"How many times has she been here?" said Leon.

"Seven."

Leon continued. "What did she want each time?"

"Information about the Registration and Investigation Bureau. Then about the free hostels. Then to find evacuees from the centre of the infected city of Trage. Then—you're out of time."

The fixer fell silent, clearly having no intention of finishing her answer. Kasper's frustration boiled over and he thumped the table again. "Can't you just finish answering that last bloody question?"

The fixer shook her pale head. Another solo jig from the topknot. "The passes cost twelve thousand."

Kasper spluttered. "Jump passes are worth four thousand each, maximum."

Leon leaned forward in his seat, knowingly violating the etiquette that prohibits any attempt at coercing a fixer. "That is unreasonable. If you want my help, you will need to be fair with us."

The dark eye-ball snapped open. The interior shifted and writhed. "You need to rethink your body language."

Kasper made to snatch for the package, but the fixer caught his hand and squeezed it. The pressure made his knuckles click, and he cursed at the pain.

Leon grabbed the fixer's wrist and applied pressure of his own. The cables in her arm pinched together beneath his grip, and the two hybrids stared at each other. Her eyeball blazed orange.

The pain in Kasper's hand became unbearable. He kicked uselessly at the floor and slapped the tabletop. "Alright, alright! I'll leave it! Let go of me!"

Without breaking her focus on Leon, the fixer slowly released her grip. Leon did the same. Kasper tore his hand free and rubbed it furiously.

She flexed her fingers once, then turned to look at him. "That was disappointing. Do you have the twelve thousand, or are we finished?"

Kasper kept rubbing his hand. They had come looking for jump passes and found a clue to tracing Alis and their missing money. The game had changed. They needed time to think.

"We'll be back with it," said Kasper.

Chapter Eleven

Gonderson laughed and took another glass of wine from a passing host bot. The three men around him, two of them commanders in uniform, did the same. Kasper didn't reach for another. His drink was still full, and he focused instead on trying to understand Gonderson's joke.

"Anyway," said Gonderson, "let's just say that I certainly never saw her mother again!"

Another guffaw exploded from the commanders. The routine was getting tiring. Bawdy story, drink, bawdy story, drink, bawdy story, and so on. Kasper smiled awkwardly and looked down at his glass. He wasn't a drinker, but Gonderson had insisted.

"So," said Gonderson, "our new, Rib-killing resident here has made quite a name for himself among the recruits. An inspiration, some say."

He grinned and slapped Kasper on the shoulder. These commanders were the third group Gonderson had steered him towards. Upon each introduction, the commanders had addressed him enthusiastically as "Rib-killer," then insisted he give them a detailed account of how he'd avenged his murdered steward. He was thoroughly sick of it.

"You've done us all a service, boy," said Jubb, the rough-looking commander of Seven Squad.

"Shows a lot of courage," said Urvey.

Urvey looked the youngest of the commanders Kasper had met so far. He couldn't have been more than a few years older than Kasper, yet here he was leading a large squad of men and women, ready to start a fight he couldn't win.

"Quick-thinking, too," said the third man. This one was supposed to be a steward from another hostel in the city, but he lacked the stoic grace of Charnell, or the zeal of Gonderson. His trouser suit didn't fit him well, and he had a dead-eyed look that made Kasper feel uncomfortable. "Have you thought about joining the fight? We could do with your help over at our place."

Gonderson raised his eyebrows and grinned, but Kasper shook his head. "I'm not really the military sort. Too many rules to follow."

Gonderson laughed and smacked Kasper on the shoulder once more. Jubb and Urvey laughed along.

But the other man didn't crack a smile. "Life has always been full of rules, Rib-killer. Power goes to the one who makes them. Death comes to the one who breaks them."

The man's eyes stayed lifeless. Something in his voice sent a chill through Kasper. Before he could put his finger on it, Gonderson placed a heavy arm around his shoulders. "Let me show you something."

He guided Kasper out of the room and into the vast space of the freight bays beyond. He lifted his arm from Kasper's shoulders, and waved it in a broad arc ahead of him. Kasper followed the gesture. In front of him stood a long row of giant armoured vehicles. He had never seen so many in one place. Each one squatted low over massive wheels, bristling with heavy weaponry, steel grillwork, and defensive spikes.

"Impressive, aren't they?" said Gonderson.

Kasper stood rooted in awe at the killing machines in front of him. Impressive, yes, but it looked as though Gonderson was planning to wage a full-scale war on the Bureau.

He fought the urge to turn and run for the exit. "Yeah."

Gonderson gave a short, humourless chuckle. "You've already killed one. There'll be many more dead in the coming weeks. The Bureau has got a fight coming!"

Despite the steward's confidence, his devoted commanders and all his hardware, the Bureau was still the Bureau. They'd made an art form out of violence. Gonderson had no chance.

"One hostel against the entire Bureau?" said Kasper. "They'll have the support of the Troopers, too. Do you really think we could win?"

That smile again from the steward. "The Bureau isn't the only organisation with friends in the Executive. And we're not one hostel, but many," he gestured at the row of death machines in front of them, "The Bureau does not expect us to have armaments and training. When they come, we'll hit them hard. They'll have to negotiate when they see they can't simply sweep us aside. Change is coming, Rib-killer. It's a new era of self-governance."

Kasper heard the self-belief in the steward's voice. He sounded both similar and different to Charnell. The older steward always held the same belief in his voice, but he only ever preached a better way of life for society.

Where Charnell had patience and wisdom in abundance, Gonderson seemed intent on revolution and glory. This made him extremely dangerous. The hostel couldn't possibly hold out against the joint might of the Ribs and District Troopers.

In fact, he thought, the Executive wouldn't need the Troopers after all. It wouldn't do for the official law enforcement arm of government to go about massacring civilians, even if those civilians were driving war machines and being led by a maniac.

The Ribs had no such political problems. He imagined the reports on screens across the city. Agents of the Registration and Investigation Bureau met with organised, violent resistance when conducting their lawful ID checks. When the smoke cleared and they reported the dead, they could simply claim self-defence.

After all, one Rib had already died while trying to do the same job in another hostel. Kasper imagined the talking heads on the screens. Doesn't this strengthen the case for martial law in these challenging times?

He turned back to Gonderson. "You're really thinking of provoking them? They don't care about the children, you know. They'll just bust right in and shoot anyone that moves."

Gonderson placed his hand on Kasper's shoulder. "Your concern for the children is admirable, Kasper. But you need to broaden your view. People are dying across the city already. Those left behind will soon see little point in leaving their homes. The Executive has failed to close the breach in the sky, so can it keep order? It has no choice but to use force. The Bureau saw this coming and has quietly moved into position. Soon it will become the brute force the Executive needs."

Kasper resented the steward's lack of regard for personal space, and fought the urge to shrug his hand from his shoulder. Gonderson continued. "Your brave action panicked them. They played their hand too early. They've assaulted civilians, and we now have the right to meet them with force. And meet them, we will."

Gonderson was obviously convinced the hostel would survive an attack. But what about a full-on siege? Kasper's mind searched for a way to save himself. "What if they don't attack at all? They could just sit and wait you out. You can't keep everyone locked in here forever."

Gonderson grinned. "This structure was built a long time ago. They built more than a front and a rear door in those days. You've already used one underground route in. If the time comes, we have plenty of options to come and go as we please."

They turned to walk back towards the crowd of officers and supporters. Gonderson finally released Kasper's shoulder. "Of course, all adult residents will be expected to join the effort. We are a co-operative community, after all."

Realisation hit Kasper like a punch. He should have seen it earlier. Why else would Gonderson accept so many mouths to feed?

He took a breath. "Our hostel just served you up a load of new recruits."

Gonderson waved a hand, as if to bat the words away. "I didn't plan it that way but, yes, thanks to you, we're much better resourced today than we were yesterday."

Kasper knew only luck had allowed him to walk away from killing the Rib. His luck wouldn't hold against a hundred more of them.

He took another deep breath. "I'm not going to join your militia and get myself killed. You've got plenty of people and resources here, but you're all trapped. I'm used to the streets, where I can move quickly, even disappear if I have to. Good luck with all of this, but Leon and I will leave tonight."

Gonderson frowned. "You mean you and that hybrid?"

"That's right, me and Leon," said Kasper.

The steward's forehead creased. Kasper had a creeping sense that he'd missed something. "Perhaps I haven't been clear, Rib-killer. We're about to go to war. The fewer rogue machines we let loose to side with their Rib cousins, the better. You want to go? Fine. But until this is over, your hybrid is staying here."

Kasper rounded on him. "You're holding us prisoner?"

Gonderson gave his now familiar, humourless smile. "Don't take it personally. All hybrids are staying inside until we've agreed terms with the Bureau. Those that have tried to leave are now, well-" he made a square shape with palms of his hands and grinned, "a little bit smaller."

Kasper thought of the waste compactors he'd seen crush metal in the city's scrap yards. He squared up to Gonderson. The man was bigger, older, and full of righteous strength, but the thought of losing his own freedom blinded Kasper to the danger. "This is a free hostel! We don't belong to you, or to anyone else. If we want to leave, we leave!"

"Security takes priority," said Gonderson.

As if on cue, Jubb walked into the freight bay. "All hybrids secured, sir."

Kasper's heart jolted. "What does he mean, 'all hybrids secured?'"

Gonderson looked hard at him. The frown was still in place, scoring deep lines across the man's forehead. "Again, security takes priority. If there's a breach, the machines are a liability. We can't have them loose in the building."

Kasper cursed inwardly. He and Leon had wasted precious time trying to get the passes. They should have found a way out straight after Gonderson's man had shot Leon. That should have been enough warning of what was coming. Now Gonderson had Leon locked up, Kasper had no choice. He had to stay.

"Is the Rib-killer with us?" said Jubb.

Kasper felt two pairs of eyes staring at him. He thought of Leon's body falling into a compactor with a load of ruined machinery. He cleared his throat and nodded. The steward's face relaxed, and he returned the nod with a wide grin.

"He's with us, Jubb. Get him kitted out like the others."

Chapter Twelve

V ivek waved his hand across the surface of his console. A hologram appeared, blurred, then quickly sharpened above it. A large, bipedal animal with rear-facing knee joints and solid blocks for feet hung in the air.

Alis shook her head, gulped down her drink, and placed the glass on the lab bench beside her. "No, no, no. It had normal human legs. Only the skull and lower jaw were like an animal."

Millan raised his eyebrows. "I thought you said they were all covered in fur? That sounds pretty animal like to me."

Alis didn't bother turning to look at him. "This one only had a few clumps of fur. The other ones were different."

Vivek switched the legs on the hologram to match human physiology. "At present, I am only concerned with the corpse."

Vivek's hands wafted over his console. Alis and Millan watched as the skull of the hologram thickened and sloped sharply backwards. A moment later, the lower jaw extended and came to rest a few inches in front of the upper jaw and nose.

"That's more like it," said Alis. She pointed at the jagged tooth resting in a clear dish on the lab bench. "Include the teeth. I'm convinced this one came out of that corpse's mouth."

"I'm inclined to agree," said Vivek.

He busied himself with refinements to the hologram. Eventually, he stood back and gazed at the creation hovering before them. The creature stood a full eight feet high and four feet across the shoulders. Dark eyeholes sat beneath its low brow, and the teeth of its lower jaw stretched upwards, sitting sharp and proud in front of its top lip.

"Looks like a badass," said Millan.

Alis nodded. "They're not all like that. Most of them are normal size. But these, they're special." She waved a hand at the length of the body. "And he's not even the biggest."

All three of them stared at the hologram. Vivek wafted a hand towards the head. "The shallow angle of the front of the skull cavity is a deformation of the original bone structure. Trauma to the front of the brain must be significant."

"Meaning what? They're stupid?" said Millan.

Vivek's neck bounced, and his head wobbled. "Not stupid. Just less able to understand context. Less able to exercise moral judgement when making decisions."

"You want to tell me why that differs from most people?" said Millan.

Alis tutted. "It looks like the infection's made some people grow teeth and hair at the same time as they're struggling to remember not to hurt people. That's not good news."

Millan shrugged. "If they're mentally deficient, it makes them even less of a match for us."

Alis placed both hands on the worktop. She stared at the hologram, and recalled faceless monsters chasing her into a ruined dark zone building. "Vivek's right. They didn't seem stupid."

Millan leaned back against the wall and nodded towards the hologram. "Accepted. But I think we can make a pretty accurate guess from that."

Alis opened her mouth to speak, but Vivek cut her off. "You said they seemed organised, that they were waiting for you?" he said.

She nodded, then drew invisible lines on the worktop with her finger. "Here's the insertion point, here's the tower and here's where I found the body. All the way from the insertion point to the body, I saw people. Nothing more than residents and a few scavengers now and then, but definitely people walking about." She pointed to a spot on her imaginary map. "But, after I moved past here, where the body is, the streets were empty until a whole gang of them jumped me. One set blocked my way and took shots at me. Another group moved up the street behind me. In any other street, I could have been down an alley or through a window before they got to me. But not this one. I had nothing but walls on either side and had to fight my way out. It was a perfect kill box. Planned, specific, and organised."

She sat back and looked from Vivek to Millan.

"Interesting," said Vivek. His hand floated across the console once more, and the hologram switched to an image of the human brain. The frontal lobe pulsed red in front of them. "The effect of frontal lobe damage on humans is the reduced ability to understand right from wrong. This is a direct result of a degradation in the ability to project forward from the present, and to consider the consequences of the decisions they make."

Millan frowned. "So, that means they can't make a decision for themselves?"

Alis shook her head. "Worse—it means they can still make decisions, but they're likely to forget that killing people is bad."

Vivek's face softened into the nearest it came to a smile. "Rather simplistic, Alis, but that definition will work for the moment."

Millan's frown stayed carved into his forehead. "If they can't understand right from wrong, how do they end up organising themselves into an ambush?"

Vivek gave a light shrug. "I do not know."

Millan's eyes widened. He slapped the wall beside him. "This frontal lobe stuff is getting us nowhere. I'm right—we're just wasting our time."

Alis pointed at the tooth lying in its dish in front of them. "So, what's your theory? Why did these things attack people? They didn't want money, or technology, or anything else. They wanted me dead, and they didn't strike until it was clear I was going for the tower."

Millan threw his arms up and held them wide open. "OK, I'll say it loud. I don't think anyone believes you. It's not called a dark zone for nothing. How can you be sure they were targeting you at all? Maybe you got caught in a turf war. You said yourself there were gangs on either side of you." He nodded towards Vivek. "And now our chief tech isn't sure, either. We've noted your opinion, Alis. Let's drop it. We've got work to do."

Vivek raised one long finger to stop him. "I merely said I do not know for certain. I can, however, offer a possible explanation."

Millan dropped his arms. "OK, please do."

The technician's shoulders rose and fell gently before he spoke, "The awareness that moral judgement exists, combined with a belief that you are not equipped to exercise it, creates a reliance on others to make those moral decisions for you. This is, of course, the basic rationale for the existence of religion throughout the universe."

Alis's eyes widened. "So, you think the mutation forced them to look for a god?"

Vivek's neck and head bounced. "Perhaps not a god. But certainly a leader, yes."

Millan pushed himself away from the wall. His eyes bulged and Alis noticed for the first time that his neck and jawline had flushed red.

He placed both hands on the worktop. "OK, OK. This is getting ridiculous. We hardly know anything about these things, let alone whether they've lost any sense of right and wrong, or they decided to look for a new messiah. It's all just guesswork. Guesswork is not how we make decisions."

The sound of footsteps made them all turn. Doron appeared, hands clasped behind his back.

He stopped beside them at the worktop, his presence filling the space. "Ah, yes, guesswork is indeed a poor basis for sensible decisions." He looked at each of them in turn. Alis felt something cold in his glare. "We might have theories, but we always need evidence before we act. Isn't that right, Alis?"

For a moment, nobody spoke. Alis looked at Vivek, then at Millan. Vivek avoided her eyes. Millan stared straight at her, a peculiar look on his face.

She felt her stomach drop. "Am I missing something, here?"

Doron continued. "The drones that recovered Irvana's body failed to recover her convertor. We now only have her prototype to use in the field. They did, however, recover the diviner she used."

He unclasped his hands and placed them on the worktop. "Unfortunately, it's damaged, possibly beyond repair. So, I asked Vivek's team to withdraw the other five and check them over."

A creeping sense of foreboding tingled in Alis's chest. She felt her cheeks flush. Millan's eyes burned into her face.

Doron cleared his throat. "It seems one of them is missing."

Millan tore his eyes from Alis. "Missing? How?"

Doron gave a small shake of his head. "The inventory had been reprogrammed to track one less diviner. It was watching five, not six."

Alis stayed quiet. She cursed herself for not preparing for this moment. Her mind raced to think of a workable excuse.

Millan guessed at the reason for her silence. "You didn't check it back in, did you?" She didn't answer. He thrust a finger at her. "You need to hand it over, right now. Or did you lose it in the dark zone?"

Alis avoided looking directly at anyone.

Doron raised a hand to calm Millan. "That one has been safely returned. The inventory was sabotaged well before

Irvana's last mission, so the one we're concerned about has been lost for some considerable time." He paused, then returned his hands to the small of his back. "Alis. Have you any idea who might have sabotaged the inventory?"

Alis felt her mouth dry up and her cheeks flush a deeper red. She tried her best to avoid anyone's eyes. "No."

He looked down at the worktop and sighed. "The techs identified the moment the code was changed. They analysed the trace energy signatures of the diviners for successive days from that point. One of them left us on a research mission without being logged."

Alis felt a cool rush of nerves in her veins. Doron had worked it out. She tried to keep the guilt from her face. He turned towards her, and she felt small beads of sweat appear along her hairline.

She swallowed. "It's safe. I thought it would be useful for my assignment, so I left it under guard back in Nasser."

Millan's jaw dropped open. "You did what?"

Alis took a deep breath. "Don't worry. It's perfectly safe."

Doron's hands came up, palms open. His voice cracked as he tried to control his temper. "How can it be safer on a decaying planet than locked away here, with us?"

Alis could feel the situation slipping rapidly through her fingers. She couldn't mount a defence on her own. "Irvana had concerns and asked me to—"

Doron signalled for her to stop talking. "Enough. If either of you had concerns, you should have brought them to me. Taking it from here was a mistake."

"Or a crime," said Millan.

Alis went to respond, but Doron's open palm pulsed at her, indicating she should stay quiet. "You will stay for the status briefing, then leave at once to retrieve it. When you return you will bring it directly to me."

She felt her face burning again. She didn't want to reveal her reasons to everyone in the room, but still needed to get back in control. "I don't think—".

Doron's hand pulsed again. "Yes, it is clear you don't think."

That felt like a slap. Her mind raced. Irvana had once suggested that people might work against their cause from within. But now Irvana was dead and couldn't speak out. Alone, Alis had very little to share at all, except for a strong feeling that Irvana had been right.

She took a deep breath. "Irvana's death is suspicious, Doron. There have been other things, too. Things that—"

"Such as?" said Millan.

She floundered, then dropped her eyes to the tabletop. She had nothing that he, or anyone else, couldn't easily shoot down in flames.

Doron sighed and shook his head. "All diviners need to be kept here, nowhere else. End of discussion. If you still want to explain yourself, you can do it once you have put right what you did wrong. Mission approval in two hours. In the meantime, you will attend Status, along with everyone else."

He turned swiftly and stalked from the room. As the door slid shut, Millan snorted his disgust. Alis ignored him.

Chapter Thirteen

Kasper's breathing came in gasps. His skin felt greasy from the fumes of battle. Drops of sweat mingled and turned to a steady trickle of sweat beneath his torn mesh-suit.

Around him the remains of Urvey's squad huddled in silence. His forearms ached, so he shifted his grip on his weapon. It did little to help. Anger billowed again in his chest. The blind arrogance of the hostel's steward had kept him here, then caused the utter carnage that followed.

The day after Gonderson had coerced Kasper to join the fight, three Ribs had arrived to discuss the peaceful registration of the hostel's residents. Instead of discussing terms, Gonderson's militia had overpowered and decapitated the Ribs.

In a move calculated to incite a violent response, Gonderson had ordered the severed heads sent back by courier to the headquarters of the Registration and Intelligence Bureau.

Within a few hours, this ancient, universal act of defiance had achieved its purpose. Faced with the murders of three agents on official business, the Executive had no choice but to grant the Bureau emergency powers, along with the extra firepower needed to bring the rogue hostel to heel.

This time there was no polite knock on the door. The first breach came from beneath the freight bay. Four huge explosions ripped through the floor, smashing, crippling, or swallowing each of Gonderson's precious war machines.

Gonderson barked orders while alarms rang across the hostel. The militia herded all the children and non-combatants to a 'safe zone' at the centre of the building. Jubb's thirty-strong squad was deployed around it for protection.

The other squads raced to cover the gaping holes in the floor of the freight bay. Fully charged weapons covered every inch of the deep holes, ready to incinerate anything that climbed out of them. But Gonderson was a hostel steward, not a seasoned warrior. He had an academic's understanding of the art of warfare.

From their position in the freight bays on the lower level, the bulk of the militia felt the jolt of a single massive blast turning a large section of the hostel roof to dust.

The Ribs had attacked the top and bottom of the building. Gonderson now needed to cover two breaches located as far apart as possible. Screens in the freight bay gave the assembled squads a clear view of roughly a hundred Ribs dropping into the newly exposed upper corridors.

Gasps of horror went up as the Ribs fired at the residents running to the safe zone. The sudden use of lethal force was terrifying. They gunned down anyone—armed or otherwise, adult or child—who did not immediately stand still.

The freight bay erupted in a riot of cursing and threats. The sight of terrified women and children slaughtered as they ran from the intruders was too much for Kasper to watch. It was the screaming that got him the most. It made him furious, but not with the Ribs.

How could Gonderson be so reckless with the lives of people who trusted him? Poorly trained militia and innocent children were dying in terror because of his stupid ambition. Outmanoeuvred and faced with the imminent death of hundreds of civilians, an experienced General would have surrendered to save those innocent lives.

But Gonderson had instead shouted at his commanders to defend the corridors. Kasper's squad, led by Urvey, was one of those redeployed to the upper levels. They had started with twenty-four volunteers. Kasper was one of the eleven still alive.

Through streams of weapons fire and thick, suffocating fumes, Urvey's squad had managed to inflict casualties on the Ribs. Eventually, their own numbers had dwindled, forcing them to retreat. Running and stumbling from the smoke and gunfire, the remains of the squad had ducked into the darkness of the hostel's jump room. Shooting and screaming continued in the corridor as the door slid shut behind them.

Now they squatted together in silence. The high-pitched, electronic whines of the Ribs' weapons grew steadily louder as the enemy advanced up the corridor.

A nearby scream made Kasper tighten the grip on his weapon. Something thudded into the door. A few members of the squad flinched.

"Easy," said Urvey. "Nobody knows we're in here."

The hostel's jump portal sat silently in the corner of the room. Its neon outline turned the eyes and teeth of Kasper's comrades into bright, hovering targets in the darkness. He stared at the dark void and the promise of safety beyond. If only he'd stolen those jump passes from the fixer, he thought.

Out in the corridor, the Ribs drew level with the room. Footsteps fell in a steady rhythm. No haste or indecision. They simply walked down the corridor without even trying to take cover.

Once they'd faded, Urvey turned to his squad and whispered as loudly as he dared. "OK. They've moved on. Where's Bersh? Ah, Bersh, run a vidwire up the door and get a view of the corridor. Hopefully we can take their rear."

At the sound of Urvey's voice, some of the squad took their cue to shift position in the darkness.

"We can't go back out there," said one. "We're dead if we do."

"He's right," said another. "We've got away with it once, but they're murderers. We need to give ourselves up now."

"Idiots," said Urvey. "They'll just shoot us, anyway. We're in it now. There's only one way out."

The rest of the squad murmured a mixture of protests and curses, but their respect for Urvey prevailed, and the protests died away.

Bersh poked his wire under the door, then moved over to Urvey and handed him the screen. From his position, Kasper could see the screen showed no sign of movement. Two bodies lay still on the ground. Their arms and legs stretched out at angles, showing that they'd hit the ground at speed, gunned down while trying to run away.

Urvey handed the screen back to Bersh. "Right. All clear. Get ready to move out."

"Shouldn't we wait a bit longer to be sure?" asked one of the squad.

Urvey shook his head. "No. We need to strike now. They know we came this way. If they get much further and don't find us, they might double-back and trap us in here."

Bersh rolled up his equipment, and the squad fell into line behind the door. Kasper tried to steady his breathing. They couldn't win. First, he had to find Leon. Then they had to get away from this place before Gonderson got them killed.

He leaned in towards Bersh, keeping his voice low. "We should be using the hybrids. We need all the help we can get."

Bersh furrowed his brow, and the sweat glinted in the faint light of the room. "You think the hybrids are going to fight the Ribs for us? Why would they do that? The Ribs are hybrids, too."

Kasper hadn't expected this level of ignorance, but he still had a card to play. "Oh, yeah. But they still hate Ribs. I know everything about killing Ribs. I'm the Rib-killer."

Bersh's eyes grew large. "Yes, you are. So the hybrids will help us take out Ribs, will they?"

Kasper nodded firmly. "Every time."

"We need to tell the commander, let's go," said Bersh.

Together they moved closer to Urvey. Bersh took out the squad's commlink and passed it to him. "Sir, we should release the hybrids. Their strength could tip the fight."

Urvey frowned at the commlink. "The hybrids? Gonderson would never allow it."

Kasper leaned towards him. "Then don't even ask him. Let's just do it."

Urvey glared at him. "Remember yourself, or you'll have to answer when this is over."

"When it's over?" said Kasper. "It's already over! We need to get more strength on our side before we're butchered."

Bersh cut in before Urvey could respond. "Commander, they hit us harder than we thought. We're on the back foot here. We should at least put the question to Gonderson."

Urvey hesitated. As Urvey's second, he had to at least listen to Bersh. As the Rib-killer and Gonderson's poster boy for the resistance, Urvey had to listen to Kasper, too. To keep the squad together, Urvey needed them to believe he was considering every angle to ensure victory.

He took the commlink. It hummed faintly in his hand, and the tiny connection lights flashed frantically as it tried to find the steward. He shook it, then moved it around in the small space by the door. It stopped flashing and fell silent. For a moment, nobody spoke. Urvey tried again, but got the same result.

Bersh sucked in a loud breath. "Gonderson's not answering us."

Urvey handed back the commlink and quietly addressed his squad. "OK. Change of plan. Communications are out, so we're going to head down two levels to join Jubb's squad in the safe zone. The Ribs that passed us are between here and Jubb's position. We're going to move up and bust through them from behind. Get yourselves ready."

Kasper looked at Bersh. The soldier grinned and leaned towards him, his teeth sparkling in the neon glow of the portal. "Don't worry, Rib-killer. The safe zone is also where the hybrids are being held," he said.

Chapter Fourteen

Vivek got out of his chair. He headed towards the glowing hologram hanging in front of the audience. The technician's long, willowy frame seemed to waft, rather than walk, across the short distance to the edge of the display.

Doron sat in the only other chair on the platform. His thick red robe of office piled up around his middle, giving him a more corpulent appearance than usual.

Vivek arrived at the hologram. "In simple terms, what I mean is this." He pointed to a 3D rendering of the urban dark zone on Trage. "The cloud arrives in the atmosphere and infects the host planet. The infection is a type of nano-compound that we do not yet understand. Beneath it, the compound contaminates all life forms, causing the indigenous population to migrate or die."

His hand wafted over a console beneath the hologram, and the image zoomed into the streets beneath the cloud. "The reduction in population inevitably leads to a decline in infrastructure and social organisation. Those left behind are forced to live at mostly at a subsistence level, only."

The audience murmured from the dimness just beyond the bright circle around Vivek and his hologram. This was all common knowledge, nothing new to see so far. But Alis, sitting beside Millan a few rows back from the stage, knew that Vivek's team always saved their latest news until last. He might be Chief Technician, but it didn't stop him from enjoying a bit of showmanship in his updates.

Vivek continued. "We also know that the dark zone erodes normal methods of electronic communication. Complete failure occurs within a year, when it literally goes dark. Even our droids struggle in those conditions."

He waved at the hologram and, around the city centre, a series of repeating waves of light flashed continually from the sky down to the streets. Each wave started short, then widened as it approached street level.

"Currently, we attribute these electronic malfunctions to a type of radiation that seeps in through the eroded atmosphere, and forms this downward spread of radiation you can see here." His long fingers traced the rapidly flashing waves from top to bottom. "Plotting a visual of this radiation is straightforward, and we have no problem in monitoring its growth over time. But," he jabbed a long finger at the waves of light, "our analysis now shows that this is not radiation, after all. It is instead massive, self-guided atomic activity."

This was his moment. Alis sensed the confusion turning to surprise around her. A ripple of hushed chatter broke out, and she smiled at Vivek's ability to work the audience.

"You mean you think the infection is alive?" said a voice.

Up on the stage, Vivek raised a hand towards the back of the room and gave a slight bob of the head to acknowledge the questioner. "Perhaps. What we are looking at is, by almost all definitions, a living organism. It is possible that it is self-replicating. That would also not be a new phenomenon."

The room buzzed in a clatter of shuffling and murmuring. On the stage, Doron raised both hands to quell the noise. "We're all aware that the rate of mutation in this particular dark zone is higher than we've seen anywhere else. It is no virus. The infection is atomic activity, absorbed by the body and disrupting DNA. Correct?" Vivek's head bobbed, and Doron continued. "This is a new development in our understanding of the cloud. It is worrying, but it is also exciting. Accordingly, I have designated this dark zone as our first excession event."

Urgent questioning broke out amongst the crowd. Doron quickly hushed them with his outstretched palm.

The waves of light in the hologram disappeared. In their place, a wide dome covered the central region of the city. Vivek motioned towards the image. "The dark zone has been growing a thick membrane around its outer edge. Today, it finally became impenetrable." He raised a hand to emphasise his next words. "Its diameter is now increasing at a rate of almost one hundred metres every forty hours." He paused. "It is now growing faster than ever before."

Urgent voices filled the room again. Doron stood and raised his hands to call for quiet. "OK. I think that brings this status update to a close. Vivek's data will be filed and available as usual. Return to your assignments. Report any similar heightened activity in your target populations."

The audience dispersed, but Doron signalled for Alis and Millan to remain behind. "Alis, you were due to see me in an hour, but I've changed my mind. I want you to come straight away." He looked across at Millan, "You come too. There is more we need to discuss."

Alis watched him leave. "What's that about?"

"Something about not bringing the diviner back, I suspect," said Millan.

Alis tutted. "I guessed that much. But what?"

Millan smoothed down the front of his mesh-suit and absent-mindedly checked a couple of his pockets. "Whatever it is, it's a waste of time. The cloud is a cloud. We just need more convertors and we'll beat it. There's nothing else to know about these dark zones."

"And you know that for sure?" said Alis.

He paused. "Honestly? I think I've been around long enough to know, so yes. It's pretty simple. Dark zones are a symptom of the infection. Remove the infection, you remove the dark zones. I don't know why everyone is making it more complicated than it is."

Alis thought for a moment. "So, you think we should react to an excession event by just doing the same thing we've always done? Does that make sense? " She spread her hands. "Even if it did, we can't get more convertors, because the only person who knew how to make them was killed. You still think this is all a coincidence?"

She breathed out and tried to stop her mind from shifting to Irvana's death.

Millan gave a smile he clearly didn't mean. "Still working on your conspiracy theory, I see. It doesn't matter either way. If we roll back that cloud, the infection dies, and the city recovers. Same as on any other planet."

But Alis shook her head. "You're not listening to me. This one is different. I can feel it."

Millan raised his eyebrows. "Are you really sure what you're feeling? You must be pretty shocked about Irvana."

She opened her mouth, then closed it again. It was a reasonable point, she realised. For a moment, she lost confidence in her whole position on Irvana's death. But the injustice wouldn't leave her, and she glared defiantly at Millan. "Yes, I'm in control of my feelings, thanks."

Millan shrugged. "OK, so Doron's waiting. You coming?"

She gave a curt nod. He turned and she followed him out into the corridor. For a moment, she felt relieved that he didn't press her about her feelings, but the relief fled when her mind turned to Doron and why he suddenly wanted to see her so quickly.

· • • ● ●· ● ● • ● ·

The doors to Doron's rooms opened, and they stepped through into the large white stone reception room. Despite Doron's position and wealth, he wasn't ostentatious. The light-coloured drapes, polished metal sculptures, and tall red-leafed plants brought the room to life with subtlety, not with grandeur.

The man himself sat beside a low table on a large, red carpet that matched the colour of his plants. A woman in a tight green dress sat across the table from him. The two of them were locked in conversation.

The woman's eyes looked too big, almost as if her face had shrunk around them. She stopped talking as Alis and Millan approached.

Doron beckoned for them both to take a seat. "Come, come. I'd like you to meet Rikka."

He didn't seem angry at all, Alis thought. The woman in green stood and faced them.

"Rikka, this is Alis and Millan. Rikka is a colleague from outside the galaxy."

"Hello," said Rikka.

The rasp in Rikka's voice sounded too harsh to be feminine, yet her deep green slicksuit had a slash high up her legs that would not have seemed out of place at a cocktail party.

Alis nodded a greeting and settled into the nearest cushion, delighting as the gel settled up around her thighs. Doron's refinements might be subtle, thought Alis, but they felt good.

Doron gave everyone a brief smile, then began to speak rapidly. "Rikka is an expert in the field of high-energy phenomena. She worked with Irvana for a while before," he paused, "well, before she died. I think it's time the three of you worked more closely."

Rikka avoided everyone's eyes and reached for a clear goblet of wine from the table in front of her. Alis watched her raise it to her lips. She looked human, mostly. Alis wondered why they hadn't been introduced before. Irvana's work hadn't been a secret.

"Right," said Alis. "Doing what, exactly?"

Rikka put her drink back on the table. "We will be working together in the dark zone." Alis noticed the inside of Rikka's mouth was deep purple. Coupled with the big eyes and the slick green body suit, the woman suddenly looked like a reptile.

Alis usually found discrimination by race abhorrent, but something about Rikka's appearance meant Alis didn't trust her. She was so focused on this thought that it took a moment for her to register what Rikka had just said.

"Sorry. What?" said Alis.

Doron answered before Rikka could repeat herself. "You're not going back to your assignment in Nasser, Alis. We need you in the dark zone, instead. Vivek needs more data, and we have to roll that cloud back."

Alis felt her pulse quicken. She preferred to work alone. If Doron thought she needed a babysitter, then he clearly meant what he said about not trusting her anymore.

Doron saw the expression on her face. "If it's your progress in Nasser you're worrying about, we can put you both back in there once your mission is over in this dark zone."

She thought about taking Rikka back to the hostel. How would she explain this raspy, bug-eyed woman to Kasper and Leon?

"I'm just not sure that will work," she said. "I had to leave fast, and that's damaged my relationships back there. I can't introduce a new face and regain their trust at the same time."

Doron dismissed the comment with a wave of his hand. "I'm sure you'll find a way, Alis." She sensed they had already agreed this without her, so tried a different approach. "But I've just come out of that dark zone. You know I couldn't get anywhere close to the source of the infection. It's too hostile. We need to leave it up to the drones."

Rikka looked up. Alis felt herself held in those large, brown eyes. "That is not possible, " said Rikka. "The environment has evolved and will no longer support drone transmissions. The only method is direct fieldwork."

Doron's face lit up in a rare expression of zeal. "Think of it as an opportunity, Alis. You get to work on an excession event! I never got the chance to study one up close. You should be itching to get down there and explore every square metre of that dark zone."

Alis glared at him. She had hoped to put the dark zone behind her, and return to her work. Kasper and Leon were good company and, for the first time in ages, she was enjoying gathering her research.

But she realised this wasn't a choice. The idea of analysing the new data had obviously got Doron excited. Plus, he'd found the perfect person to keep an eye on her.

"Of course, it won't just be the two of you," said Millan. "I'll be coming, too."

Alis must have shown the shock on her face, because Millan laughed. She jerked a thumb towards him and looked at Doron. "How does he know about this before I do?"

The zeal slipped from Doron's face, but he continued to smile. "Don't worry. This time you have missed nothing. Millan knows about the mission because he is leading it."

Millan gave Alis another of those grins she hated. "And I hand-picked you to come with me."

"I'm flattered," she said, "but an hour ago you told me this dark zone had nothing to hide."

"And this little trip will prove me right," said Millan.

"It'll prove you can get us all killed," she said. She threw her hands up and raised her face to the ceiling. "I can't follow this guy, Doron".

Rikka had been sipping at her drink. She put it down on the table and looked at Doron. "Am I permitted to speak openly?"

He nodded. Rikka turned and stared straight at Alis. Those eyes were going to take some getting used to, she thought.

"My home is not in this galaxy, but it suffers the same infection as Trage," said Rikka. "Understanding your excession event is critical if I am to stop it. From what little I have learned, you, Alis, are a liability. You are prone to acts of recklessness. This makes you a threat to the success of my work. Despite that, I am prepared to work with you to achieve a higher aim. You could perhaps now do likewise with your own personal preferences."

The cool delivery stunned Alis into silence. The woman stared at her without blinking, clearly waiting for a response. Doron and Millan also sat in silence, waiting for Alis's reaction. She slowly realised that, at least for now, she was alone and out of options.

She shrugged and raised her hands. "OK. Looks as though I don't really have a choice. No more objections."

Rikka picked up her glass. Doron grinned at them all. "Good. You're now a team. Your objectives are to reassemble Irvana's convertor, go and find the tower, then roll back the cloud. We've learned the hard way not to underestimate whatever is in that zone, so keep it tight."

Millan rubbed his hands together. "No drones will work in there, so we'll need to travel light. We will of course need the diviner before we go."

Alis's stomach dropped at the mention of the diviner. "I know, I know. I'll go and get it." Rikka frowned. "It's not here? It is essential. Without it we cannot target the convertor."

Alis waved a hand at her. "We've already done this routine. I'm going to get it and bring it back. It won't take long."

But Rikka didn't seem convinced. She turned to Doron. "It needs to be here. Where is it, exactly?"

"Alis has it secured on the target planet," said Doron.

Alis nodded. "It'll be back shortly."

Millan slapped the side of his chair. "I should go with Alis to get it. It's too precious to leave to chance. We need to ensure it gets back here in one piece."

Alis threw her hands up again. "Why would it fail to arrive in one piece?"

"I just think I should be around to ensure it's safe," he said.

Doron waved a hand at Millan. "No, you need to be here to oversee the mission prep. Rikka can go."

Rikka nodded. Alis kept her hands up. "I don't need to be chaperoned."

"I'll decide that," said Doron. "You've proved your judgement is questionable. I feel happier having two people going to get it."

Rikka put down her glass and stood up. The hem of her skinsuit unfolded and slid down to her ankles. "We should leave immediately."

Doron placed two hands on the table and pushed himself up to his feet. "Agreed. Report straight to me when you return."

Alis and Millan took their cue and stood. For the second time in only a few minutes, Alis felt she had no control over the events going on around her. "You're wrong about my judgement, Doron."

Doron shook his head. "Not this time, Alis."

Alis thought about answering him, but it was clear from his face that she had nothing to gain. Instead, she turned and headed to the door in silence. He would listen to her when she brought back the Diviner. The one-eyed fixer would have kept it as safe as anywhere in the galaxy.

Chapter Fifteen

U rvey's squad jogged silently in single file. They moved too slowly for Kasper's liking. He had to check his stride several times to avoid stepping on the heels of the man in front. He fought the urge to just sprint past them. That would be stupid. The next corner could hide a group of waiting Ribs.

He passed shattered doorways and scarred walls on either side. Some of the door numbers were difficult to see, but he managed to pick out a few. His stomach leapt. This was the fixer's corridor. He wondered whether the hybrid had avoided being locked up. Either way, her room would most likely be empty.

He looked at the doors to his right. Lab six, then lab five. The fixer's door was only a short distance ahead. His scavenger instinct couldn't let this golden opportunity pass. Besides, he was faster than most of his squad, so he could get in and out and back in line before they got too far ahead of him.

Lab 3 appeared beside him. He took a breath and stepped out of the line. The squad passed him with questions on their faces, but none dared break the silence and say them out loud.

He rummaged through his pockets and pulled out a set of spring gauges. He selected one, and sprung the mechanism on the lab door. Pulling the door open a short distance, he slipped inside and closed it quietly behind him.

The room was precisely as he had last seen it, except without a one-eyed, scarred fixer standing in front of him. He picked his way through the items strewn about the room and arrived at the locker embedded high in the wall.

A second spring gauge overrode the lock, and he opened the door with ease. He reached inside, then stopped. A tapping sound had struck up behind him. Panic rose in his throat. With both hands stretched high and his weapon dangling at his waist, he suddenly felt very exposed. He let go of the door and slowly turned around.

On a table on the far side of the room, with one foot up on a pile of looted items, sat a muscular, wide-faced man. He wore the unmistakable black skinsuit of a Rib.

"Hello," said the Rib.

Kasper felt the urge to run for the door. Instinct told him to stay still.

The tapping continued. He watched the Rib roll a short blade through his fingers. Each time it completed a turn, it tapped against something he held in his palm.

"You're in the militia here?" he said.

"Yes," said Kasper, his voice cracking with the tension in his throat.

"You've over-estimated yourselves. You know the Bureau will prevail."

He waited for an answer, but no words came to Kasper's mind. The Rib laughed at him.

"Your silence gives you away. You know you cannot win." He nodded at the weapon dangling at Kasper's waist. "Why not give it a go? I've only got a knife. You might get a shot off before I can reach you."

Kasper's mind fought to respond. Engaging with the Rib on some level, any level, could be his only chance of survival. He opted for the truth. He steeled himself to talk, but his voice sounded weak.

"I'm not your enemy. I knew they couldn't win. I didn't even want to be involved," he said.

The Rib flipped the blade and caught it by the hilt. The tapping stopped, and the silence felt somehow worse.

"I'm not your enemy?" he said. "Funny. I heard that same statement only a few minutes ago. Wait a second."

Without taking his eye off Kasper, the Rib reached down behind the pile of loot in front of him. His hand slowly raised a large object above the top of the pile. "That's exactly what she said!"

The Rib gripped the fixer's topknot, and let her head dangle freely beneath it. Kasper's stomach dropped. Blood and dark yellow fluid dripped from the freshly severed neck. Both eye sockets were empty, and a fresh, red streak on her good side matched the older one on her withered side. He felt the bile rise in his throat.

"What?" said the Rib, looking into the fixer's face. "No comment from the wise-woman?"

He laughed again and tossed the head onto the floor between them. It gave a single dull bounce, then came to rest. The neck wound left a dark, wet smudge on the floor.

The Rib stood up. Kasper pressed himself against the wall. His mind worked furiously.

"Here," said the Rib.

He tossed the object from his palm towards Kasper. With a life-preserving obedience, Kasper reached out and caught it. Opening his palm, he looked down at the greasy black orb that, until a short while ago, had been part of the fixer's face. Bile shot up into his mouth. He spluttered and tried to force it back down.

"Nice, eh? Your turn now, I think," said the Rib.

He took a step closer, and Kasper shook. He felt like dropping to his knees and curling into a ball. Emotion pressed up into his face and made his eyes strain with an urge to cry. His hands came up involuntarily, and he waved them in a pathetic attempt to convince the Rib that he should live.

The Rib moved closer and laughed again. He kicked the fixer's head to one side. Kasper looked down at the face. He didn't want to see the Rib's blade coming at him.

It was then that the fixer's withered socket sparked. An orange glow sprang up deep inside it. The orb in Kasper's hand snapped open, and the Rib stopped. Puzzled, he laughed again, his mouth wide open.

The orb shot out of Kasper's hand and fully into the Rib's mouth. Wide-eyed, the man clutched at his throat and staggered backwards. With the Rib off-guard, Kasper found his courage and reached for his weapon. The Rib flicked out his hand.

The small blade came streaking towards him. He dived to the floor and fired wildly in the Rib's direction. The Rib ducked, then span out of view.

Random circuitry, artefacts, tools, and clothing jumped in the air as the shots smashed and ricocheted around the room. The roar of the blasts was deafening in the confined space, but Kasper didn't dare stop. His weapon jumped and clattered, sending burst after burst towards the Rib's position.

Fumes stung his eyes. The muzzle flashed and blurred his view. No movement came from the other side of the room. He stopped firing. His arms quivered and his breath came hard. He blinked rapidly to clear his eyes.

Kasper didn't think the Rib would die easily, despite the fixer's attack from the afterlife. He dropped to a crouch, stuck his weapon out, then inched slowly across the floor.

At first, he could see nothing, just piles of smashed and upturned objects, partially obscured by floating dust and the water in his own eyes. He gripped his weapon. It took him a moment or two longer before he noticed the skinsuit amongst the decimated junk.

The muscular body of the Rib lay in a buckled heap against the rear wall of the room. His right arm and shoulder were missing, and a deep hole in his chest fizzed loudly as the last of his human blood mingled with his fading electronics.

Kasper waited for movement, but none came. He relaxed and lowered his gun. Without taking his eyes off the corpse, he got to his feet and backed slowly away. He kept his eyes forward until he drew level with the fixer's head.

He felt pity for her. The slack-jaw and empty, bloody eye sockets were so grotesque that her face was like a caricature of death. Whatever life had sent the orb flying towards the Rib had now gone. He turned, grabbed the leather package from the locker, and ran for the door.

Adrenaline thumped in his veins, keeping him moving and suppressing the fear of running straight into any Ribs. He strained for sounds up ahead. Muffled thuds and shouts came to him sporadically, but he met nobody between the lab and the end of the corridor.

Gonderson had cut power to the lifts as soon as the assault started, so Kasper headed into the darkness of the stairwell. He worked his way slowly down the staircase, arrived at the next level, then peered into the corridor ahead.

The smell of weapons floated on the air. Patches of dim light dotted the walls and floor, but did little to lift the darkness. He started up the corridor, keeping one shoulder tight to the wall.

Bodies lay on the edge of the first patch of light. Nearest to him were two young women in militia uniforms. The rest of the corpses were unarmed residents. All of them stared empty-eyed at the ceiling.

He crouched beside each body and gently closed their eyes. He reached for the last body and pulled back his hand. A dead Rib stared up at him. In his head, Kasper gave a silent cheer for the dead militia around him.

He pressed his hand onto the head of the dead Rib then ran it down onto its shoulder. The human sections were as cold as the machine sections. He thought back to the Rib's indifference at the murder of the fixer. He saw why Gonderson believed all hybrids turned fully machine in the end.

But Leon remained an obvious example of where Gonderson was wrong. Kasper's anger simmered again at Gonderson's arrogance. Raising his boot, he kicked the dead Rib as hard as he could.

He reached the next stairwell, descended slowly, and stepped into a heavier stench of battle. He heard a shout somewhere ahead, followed by a burst of gunfire and the high, electronic whine of Rib weapons.

Screams echoed towards him. He stopped short of the next bend, and slid his helmet's monocular over his eye. The battery told him he only had a few minutes remaining. He inched to the bend and peered ahead.

The tiny screen showed three bright dots advancing on a larger group. The large group stayed in place, arranged in two ragged lines across the corridor. This had to be Jubb's squad, defending Gonderson's so-called 'safe zone' against the Ribs. Kasper seethed at the name. How could that idiot have thought anywhere would be safe once the Ribs arrived?

He flipped the screen up onto his helmet. He had a decision to make. Behind him, the darkness offered a silent route away from the fight and out of the madness. Ahead, Leon sat in the cells, with three murderers heading towards him. Nerves spread like ice through Kasper's chest and down his arms. Whatever the odds, he couldn't leave his friend to die.

He took a deep breath and inched his way towards the battle. Around the next corner, he found more shapes littering the floor. He bent and turned one over, recognising it instantly as one of his own squad. The dead man's mouth sat wide open, locked in a frozen scream. He closed the man's eyelids, bit back his own fear, and moved up the corridor.

The lights of the safe zone carved up the darkness, throwing long shadows behind the advancing Ribs. They sent heavy fire smashing into the barriers, each blast flashing on impact and forcing the defenders to stay low.

One defender blasted wildly and caught a Rib across the thighs. The other two Ribs returned fire. The man took a second too long to duck out of sight. Kasper watched his body take the blasts and spin away into the darkness.

The injured Rib sat on its knees in the open, firing in short bursts while struggling to get back up. The other two took defensive positions behind broken doors and emptied multiple blazing rounds into the defenders' position.

None of them seemed to reload. Kasper wondered at the amount of ammo they must be carrying. As if in answer, one of them stopped firing. Multiple blasts flared at once from the barriers, hitting the stricken Rib still sitting on the floor. He broke apart in a bright plume of fluid and sparks. The other Rib returned fire, sending another defender spiralling into the air.

Kasper stepped forward. The Ribs stayed focused on their assault on the barrier. He crept towards the nearest one, pausing in the shadows, then timing his movements with the blasts from its weapon.

A doorway hung open a short distance behind the Rib, leaving a narrow width of the door jutting into the corridor. Kasper settled behind it, dropped to one knee, and took aim. Recalling Urvey's advice, he took a single, long inward breath, then exhaled slowly as he squeezed the trigger.

The blast flashed, then screamed towards the Rib's exposed back. It tore through flesh and metal, splitting the man in two. The figure swayed, then collapsed onto the ground.

Kasper switched his aim to the Rib on the other side of the corridor. Taking a breath, he squeezed and fired again. But the Rib was already moving. He dived to one side, rolled smoothly and came up firing.

A red-hot spike punctured Kasper's leg. He cried out, and felt his weapon slide from his hands. Two thuds hit his helmet. The corridor spun. He tried to bring his hands up, but his arms refused to move. Blue flashes hurtled towards him, and he threw himself onto the floor.

He felt a massive thump through the ground, then a roar filled his ears. The floor fell away, and the bright lights of the safe zone slid out of view.

Something punched him in the stomach. He struggled to pull air into his lungs. Something else crashed into one side of him. Pain set his nerves ablaze. He cried out again. Something told him it would be a good time to fall asleep and, grateful, he closed his eyes.

Chapter Sixteen

Alis and Rikka stood at the edge of a high platform, the only people visible in the dark courtyard. The Salient had provided nothing else but the space and height they needed to start their journey.

The air in front of them rippled. A patch of the darkness shifted. For a moment, it seemed to reach out to them, then shrank back and formed straight edges around an empty centre.

Alis felt a familiar tingle of adrenaline as sharp steel corners appeared, quickly followed by broad metal surfaces studded with blinking lights. The pentangle, fully materialised, hung quietly in the middle of the courtyard.

A breeze ruffled her hair, and the centre of the pentangle turned into a swirl of colour. She looked over at Rikka. The alien woman seemed unimpressed. She looked straight into the swirling centre, oblivious to the wonder of the technology in front of her.

"Ready?" said Alis, raising her voice over the breeze.

Rikka nodded. Crouching, they both pushed hard against the platform and leapt straight into the churning core in front of them.

Sucking them in whole, the pentangle threw a signal to its partner on the surface of the planet below. If its partner had been sentient, it would have breathed a sigh of relief. It had been in position and waiting patiently for its passengers for over an hour.

Acknowledging the signal, it materialised in the night air, holding itself steady above the broken roof of the besieged free hostel. A few seconds later, Alis and Rikka burst out of its centre and rolled smoothly into a feet-first descent to the hostel below.

Air-boosters hissed and spat like snakes on the soles of their boots. They steadied themselves and floated down between the broken ends of two vast joists.

The remains of the hostel roof lay on the floor of the room in piles of twisted metal and torn insulation. Small pools of rainwater lapped at their feet.

Rikka stood in the centre of one of them, the hem of her skinsuit disappearing beneath the surface. "This hardly seems a safe place to leave something important."

Alis stared at the devastation, unable to speak.

Rikka kicked some debris with her foot. "I trust you didn't hide it somewhere on this level?"

The question brought up an image of the fixer in Alis's mind. Fixers were not known for their weakness. "It'll be safe."

They picked their way across the room, and Alis peered into the corridor. Rikka held two fingers over a narrow panel on her sleeve.

After a moment, she shook her head. "The building is dark. Networks and power are mostly dead. Wherever it is, the diviner is at risk. Assuming, of course, it is still in the building at all."

Alis felt the criticism and ignored it. The corridor lighting blinked uncertainly, lighting up the debris and the walls every few seconds. A deep groove in the wall caught Alis's eye, and she walked over and ran her hand over it. She muttered a curse as she felt the rough, undulating edge of the blast mark on the wall.

"What is it?" said Rikka.

Alis's cheeks burned. For the first time, she thought the others might have been right. The hostel hadn't been safe at all. She should have paid more attention to what that damn steward had been crowing about.

She swallowed hard before answering. "It's a scar from a weapon blast."

Alis stood back as the other woman traced the curve with her finger. She turned to face Alis. "This is your idea of a safe place? Someone blew a hole in the roof and started firing weapons in here."

Alis refused to believe there was no hope left, but she felt the guilt spreading to her fingertips. If Rikka had intended to punish her, she was doing an excellent job.

"I know where to go," said Alis.

They clamped scopes over their eyes, and the corridor turned into a world of grey and green. Stars glinted through great holes in the roof, and debris crunched underfoot as they plunged through the darkness.

Alis processed the surrounding damage. The destroyed roof and scarred wall suggested an attack of significant force. Although she knew Gonderson was a loud opponent of the Bureau, behind all his posturing he had never seemed brave or foolish enough to start a war.

Alis concluded this was not about maximising revenue, nor about politics. There was no trigger in all that for a sudden shift to this kind of atrocity. Something specific must have tipped the whole thing into violence.

"The steward here is a madman, but the Bureau didn't need to smash their way in and shoot the place to pieces. This is a deliberate move to take control of the free hostels," she said.

Rikka looked blank. "I am not familiar with events here in Nasser. Is this the same Bureau that was active in Trage?"

"They're the same outfit, but here they're still trying to take control of the city," said Alis.

They both walked quietly in the darkness for a few moments before Rikka spoke again.

"And the Bureau are tagging citizens for civil obedience?"

Alis stopped. "Yes. How is that you don't know this? I thought you'd been working with Doron on the dark zones?"

The view within the scope washed away Rikka's expression, but Alis felt her hesitation. I do not study societies, only the dark zones that infect them. I simply have no data regarding the civil arrangements in the cities."

Alis squinted at her but still couldn't read her face. "Cities are the same everywhere. There's always someone trying a power grab of some kind."

She sighed and walked on. Rikka fell into step. "Not on my planet."

"And where is your planet, exactly?" said Alis.

"Several light years from here. Cities are not something we create. All structures are equidistant, to maintain the balance," she said.

Alis gave her a sideways look. "No power struggles at all? Does nobody want anything more than they've already got?"

"Not all power struggles arise from wanting more of something, Alis."

Alis didn't have time to consider the statement before they reached the end of the corridor. Ahead of them sat a series of wide steel walkways. The light was still working in here, and they removed their scopes to take in the view.

Below them, walkways ran a full circle around the walls of an atrium three levels deep.

Rikka pointed to a section of the walkway on the level below. "Look there."

Alis followed Rikka's finger, and saw the marks of small arms fire on the steel railings. Her eye moved a little further along until she saw what Rikka had been pointing at. A pile of cloth and debris sat on the floor of a walkway. It looked high, perhaps head height. She could pick out rough, pale strips jutting out from the centre, possibly bearers, or some part of the hostel's pale walls.

"Someone's been cleaning up," said Alis.

Rikka nodded. "Look again."

Alis dropped her scope over one eye and focused on the pile. The sight made her gasp. Rikka grunted in agreement.

The pile of rags and debris had legs and arms protruding from it. Some of the pale strips she'd seen at first still had shoes on them. Her heart dropped.

To Alis's relief, Rikka didn't make any more 'I told you so' comments. She simply glanced around the rest of the atrium then paused. "How much further?"

Alis thought for a moment. "Down three more levels to the ground, then we head west. There's a shortcut, though."

She gripped the handrail in front of her, vaulted it, and dropped into the wide, open space of the atrium. She felt the rush in her stomach, and allowed herself a moment's delight as she plummeted past the levels below. At the right moment, she hit her boosters and landed confidently on the floor of the atrium.

Rikka landed beside her a moment later. She didn't look pleased. "We are in a war zone. It would be better if you avoided impulsive decisions like that."

Alis smiled. "You said we needed to move quickly. You can hang back if you like. I'll be quicker on my own."

Rikka didn't return her smile. "We are better off staying together. Doron wouldn't want to lose anyone else."

Alis briefly wondered what Doron might have told the alien woman. She dismissed the comment, and headed into the dark opening of the western corridor. But after only a few steps, a group of figures in black skinsuits emerged from the shadows.

Alis cursed herself for being distracted. The adrenaline surged in her veins. She noticed Rikka shift her weight onto her back foot. It looked as though Rikka could take care of herself.

The small group of Ribs fanned out in front of them, blocking their path up the corridor. Each one gripped a weapon, and their torn and dusty clothing made it clear they'd seen some action already. But despite the marks on them, they still stood straight and proud, every inch the winning side.

"Hello," said Alis.

A tall, thin woman cleared her throat in a way that said she expected everybody's full attention. She had scarlet hair, cropped short over her ears. It reminded Alis of the fixer. As the Ribs settled into position, the red-haired woman looked Alis and Rikka up and down.

"You are not residents here, I assume?" she said.

Alis let the superior tone wash over her. Keep it casual, she thought. "No, we're just visiting. We've come here to see a friend."

The woman's tone remained superior. "Well, the hostel is closed. You should leave."

Alis gave her the best conciliatory smile she could muster. "Why is that?"

The Rib woman paused, as if considering whether to provide an explanation. "The hostel failed to comply with registration regulations. It put up hostile resistance when agents of the Bureau arrived to conduct their lawful duty."

Alis made a show of looking up at the heavens. "Was it necessary for the Bureau to arrive through the roof?"

A few of the Ribs glanced at each other and shifted the grip on their weapons. The thin woman nodded. "Sadly, yes. Our work here is almost complete. You can contact the Bureau to find a record of your friend. Now you should leave, unless you would like us to check your registration status?"

Alis slowed her breathing. "We don't need our registration checked, thank you. But we've come a long way. It would be a shame to leave without seeing our friend."

The woman didn't speak. Her eyes flicked over to Rikka, ran up and down the stark green of her outfit, then returned to Alis's face. It occurred to Alis that Rikka looked unusual in defiant green amongst the greys and blacks around them.

"As I said, you will have to leave now," said the woman.

Alis smiled again. She'd just come back when this group had moved on. "OK, no- problem. We'll head out the way we came in."

Alis turned to go, but the Rib woman held up her hand. "And how exactly did you get in? We have agents on every door, and I heard no reports of anyone entering the building."

Alis could see the other Ribs starting to look tense. One of them fingered the trigger chamber on his weapon. Another looked to his leader and back again. She remembered the bodies piled on the walkway above them.

"We came in through the hole you'd made in the roof. It was very convenient," said Alis.

She turned to step away, but the woman's voice came again. "I think it will be necessary to check your registration, after all."

Alis stopped but didn't turn around. The Rib woman produced what looked like a small joystick. She pressed the top and pointed it towards Alis's back. Rikka brought her hands up, thinking it might be an attack. The Ribs responded with a clatter and whine of raised weaponry.

Alis recalled the kiosk she'd knocked off with Kasper and Leon. She'd been ID'd by the owner. She prepared herself for what was about to happen.

"I see you were recently identified as unregistered," said the woman. "You will need to come with us."

Alis flicked her eyebrows at Rikka, then slowly turned to face the Rib. "I'm afraid we won't have time for that."

She could almost hear the Rib woman's processors trying to calculate why someone would be so cocky when they're clearly unarmed and outnumbered.

The Rib woman frowned. "Fine."

She dropped her hand, and the place erupted in a roar of weapons fire. But Alis and Rikka were already moving. The blasts passed harmlessly through the air, smashing chunks out of the opposite wall.

Alis's whip hissed across the corridor in a single streak of gold. The Rib woman froze as the cord wound around her neck. She opened her mouth to cry out, but the cord cut through her throat before she could make a sound.

Alis moved again, focusing on three Ribs closest to her. Like pack animals, losing their leader left them without a plan. They fired at random. Alis blurred her arm into a short tube. She ducked and rolled, coming up on her haunches and firing in a single smooth movement. Three tiny missiles flew towards the Ribs. Three cries of pain went up, followed quickly by three dull thuds as the explosions ripped them apart.

She turned to help Rikka, but found her standing calmly among the bodies of the other Ribs.

Rikka nodded towards the three Ribs Alis had killed. "Impressive."

Alis shrugged off the compliment. "They weren't very well trained."

She looked down at the corpses lying in disarray around Rikka. All five of the bodies were headless. "I thought you might need some help. But it seems you can handle yourself."

Rikka kept her eyes on Alis. "I had thought the same of you." She waved her hand at the corpses then again to take in the whole atrium. "If you can fight like you do, explain to me why you didn't see the danger in leaving the diviner here."

For a moment, Alis considered telling Rikka about Irvana's warnings. About how her death makes them seem more urgent. She dismissed the idea. "Let's just focus on collecting it."

But Rikka's expression hardened. "We are in this mess together now, so if there is something I should know, I would rather hear it before you end up getting yourself killed in here."

It hadn't even crossed Alis's mind that she might be injured, let alone be killed. A fight with a few Rib agents hadn't changed that. She suddenly felt patronised by Rikka's worrying—hadn't she just proved she can look after herself?

Alis sighed. "Well if something does happen to me, at least it'll be a relief from all your questions."

Rikka exhaled and shook her head. She started off for the corridor. Alis let her take a few steps before following. She stepped around a headless Rib, then something about the stump of its neck made her stop.

She bent and looked closely at the wound. The skinsuit fabric around the neck had melted from the force of Rikka's blasts. The damage looked the same as on the neckline of Irvana's corpse.

Chapter Seventeen

The hostel's doctor had no military experience. What little medical equipment and ability he had were not helping him with the war raging in his corridors. The cramped hallway of his surgery overflowed with slumped bodies, cries of pain, and pale, terrified faces.

Leon stared at the doctor across the body bag on the bed between them. The doctor's white coat had the grime of war smeared generously down the front. He looked exhausted.

He shoved his hands into his pockets, stretching the fabric of his coat and pulling his shoulders into an unflattering slump. "It's not easy to accept, I know. He hasn't been conscious since he rambled about you. He's a mess. Critical. He could still make it, but—"

"Is he going to die?" said Leon.

Leon's hands hung in front of him. A buzzing green light encircled his wrists. An armed woman in combat gear stood next to him. Her weapon hung loosely from her shoulder, and her eyes never left him.

The doctor shrugged. "Hard to say. The Rib's body shielded him against the worst of the blast. But his legs and upper right side are mostly gone. The shock and blood-loss alone should have killed him, but he's still with us. He's lucky it happened right outside our doors."

Leon kept his face blank under the watch of the guard. "What will you do now?"

The doctor shrugged again. "Hope for the best. He's got a serious concussion, and what's left of him is probably bleeding internally. We've pumped him full of every kind of drug we can give him. He needs proper care. If he can avoid an infection until this madness is over, a proper hospital might save him." The doctor allowed himself a small smile. "Brave guy, though. Stopped that attack and nearly killed himself doing it."

As if on cue, the guard dug Leon in the back with the nose of her rifle. "OK. You heard him. Nothing more to be done. Back to holding."

Leon ignored her. "If he is moved right away, his chances improve, correct?"

The doctor's forehead creased. He gave Leon a tired smile, but his eyes sparkled. "Thinking of taking a day trip?"

Leon nodded towards the sound of firing coming from somewhere in the hostel. "We all might need to get out of here fast."

The doctor's eyes widened. "Get out? How would we get out? We're stuck here until Gonderson either gives up or gets killed."

The guard nudged Leon a second time. "Enough of the chit-chat, big guy. Get moving."

Leon ignored the guard again. He looked over at his friend, lying in a bag on the bed. Kasper's head and shoulders were obvious within the sterile wrapping. His body sloped away from his chin and down over the contours of his torso and waist. But those contours stopped sooner than they should. Not far below his waist, the bag continued down his thighs, then dropped abruptly to the bed. The image reminded Leon of Charnell.

The doctor nudged his glasses further up his nose, then returned his hand to his pocket. "It's not easy seeing a friend in that state."

Leon looked at the doctor's tired face. For a moment he thought he should thank him for his kindness, but then it struck him: he didn't feel upset.

In truth, he felt strangely unmoved by what had happened to Kasper. An acid rush of nerves flared in his stomach. Perhaps Gonderson was right. Had his treatment as an unfeeling machine in this hostel tipped the balance for him? Surely any human would be horrified and distraught at seeing a friend blown to pieces. So why didn't he feel anything?

The doctor cocked his head and frowned. "You sure you're OK?"

"I am, thank you," said Leon.

The guard reached for Leon's arm. "Now we go."

Before the hand reached him, the room fell into darkness. Leon froze. The coloured glow from powered devices and displays speckled the black room. From the hallway, he heard the residents chattering nervously. Shouts rose from the barrier outside. The militia clattered loudly, preparing for whatever came out of the darkness.

Leon's guard made a grab for the cuffs glowing green in the darkness. She pulled and one cuff came away empty. Before she could un-shoulder her weapon, Leon's free hand caught her squarely on the side of the head. The impact knocked her across the room, and she lay silent where she fell.

Leon flipped open a panel in his stomach, and two bright white beams shone across the room. The doctor raised his hand against the dazzling lights. "Good god! What are you doing?"

"You suggested a day trip," said Leon. He reached inside the panel and removed one of the lights. "Take this. Go and care for your patients."

The doctor snatched the light and hurried over to his patients squatting in the corridor. Outside, a barrage of small arms fire rang out, as though the entire militia had opened fire at once. Two large thumps shook the room. The firing stopped. Then he heard screams. Grown men and women, terrified and scattering in panic.

He pulled his tablet from his pocket. Scanning the room, he found an infuser in the nearby units. Pulling at the doors, he grabbed the infuser, flipped off the cap, unzipped Kasper's bag, and pressed it to his friend's exposed shoulder.

Kasper's body jolted as the serum entered the bloodstream. Moving fast, but with great care, Leon strapped the bag containing his friend's body onto his back—an action that would have given any human pause for thought, but Leon remained focused on the task at hand.

He opened Kasper's pack and took out the battered leather wallet. The passes sat securely inside, nestling against the surface of the silver box. He put the wallet away and switched off his lights. The room returned to black, speckled with the lights of instruments.

Next, he took Kasper's scope out of his pack and let it mould to the shape of his face. It gripped his skull and calibrated the gloom, giving him a clear thermal picture of his surroundings.

He checked his systems and equipment. He would not be an easy kill for anyone, but he had a higher chance of survival if he could free the other hybrids to help him find a way out. If it came to a fight with the Ribs, they would be far more effective than a human militia.

The sounds outside the medical centre stopped. Leon stepped into the corridor and watched the doctor swing his light back and forth. With little else to offer, the doctor patted shoulders and muttered reassurances to the anxious faces staring up at him. Without a word, Leon squeezed past him and stepped through the exit.

The doors slid shut behind him, and the sounds of the living fell silent. The smell of sulphur filled the air, although he couldn't pinpoint its source. Blackness hung around him in all directions. He had expected Ribs to be nearby, but no trace of movement reached him.

He tried to connect to the hostel's net, but none of the protocols he knew—including some he shouldn't—would give him a response. He scanned as far as he could for signals, but nothing came back. Nothing around him but absolute silence. Where were the Ribs? His processors didn't like it.

He set off towards the cells where Gonderson had imprisoned him, along with the other hybrids. The scope's sensitivity helped him pick a route around the medical centre and down through the darkness. His feet clunked in a steady rhythm, and warm air flowed around him. He felt strong. He'd be stronger still with the other hybrids beside him.

The warm air still carried the smell of sulphur. It hung around him like a question. He processed explanations for the silence outside the medical centre, settling on the one scenario with the highest probability, albeit the most inexplicable: the Ribs and the militia were all dead.

This conclusion left only two explanations for such an unlikely outcome. Either the person firing the last shot had died a moment later, or something else killed the last fighter standing. He'd heard two large thumps outside the building. Perhaps it was an explosion that had killed everyone. He ran the facts again, but still it came out inconclusive. He didn't like inconclusive outcomes.

He drew closer to the holding cells and slowed his pace until his footsteps fell silent. Dropping low, he gently placed Kasper's drugged body on the ground and prepared to tackle the cell guards. At close range, his size, strength, and speed should be enough to take them both out with no chance of retaliation.

Inching forward, he scanned for traces of body heat. The scope clicked and whirred gently, but registered nothing. He moved forward and tried again. Same result. He stood and peered round the last sweep of the bend. Nothing. Zero sign of life.

The scope showed the cell doors wide open, and he saw the outline of two bodies on the floor. The two guards lay in crumpled heaps, killed where they stood.

At first, he felt pleased that the hybrids had broken free. But then he noticed an arm lying drooped over the threshold of the cell doorway, its shoulder disappearing into the darkness beyond.

He walked over to the cell. The scope penetrated the gloom and showed multiple small objects strewn around the floor inside. They stayed monochrome in the scope's view, showing they were as cold as the metal on which they lay.

A closer inspection showed five hands, three arms, and eight legs—all of them tattered and bloody. Leon felt a rare, deep flash of fear. There had been eleven strong, fast, and capable hybrids in that cell. Now only a few pieces of them remained.

He turned to leave and registered another thick wave of sulphur. The source still wasn't clear, but it seemed to hang over the carnage. He committed the attributes and structure of the aroma to memory and turned his attention to finding a way out of the hostel.

Without his small army of hybrids, he might not make it past the remaining Ribs and out of the exits. His mind turned to the jump passes. The jump portal would take a long time to find without the hostel's net to guide him. He needed to reach it fast.

He hefted Kasper's weight onto his back and headed up the corridor. His mind ran the probabilities of his friend surviving the night. The answer that came back made him increase his speed.

The medical centre still sat in darkness. He passed it and picked his way through the debris of battle littering the corridor. His scope lit up the outline of a repeating rifle on the floor. He stooped and picked it up. His processors reported an approximate density of sixty percent in the fuel chamber and he decided to keep it.

After a few hundred metres, he climbed the next stairwell and emerged onto a new stretch of corridor. This one seemed to have avoided the battle.

Lights still turned gloom into daylight at regular intervals along the walls. The scope modified its brightness to avoid blinding him, and he covered ground much faster than before.

He saw nobody and no signs of battle for a full twenty minutes. The silent walls seemed oblivious to the carnage elsewhere. He tried to visualise the other corridors hidden behind the surrounding walls. He wondered if they were scarred and filled with death, somehow compensating for the clear route he now had ahead of him.

The corridor took a long sweep to the left. He squatted in the gloom between two pools of light, then sent an electronic ping flying around the arc of the bend. The tiny pulse dutifully disappeared into the darkness.

He waited a few moments, then felt it register back on the scope. Blue. He took a breath and checked again. The meter clearly showed blue in the result field. Not green. Blue. Something ahead of him had a life of its own.

Leon sent another ping, this time on a slightly different trajectory, aiming to plot the size of the energy source. That came back blue as well. The energy source looked wide. He rose to his feet, shifted Kasper's bag clear of his arms and walked forwards, scanning the corridor ahead.

The bend soon straightened. The walls and floor still seemed untouched by the battle raging elsewhere in the hostel. A flash of light in his scope made him stop dead. Something ahead flashed again.

He crept forward a short distance, and the scope rendered the outline of two tall figures standing over two others on their knees. He didn't need his logic unit to help him decide what this was: two Ribs, standing over two prisoners.

The jump portal lay on the other side of the group ahead. He had to go through them. He kept his eyes on the scope's display and ran some scenarios to help plot his approach. With no military mods or training, all he had was his strength, the element of surprise, and a loaded gun.

As he watched, the two Ribs raised their arms. A moment passed, then the kneeling bodies jerked and fell sideways. The sound of two loud shots rushed down the corridor like fleeing souls.

The sight made Leon feel sick. But not, he realised, at the deaths. Again, he felt neither sympathy nor outrage. Instead of compassion, he focused on the lack of purpose, or reason, for executing two people who had surrendered. Why would anyone who is trying to restore order carry out such a pointless act? It made little sense to kill people, to become figures of terror, if the aim is to return everyone to a system of law and order.

Frustration gripped him. Why were they doing that? All of this would just continue to stay broken if they kept doing it. He moved towards the Ribs, holding his weapon out in front of him.

As he approached, one of the tall figures raised a hand to the side of its head. It paused for a moment, then nodded. Turning to the other, it gestured up the corridor in the opposite direction to Leon, and the pair of them broke into a run. Leon's frustration reached a tipping point, and he sprinted after them.

The Ribs were lighter and could move faster than he could. He watched them edge out of range of the scope and urged his thighs to pump faster. The lights on the walls whipped past him like a stream of glowing bullets. He closed the gap slightly, and watched the Ribs grow larger on his screen. Within a few seconds, he'd be able to see them clearly with his own eyes.

Then they disappeared. Both figures just seemed to walk off the edge of the scan. There were no exits to the sides, so they couldn't have left the corridor. He slowed to a walking pace. Pulling the scope from his face, he checked it over. Satisfied, he replaced it and worked his way cautiously down the corridor.

It narrowed as he went, ending in a broad, steel door lit from above by a single dim bulb. He reached out and ran his hand over the door. They hadn't disappeared, they'd just gone through a door too dense for the scope to penetrate.

He examined the frame and found a panel showing a single red light. Locked. He needed to get through it, but without a working scan, he'd have no idea of what waited for him on the other side.

Kasper's body bag shifted on his back. A low, stuttering moan sounded from inside the folds. The noise bounced off the walls, then chased away down the corridor. Leon froze. He realised that someone could approach from behind without him knowing. They might already have heard Kasper groaning. For that matter, he also had no idea who might come through the door at any moment. He suddenly felt very exposed.

Kasper moaned again. He had to keep him quiet. Reaching into a pocket, Leon pulled out another infuser. He lowered the bag to the ground and unzipped it, trying to expose as little of his friend as he could. In this state, an infection could be lethal.

The scope painted Kasper's skin a greyish pink, showing low body temperature. As if on cue, Kasper shook. Another moan drifted out and bounced down the corridor. Kasper's body shook again, harder this time. The hem of the body bag whipped out of Leon's hand, sending the sound of rustling plastic chasing after the moaning. He grabbed it and pushed the injection into Kasper's shoulder. Kasper's body instantly relaxed.

Leon sealed the bag quietly and reached out to lift it. A soft click made him stop dead. From the corner of his eye, he watched the red light wink out and the green one spring into life in its place. The door slid back. He span round and raised his weapon.

In front of him, a small girl appeared, her eyes wide and her face streaked with dirt. Her dress had once had a picture on the front but now had so much filth across it he couldn't see it clearly.

He lowered his weapon, removed the scope from his face, and crouched to her level in the dim light from the doorway. "Prue?"

Prue burst into tears and ran to him. He caught her in his arms and cradled her against his chest. She cried uncontrollably, her body shuddering from head to toe. They sat like that for a full minute. Prue sobbed, and Leon scanned the corridor for any sign that the noise had brought the Ribs running.

Prue looked up at him and tried to form words with her mouth, but all she could manage were gasps and more strangled sobs.

Leon smiled. "It's OK now. I've got you."

His words only made her cry harder. Still conscious of the threat from the door, he turned his attention to whatever lay past it. The door had a dim light on the other side, but beyond that he could only see more darkness.

No Ribs appeared in the room but, to his relief, traces of energy from the jump portal floated towards him. Something else floated with it, too. The trace odour of sulphur. His processors pushed an image into his mind of the hybrids' cell back at the safe zone. The same odour had been in the air there, too.

Leon picked Prue off his chest. Her crying lost its desperation, but her face didn't. Her wide eyes made her look feral. "You have to listen to me now, Prue. We're not safe here. You need to try to be quiet."

Prue nodded through her tears, but her face creased and her body shook. Leon tried again. "We have to be strong, OK? Kasper is hurt and we must get help. Do you think you can stop your crying?"

She clamped her mouth tight, but a few loud sobs still burst through. She breathed in and tried again. This time, only a few whimpers sounded through her cheeks.

He gave her another smile. "Better. That's better. Well done. Keep taking those big breaths. Take your time."

He let go of her and reached down for the body bag. Lifting it up, he swung Kasper onto his back. The fascination of the bag distracted Prue. For a moment she forgot about crying and focused on Kasper, trapped inside the plastic.

She reached out a hand and stroked the smooth skin of the body bag. Sniffing and coughing, she rubbed her face, spreading dirt into wet swirls across her cheeks and forehead.

Leon crouched, and the pair of them looked at each other. "Feeling a bit better?"

Prue nodded. Her curls wagged in the dim light from the door.

Leon tried to talk as softly as he could. "Where are you going?"

"I don't know," she said.

"Where is everyone?" he said.

"Gone."

Leon frowned. "Did they leave you behind?"

Prue shook her head, and her curls bobbed again. "The man made them disappear."

Leon scooped the little girl up in his arm. "Which man?"

All he felt was bones. He made a mental note to find her some food.

Her mouth trembled again. "The glowing blue man. He made them all disappear. She clamped her eyes shut to fight back the tears. "I was all on my own."

She screwed up her face, but instead of collapsing into more crying, she sobbed a few times then sniffed and rubbed her eyes clear.

Leon tried the softest smile he could muster. "You are a tough girl, Prue. Kasper would be impressed if he could see you now."

Her eyes brightened a little, and she looked across at the bag poking over Leon's shoulder. "Is he really hurt?"

Leon shook his head. "He'll be fine. We just need to get him to a hospital."

He peered at the open doorway. The darkness beyond the dim light could hide anything. Somewhere on the other side of it sat a jump portal. He had two passes that would take two people away from all this death and madness. Now Prue had joined them, two weren't enough. He needed time to think.

He put the scope back over his face and felt it settle into position. Retracing his steps, he scanned the nearby rooms. He found one that had a separate bedroom within it. A box within a box would be easier to defend.

A gentle shift in Prue's weight made him wonder at how such a tiny, defenceless girl could last this long in the middle of a war zone. He stepped over the threshold, and into the shell of someone's ruined home.

Furniture and belongings lay about the floor, broken and violated, leaving only empty surfaces and a bare mattress laid out in the back room. He sat on it and laid out Kasper's bag as gently as he could. Prue plopped down gratefully beside it.

Leon smiled at her, "So, what was this man like, the one who was glowing blue?"

Prue creased her face in concentration, but she didn't seem upset by the memory. Again, Leon thought her resilience was impressive for a human so young.

"He was smaller than you. Same size as Kass. He came up to us all and talked to the big men with guns. Then he just went blue all over. It got too bright. I closed my eyes. Everyone said run really fast, so I did." She stopped and looked out of the doorway, "There was a bad smell, too."

Leon nodded, "Was it a rotten smell, maybe like old food, or something you would never eat?"

Her face scrunched up and she nodded vigorously, "It's still in my nose."

Leon searched his memory and examined the odour once more. It was most similar to sulphur. Possibly from a chemical reaction to create heat, his processors told him.

He briefly considered whether it might be a new Rib technology. "What happened to the people when the man was glowing?"

Prue rubbed her hair against one cheek. "They weren't there anymore."

"You mean they ran away?" he said.

Her head shook. "Nooo. They went like smoke."

Leon paused. No immediate explanation arrived in his mind. "And what about the glowing man?" What did the glowing man do when they turned to smoke?"

"He stopped glowing," she said.

They sat in silence for a few minutes while Leon tried to make sense of what he knew so far. Back at the cells, only pieces of bodies remained after the attack, no full corpses. The trace of sulphur there and around here was the same, except at the cells it had been a lot stronger. *Did those hybrids also 'go to smoke,' as Prue put it?* He challenged his logic unit to supply an answer.

Prue sighed and smacked her lips. She let her head roll to one side, and it bumped gently against Kasper's bag. He watched her fall to sleep beside Kasper and reflected on Gonderson's opinion of hybrids as inhuman machines. Here were two vulnerable humans, resting under his protection, trusting him with their lives. What would that fool say now? *Silly question*, he thought. *Gonderson's probably already dead.*

The lock did not respond on either the door to the corridor or the door to the bedroom. Both doors stayed stuck wide open. Deciding that one more ransacked room was less likely to draw attention than a room with a locked door, he left them that way, and instead quietly began rearranging the furniture and debris around the room.

A room with a barricade across the door would draw too much interest from the corridor, but he could probably risk mocking up a fallen cabinet across the entrance to the bedroom. He found one, turned it on its side, and quietly placed it across the outside of the bedroom doorway.

He sat down on the floor of the bedroom, behind his barricade and out of sight from the corridor. The bedroom was small and even with his back wedged against the wall, he still had to push his feet under the bed.

He looked at Prue and Kasper. Stopping had not been part of the plan. The delay had reduced Kasper's chances of survival. He couldn't risk running into Prue's blue man, but he needed to make a jump and get his friend to a hospital as quickly as possible.

He leaned back and closed his eyes. Fatigue throbbed in his organic flesh and bone. He felt sleep coming, and set his sensors to wake him should anything move outside in the corridor. Then he asked his logic unit to work on a fresh problem: how might three people pass through a jump portal with only two passes? The answer came back instantly: they could not.

Chapter Eighteen

A lis and Rikka jogged along the hostel corridor in silence. Alis went back over events in her mind. The melted neckline on the suits of the dead Ribs continued to trouble her. She hadn't seen how Rikka had done it, but the alien woman had killed five opponents before Alis had killed two. Did Doron know Rikka was that good?

"It's up here on the left," said Alis.

"Good," said Rikka.

The door to Lab 2 was shut, but unlocked. They quietly opened it and stepped inside. The chaos in the room caught Alis by surprise—the fixer must either be dead or long gone. Her stomach churned.

She walked to the wall locker where she knew the fixer kept the diviner. She noticed the locker was open, and looked for something to step on to reach inside it. At her feet, resting on a small pile of valuables, lay the severed head of the fixer.

Alis gasped. The sight of the eyeless skull removed any last hope she had of finding the diviner's package in the locker.

She checked anyway and found it empty. "It's not here."

"You seem very sure," said Rikka.

Alis felt like she was peering over a cliff, staring at the rocks below with no choice but to hurl herself over the edge. "I am."

Rikka's expression hardened. She stared over at the locker. A few seconds later, she relaxed and shook her head. "You are right. Traces of it remain in that locker, but it is no longer in this room."

Alis caught herself staring. What had Rikka just done?

Rikka ignored the look. "It's been gone a long while. If it's still in the building, I can use this trace to help locate it."

Collecting herself, Alis joined in, grateful that Rikka hadn't rubbed her face in the disaster. "OK. So we keep looking."

But Rikka glared at her, wide eyes looming large in the small space between them. Alis thought she saw a flash deep inside them. She looked furious. "You make it sound simple, but it is not. The simple thing would have been to return the diviner as expected." Rikka's jibe stung. Alis felt frustration rising in her throat. But Rikka hadn't finished. "What we have now is a very slim chance of finding it ever again. That's a significant problem. A problem for which we have you to thank."

It felt vindictive now. Alis could take a few jibes, but Rikka seemed to have missed the fact that Alis had hid the diviner here for a reason. "Can you change your tone? You're here to help, not judge, so stop with the accusations."

Rikka stared for a moment, then did the last thing that Alis expected. She laughed. The sound was rasping and harsh. It was brief, but Alis could tell from Rikka's eyes that it was pure amusement.

Rikka cocked her head to one side. "And what will happen if I continue? Should we part company? Without me you cannot find what you've lost, so I think not." A little of the humour left her face, and she frowned, but the smile remained in her eyes. "Perhaps you'll attack me? That would be another poor decision."

Alis snapped. Her whip sliced through the air and looped around Rikka's throat. Rikka's eyes flashed. She raised a hand to grab the cord but stopped, staring at the grip charge in Alis's hand.

Alis raised her eyebrows. "Enough of your bullshit, OK?"

She drew the whip in a fraction, letting it tighten against Rikka's skin to drive the question home. Rikka didn't respond. Instead, she closed her eyes.

The whip vibrated in Alis's hand. Her gold cord dimmed, faded, then shone a bright blue along its full length. She watched wide-eyed as it went dark, fell away from Rikka's throat and pooled on the floor between them. Rikka opened her eyes.

Alis took a step backwards. "What did you just do?"

Rikka ignored her. "I am not your enemy, Alis. I am here to make sure you put right what you did wrong. But if you attack me again, I will not hold back."

Alis squeezed the grip charge in her hand and the whip jumped into life. Rikka didn't flinch.

Alis retracted her whip. "You're threatening me?"

Rikka nodded. "Yes, you could say I am threatening you. But only because you attacked me. You now know that if you do it again, you will lose."

"So why hold back at all?" said Alis. "You can track the diviner without me. I'm no use to you."

"All of you are useful to me," said Rikka.

Her choice of words made Alis pause. "What do you mean? What do you mean *useful*?" But Rikka again ignored the question. Instead of answering, she looked around the room, then over at the door. "We need to find what is lost. Speed is important. We should separate and search alone. We'll split the levels evenly between us to cover them all. How many levels in the building?"

Alis had finally run out of words. She couldn't remember ever seeing the type of energy control that Rikka seemed to perform at will. She didn't trust the alien woman, but she couldn't beat her in a fight, and they both wanted the same thing. But the shift of power made Alis feel weak. It was not a feeling she liked.

"28," said Alis. "There are 28 levels."

Rikka looked down at the left side of her skinsuit. A neat rectangle, about the size of Alis's hand, gently pushed outwards from beneath the surface of the fabric. Alis watched as the material stretched so thin that it would surely tear. Instead, it seemed to sense it had reached its limit and shrank away to reveal the object.

Rikka caught the object as it fell free. The gaping hole at once filled with a green gel and disappeared. She handed the object to Alis. "You can use this."

Alis took the object. It felt flat and solid, but somehow seemed too light for its size.

Rikka motioned towards the door to the room. "It'll go live as soon as we part company out there. If it detects the diviner, it will guide you to it."

Alis ran her fingers over the alien guide. It had thousands of lines crisscrossed over each surface. Some seemed alive, shifting position as she turned it over in her hands. "Did Vivek give you this?"

Rikka shook her head. Alis frowned. "It's yours? Does Doron know you own a secret device for keeping track of our most important equipment?"

Rikka shook her head again. "I configured it when I realised what you had done. There seemed to be a high probability that we would need it."

"And where did you get it? How many more are there?" said Alis, "If our enemies have them—"

She stopped. A minute ago Rikka had claimed they weren't enemies. But why have a device like this? She tried to remember for certain whether coming to find the diviner had been Rikka's idea.

Rikka sighed. "I built only one. There are no more like it, so you need not feel threatened by its existence. We're just wasting time, now. We must begin our search."

Alis squinted at her. "So, if we split up, and I have the only one of these that exists, how will you find the diviner? I can't see you doing that without a second device."

Rikka's face hardened. "I do not need a device. You are wasting time. Let us go, now."

Alis realised Rikka was right. The state of the hostel meant they needed to move fast. She decided to let the matter drop. "Fine. But this isn't finished. You will need to explain yourself to Doron when we get back."

Rikka ignored her. Instead, she pointed at the slim device shining in Alis's hand. "That will tell me if you find the diviner. If I find it, then it will tell you. Either way, when one of us has found it, we should both know. Then we meet back on the top level to leave."

"Fine," said Alis.

"Good," said Rikka, "then there is no reason to stand here talking. You take 1-14 and I will take 15-28."

Without a pause, Rikka turned and left the room. Alis looked down at the head of the fixer. She wondered how she had met her end. With her death, Alis had lost a useful source for digging into Rikka's background. The alien woman had a worrying affinity with energy.

Something moved against her hand and snapped her out of her thoughts. Rikka's device glittered and shifted in her palm, as if eager to get started. She took the hint, turned her back to the severed head, and left the room.

Chapter Nineteen

Leon's eyes snapped open. The sound of running came from somewhere in the corridor. He glanced at Kasper and Prue. They lay motionless on the bare mattress—Kasper barely alive in his body bag, and Prue sleeping soundly beside him.

Leon placed the scope over his eyes. The dark walls in front of him turned a translucent green. For an instant, the dim light from the corridor flared like the sun, then the lens adjusted to let him see over the cabinet and into the main room.

The running reached the doorway, and two men in hostel militia uniforms raced into the room. Leon didn't move. The men were unarmed, but he still wished he was holding his rifle.

They flattened themselves against the wall on either side of the door, both panting like sprinters at the end of a race.

"What is he? What is it?" said the taller one.

He was breathing so hard that the words came out in gasps. The shorter one put a finger to his own mouth and shook his head. When he spoke, he lowered his voice to a breathless whisper. "Quiet. I don't know. I don't know. But we can't stop here. It's coming this way."

The other man dismissed him with a flap of his hand. "Are you crazy? I'm not going back out there. We can hide in here. It'll go straight past."

"And if it doesn't, we're dead!" said the other.

The two men stopped talking. For a moment, the only sound was the pair of them trying to catch their breath. Leon's fingers slid over the handle of his weapon. He willed Prue and Kasper to stay quiet.

After a few moments, the shorter man shook his head. "I can't just stand here and hope I don't get obliterated. We're trapped. We've got to keep moving."

He gripped the edge of the doorframe, pulled himself over the threshold, and disappeared in a clatter of wild footsteps. The taller man cursed, then followed, gripping the doorframe and launching himself into the corridor like a paratrooper jumping from a plane.

Leon relaxed his grip on the weapon just as a third figure sprinted past the doorway. He tensed, but the man had already disappeared. Leon noted he wore a light-coloured, loose suit. Not a militia uniform. And not a Rib outfit, either.

He wondered for a moment how he hadn't sensed or heard the man approaching. Then two screams split the silence in the corridor. Light flooded the room, forcing him to clamp his eyes shut against the glare inside the scope. The screams started again, then abruptly stopped.

Darkness returned to the room. Leon opened his eyes and locked his gaze on the doorway. Nothing moved in the corridor, but still he kept staring. The smell of sulphur wafted into the room, and he felt the electric surge of fear in his stomach. He filed it away somewhere secure in his mind. If it came to it, he would not let fear stop him from facing this blue man.

He gave Kasper another injection. His friend moaned quietly as the drugs did their work. Leon took any evidence of life as a positive sign, so revised up the remaining time before Kasper became critical. He moved over to Prue, checked her breathing, then left her to sleep. She would need all her strength for the journey ahead.

As he sat back down on the ground, Leon's processors informed him he could not track the blue man with any combination of equipment or skills currently in his possession. The human part of him uttered a sarcastic acknowledgement.

He thought briefly how Kasper might have laughed at the idea of his two sides bickering. He missed his friend's unorthodox approach to problem-solving. Without him, he now had a near impossible task. Kasper would die soon without proper medical help. The best way to get it was by jumping to a suitable hospital. But they only had two passes, and he couldn't leave Prue alone in this madness.

The solution was obvious to his human brain, although his processors, programmed for survival, recommended an entirely different course of action. He ignored them. His processors did not factor ethics and honour into their calculations. The decision he made was the only real option. It was simply the right thing to do.

His mind made up, Leon lifted the cupboard to one side as quietly as he could. He hefted Kasper across his back and scooped Prue's sleeping form off the bed. She stirred, frowned, and wriggled as she found a more comfortable position in his arms.

Carrying both his wards, he crossed the main room and paused at the threshold onto the corridor. The scope was useless at detecting the greatest threat to them, but it could still detect everything else.

Pushing all logical protests out of his mind, he stepped into the corridor and set off for the open doorway where he'd found Prue. The smell of sulphur was faint now, but strong enough to make him fearful.

He thought again of Gonderson's words. You're wrong, steward, he thought to himself. I'm afraid, so I cannot simply be a machine.

The room beyond the door turned out to be one of the large refectories in the hostel. Several long tables ran in a ragged line down the entire length of the room. Benches lay scattered about the floor. Beyond them, the shutters over the servery showed dents and tears from weapon blasts.

Lights were on ins the kitchen, but nothing moved inside. Here and there were the dark shapes of dead bodies on the ground. He did his best to avoid them, in case Prue woke up and thought of her earlier horrors.

Clearing the room, he found himself back in a long, dark corridor. He saw patches of light up ahead, but otherwise the entire scene was familiar. The jump room should be on the next level up, but he couldn't tell for certain where it would be, or how far he had left to go. He tried again to access the hostel's net for help. Nothing came back.

Lights came and went as he trudged along the corridor. Other than the glowing blue man and his two victims, Leon still hadn't seen a living soul since leaving the doctor at the medical centre. Realising the jump room was also likely to be deserted, he began searching his memory for information on how to work the portal.

In the crook of his arm, Prue stirred. She let out a few long breaths, screwed up her face, and blinked up at him. Her head rocked gently in time with his strides.

He smiled at her, hoping she didn't cry out. "Nearly there. We still need to be quiet. Maybe stay sleeping until we arrive?"

She yawned, but said nothing. He didn't push it, opting instead to model the silence that he was hoping for. They passed under a light, and she put a hand over her eyes to block the sudden brightness.

He bounded up the next set of stairs and stepped out into the new corridor. To his surprise, the corridor looked completely intact. All the lights were working, and some doors sat closed, with locking lights sparkling as usual.

"OK, Prue," he said, "we've almost done it. This corridor looks safe, but I still want you to stay quiet until we reach the right room. Can you do that?"

Prue still looked sleepy, but she managed a brief nod. He gave her his best reassuring smile. Buoyed by his progress, he started swiftly, with Kasper's body bumping softly to the rhythm of his footsteps.

The corridor was well lit, but it twisted and turned at frequent intervals, so he couldn't see too far ahead. Eager not to waste time, he sent out continual pings to check for obstacles.

After a few hundred metres, his scans showed an increase in the jump portal's energy trace. He could soon pinpoint the room he needed. He looked down at Prue and gave her another smile. This time, her eyes seemed to smile back.

Leon felt pleased with his decision. He had made peace with what he was about to do. Prue would be safe, and his friend would have a strong chance of survival. Then his ping failed to return. Before he had time to think about why, the corridor went dark. Prue squealed and gripped his arm.

"It's OK," said Leon. "The power comes and goes. We will be fine. Just try to keep quiet, like we agreed."

Prue didn't make another sound. Instead, she just looked up at him as he peered into the darkness. The scope showed nothing, and his processors raced to calculate an explanation for the fluctuating power. He moved Prue gently to one shoulder and trained the barrel of his weapon on the empty corridor.

He walked a short distance and stopped. Two figures came into view on the scope: one of them male, and the other female. As he watched, the woman threw the man against the wall. The man ducked in time to avoid a punch to the face, then threw himself back at the woman. They both fell to the ground, spilling apart, then scrambling to get back on their feet and face each other.

The man caught the woman with a blow to the shoulder, and a bright flash lit up the surrounding walls. They came apart briefly, then locked together as the struggle renewed. Despite the obvious frenzy, all of Leon's readings continued to deny the existence of any movement in the corridor.

The deadlocked pair hadn't noticed him, so he took a few cautious steps closer to see what he could pick up. The readings stayed blank, but his human half shivered as he finally recognised the man that had chased and obliterated the two panicking militia men.

The woman battled hard. Her long green skinsuit flashed in the bursts of light. But, despite her efforts, the man brought his hands to her throat and press her against the wall. Leon knew he had to find a different route to the jump room. Whoever survived this fight could still choose to turn him to dust.

He took a step backwards and felt something under his foot. He shifted his weight just in time to avoid falling over it, but he squeezed Prue as he did so, and she cried out. Without shifting his hands from the woman's throat, the man turned his head and looked straight down the corridor at Leon.

He held Leon's eyes for a moment, then turned back to the woman. He pulled her head forwards then slammed it against the wall. Her hands dropped to her sides. He let go, and she slowly slid to the floor. He turned back to Leon and began walking towards him.

Leon opened fire. The corridor burst into life. Deafening blasts flashed and lit up the walls. The shock made Prue scream, and she struggled to get away from the weapon. Her flailing legs ruined Leon's aim. Most of his shots missed and bounced erratically off the walls.

"Keep still, Prue. Just keep still," he said.

Ahead of him, the man swiftly and calmly dodged any blasts that came close. Leon didn't need his processors to tell him it was time to run. He fired a few more shots, then turned and ran in the other direction.

He flew down the corridor, convinced that any delay would kill all three of them. His processors worked to find an escape plan while he ran blindly from the danger behind him. The smell of sulphur crept up on him. Already running at maximum speed, he couldn't go any faster.

The scope showed an exit within fifty metres on the east side of the corridor. The wall beside him glowed like a great blue cloak.

The exit arrived, a narrow doorway set into the wall. The door was shut, probably locked. The air thickened. He felt the man closing in. The flesh on his human half screamed to get away. Aiming his weapon, he blasted the door. Half of it blew apart.

Prue screamed. ""Stop! I want it to stop!"

The floor beneath Leon's feet glowed blue. The scope fizzed and went blank. Dipping his head, Leon used the hand holding Prue to tear it from his eyes. The air pressure rose, squeezing Leon's head like a vice. Prue screamed again and began to cry. He threw himself sideways and crashed through the broken doorway.

He twisted to keep Kasper and Prue clear of the impact, and felt a jolt as his leg caught his weapon against the wall and snapped it cleanly in two. He dropped it and backed away from the door. The floor beneath his feet shifted, and his legs gave way beneath him. He reached out to steady himself and lost his grip on Prue. She tumbled to the floor.

Beyond the doorway, the air was on fire. A vivid blue flame burst across the threshold, reaching towards him like an open hand. He tried to stand, but couldn't raise his leg. He looked down and saw his knee joint throwing out sparks. Below it was nothing but empty air all the way to the floor.

He grabbed Prue and dragged her away from the door, hobbling as fast as he could. His processors screamed at him to repair his severed leg.

The remains of the doorframe exploded behind them. In the middle of it stood the man, glowing blue from head to foot and surrounded by billowing flames, like a mythical beast raised from the underworld.

Sulphur filled Leon's throat. Maimed and stumbling, he pushed Prue ahead of him. "Run! Run!" Prue stood still in the choking passageway. She clamped her lips tight and shook her head. Leon was frantic. "Prue, go! I'll catch you up. Go, now!!"

She shook her head again. He tried to push her, but she resisted. Before he could shout again, she looked past him and screamed.

He reached for her but stopped, his arm in mid-air. It glowed bright blue from his fingertips down to his elbow. It shone like a streetlamp, throwing a wave of light around the small passage.

The light faded almost as quickly as it came. To his horror, it left behind only dark space. Dumbfounded, he looked from the stump to the other hand. He watched in despair as his fingers turned bright blue. His processors fell silent. They'd run out of ideas.

He saw Prue's mouth open wide and screaming, but could hear nothing.

A voice sounded inside his head, clear and commanding. "Give it to me."

Leon tried to push himself away, but his maimed leg flapped uselessly at the floor. The man drew closer. Flames raged around him. He stretched out his hand, his fingers shining with the same iridescent blue that now ate Leon alive. "Give it to me and you can live."

The man's mouth didn't move when he spoke. Leon barely noticed. His logic unit convinced him he could no longer protect his friends. Somewhere in his flesh he felt a warm rush of panic. "Give you what?"

The voice came again. "The box. You have one hand remaining. Pass it to me while you're still able."

Leon's panic rose. He felt the pulse hammering in his human half, threatening to make him pass out. He struggled to form the words to respond. "I....don't have a....box. I don't know what you're.....talking about."

The man pointed a finger at Leon's remaining foot. It glowed, faded, and left only dark floor in its place. Leon's human flesh crawled in horror. No pain, just the horror. "I don't....know what it is.....you want!!"

The man's expression didn't change, and his mouth didn't move. "You have a silver box. You have it with you right now, inside a package."

Leon's thoughts came slowly. He remembered the leather package with the jump passes. It had a silver box inside. Reaching into his pocket was difficult. Just opening the flap and inserting his hand seemed to take him an hour. He pulled the leather packet free, and held it out to the man.

The man nodded. "Throw it here,"

Leon saw the man's outstretched hand. He prepared to toss the leather packet, but stopped. A gold flash lit up the man's left side. The hand continued to reach for Leon, but the blue glow vanished. The voice in Leon's head screamed.

Four more flashes arrived in quick succession. Each one slamming hard into the man's body. He staggered and fell backwards, swallowed whole by the flames and smoke behind him.

Sound returned. The roar of the fire and the screams from Prue rushed in to fill the silence. He felt a hand take a firm grip of his wrist, while another snatched the leather package. The hand pulled his wrist backwards, and he felt his body sliding away from the flames. His mind was fogged, but he knew it couldn't be Prue pulling him.

The sensation felt pleasant. He relaxed, welcomed the gentle rhythm, and watched the flames and shattered doorway recede as his body slid up the passageway. Before he fell unconscious, he saw Prue walking beside him. Her hair bobbed around her cheeks. He felt happy that she had stopped crying.

Chapter Twenty

Alis dragged Leon up the corridor. Her arm ached from the effort, and she made slow progress. She cursed Rikka under her breath. The glistening alien device had lit up and directed Alis here, but the other woman was nowhere to be seen. Now she had no choice but to reach the roof alone.

She suspected that Leon's attacker probably wasn't dead. She looked back for any sign of movement. A replay of the man erasing parts of Leon's body flashed up in her mind. She had nothing to explain it. The iridescent glow, the calculated violence, the disregard for life. It was all new.

She had to move faster. She set Leon down and looked into his face. "Leon?"

Leon's voice came thick and slow. "Alis?"

"Yes, yes, it's me. What sort of state are you in? Can you see me?"

His head swept slowly from side to side. "I can see nothing."

Alis flicked a worried glance back up the corridor. Nothing yet. "Why was that thing attacking you? What was it?"

Leon's voice dropped too low to hear, and she had to lean in. "Say that again, I can't hear."

He took a breath. "Do not know. Wanted the package, the box inside."

Alis felt her stomach drop. That blue thing knew about the diviner. She had found it using Rikka's device. But how did that thing know Leon had it? Rikka's voice resounded in her head, telling her that the hostel wasn't a safe place to leave the diviner. She shook it away. Rikka didn't know about Irvana's warnings.

The blue being was the immediate problem. Doron could dismiss her idea about the cloud defending itself, but he 'couldn't ignore attempted theft by a murderous alien being.

She put a hand on Leon. "OK, look. You're in terrible shape. But we must move faster. I'm going to lighten your load, but you'll have to help me move you. I can't go any quicker alone."

Without waiting for a reply, Alis set about unbuckling the large black bag that bumped and slid alongside Leon. Pushing it to one side, she grabbed hold of him once more and pulled him along the floor. Prue stayed still.

Alis flapped at her to hurry. "Come on. We need to move fast."

Prue pointed down at the discarded bag. "You can't leave him."

Alis stopped. She looked again in the direction they'd come from. "Him? You mean there's someone in there?"

Prue nodded. "It's Kasper."

Alis dropped Leon's arm and rushed over to the bag. "This is a body bag." Prue nodded. Alis felt sick. "Is he dead?"

Prue shook her head. "We're taking him to hospital."

Alis took a deep breath. The odds were overwhelming. Her blasts had most likely just slowed the attacker down. He could soon catch up with them. When he did, she couldn't protect everybody at once.

Faced with no choice, she buckled Kasper back onto Leon's body. She looked down at Prue, and felt a pang of sympathy for the dishevelled little girl. She had already suffered more trauma in her limited years than many people do in their entire lifetime.

"We've got him, Prue," she said. "We'll find somewhere safe. Try to keep up now."

Together they made slow progress through the deserted levels. The stairs were the most difficult. Alis had to carry Kasper and Leon separately each time, which doubled the effort for each flight.

Leon pushed himself up where he could, but he had no purchase with what remained of his body. Prue tried to help and would guide Leon's mutilated limbs to the next step, or run up to get the buckle ready to reattach Kasper when he arrived. But the further they travelled, the weaker he got.

By the time the four of them reached the upper level, Alis felt her muscles telling her to stop. Prue dropped to her knees, her chest heaving as she gathered her breath. Alis set Kasper down on the floor, relieved to have made it to the broken roof, but still nervous about who, or what, might come after them.

The remaining lights picked out streams of rainwater falling through gaps in the broken roof. Alis sent her transmission, telling the pentangle she needed extraction for two people on foot and two unable to move. The confirmation came at once and she sighed, grateful someone was still out there listening.

She piled a few larger pieces of debris across the top of the stairwell. It wasn't enough to block the entrance, but it would at least slow down anyone coming their way.

She sat on the floor next to Prue, and gave her a smile. "Hey, you've done really well. We'll be out of here in a few minutes, and we'll find you a nice bed to sleep in. When you wake up, you can have anything you want to eat."

Prue looked up. She had fresh wet streaks down the side of her nose. "What about them?" She pointed at Leon & Kasper, lying heaped and broken against the opposite wall.

"I have friends who will help them," said Alis. "They'll get better, don't worry."

But Prue shook her head. "They won't. When grown-ups get sick, they die."

Alis felt her own smile fade. The world was a bitter place in Prue's eyes. It was dark and raining. Her parents were dead, her carer was dead, all the adults were fighting, and now her friends were so badly hurt they couldn't move. Around her was nothing but fear and loss. It was simply too much for a child to bear.

A small, green light flashed on Alis's suit, distracting her from her thoughts. She jumped to her feet. "Time to go."

They heaved Kasper and Leon into a space beneath the gaping hole in the roof. Shielding her eyes from the rain, Alis looked up at the black sky and waited for the shimmer of the arriving pentangle. Behind her, something clattered in the stairwell. Prue gasped.

Alis held up a hand. "Don't move."

She quickly crossed the room and peered into the corridor. Another clatter sounded on the stairs, followed by a jolt against a piece of debris. She morphed her right arm into a wide tube. The wall to her left had a large hole in it. She took up position behind it, using the hole to cover the top of the stairs with her weapon.

Her suit blinked again. She looked up to see lights shimmering into view above her. The pentangle would expect her in a few moments. She looked back at the doorway. Her stomach leapt. The debris now lay flat across the corridor. She stood up and backed away from the wall.

"Were you waiting for me?" said a voice.

Alis held her breath and spun around. Rikka stood calmly next to Prue, a slight frown over her big eyes. Her concern seemed mocking rather than genuine.

Alis breathed out. "Where the hell have you been?"

Rikka raised a hand and showed Alis a strip of fabric from a light-coloured trouser suit.

"Finishing the job you started on our bright blue friend," she said.

Chapter
Twenty-one

The little yellow bird sat in the sun, on a deep red branch of the Dragon Tree. It sang so beautifully that people stopped to listen. Each note sent a ripple of orange light flowing over its wings and down to its tail, like ink released through water.

The walls of the courtyard provided perfect acoustics for the bird's song. The small knot of admirers beamed with delight, nudging each other and pointing at the new patterns flowing and twisting over its folded wings.

Behind them, a small, dark cube floated silently through the entrance to the courtyard. No larger than the palm of a child's hand, the shape moved smoothly, keeping a precise height of two metres above the floor.

Despite the sunlight striking its surface, the cube stayed dark, as if refusing to reflect the warmth above it. It moved through the air like a small patch of gloom in a bright world filled with joyous song.

Four figures followed behind it. Over their clothes, each of them wore a full-length, black, hooded robe. One of them was the size of a child, and the arm of her robe fell to her elbow as she reached out for the hand of the nearest adult.

The cube led the group in silence, moving ahead of them at a steady height. Together, the procession moved across the courtyard and drew level with the solo performance of the little bird.

The bird stopped singing and cocked its head to one side. People looked at one another, then noticed the procession moving behind them. Without a word, they turned to face the passing figures, then bowed their heads. The procession didn't acknowledge them, except for the child, whose pale face stared blankly at the respectful group from under her hood.

The procession crossed the courtyard, and approached the wall on the far side. A small section of the wall's surface shifted and melted until it formed a perfectly square hole. Without hesitation, the cube slid neatly into the hole and stopped.

The fit was so precise that the rear face of the cube joined with the surface of the wall. The robed figures halted. All except the child, who wrestled to adjust her hood with her free hand.

After a few moments, the rear edge of the cube flashed. The wall faded to reveal the entrance, and the cube already travelling down a short passageway.

The bird's audience turned back to their show, hoping it would continue to delight them with its song. But when they looked up at the blood red branches, the bird was no longer on its perch.

At the end of the passage, Doron removed his hood. Alis and Rikka followed suit. Alis bent slightly to help Prue slide the cloth evenly off her head. Freed from her hood, Prue stared up at the domed ceiling of the vast, circular room in front of them. Low lights sat in niches on each spine of the dome, but they did little to light the large space.

"It's too dark," she said.

The others looked down at her, surprised that hers was the first voice they heard. Doron smiled. "This is a place of rest, young lady. We can't have it ablaze with light."

Prue looked puzzled. "But they're all dead. They don't care about lights. They can't see."

Doron sighed and went to speak again, but Alis got in first. "It's dark out of respect for people who come here to think quietly about those they've lost, Prue. That's just the way they like it."

Prue didn't reply. Instead, she walked over to look at the rows of black cubes bristling from the surface of the stone walls around them. Their own cube had come to a halt, and now hovered in front of an empty slot close to where they stood. It hung there obediently, as if awaiting instructions.

The three adults moved closer to the cube's empty slot and hung their heads. After a moment, Doron addressed them as though holding a sermon for a much larger audience. "We stand here to mark the passing of a friend. A defender of the weak and the sick. A victim of circumstance, who never sought to save himself. Instead, he laid down his life for those who could not help themselves. His courage and compassion have earned him eternal rest with us here, among others who made that honourable choice—the choice to give up their life so that others may keep theirs. Here, he shall rest in peace."

The three of them watched the cube move towards the wall. It paused for a second, then slid into place. For a few moments nobody moved. The only sound was the scuffing of Prue's feet on the floor as she shifted from foot to foot.

Rikka slipped the funeral robe off her back and waved a hand around the tomb. "This room is testament to the genocide. For every one of these cubes, tens of thousands have died in the struggle on their home planets."

Doron shrugged off his robe. "It's always been the same. With the infection comes the sickness, and with the sickness comes the inexorable decline."

But Rikka shook her head. She pointed at Leon's cube, now lodged permanently among the rows of others protruding from the wall. "This one died because of a mistake. He wasn't killed by the decline of a city."

Alis felt the sting of Rikka's accusation. Her anger flared. "He died because something is trying to stop us, not because anyone made a mistake."

Doron raised a hand for silence. "This is not the place to discuss this. Come."

He strode back up the passageway, leaving the dimness of the mausoleum behind him. Rikka followed, but Alis hung back. She walked over to Prue and tapped the little girl on the shoulder. Alis recognised her empty stare, and felt a familiar pang of despondency on her behalf. She beamed broadly to hide it. "Let me show you something."

Alis waved her palm near the edge of the cube and a hologram burst into life. The little girl slowly moved closer. Standing on the protruding edge of the cube was a hologram of Leon. Alis looked at the hologram, and spoke clearly and slowly to it. "April 3rd, 2307."

The hologram vanished, and a new one took its place. It was a perfect image of Prue sitting beside her friends at the hostel. She was clutching her bear, and her friends were smiling and talking.

Alis reached put an arm around Prue's shoulders. The little girl blinked, and her eyes widened as tears welled up inside them. The image expanded, and showed Leon walking over to her and her friends. He reached them, bent at the waist and whispered into Prue's ear. Her face lit up, and her mouth flapped with laughter.

Alis leaned in and whispered to Prue, copying Leon's last act in the hologram, "You can come here and see him whenever you feel like it."

She felt Prue's hand in hers. She bent and lifted her up, clasped her close, and felt the first sobs leaving her. Her cries flowed unchecked, filling the room and bouncing back at them both in waves. Alis pushed her own tears aside and walked back up the passageway, carrying Prue and leaving Leon's small cube of memories playing out happier times.

Chapter Twenty-two

"Why did you take it?" said Doron. "It's a simple question."

Alis shifted in her seat, avoiding his stare. She looked past him at the small forest of plants covering one side of the room. A few early flowers sat in blots of red and pink against the green canopy.

Doron nurtured the plants himself, expressing his delight to visitors at the contrast between the stout, dead walls of the room and the eternal, self-propagating life blossoming before them.

Alis admired Doron's effort to celebrate life. They all needed to stay positive somehow.

She took a breath and looked up at him. "I took it because I didn't judge it safe to leave it here."

Doron's eyes didn't move. "You've said that already. You just haven't told me why you thought that."

Alis felt a rush of nerves in her stomach. "I believe someone here is working against us."

Doron sighed and leant back in his seat. He exhaled slowly and raised his chin to the ceiling. "You think someone here is a traitor."

Alis knew she had a reputation for unusual theories. She couldn't be sure whether his question was genuine, or just resigned disbelief. "Yes."

"And you chose to keep that to yourself," he said.

She nodded. "I would have come to you, but I didn't have a name yet. If you spoke to anyone about it, it could have alerted them."

Doron dropped his chin and met her eyes. "So now you have a name?"

Alis nodded. "Yes."

"Who?" said Doron

She paused. She knew he would not be happy with her next answer. Irvana's warnings felt justified now more than ever. Ty had warned her too, but neither he nor Irvana could back her up now.

She checked her reasoning. It was watertight. "Rikka."

Doron's face twitched, as though the word had bumped the side of his head as it went past. "Rikka." He paused. "You think Rikka is our traitor."

Alis pressed on, ignoring his reaction. "We know little about her. She arrived at the same time as Irvana turned up dead. That alone is suspicious."

Disbelief hung on Doron's face. "We share a common enemy with Rikka. I can see no reason to doubt her."

Alis spread her hands. "Ok, ok. But why come and watch us saving lives here, when her own people are dying? It makes no sense. You know she has a device that can track the diviners? She lent it to me in Nasser. A device like that makes our diviners much easier to steal."

Doron shook his head. "That is not her purpose. And if it was, why lend the device to you rather than keep it a secret?"

Alis felt her chance slipping away. She reached for her one piece of hard evidence. "There's something else. Remember the melted fabric on Irvana's suit? Rikka and I had a fight with local law enforcement. She killed a few with some sort of energy weapon. I didn't see it, but she took their heads off their shoulders. When I looked, each of their suits had the same melted fabric marks as Irvana's."

Doron waved the words aside. "All weapons leave blast marks, Alis. Do you have any hard evidence that shows her intention? Anything at all that makes it look less like personal resentment, and more like something we can act upon?"

Alis dropped her eyes. "Resentment?" She hadn't expected that. "No. Nothing hard yet, but—"

"Then forget it. Currently, the only proof we have of wrong-doing around here is your theft of the diviner."

She sat up. "It wasn't theft."

Doron raised his eyebrows. "Then what shall we call it? You took it without asking. What is that if not theft?"

"As I tried to explain before, Irvana was worried. She thought we might be betrayed. She asked me to keep a diviner safe in Nasser."

"How do I know that's true?" said Doron.

Alis felt her cheeks flush. "Why would you think it isn't?"

Doron crossed his legs and smoothed his trousers over his knee. He pursed his lips, then nodded once. "Right. So you think Rikka is the traitor Irvana was worried about?"

"Someone had to leak the location to that blue thing, didn't they? Nobody tried to steal it until after I told everyone where it was. That means the location was leaked by someone here. As I said, Rikka looks very guilty right now." Her eyes blazed. "Why have that device for tracking our diviners? What's the link between her and that blue being?"

Doron didn't speak. He got up and wandered across to the flower-dotted canopy of his silent plants. One hand scratched gently at his cheek. She could almost hear his mind turning over the facts. He hadn't immediately dismissed her reasoning. This was all positive.

"I see," he said. "And how do you explain the fact that your chief suspect then killed this blue being?"

Alis paused. The questions was obvious, yet she hadn't prepared an answer. She felt her cheeks flush. "Well, I haven't worked that out yet, but there will be an explanation."

Doron smiled in a way that made her feel stupid. "Indeed. And not only did she kill it for us, but the clothing she brought back shows high quantities of the same matter that infects the dark zone. It seems there is indeed a link between the blue being and the cloud, as you originally suggested. Vivek believes there will be more of them. Ghosts, he calls them. In truth, Rikka's done you and the rest of us a great service, don't you think."

The zeal dropped from Alis's face, "Ghosts? I suppose that fits. But as for Rikka, I think—"

Doron raised his hand. "I know what you think, Alis. But you're wrong about Rikka. In fact, your judgement in general concerns me. I'm struggling to see how I can rely on it. "

Alis felt the conversation slide in a direction she wanted to avoid. She opened her mouth to speak, but Doron gestured for her to wait.

He stretched his arm and drew an arc around the room. "Our judgement either saves or destroys the lives around us, Alis. Rikka is no traitor, and you should never have taken the diviner from here. It doesn't matter who told you to do it, you made the wrong decision. For the time being, you are not to work alone."

The drop from hopeful sleuth to untrustworthy felon caught Alis by surprise. Her face froze in disbelief.

Doron continued. "Think about it. We almost lost a diviner because you hid it on a whim, inside a hostile location."

Alis threw up her hands. "But I wasn't to know some crazy, megalomaniac hostel steward would start a civil war!"

"Precisely my point," he said.

His words hung in the air between them. Alis let her shoulders sag. She finally grasped how it all looked. In his view, any risk to the diviner was obviously too great for one person to handle alone. Yet she'd told no one. He couldn't be sure what she might do next.

But the threat hadn't disappeared simply because Doron wanted hard evidence. Frustration welled in her chest, and her foot tapped a rhythm on the floor. "Whether you believe me or not, there is someone here working against us. They killed Irvana. I can feel it."

"Then bring me your evidence. Your chief suspect has helped us enormously. Blast marks and suspicion are not enough to prove otherwise."

She couldn't find an answer for that. He sighed and waved his hand. "Having you on form is important, but with Irvana gone, we're short of people. We need to bring someone else onboard."

Alis frowned. "You mean recruit someone?"

Doron nodded. "Tell me more about Kasper."

Chapter Twenty-three

K asper looked at his mother. She had her back to him, busying herself in the bathroom. Her dark hair bounced while she scrubbed furiously at something in the sink.

She wore her favourite dressing gown, the old pink one that used to feel thick and soft against his cheek. Nowadays it looked thin and faded. Despite several presents of thicker and softer gowns over the years, she always threw on the old pink one from the back of the bedroom door. Kasper felt himself smiling at the memory.

His mother said something he couldn't quite hear. He asked her to repeat it, but she didn't answer. He caught sight of himself in the mirror over the bath and stopped dead. Staring back at him from the mirror was Leon. His friend looked worried. His mouth was moving frantically, but Kasper couldn't make out any of the words.

He turned back towards the sink and found his mother facing him, her lined face filled with disgust. She raised a fist, shaking a dripping wet shirt at him. "I've been trying to get the marks out of this for hours! What a waste of time! I can't believe you'd be so careless!"

Kasper didn't recognise the shirt. His mother rarely shouted at him. He must have done something terrible.

She continued raging at him. "What is the point of me trying to clean it if you're never going to wear it? What a selfish boy! You need to wake up and learn that the world doesn't spin around you. You're not put here to do whatever you want, whenever you feel like it! How about thinking of someone else for a change?!"

He had no clue what he'd done wrong. He hadn't seen her so angry before. In the mirror, Leon mouthed his silent monologue. Kasper dipped his head to one side, then bounced his eyebrows, one after the other. Leon did the same at precisely the same moment and without once pausing for breath.

His mother's voice interrupted him. "Are you listening, Kasper? Are you listening to me?!"

This time she held up a pair of trousers with both hands, her fingers hooked into the waistband, stretching them wide so he could see them clearly.

Beneath the waistband, the trousers hung like ribbons. She thrust them so close to his face, the only other thing he could see was her eyes glaring over the top of them. "I asked you if you're happy with what you've done?"

She dropped the trousers at his feet and bustled out of the bathroom, muttering as she went. "Selfish, selfish boy."

He looked down at the destroyed trousers. Something about the shredded legs was familiar, but the memory hovered just out of reach.

Above the bath, Leon had disappeared from the mirror. In his place was a clear reflection of the bathroom wall opposite. Kasper's brain struggled with the empty reflection. He leant towards the mirror and ran his fingers over the glass. But their counterparts failed to appear. He swallowed. His heart beat faster in his chest. The light in the bathroom switched from dim orange to bright white.

He heard faint voices. He closed his eyes, braced both hands on the wall, and shook his head. The voices grew louder and a steady electronic 'beep-beep' reached him from somewhere. Something was very wrong, indeed.

The lights penetrated his eyelids, so he squeezed them shut and tried to leave the bathroom. But heavy objects pressed hard against the skin on his legs, and they refused to move.

An icy chill flooded everything below his knees. The shock of it made him gasp. The lights seared into his head, and a lone voice rose above the others.

"Kass, Kass!"

It sounded female. He knew the voice, but couldn't place it. He still had his eyes clamped shut. Noises crashed in on him —people talking, busying themselves with tinkling metal objects, the monotonous 'beep-beep' coming from somewhere behind him.

"Nod if you can hear me," said the voice.

His whole body felt slow, as though he'd woken too early in the morning. He opened his eyes, and bright lights stung them from somewhere above him. He tried to block them out, but his arms wouldn't move. A rush of panic chased away the final fog of sleep.

He tried to look at what was obstructing his arms, but a strap pressed into his forehead, keeping his head firmly in place. He thrashed to pull free, but neither his arms, legs, nor head would move.

The feeling brought back a childhood memory of placing stones on a spider's legs to see how strong it was. The spider pulled away easily, but not without losing two of its legs. Kasper had felt bad afterwards, and worried about how the spider would cope without a quarter of its legs.

"It's alright, Kass, you're OK," said the voice. "Just nod if you can hear me."

Kasper tried to nod, but the brace on his forehead cut it short, reminding him he couldn't get free. The voice came again. "He's awake, he can hear me."

More clanking reached him, louder this time, then a hand gripped the side of his face. He yelled and tried to pull away, but failed again.

"OK, he'll need sedating for the next part," said another voice. This time a male. "Pass me that, please?"

Kasper tried again to open his eyes. He squinted and blinked against the lights, but his eyes moistened and the shapes just blurred into patches of dark and light. Something that looked like the head of a woman loomed nearby. He blinked and squinted until the face finally came into focus.

"Hi, Kass."

Alis.

Her voice triggered something in Kasper's head. Everything rushed into his groggy brain at once: The money, Charnell, the Rib, Gonderson, the fight in the hostel. The gaping holes in his memory snapped shut. Now he was Alis's prisoner.

He glared at her smiling face. "You. Stole. Our money."

Her smile faded, and he saw her mouth moving, but a hissing sound drowned out the words. Chills spread in streaks across his chest. His vision dimmed, and he felt a rhythmic pushing against his thighs and upper arms. Again he thought of the spider he had tortured. He imagined himself splayed on the ground, giant hands placing enormous boulders on his limbs.

The pushing stopped, replaced by a sudden rush of heat into each limb that made him cry out. In his mind, the spider's legs were ablaze, set on fire by another cruel young boy.

The male voice came again. "That's it. Everyone clear, I'm bringing him out."

Another loud hiss nearby. Kasper's mind cleared. He felt more awake. Hands appeared near his eyes, and he flinched as someone worked to free him from the pressure on his head.

"Head's free." said the man.

Kasper could see beyond the lights. A broad ceiling and the edges of nearby machinery. Plus, in at least two directions he saw brighter patches of spilled light that must be doorways. He prepared for his arms and legs to be freed.

The man's voice again. "OK, bring him up."

Something hummed behind his back, and his body tilted forward. The full view of the room was a shock. Medical equipment, cables, screens, and blinking lights crowded the surrounding space. A group of about 10 or 15 people in loose white and blue clothing stood looking at him in silence.

Nearest to him, he saw Alis standing with two men. One of them looked thin and serious, while the other seemed to smirk at him. Tipped up on this bed, he felt like a work of art, presented for inspection to a crowd of critics.

The thin man nodded rapidly. "Excellent."

The room exploded with applause. People slapped shoulders and shook hands, smiling and laughing with each other. Only Alis and the two men continued to look directly at him.

All three were smiling now. Kasper thought they looked pleased with their prize. The thin man turned slowly to the delighted crowd, raised his arms, and smiled. "Quiet now, everyone."

The room fell to a murmur. The man waited until the last of the chatter faded completely. "I am delighted to celebrate with you, once again, the success of our team here in transformation. Of all our endeavours, this is surely our most impressive."

The man paused, and Kasper's eyes searched Alis's face. She met his gaze and smiled. He imagined grabbing hold of her throat and squeezing until she said she was sorry and promised to hand back the money.

The thin man continued. "Our enemy ruins planets, pushes entire races to extinction in a relentless thirst for destruction. But here is another life you've saved. A marvellous ally and a show of defiance in our fight to push back the menace and bring peace to the universe."

He turned and beamed a broad smile at Kasper. Unable to move, Kasper could do nothing but stare back. He was racing to catch up with the brief speech he'd just heard. What was this menace? How was he 'a marvellous ally'?

The man clapped his hands, and the room exploded once again into applause and cheering. The image of the spider left him. In its place came the memory of a group of hunters whooping and clapping around the feet of a huge, snarling bear caught in the fizzing bonds of their i-net.

The sight of the captured bear had troubled Kasper. A powerful predator reduced to a trophy, while it's weaker, technology-rich captors revelled in their tiny orgy of self-congratulation. He'd carried on walking as a single crack of gunfire brought a cheer from the group. He remembered feeling sickened.

Now, presented on this upright platter, Kasper looked down at the revellers in front of him. If he hadn't heard the thin man call him an ally, he might expect the same crack of gunfire to be the last thing he heard.

"Time for him to take his first steps. The show is over. Thank you," said the man.

He flapped an arm, and the crowd emptied out of the doors. With a nod to Alis, he and the third man followed suit. The room was empty within a few minutes, leaving Kasper alone with Alis.

She walked towards him and smiled. "You look good."

Kasper tried to lift his arms, but they wouldn't respond. Trapped like the bear, unable to pounce on his grinning captor, frustration surged through him. "Get me off this thing!"

Alis walked out of sight behind him. He felt the same hum and vibration through his back and he slowly tipped back to horizontal. Something hissed from the direction Alis had gone. The strap fell away from his forehead and his arms came free.

"There," she said. "Take it slow, though. You're going to be weak for a while."

He lifted his head, and felt his brain take a moment to catch up. His eyes blurred, and he blinked fast to clear them.

Alis stretched out her hand. "Slowly, slowly. You need to take it slow. You've been through a lot. Most of it you'll never remember."

He looked down at himself. Someone had dressed him in tight, black clothing. It flowed over every contour of his body, pressing so intimately that he looked naked. He felt Alis standing behind him and tried to pull his knees up to hide his form.

His legs felt peculiar. They didn't seem to move in a single motion. He could see his legs were bare, except for a thin layer of fabric, but in places his thighs, calves and feet felt like something pressed against them, as though he had full pockets weighing heavily against his flesh.

His nerves told his knees to come up, but he had to work hard to get them to move. The effort was immense. A few drops of sweat broke out on his forehead.

Alis motioned for him to stop. "Relax. Relax. You're pretty much healed, but you've still got to get used to moving about."

"Where am I?" said Kasper, "What have you done to me?"

Alis moved into his field of vision, her face partly shaded by the lights above. Her hair was shorter, about shoulder length, but he knew her smile and the plane of her cheek. He felt the briefest glow of delight at seeing her, before his anger came flooding back.

"You're fine," she said. "You're among friends now, on board a ship orbiting your planet. You're perfectly safe. There's a lot to tell and a lot to take in. Some of it—" she paused and looked past him for a moment, before looking back into his face again, "—all of it, will most likely be a shock. You need to be prepared to adjust."

He shifted his knees and tried to raise himself up onto his elbows. His arms felt like they were lifting weights. He couldn't think of anything except moving off his back. "Take these things off me."

Alis pulled up a stool. The sudden scraping of its feet on the floor startled him. She sat down and shifted herself into position so he could see her. "There's nothing holding you, Kass."

He creased his face at her. "Well, I can't move! How are you keeping me on here?"

She smiled gently. "I'm not holding you on here. There is nothing holding you at all. You were mostly dead when I found you. We had to rebuild your limbs, as well as a good chunk of your chest and shoulder. It's still going to be a few days or more before you can move freely again. You're going to have to learn how to talk to your new body."

Kasper bristled. Build? Learn? The dim corridors of Gonderson's hostel took shape in his mind. He could hear the screaming of injured people and the smell of warm, greasy weaponry.

Bright flashes tore away the shadows. Men with guns ducked behind barricades. The pictures came and went. He knew something had happened but couldn't make it take shape in his head.

The bones in his legs felt cold. It was an odd sensation, like they were hollow from the knees down and the chill poured in to fill them.

"I know it's confusing," said Alis. "You'll feel different for a while. Your body's been through an enormous amount of trauma. We just need to get your head into it."

"You're making no sense!" he said. "What trauma? And what do you mean learn to talk to my body?"

Alis looked down at his feet, then back at his face. She took a breath and frowned. "OK, but brace yourself. I was in your place once. I know first-hand this is not easy to hear." Kasper said nothing. She took a breath and continued. "You were badly hurt at the hostel. Both your legs and most of your right side were blown to pieces in the fight. Your right arm and shoulder,

plus your lower left arm, suffered so much damage they had to
be removed by the hostel's doctor before I got to you. The good
news is your suit shielded you from the worst of the blast on
your left side, just enough to protect your upper stomach and
chest."

She smiled and spread her hands as though presenting a tray
of cakes. "Your suit saved your heart and lungs, Kass. It saved
your life."

Kasper frowned again. He mentally checked his body. It
seemed fine. No pain, no sense of anything missing. He could
see his knees, fine and healthy, pointing up to the ceiling.
Everything seemed in place. And yet, he could barely move, and
he had a cold, disjointed feeling inside his legs. It came back as
he thought about it, throbbing and pulsing. Then his arms did
the same. They felt like hollow tubes, slowly filling up with the
same severe chill as his legs.

Alis seemed to guess what he was thinking. "They feel cold,
don't they? Empty, maybe?"

He nodded, and Alis moved a hand towards him. He watched
her hand come to rest on his forearm, but he didn't feel it land.
"I can't feel a thing! Why can't I feel anything?"

"You will in time. The recovery can be slow, but you'll get
there. Everyone does," she moved her palms onto her chest. "I
did."

Then, in a complete change of pace, she raised her hand above
her head, balled a fist, and slammed it down onto Kasper's arm.
He flinched, but felt nothing.

Alis laughed. "Got you worried there! It's simple, you've lost
the connection between your brain and your arm. In fact, it's
really because you've lost your arm, not the connection. It's just
that you now need to build that connection with your new arm.
The good news is that your new arm is much, much better than
the one you were born with."

Kasper's anger surged. Alis wasn't making sense, but she
seemed delighted with herself. So he'd survived a grenade blast.

But she'd gone ahead and replaced large parts of his body without his say so.

His body belonged to him and him alone. He'd grown his body himself, nourished it with his choice of food, developed his limbs and muscles by running, jumping, lifting, and carrying. Where were those carefully nurtured pieces of life now? Ripped from his bones, then sprayed in wet lumps across the corridor. He suddenly wanted to go back and scoop them all up.

"Why can I move my legs, but nothing else?" he said, "I have to get up."

"You need to reconnect with your body. I know it's difficult to understand. But just take a deep breath and we'll try the basics," said Alis.

Kasper's anger finally spilled over. "How can you know?! I'm stuck on here and you're just talking crap, telling me I'm not even human! *Reconnect, learn, take it slow*! That's it. Get me off here. Now!"

He pushed his legs to one side, but they moved slowly and the veins on his neck pulsed with the effort. He pulled his shoulder towards them, trying to use the momentum of his falling legs to help roll his upper body to the edge of the bed. His shoulder didn't respond, but his legs continued to fall.

Alis reached out and caught them. "You need to calm down. You're going to hurt yourself."

She pushed his legs back onto the bed.

He tried to resist, but couldn't move them. "Calm down? I'll be calm when you give me the kiosk money. Where is it? You stole it!"

Alis frowned. "That? Didn't it go through? You can have it. I had to leave suddenly to come here, so I don't know, maybe it's stuck somewhere. We don't really use currency, so I'll try to find it if you want it."

Kasper groped around for something to say. He'd expected her to protest her innocence, maybe even accuse him of lying and taking the money for himself. But he hadn't been prepared for her to just offer it to him, like it had no value. Who doesn't value money? "You didn't take it?"

Her frown faded, and she smiled again. "OK, definitely time for you to relax."

Another hissing sound reached him. He felt warmth spreading from the centre of his back and out through his limbs. The space between his shoulder blades relaxed, and he filled his lungs in a single, long breath. The lights above him softened, and he felt a gentle tide of pleasure wash over him. "What did you just do?"

His tongue felt fat, and the tide flowed constantly from cool to warm as it lapped at his senses.

Alis gave a short laugh. "It has a very complex name, but I call it the happy juice. You'll be high on life and feeling great for a while. So, try to listen to what I'm saying. Nod if you can hear me."

Kasper nodded. He couldn't form words, but it didn't bother him. He didn't feel angry anymore. The juice was too nice. He was content to just lie still and listen.

Alis flexed her fingers. "Good. So—" She laid both palms on his arm. He felt nothing. "You asked me how I know? Well, because I was once where you are now. I was brought here, like you, mostly dead. And, as with you, they wanted to rebuild me." She smiled and let out another laugh. "Although I think they might be regretting it."

Kasper thought that was funny. He smiled and laughed with her.

That made Alis laugh loudly. "I'd forgotten what the happy juice does to you. That's really funny. It's hard to stop yourself laughing, isn't it?"

Kasper laughed louder. Alis laughed harder. Then Kasper laughed harder, too.

"Ok, ok," said Alis, recovering herself, "alright, so, I got rebuilt." She held up her arms and waved them in small circles.

"These are not mine. Well, that's not quite true. They can't be anyone else's, so I suppose they must be mine. But they're just not the ones I was born with. No, they were grown for me, bioengineered using my DNA then grown in a lab by some brilliant people here, on this very ship."

Kasper imagined a vast spaceship floating in star-studded blackness. Alis leaned in closer to his face and smiled. Kasper smiled back at her. It was nice to see her up close after so long.

"Do you want to see something really special?" she said

He nodded, and Alis stood up. She stretched out her right arm over the bed, palm flat, facing down towards his legs. As he watched, she dropped her hand down at a right angle to her wrist. But it didn't stop there. It kept going and slapped against the underside of her forearm. Kasper laughed. It looked ridiculous.

The skin of her hand, wrist and arm shifted, changing shape and melting together into one large, round stump on the end of her arm. Kasper yelped with delight.

The lump collapsed inwards and revealed a cluster of short tubes. Kasper whooped and laughed like a child at a magic show.

He worked hard to get his words out. "What is it?"

Alis grinned. "It's a gun."

Kasper giggled and stared. His eyes widened at the stunted, reshaped arm hovering above him. Questions floated somewhere, but he couldn't reach them. The arm-gun was amazing. Her hand turned into a gun! She was incredibly lucky. He giggled again.

Alis laughed with him. "I can see you're impressed."

They both laughed at each other. Tears appeared at the corners of Kasper's eyes. Alis leaned over and wiped them away with the fingers of her other hand. Her laugh turned to a soft giggle, and she dragged her fingers gently across the fringe of his hair. "It's good to see you again, Kass."

Kasper felt another fleeting question, but couldn't quite capture it. He'd been unhappy about something, but now it didn't seem to matter so much. He giggled and nodded, trying to convey his joy through his eyes.

Alis let her fingers linger on his cheek, then dropped her hand and leaned in towards his face. "Guess what? *Your* arms can do it, too."

Chapter
Twenty-four

"I'd better move that," said the old woman.

Her outline flickered as she bent to pick something off the floor. She straightened, and her arm disappeared from her elbow to her fingertips as she reached to place the object somewhere outside the width of the shimmering frame.

"Can't have that lying there, someone'll fall over it, no doubt," she said.

The woman continued chatting, disappearing beyond the edge of the hologram every so often, then reappearing like an actor on stage wandering in and out of the wings.

A thin woman sat on a stone bench in front of the hologram, staring at the scene unfolding in front of her. She sat up high and tight under a black dress, both her hands gripping the top of her thighs.

After a few moments, her lips pressed together, and she pushed her chin down into her chest. Her shoulders shuddered, and she brought her hands up to her face. She wept quietly as the old woman began a fresh conversation about the weather with someone hiding somewhere offscreen.

Kasper watched the woman sobbing on the bench. He stood rooted to the spot, aware that he had walked, uninvited, into a very private moment.

She pulled her legs up and tipped herself sideways to lie on her side. She shut her eyes tight against the tears, as though trying to block out the chattering of the hologram. Defeated, she waved her hand at it. The whole play snapped out of existence, and silence fell.

Kasper left the woman to her grief and peered at the rows of dark cubes embedded in the walls. The tiny, silent coffins looked serene, all of them confident their solitude would stand the test of time. One of them held the last resting place of his friend. Alis had told him where to look, but he wasn't sure he'd find the right one. He also wasn't sure how to work the hologram.

He missed his friend beside him. He missed the company, and the unusual way the hybrid viewed the world. Mostly, he missed the thrill of planning their days, knowing they'd go out scavenging together, skilful and unbeatable.

He sneaked a look at the woman lying alone on the bench. She hadn't moved. The old woman's chatter had gone, leaving her alone in the dark with her grief. He realised that when Leon's hologram disappeared, he would just lose his friend all over again. For the second time in two days, he stopped his search, turned around, and left the mausoleum.

Outside, the courtyard was empty. He chose a bench on the other side and slumped onto it, grunting as he landed.

He lifted his arm. He pictured the palm of his hand twisting forwards until it pressed against the underside of his forearm. His hand obeyed. It slapped into place and turned his wrist into a smooth, rounded stump.

He'd seen his hand do that many times now, but it still looked unnatural. Its shape was all wrong. Tendon and muscle shouldn't do that. Most people couldn't get their fingertips close to their forearm, but his entire palm now lay flat against it. It was grotesque.

It was still his wrist, still his arm, but to see it flip round and clamp against his forearm— without the slightest discomfort—still filled him with fascination and revulsion, in equal measure.

Alis had called it 'teleo-psychokinesis'. But when he pushed her for an explanation, she'd just said 'it means you shape things by thinking about them'. So now he sat on the edge of the bench doing exactly that.

He watched his hand blur and melt into his forearm. It flowed and hardened into a short tube. He peered down its length, taking aim at the dragon tree.

Charnell's bloody corpse flashed into his mind. The Ribs wouldn't stand a chance now, he thought. He pictured a large, multi-barrelled weapon and watched as the single barrel disappeared into his flowing skin and his arm hurried to redesign itself. But instead of forming barrels, it stopped. It hung completely still in front of him, just a partly formed, twisted mess.

He frowned and thought again of the shape he wanted, focusing on the details in his mind. The flesh rippled, then fell still again. Panic rose inside him. It wasn't working. What if he couldn't get his arm back to normal?

He pictured his own hand in as much detail as he could. The surface of his arm bubbled and rolled until a few fingers reappeared. A few seconds of movement passed and his hand formed, then flipped back to its usual place above his wrist. He breathed a sigh of relief and leant back in his seat. It had been weeks since he first started learning how to use his arms. They'd never been stuck before.

Footsteps tapped on the flagstones of the courtyard, and he looked up to see Alis approaching.

She looked serious. "You OK? Did you go inside?"

Kasper glanced at the mausoleum. "I did. Not for long, though."

She nodded and murmured her understanding. "It's not easy, is it? Seeing him again like that."

Kasper felt the pressure at the back of this throat and pushed it back from where it came. He didn't admit he had avoided running the hologram. "No, it isn't."

Alis sat beside him and pointed at his hands. He realised he was holding them flat on top of his thighs. It looked unnatural.

"Everything OK here?" said Alis.

He flexed his fingers and shook them out. "All good. Just been practising a bit."

Alis smiled. "Good. Practice is important. I still practise, even now. It keeps you sharp."

He frowned at the backs of his hands. "I still don't really understand how it all works, this teleo-psycho-stuff."

"Psychokinesis," said Alis.

Kasper nodded. "Yes, that. I mean, I understand that it's all connected to my brain, but how does it keep on working? It's just tiny machines, right? Don't they need a battery or something?"

Alis grinned. "The key word here is 'nano,' Kass. They are nanocells. They each have a nanogenerator. This harvests movement and turns it into energy. You then use that to power what you need."

He stared at his hands. "What, forever?"

She shrugged. "Maybe. All I know is those little things will run a lot longer than the cells you were born with."

Kasper's eyes widened. He raised his hands in front of his face. "You mean when I die of old age, these things will still be alive and well?"

She laughed. Kasper liked the sound of her laughter.

"Yes, although they'll have very little to do once your brain stops giving them instructions," said Alis.

He let his hands drop. "That makes them feel even more alien."

She laughed again. Kasper frowned.

"What about the ammo? You said there's a store we go to?"

Alis nodded. "Q-stores. It's just for the heavy ordnance when we're heading out on missions. Your tools and blasters work fine with no ammo."

"Power from the nanocells?" he said.

Alis shook her head gently. "Nanogenerators."

Kasper rolled his eyes. "Right, nanogenerators. Got it."

A thin man appeared at the other side of the courtyard. Kasper switched his attention to watch the man walk swiftly towards them. "Is that Doron?"

Alis nodded. "He mentioned he wanted to speak to you. Keep an open mind."

Her advice caught him by surprise. She clearly knew something about what Doron was about to say. He looked at her, but she kept her eyes on Doron's approaching figure.

Doron arrived at the bench and nodded a greeting to them both. "Forgive my intrusion."

"No problem," said Alis.

Kasper didn't answer. Doron nodded towards the mausoleum. "I hope this isn't a bad time?"

Kasper stood up and shook his head. "It's fine."

Alis moved off the seat and the thin man sat down, indicating Kasper should do the same. "Sit. Let's talk."

Kasper obeyed. Conscious of the lack of personal space between them, he pressed himself hard against the arm of the bench, grating his ribs painfully against the cold stone.

"You've been through a lot to get to this point. How are you feeling?" said Doron.

Kasper didn't quite know how to answer the question. Doron had barely spoken directly to him in the weeks since he'd arrived, but now he'd deliberately come to find him. A small alarm bell rang in the back of his mind. "I'm fine."

Doron grunted softly and smiled. "That's twice you've used the word fine. It is highly unlikely that you are *fine*." The smile seemed to widen the man's face. The change of shape softened his features, and Kasper noted the glitter of intelligence in his eyes. "I am sorry about your friend. Many of us here have lost someone. It's never easy, although the holo-stones can help a lot. How are you finding his?"

Kasper went to answer, but Doron raised a hand. "Actually, don't tell me. I already know you think it's fine." He smiled again.

This time Kasper smiled with him. He didn't know what this surprise visit was really about, but Doron seemed very relaxed. Or, at least, he wanted to put Kasper at ease.

Doron smoothed the fabric of his trousers and cleared his throat. "You might not realise it, Kasper, but you have done us a great favour."

Kasper couldn't think what that might be. Doron continued. "In your haste to escape the hostel, you helped retrieve an essential tool in our fight."

Something clicked into place in Kasper's head. The image of Alis on a jump pass, the worn leather package, and a hard, silver edge within it. "That box with the jump passes."

Doron nodded and flashed another smile. "Yes, indeed. We're very grateful to you," he said. He took a breath. "What has Alis told you about our work?"

Kasper hadn't expected such a direct question. It made him pause before answering. "Not a lot. You're trying to save people on different planets, in different colonies. I know it's to do with some poisonous cloud that starts above a city, then spreads and kills everything. It's already happening where I come from."

Doron grunted. "Something like that, yes. A few of us lost our loved ones, our homes, and ultimately our planet to this," he paused, "what's the best way to describe the cloud? I suppose *alien invader*. So, with the last of our resources, we devoted our lives to doing something about it. As more planets fell, our numbers swelled."

Kasper had already struggled to grasp the size of the ship, the Salient, but couldn't imagine what other resources Doron might mean. "So this is your ship? You brought it from your planet?"

Doron shook his head. "In truth, we found it. Or perhaps it found us, I'm never sure. We set off in a modest sized shuttle from the surface, then almost crashed straight into the Salient less than hour after launch. Like it was waiting for us, empty and ready to help us in our sworn cause."

Kasper raised his eyebrows. It sounded like the stuff of child's stories. "You mean someone just flew it there and abandoned it?"

Doron nodded. "That's what we think. Although, it wasn't entirely empty. We found Vivek inside, locked in cryo-sleep."

Kasper felt the obvious question forming on his lips, but Doron raised a hand to stop him.

"I know what you're about to ask. And no, he could remember nothing of how he came to be here. We gave up asking him and the Salient for answers a few years ago. In truth, we know as little about our ship as we do the alien substance it's helping us to destroy."

"But Alis said you'd all made a breakthrough. You know enough about the cloud to destroy it now, right?" said Kasper.

Doron sighed and cleared his throat. Kasper noticed a change in his voice as he spoke. "Yes, we will win more battles, but we're still losing the war. There is too much we don't know about this cloud, and too few of us to roll back the tide."

Kasper wondered if this would be the moment he was told to return home. To get out of the way while the rest of them plan what to do next.

Doron let his revelation hang in the air for a moment longer before he spoke. "Which brings us back around to you, Kasper. You represent an enormous investment for us. Not only in the technology we've gifted you, but also in the training, development, and teaching that comes along with it."

The thin man smoothed his hands over his knees, then looked over at the dragon tree. Kasper followed his eyes, and wondered briefly at how the Salient had created such a perfect replica of a living thing. Probably all to do with nanocells, he thought.

Doron was speaking again. "I don't say that because I want you to be grateful, you understand, but because I want you to be very clear about our relationship. We pulled you back from the brink of death, but you're not simply a patient here. You're also not a visitor." He waved his hand at Kasper's legs, then up his body. "All of these changes mean you are one of us and, as one of us, you must decide whether you share our values."

Kasper opened his mouth to speak, but Doron raised his hand again. The man clearly wanted to finish what he had come to say. "It's a risk for us, this investment. You're an uncertainty. An unknown." His hand waved again at Kasper's cyborg body-parts. "But this is not our biggest investment in you. Do you know what is?"

Kasper shook his head. He wouldn't risk a guess when he was clearly about to be told.

"Our faith," said Doron. "We have invested our faith in you. The faith that you will share our belief in our great mission."

Doron fell silent, and it took Kasper a moment to realise it was now his turn to speak. He groped around for a response, trying to guess where Doron had been going with his monologue. "So, what exactly is your mission?"

Doron didn't crack a smile. "We're saving the universe."

Kasper looked at him. He couldn't tell if the man was being honest or sarcastic. Either way, he had expected a proper answer. They'd effectively turned him into a cyborg without asking. The least Doron could do now was to be straight with him. "You're right, what I'm feeling is more complicated than fine. There's a lot of new stuff here. To be honest, I don't know what to think. I'm grateful to be alive. I know I'm in your debt for that, but this change." He lifted and rotated his arm, as if Doron needed confirmation of what he was talking about. "I can't use it. It doesn't always do what I want. It's just lumps of dead metal bolted to my body. I didn't ask for that. You could have grown new body parts from my skin. But you didn't. You did this, instead."

Doron smiled again. This time, Kasper found it irritating. "You will come to master them in time. And, yes, we could have grown new body parts. But have you ever seen second-gen body parts up close?"

Kasper shook his head. "No, but I know people who've had it done. They're walking around just fine."

"Those parts are lighter in colour," said Doron, "so they don't match the skin of their host. They also seem more," he frowned and looked over at the mausoleum, "how can I put this? Vulnerable!" he said.

"Vulnerable?" said Kasper.

Doron nodded. "Second-gen parts are weak. They also age faster than the host body. Believe me, you wouldn't have wanted them."

"How would you know?" said Kasper.

Doron clearly wasn't expecting a challenge. His mouth hung open, but nothing came out. Kasper pressed his point. "I would have been happy with that. I would have settled for being whole, even if I was a little bit weaker. It's better than these lumps of tin you've stuck on me."

Doron found his voice. "Perhaps you would. We, however, would not," he pointed at Kasper's chest. "We put millions of nanocells inside you. They saved your life. They're now sitting there, waiting for you to command them to do amazing things. These things, these skills, they will help us overcome our enemy."

Kasper's temper rose. *Doron was avoiding the obvious issue.* He tried his best to avoid shouting. "And what if I don't care about your struggle? What if I have a struggle of my own going on elsewhere? You've forced me into this when I was too dead to say no!" He lifted his arms and legs and shook them. "These things are not mine! They belong to you, not me. You've just stuck them on me so you can force me into fighting your battles!"

Doron ignored the display. "We are all forced into fighting battles eventually, Kasper. The difference now is that you are more likely to win."

Kasper spread his hands. "Sure, but I prefer to choose the battles for myself, thanks."

Doron sighed. "It feels like we've tricked you. Taken your body and compelled you to join us, yes?" Kasper didn't reply. Doron continued. "The power to choose is gone from this galaxy, Kasper. We all have the same enemy, and it is dedicated to our utter destruction. There is no free will anymore. There is no choice to be made. Other galaxies have fallen. If we want to go on living, we all need to fight."

Kasper glared at him. "You've done this to me without my say so. If every living thing has no choice but to fight, then at least I can choose to go home to do it."

Doron returned Kasper's glare. "When is the right time to fight? When the enemy is at your door, or before they draw close?"

Kasper thought of Charnell's body, and the tiny cube of AI that used to be Leon. He thought again about how close he had come to death at Gonderson's hostel. The Bureau, the welfares, the free hostels, all of it came from the rising sickness. All of it came from the cloud over Trage.

Alis had stayed just out of view, but chose this moment to step into the conversation. Kasper had almost forgotten she was standing beside them. Her interruption broke his anger, an impact she was probably hoping to achieve.

She cleared her throat. "Sorry, Doron. When you said you were going to speak to him, I hadn't thought you meant at once."

Doron shook his head and smiled. "Yes, you're right. I've taken too much of your time. Let's leave it there for now. I think we've reached a natural conclusion." He gave Kasper a brief nod. "I'll leave you to Alis and your training."

He stood and left without a backward glance. Alis waited until he was out of sight, then gaped at Kasper. "Did you *need* to be that aggressive?" she said.

Kasper threw up his hands. "He just told me I should be grateful for the violation of my basic human rights."

She laughed. Kasper smirked, partly at himself and partly out of relief from the crushing intensity of Doron's visit. With the big man gone, the two of them were alone in the fading light of the courtyard—both connected by the same master, and the same dead friend.

Alis dropped into Doron's vacant spot on the bench. She took up no more room than he had, but somehow still seemed closer to him. She threw a leg over her knee and looked up at The Salient's reproduction of a reddening sky.

"If you're making a joke after one of Doron's little chats, you're doing better than I was by this point. It took me a lot longer to adjust to this life," she said.

Kasper sighed. "You told me to think of the greater good. I'm used to looking after myself. That's my greater good."

"I only said that when you asked me about the kiosk. Truth is, I needed that money for the fixer. I had to pay her to hide the box Doron was talking about. That was the greater good back then, not you and Leon." She shrugged. "But it's not always that obvious. I tried to aim for the greater good here, and that hasn't worked out too well so far."

Her eyes wandered down to his arms. "Are you ready to use those? Doron wants you with us when we go out again. Dark zones are nasty places. You need to be sure."

Kasper snorted. "I grew up in a rough neighbourhood. I can handle myself on a street, even without these new toys."

He'd intended to come across as self-assured, but Alis didn't seem convinced. "Maybe. But it won't be like the streets you're used to. The air's thick, most people have left, and those that couldn't afford to leave are not the same as they were."

A grin spread across Kasper's face. "Not the same? You mean they had to drop the wage-earning and start scavenging? That already makes them my kind of people."

Alis shook her head. It made her hair bounce. "No, I mean they've changed. Properly. Some physically, some mentally, some both. If you live in a dark zone, you change fast."

"So, why don't they leave?" said Kasper, "They're not stupid. They should just walk out and get help."

Alis shook her head again. He noticed the same bounce of her hair. "We tried that. We went in and brought out an entire group of people. Few hours later they were dead. Suffocated right in front of us. It like pulling fish from a river, then watching them flip around on the bank until they lie still."

An image leapt into Kasper's mind of people writhing and clawing at their throats, trying to get air into their lungs.

Alis looked off across the courtyard as she spoke. "The people in those zones are doomed. The poison twists you until you're ready to do anything to stay alive. It's just a long slide into hell."

"OK, I get it. Not like my neighbourhood," said Kasper.

"Not one bit," said Alis. Kasper caught the change in her face. She lost the hint of a smile and gained a gentle crease beneath her eyes. "And this one is different. Droids can't support us. We've already lost someone. One of our best."

"Lost? You mean someone was killed?" said Kasper.

Alis pulled her lips tight and nodded.

He frowned at her. "But you—" he looked down at his own arms, "*we* are invincible, aren't we? We're all modded up with tech. Nobody in those zones can touch us, right?"

"We have an advantage, Kass, but we're not invincible. We're still flesh and bone, and need food and equipment to survive."

Kasper turned slightly on the bench so he could look into Alis's face. She was so close to him that he could almost feel her warmth on his cheek. "So someone wasn't careful?" he said.

"Something like that," she said.

Kasper paused. "What does that mean, exactly?"

"It means you need to remember you're not a god in there, Kass. Trust me, you can still be killed, and you'll be a constant target until the moment you leave."

He screwed up his face. "Without being asked, I'm getting sent into a, what was it you called it? A 'slide into hell' that killed one of your best people. And now you're holding back on the full story. Why is that? It doesn't exactly help build the trust."

Alis slumped back on the bench. He could see she agreed. They were putting his life at risk, and nobody had even asked his permission. He'd basically been conscripted.

"I don't know for certain how she was killed," she said.

"Do you mean you don't know how her life ended, or you don't know who made her dead?" said Kasper.

Alis looked thoughtful. "I don't know who did it. The inquiry said it was a local. But she was too smart to let that happen. Something wasn't right."

It was Kasper's turn to slump back in his seat. His frustration passed. He found it increasingly difficult to be angry with Alis. For the first time, she seemed genuinely conflicted.

"Who was she?" he said.

Alis kept her eyes staring ahead. "Her name was Irvana. She was a real talent. Loved logic, tech, science, and anything else that brought us closer to winning. Great fighter, too."

"Sounds impressive," said Kasper.

Alis nodded, but her face was blank. "She built something that she called her converter. That box inside the leather wrap, the one you stole from the hostel, is a diviner. The convertor is basically a weapon we fire into the cloud to roll it back. The diviner finds the centre of the cloud, so we can target the convertor. But it takes a long time to destroy one of those clouds. Meanwhile, we get our butts kicked by whatever is still lurking in the dark zone."

She smiled. Kasper felt himself smiling back. Her eyes sparkled.

"She turned the tide for us, Kass. We used to fire chemicals into the sky. They didn't really work. We looked like fools. But Irvana's convertor shot a new compound, using a kind of energy beam." She shrugged. "She never explained it to me properly, but it tore a hole right through the cloud." Her eyes flashed. "The longer the beam stayed on, the bigger the hole got. It eventually disappeared, like the sky grew back into place. For the first time, we removed the infection from an entire city!" She shook her head, as though still in a state of disbelief. "It was incredible."

"So, what happened? She took it somewhere, and it didn't work?" he said.

Alis shook her head. "No, she took it up a tower, and it seems to have fired just fine. Next thing we know, the droids find her dead on the street below."

Kasper breathed out. He turned the statement over in his mind. "It *does* sound like some locals attacked her."

A clump of hair fell across Alis's face, and she batted it away. "She was too smart. Someone set her up."

Kasper raised his eyebrows. "Really? Who?"

Alis shrugged. "Don't know yet."

"So, it's just a hunch?"

"It's more than that, Kass."

"What evidence have you got?"

"Nothing solid, but—"

"So what makes you think someone else did it?"

Alis slapped a hand on her thigh. "I know someone killed her, OK? I can feel it."

Alis rarely had outbursts. They both fell quiet and stared out at the cool, dark stone around them. Kasper thought about the people he had met in this place. If Alis was right, she was the only person he could trust. Yet she sounded irrational. Irrational people were often wrong.

She shifted on the bench beside him. "Sorry, Kass. I'm still not good at thinking about Irvana's death, let alone talking about it."

Kasper smiled into the darkness ahead of him. "Don't worry about it. I'm feeling pretty emotional right now, too."

He felt the warmth of her hand on his arm. Something stirred in his chest and she smiled, as though she had felt it through his shirt.

She broke away and crossed her legs. They didn't speak for a few moments, then Alis tapped her dangling foot gently against the bench. "We'll be spending a lot more time together, Kass. We should be clear with each other about what that means."

He looked away, trying to scramble from a personal cliff-edge he hadn't seen coming. "Sure, sure. We've got a lot to do. Doron was saying how important it is and—"

Alis's hand returned to his arm, stopping him mid-sentence. "You've been through a lot, and there's more coming. Now is not a good time for us to get confused."

He nodded. His throat seemed to have closed entirely. Alis sounded resigned, like someone forced to accept a bad bargain. "Let's just stay focused on your training."

Kasper took a deep breath and stretched his arms above his head. Inside, his emotions flew around like leaves in a storm. He managed a small grin.

"Sure. It'll be good to focus on that. There's still a lot for me to learn."

She smiled. "There's a lot for both of us to work out."

He brought his arms down and breathed out. "You can tell Doron I'll be ready. If you're going into that dark zone, I'm coming with you."

Chapter Twenty-five

Two young men stood at one end of a wide, flat rooftop. They looked odd, stood side by side. Roddi was taller than Jobe, broad-shouldered, with one arm much thicker and more muscular than the other. Jobe was small, pale, and padded constantly from one foot to the other, as though he couldn't stand still.

Jobe watched Roddi throw the stone he'd been fingering for the last few minutes. It looked a good shot. Roddi had been getting better and better at this game. He creased his eyes against the sky as it dipped towards an empty can at the other end of the roof.

Transfixed by the flight of the stone, they didn't see another man appear from the nearby stairwell.

"LOOK OUT!!" the man shouted.

Roddi and Jobe leapt into the air. The man stopped and guffawed like an animal. The two of them spun round to see him standing with his head thrown back in delight.

"Laine!" said Roddi.

"Ha, ha," said Laine. "You shat your pants!"

A dark pink scar sat directly across Laine's face, splitting it from ear to ear. The healing had scrunched the skin on both sides of it, making it look as though someone had stitched a huge, tight seam across the middle of his face.

Jobe stood rigid with fright, but Roddi regained his composure as quickly as he'd lost it. "Hilarious."

Laine's laughter faded. He looked Roddi up and down. "Yeah, it was. Looks like you need a sense of humour."

Jobe kept his eyes on Laine as he walked slowly towards Roddi. He thought Laine's scar made him look dangerous. He turned over the contradiction in his mind. If someone had a scar, it meant they'd been injured, so they should seem weak, or at least weaker than a person looked without a scar. But on Laine, the scar looked like proof he'd done something crazy. Maybe he'd left a corpse behind that looked even worse than he did.

Laine reached Roddi and jabbed his finger into his chest, emphasising every word he spoke. "What. Are. We. With. Out. Hew. Muh?" he said, "Nuh. Thing. But. An. Nee. Mals."

The last jab was harder than the rest. Roddi rocked back on his heels. He held Laine's eyes, but did nothing. The bigger man looked him up and down. His eyes settled on Roddi's large arm. He burst into another roaring guffaw. "What's that? You been working that arm pretty hard. You need to get yourself a girlfriend!"

He threw his head back and roared at his own joke. Still laughing, he turned his attention to Jobe. "Hey, little fellah! You look like you're shittin' in your pants!"

Jobe's eyes danced from Laine to the edge of the roof. If Laine wanted to, he could charge at him and knock him clean off the top of the building. "Yes, I mean, you frightened me. I wasn't expecting it, you know? The shout and all that. Especially when nobody ever comes up here, and it was so quiet before. Sort of a surprise, that's all. I mean it was pretty funny, I guess, really, sort of."

Laine kept his smile in place and walked towards Jobe. "I forget how fast you talk, little squeaky man. You thought it was pretty funny, yeah?" He looked back at Roddi. "See? It was funny. You need to get a sense of humour like squeaky, here."

Laine placed his hand on Jobe's shoulder and gripped it hard. Jobe couldn't keep from showing the discomfort. Laine gave him half a smile and walked him backwards, towards the edge of the roof. "You like jokes, huh? You like to laugh, do you?"

Laine guided him closer to the roof's edge. Jobe felt the void looming behind him. He heard words tumbling out of his mouth, and cursed inwardly at his own affliction. "Roof edge, funny isn't it? Don't want that, though, eh? To think that about it, I mean, do you?"

Laine laughed at the gibberish coming out of Jobe's mouth. "There he goes again. Can't control his words, can he? You're a funny guy. Fancy going flying? That would be funny, wouldn't it? C'mon, let's see if you can fly. Just for fun!"

Jobe's heart banged in his chest. His lungs refused to take in any air. He didn't know if Laine was really going to do it. He didn't want to risk pushing back and annoying him. Laine might get angry and decide to do it.

"Leave him alone!" said Roddi.

Laine stopped and turned his head. His grip stayed painfully tight on Jobe's shoulder. "Make me."

Roddi looked at Jobe, then back at Laine. "How about a contest? Maybe you can beat us."

Laine didn't move. "Sounds boring."

Laine started walking Jobe closer to the edge. The emptiness yawned at Jobe's back. He let out a squeal, then cursed and clamped a hand over his mouth.

"It won't be," said Roddi. "It'll be a wager."

Laine stopped. Jobe's legs gave out, and he sagged. Laine's hand was the only thing keeping him upright. "You mean that when I beat you, I get your money?"

Jobe stared at Laine's feet, his head bobbing as he mouthed a steady stream of nonsense to himself.

Roddi nodded. "If you beat me, yes."

"*When* I beat you," said Laine.

Laine released his grip and headed over to where Roddi was standing. Jobe sank to his knees.

"Alright, let's do it," said Laine. "What's the game?"

Roddi opened the palm of his hand and revealed three small stones. He snapped his fingers shut and pointed to the far end of the roof. Three cans stood in a ragged line. Each one had its mouth open wide to the heavens, waiting to catch a falling stone. "It's simple. Best of three into those cans."

Laine squinted at the cans, then looked back at Roddi. "Easy. How much?"

"50," said Roddi.

"Done," said Laine.

Laine held out his hand for Roddi to give him the stones. But Roddi kept his fist shut. "You need to find your own stones."

Laine shook his head. "No, *you* need to find your own stones. I'm having your ones in case they're fixed. How do I know they're not magnets, huh? I just turned up. You could have been cheating the little guy all day."

Roddi paused, then thought better of objecting. He opened his hand and tipped the stones into Laine's palm. "Sure."

Jobe still knelt where Laine had left him. Laine looked at him and grinned. "Come here, little guy. Come where I can see you. Don't want you cheating somehow, do I?"

Jobe felt weak, but got to his feet and walked slowly over to stand next to Laine. The scar on the man's face made him feel worse.

Laine turned to face the cans. "You first."

Roddi finished selecting his stones and peered over at the cans. He felt confident. He locked his eyes on the target and shuffled his feet into position. Breathing slowly through his nose, he wound back his arm and let loose his first shot. It rose fast and high, then came down smoothly, landing in the first can with a dull clank and a brief rattle. "One." he said.

He threw his second stone. It flew in a high, unswerving arc across the roof. Another clank, followed by a rattle. "Two," he said.

He pulled his arm back to send his third stone soaring towards the last open can. Just as he threw it, Laine slapped him on the back. The stone stayed level and pinged uselessly off the ledge at one side of the roof.

Furious, Roddi span round. "What the fuck was that?"

Laine didn't flinch. Instead, he curled his lips and rocked his head from side to side, mimicking Roddi's outburst. "Whan da fick wad dat?"

He stuck his face out towards Roddi. His grin stretched as wide as his scar, making him look like a frog with two mouths. "I didn't see 'no hitting' in the rulebook, did I? Did you say to me 'No punching allowed, Laine'? No. You did not. You just said," he mimicked Roddi once more, "'Id bimpel. Bezt o free indo dose canfs', didn't you?" He laughed again and took up his throwing position. "Now it's my go."

He raised his right arm behind him, but instead of throwing the stone, he broke into a run. Roddi and Jobe stared open-mouthed as he stopped in front of the cans, brought his arm over in a slow, exaggerated motion, and dropped a stone into the first can. "One!"

The second and third stones fell into the cans with the same exaggerated motion. Before the final rattle faded, Laine leapt into the air. "That's three! I win!"

He jogged back towards Roddi and Jobe with his scar-wide grin fixed in place. "50 it is, mate, pay up."

Roddi stared at Laine's open hand. "You're joking, right? Dropping them in doesn't count!"

Laine's grin disappeared. "You saying I cheated?"

Roddi didn't answer. Jobe looked down at his own feet, trying to avoid Laine's glare.

"I asked you a question. Are you saying I cheated?" said Laine.

Roddi took a breath to speak, but he was too slow. Laine's hand whipped out sideways and smashed Jobe across his face. Pain exploded in Jobe's skull. He howled and dropped to the floor, both hands clutching his nose.

Laine's eyes didn't move from Roddi's face. "You saw me throw them. I made it really clear I was throwing them. You owe me money. Now pay up."

Roddi lunged for Laine's throat with both hands. Laine grabbed one wrist, but Roddi got the other hand through and clamped it around Laine's windpipe. He squeezed it as hard as he could, then a boulder slammed into his stomach.

He gasped and loosened his grip. The same boulder smashed into the side of his head, blurring his vision and taking the strength out of his legs. He crashed to the floor, just in time to see Laine's boot connect painfully with his shin. Like Jobe before him, he howled in pain.

"Now, you dog shits, you owe me money. Hand it over," said Laine.

Roddi and Jobe moaned and rocked on the floor of the dusty rooftop. Laine stood over them, so pumped with adrenaline that spit flew from his mouth as he spoke. "Shut up moaning and hand it over!"

Jobe's eyes streamed and his face throbbed, but he could see Roddi was unable to speak. An idea came to him. "We don't have it on us now. We can get it for you, though."

Laine laughed. "Ok, little fellah. Jump up. Let's go now."

Jobe thought fast. He had spent most of his life avoiding getting beaten up and, nowadays especially, he was a quick talker when things got dangerous. "It's at my place. You can't come over there, though. Everyone else is there and they'll know, won't they? They'll know."

Laine lashed out a boot and connected with Roddi's other shin. Roddi howled. "I fuckin' want it. When am I going to get it?"

Jobe's mind whirred again. "Tonight. I'll get it and bring it here tonight. Just before dark, tonight."

Laine didn't move. "Deal. But any funny stuff, and I'll find you. Don't matter where in the city you are, I'll find you. You hear me?"

He drew his foot back to kick Roddi again. Roddi flinched, and Laine laughed. He turned and walked away from the two prone bodies, shouting as he disappeared down the stairwell.

"See you losers later. And don't keep me waiting!"

Chapter Twenty-six

K asper stared at the empty buildings in front of him. Their outlines blurred in a purple haze that tainted everything around. Nothing moved. The entire city seemed asleep.

His eyes followed the line of the rooftops, and up to the sky. Vast blots of deep purple hung above him, stealing the light and plunging the city into a permanent dusk. Narrow streaks of infection crept between each of the blots, carving dark paths in the sky like veins pushing through skin.

Standing beneath it, he realised for the first time that his own city was going to die. Charnell's dream was just a fantasy. This infection would swallow everything. Nobody would emerge in a new dawn once the infection had passed. Ribs, welfares, troopers, and hostels— nothing would survive.

The air felt too close around him. He realised he had been trying to take shallow breaths to keep the air out of his body. He remembered Vivek's advice that they'd need to breathe it for several days before they were seriously harmed. Still, he didn't feel like filling his lungs with it.

Behind him, the veil of the dark zone thickened and closed, shutting out the pentangle that had brought him and the others here from The Salient.

"Fascinating," said Rikka.

"It's got a lot worse," said Alis.

Millan raised his voice. "We need to form up! I'll take the lead. Rikka, you take the rear. Alis, you and newbie flank the karyack."

They fell into place on either side of the smooth, domed body of the hovering karyack. Kasper stared at the floating equipment store as it waited patiently for instructions. It hung in the space between them all like an enormous insect, the constant correction of its anti-gravity field making it bob gently, as though eager for the command to move on.

Kasper wondered why they couldn't just ride the karyack all the way to the tower, but apparently it was the only self-powered unit that would work in the dark zone, and it was too small to take their combined weight. So, it carried their equipment locked safely inside its steel hull, while they walked beside it like targets in a shooting gallery.

Alis cleared her throat. "We're a team. Decisions should be made by discussion, not by order."

Millan looked at her over the top of the karyack, and smiled. "Sure, Alis. I'm all for a team vote before making decisions. As long as you remember that I'm leading this mission, and the casting vote is mine." Alis didn't reply. Millan's smile faded. "Let's go."

They moved down the silent street in a neat diamond formation. Grey buildings rose silently around them, reaching for the infected cloud above. Abandoned vehicles littered the road like carrion, stripped bare of their parts and left to rot.

Kasper held his scope to his face. It clamped onto his skin and tightened its grip. Fear flickered in his chest, but again, it stopped just as he felt the first twinge of panic.

The view in the scope shook. The focus refused to settle on any of the objects ahead of him. He fiddled with the calibrations on the lens, but it only made matters worse.

He ripped it from his face. "Damn it."

Millan looked back from his place in front of the karyack. "What's wrong?"

"My scope's playing up," said Kasper

"My scans are no good, either," said Alis.

Kasper threw up his hands. "Maybe we're being blocked."

Rikka shook her head. "No. It seems Vivek's theory is correct. The atmospheric activity in here is greater than outside. We cannot rely on signals to pass through the air."

Millan raised a hand, and the karyack stopped. The rest of the group stopped with it. He turned and faced Rikka over the shell of the bobbing vehicle. "OK. So you're saying we've got no scans?"

"No accurate ones," said Rikka.

"What about using the diviner?" said Millan.

Rikka shrugged. "It's not strictly a machine, so it should be fine."

Alis waved a hand at the air around them. "And you can't use your skills to shift some of this stuff around a bit? Maybe break it up to improve signals?"

Rikka gave one of those smiles that did not warm her eyes. "That is not quite how it works."

"Then how does it work?" said Alis

"Differently," said Rikka, "It is complicated."

"Too complicated for us simpletons?" said Alis.

Rikka opened her mouth, but Millan cut in before she could speak. "Drop it, Alis. Rikka, what can you do to improve navigation? Anything?"

Rikka shook her head. "Once we're closer to the tower, the diviner will pick up traces of the source, and we can follow those. Until then, I can do nothing."

Alis span three hundred and sixty degrees on the spot. "I don't recognise a thing in here. We're going to be walking around for weeks if we don't find a route to the tower."

Millan rubbed at the stubble on his cheeks. "We need to look for landmarks. Anything you think you remember?"

Kasper took a deep breath. "I think I might be able to help."

Millan's eyebrows shot upward. "OK. How?"

"Well," Kasper felt a small rush of nerves in his stomach. He was sure he'd made the right choice, but Millan was obviously someone who wanted everyone to follow rules. Kasper was about to reveal he was not one of those people. "When you grow up forced to scavenge a living, you learn to spot things you might need later. Because, more often than not, they're not going to be there again when you need them," he said.

Millan frowned. "Thanks for the tip. Now tell us how you can help."

Kasper took a breath. "OK. I took a clone of Vivek's map."

Millan's eyes widened. "You stole a holograph from Vivek?"

Kasper felt an odd sense of pleasure at seeing Millan's surprise. He shook his head and gave a brief shrug. "You call it stealing. I call it planning."

Alis threw her head back and laughed. "Once a thief, always a thief."

Kasper raised an arm and a perfect copy of Vivek's three-dimensional holograph rendered in front of him. Bright lines marked out the streets and building and their location pin bounced on the spot where they stood.

Millan shook his head. "Make sure this gets back to the Salient in one piece."

Kasper nodded, delighted his decision had paid off.

As the map built out, the tower came into view. Millan began examining the lines suspended in front of him. He followed the shortest route to the tower with his finger. "We go this way. But without scans, we've only got our eyes to rely on, so let's stay off the highways. They're too open, and we need to see what might come at us."

Rikka nodded and pointed to a set of parallel lines running east to west above Kasper's arm. "These routes are narrower. We should take those where we can."

Kasper shook his head. "Surely narrow streets are more dangerous? We can easily end up trapped single file in a backstreet or basement somewhere."

"It's a simple matter of scale," said Rikka. "With no alert from our equipment, we could get caught in the open by vehicles, heavy weapons, or overwhelming odds. Smaller places mean smaller threats."

Kasper thought about the many times he and Leon had been successful because they were just two people using well-practised tactics. Small teams in small spaces were still a significant threat.

As if reading his mind, Alis shook her head. "Smaller doesn't always mean weaker. It only took one ghost to kill Leon and a whole load of other people. None of them stood a chance."

"Ghost?" said Kasper.

Alis frowned at him. "Did you read the mission notes I gave you? The blue glowing things. Vivek's calling them ghosts. He thinks there'll be more waiting for us in here."

Kasper immediately regretted not reading the notes properly. He tried to commit the idea to memory, although ghosts conjured up a different image to him than blue, glowing people.

"Indeed," said Rikka. "Their link with the cloud is clear. I agree we need to be just as cautious in the backstreets as we do in the open, but the smaller routes still remain the safer choice."

Millan nodded and pointed at spaces between the edges of buildings. "Fine. We can estimate distances between buildings and avoid dead ends. Provided we don't end up trapped without an exit, we should come out of this alive."

Alis crossed her arms. "I'm not so sure about that. How long should it take us to cross the city?"

Millan stared at the dark buildings for a moment. "Barring any serious setbacks, I'd say less than six hours."

Alis said nothing. Rikka shook her head. "It will be close to dark by then. Travelling at night with no scanning equipment would be unwise."

Kasper shrugged. "I don't know. In my experience, the dark helps you move without being seen."

"Either way, we should just get on with it," said Alis.

Millan grinned. "Agreed."

He raised his hand and the karyack slid forwards. Setting off ahead of it, he glanced over his shoulder at Kasper. "Remember to keep your stolen goods out of harm's way, ok?"

Kasper didn't reply, but made a mental note to be careful where he put his arm.

Signs of decay rolled past them from junction to junction. Hours went by, and he saw plenty of evidence of people scavenging a living, but they saw nobody. They occasionally heard movement and clattering from inside the buildings, even a door slamming shut, but not a single person appeared.

At first, Kasper reacted to each sound, searching the buildings with his eyes. Twice, he thought he caught movement in the windows, but the haze hampered his vision and he couldn't be certain. "I think I see movement. Those sounds are people moving around."

"Indeed they are," said Rikka.

Millan called back over his shoulder. "It's always the same in these places. They stay well out of sight, but they're curious. They're trying to get a peek at the strangers."

Another clatter sounded, this time off to Kasper's right side. It sounded like metal bouncing on concrete. His head flicked round to search the gloom, but he saw nothing. "Why are they scared of us? We're not even showing our weapons."

Alis looked at him across the roof of the karyack. "Now you really do sound like a newbie."

She grinned, but Kasper frowned back. "Why hide if you need help?"

"It is not us they are hiding from," said Alis.

Millan nodded. "Yep. There are scarier things in here than us. They're staying safe and just waiting for the show to start."

They arrived at another junction, turned east, and headed up a slight gradient. The buildings on the left gave way to waste ground. Rubbish covered it entirely. It looked to be several feet deep, and took on shapes and curves that both caught the light and cast deep shadows in equal measure.

The rise and fall of the vast pile pushed right up against the buildings on three sides. It was an ocean of rot, and its stench hung thick in the air around them.

Millan threw a hand up and everything came to a halt. He pointed to a peak in the rubbish, roughly in the centre of the pile. "What do we have here?"

Kasper followed his finger and saw a black, wedge-shaped object. It moved from side to side in a halting rhythm, as though stuck inside an invisible box.

"Looks feline," said Alis.

"*Big* feline," said Kasper.

The shape froze and lifted its thin end off the ground. It wagged slightly, then a loud screech flew across the waste ground, shattering the silence and slamming into the four of them.

Millan raised an arm as if to ward it off. "That's no feline."

Rikka pointed at the buildings on the west side of the waste ground. "There."

More black shapes appeared from the doors and windows. A torrent of lurching, screeching black shapes poured out of a building and came scrambling and rolling through the rubbish towards them.

The sound pulsed in Kasper's ears. "They're coming towards us."

"Weapons up," said Alis.

Millan waved an arm downwards. "Not yet. We're vulnerable out here. We need to get to higher ground." He span round and pointed at the building behind them. It had double doors and several floors above ground level. "That one."

The teeming mass of black bodies surged towards them, screeching as it tore across the garbage. Rikka broke into a run towards the doors. She threw her shoulder against the gap in the middle and burst inside. Alis and Kasper cleared the threshold and found themselves in a wide entrance hall. Ahead of them, a broad staircase led up to a mezzanine fringed with tight railings.

Behind them, Millan urged the karyack through the doorway. He grabbed the doors, slammed them shut, then glared at Kasper and pointed at the blacked-out lock screen. "Lock it! Quickly!"

Kasper ran to it and tapped its surface with his fingers. Nothing happened. He tried again. The steel bolts sat stubbornly in their barrels, refusing to shoot into the waiting slots in the doorframe.

Frustrated, he slapped the dead panel. "Power's out."

Millan cursed and waved a hand at Rikka and Alis. "Help us block this door!"

Alis gripped the edge of a large table, and Kasper helped her drag it to rest against the doors. Rikka and Millan pushed two steel cabinets over, and the four of them heaved both into place, wedging them between the floor and the back of the doors.

The sound of screeching filled the hallway. Something thudded into the door. Kasper's heart leapt. The second and third thud came close together, rattling the door in its frame. The next thuds turned into a frenzy of clawing and banging that made the doors strain on their hinges.

"Upstairs," said Rikka.

Kasper and Alis went straight to the top of the stairs . Millan and Rikka kept pace with the karyack as it glided smoothly up the steps. Behind them, the doors bowed inwards. Kasper saw black fur bulging through a gap where the doors no longer met. A rush of nerves flooded his stomach. "They're getting through!"

"Weapons up," said Millan. "We'll hold them back from the top of the stairs."

Kasper crouched behind the railings on the broad mezzanine. On each wall around him, two doors sat quietly, presumably leading off into more corridors or rooms. At either end, where the mezzanine curved around the entrance hall and met the front wall of the building, a large window looked out over the waste ground.

The sound of screeching swamped the landing. Alis and Rikka ran over to one of the windows and peered down at the scene below.

"They're intelligent," said Rikka. "They're using their combined weight to break through the doors. That means they are communal."

Millan and the karyack reached the top of the stairs. "OK, great. Now tell us how to get rid of them."

Kasper moved over to the window. He stared at the seething mass growing outside the building. Flashes of pink and white dappled the black pile as the creatures scrambled across each other's backs.

Long, scaled tails whipped up and slapped down onto bodies. Yellow incisors stuck out over small rows of spikey grey teeth, all wrapped up in dark, furry jowls. Beneath him, the doors groaned and shifted. He began to imagine the beasts bursting through and landing on him. Heavy, stinking, thrashing and biting.

Millan's voice jolted him back into the moment. "Kasper! Get back over here. Weapons up."

Kasper rushed away from the window and took a position on the opposite side of the stairs to Millan. A loud crack came from the doors, followed by a harsh scrape of table legs dragged across stone flooring.

Millan's forearms twisted, then blurred into straight lengths capped by multiple short barrels. He jerked his head towards Kasper's hands. "Get yourself ready."

Kasper held up his arms and willed them to change. He pictured his most reliable weapons and watched as the palms of his hands twisted, then clamped flat against his forearms. His mind shrieked silently at the sight of his broken wrists. He braced himself for the pain, still unable to accept that it wouldn't hurt. Instead, his arms moulded smoothly from their usual shape into a pair of barrels.

Millan gave him a quick nod. "That's it. Now, nothing comes through those doors. Understand?"

"I get it," said Kasper.

Millan crossed over to the windows. Alis pointed through them to something Kasper couldn't see. "What are those three doing over there?" Why aren't they joining in the fight?"

Millan leaned closer to the window. "Hard to say. Looks like they're watching."

"That might be true," said Rikka. "Or perhaps they're directing."

Alis grinned. "You think they're running things?"

Rikka nodded. "It is possible. These creatures could have a higher level of intelligence than we think."

"In that case—" said Alis.

She blurred her right hand and punched through the window. Shards of shattered glass clattered to the floor. The heavy stench of warm, fetid bodies surged through the hole into the room. Alis extended her arm and took aim.

Another loud crack pulled Kasper's attention back to the doors. A fat, hairy body slid free of the gap and landed in a heap on the tiles. It kicked and thrashed for a few moments, then righted itself at the foot of the stairs.

Kasper raised his weapons. "One got through!"

Millan shouted across from the window. "Kill it then!"

The thing shambled up two steps, cautious at first, testing the grip of its claws on the smooth floor. Its long, scaly tail jerked and flicked behind it. Then it picked up Kasper's scent. Two long teeth appeared, and a piercing screech destroyed the last illusion of safety on the landing.

The staircase wasn't long, and the creature was large. Kasper's shoulder jolted with three short, rapid blasts. Each blast found its mark easily, shredding the creature's flank in a bright plume of red and black. The force lifted it clear off the floor, and sent it smashing back against the doors. It sagged onto the floor in a heap of wet fur and flesh.

Kasper waited a moment, but the beast didn't move. A mixture of relief and adrenaline flooded his veins. He whooped in triumph. In answer, the doors bowed further inwards with the weight of the dead thing's brothers and sisters.

Millan grinned, but shook his head. "Don't get excited, it's not over yet!"

Alis fired something out through the hole in the window. For a split second, nothing happened. Then she let out a whoop as triumphant as Kasper's.

"And they're gone!" she said.

Kasper resisted the urge to look away from the bulging door. A few seconds later, Alis laughed. "They're breaking ranks! Look at those in the middle, they've got no idea what to do with themselves!""

The doors in front of Kasper straightened and relaxed on their hinges. The scraping faded, and the screeching descended into multiple low squeaks and grunts. It was as though someone had switched off the madness.

Rikka moved closer to the shattered window. "Remarkable. A hierarchy of intelligence with complete control over lower orders."

Millan pointed to the street directly below them. "They're dropping off the pile at the doors, too."

Alis turned and looked across at Kasper. "How's it looking down there, Kass?"

He gave Alis a broad grin over the top of his outstretched arm. "It looks like they've lost interest."

Millan walked towards him. "You got one, right?"

Kasper nodded towards the door. "Yep. I did."

The corpse sat in a soggy heap at the foot of the doors, its blood leaking out across the tiles.

Millan looked pleased. "Good. Stay where you are, there are still plenty out there."

Alis and Rikka watched through the window. Kasper imagined the creatures bumbling around on the rubbish.

Alis chuckled. "I wouldn't worry, they're confused and heading home."

"Maybe, maybe not," said Millan. "Rikka, you keep an eye on them. Alis, go and examine the one downstairs."

Alis headed towards the stairs, flicking her eyebrows at Kasper as she passed. "Coming to take a look?"

He glanced at Millan, then got to his feet and followed Alis down to the ground floor. Together they stepped around the dark pool of blood and peered down at the corpse splayed on the floor. Its head lay almost face down, forcing them to move in closer to see it fully.

Two dull, oval eyes, both as big as fists, stared back at him. Beneath its eyes, thick whiskers stuck out like plastic rods around its muzzle. The creature's pudgy tongue bulged and glistened behind two incisors, like a wet sack shoved between two large, yellow bars. A thick stench of dirt, blood, and faeces caught in Kasper's throat. He gagged and coughed to clear his mouth.

Alis looked thoughtful. "Some kind of rodent."

"Bloody big for a rodent," said Kasper.

With the fingers on her left hand, Alis prodded the head of the dead creature. It stayed still.

Kasper snorted. "You don't think I killed it?"

Alis tutted in mock annoyance. "Just checking the weight of the head. It's fairly light."

"Because it's dumb," said Kasper.

To his delight, the quip earned a short laugh from Alis. She dug into a pocket on her suit, pulled out a small metal plate and pressed it to the side of the dead rodent's skull.

"What's that?" he said.

"Sampler," said Alis.

The plate clamped itself to the rodent's skin and Alis released her grip. It reminded Kasper of the way his own scope moulded to his face. The head of the corpse jolted, and a row of tiny lights sprang up on the surface of the plate. Each one winked out as the sampling progressed. Thirty seconds later, the plate went dark.

Alis peeled the sampler from its head and walked towards the stairs. "Let's see what we've got."

Kasper stood up to follow, then stopped. Above them, he could hear agitated voices. Alis heard them, too, and they both ran up the stairs, blurring their weapons as they went.

Arriving at the top, they saw Millan and Rikka standing in the middle of the landing. Both had their guns trained on the karyack.

"What is it?" said Alis.

"Listen," said Rikka.

They listened. Kasper could hear nothing. The karyack sat silently in the corner. He was about to ask what he was supposed to hear, when a banging sound came from inside the karyack. It bobbed up and down like a boat on the water.

"Something's got inside it," said Millan.

All four of them stared at the vehicle. Another bump sent it rocking again.

"How could anything get in?" said Kasper. "It's sealed shut."

Rikka caught his eye. "Remember this is not an ordinary dark zone. We do not have all the answers yet."

Millan waved the words away. "Whatever it is and however it got in, we need it gone."

As if in response, the karyack rocked with two loud thumps against the interior. Alis pulled out her grip charge. The long cable unfurled onto the floor and crackled into life at her feet. "Open it."

Kasper raised his weapon and trained it on the karyack.

Millan raised a hand. "Don't hit the equipment with that."

Kasper nodded. Millan spread his fingers and the karyack hummed in response. The dome slowly split into two half-shells, like an insect preparing its wings for flight.

Inside, the cargo lay strewn about in piles, but nothing moved. Then Kasper saw something shift quickly at one end. His heart leapt and he aimed his weapon.

"I see it," he said.

"Get it then!" said Millan.

A gold flash flared in Kasper's eyes as he fired. His arms jerked upwards and his blast slammed into the wall above the karyack. Stumbling, he saw Alis's whip slither off the end of his weapon.

Shock turned to anger. "What the hell are you doing?!"

Alis pointed at the karyack. "Look."

Inside, the shape crawled slowly forward into the light. Mostly hidden by the shadow of the karyack's fanned doors, the creature was difficult to see. But once its head poked into the light, he relaxed. "Prue!"

Alis stooped to help the girl get free of the equipment. She pulled aside the last of the straps, and lifted her out of the karyack. Setting her onto a chair, she swept strands of hair from the girl's face and smiled. "Are you OK, Prue?"

The girl's chest fluttered as she gasped for air. "I just wanted to be with you and Kass. I didn't want to stay back there."

Alis gave her a hug then pulled back to look into her face. "OK. That's ok. How do you feel? Are you short of breath?"

Prue screwed up her nose and seemed to struggle to hold back a sob. "I couldn't get my breath to come."

Alis sighed and ruffled Prue's hair. "The karyack is air-tight. You're lucky we heard you moving around. You were starting to suffocate."

Kasper blurred his hands back into shape. He stepped forward so she could see his face. Her eyes widened as soon as she saw him. "Hello, Kass."

Kasper smiled as warmly as he could, but he felt a pang of annoyance that she'd chosen to get stuck with them in this dead city. "Hello, young lady. You gave us all a fright there. We thought you were some kind of monster."

Prue gave him a weak smile. He jerked his thumb towards Millan, "But he's already the biggest monster around here."

She smiled again and Kasper laughed, hoping to put her at ease.

"Alright, newbie," said Millan. "It's good the girl survived, but she gives us a problem. We still have a long way to go and she's going to slow us down."

Alis shrugged. "And what else do you suggest? We can't just put her in a taxi, can we? She can stay in the karyack. We'll leave the top open a bit. She'll be able to breathe just fine."

Millan shook his head. "Makes no difference. We're now compromised. She doesn't have the resources that we do," he waved a hand towards the windows at the far end of the landing, "if we get caught in the open with more of these things coming at us, we don't know if we can protect her."

Kasper looked at Prue and he gave her the most reassuring smile he could muster. This time, she didn't smile back.

Rikka's voice struck up behind him. "Then it's even more important we get this over with quickly. We must get out of the dark zone before nightfall."

"I thought we couldn't do that. You said it's not possible," said Kasper.

Rikka gave a half smile and nodded. "Yes, I did say that. But one of us could go on ahead. It's much quicker to move alone."

Millan shook his head again. "I can't see why splitting up is a clever idea. We're stronger together."

"It stands to reason," said Rikka. "One of us moves light and fast to set up the convertor. The others travel straight to the portal. That means we are two targets moving through the city, rather than one. This splits any hostiles, and increases our chances of success. By the time the main body of the group arrives at the tower, the lone person has already achieved our objective."

Millan waved away her words. "That still means the main group moves at the same pace. It doesn't solve the problem of travelling at night."

"But improves the chances of achieving our objective," said Rikka, "I am the most qualified to work with energy traces. I should go."

From her kneeling position next to Prue, Alis stood up and squinted at Rikka. "Why are you so keen to go? Millan and I have both used the diviner successfully on other planets. The convertor is easy for any of us to set up. I can't see why you'd be the first choice."

If Rikka was annoyed by Alis's challenge, she chose not to show it. "I read energy patterns. We're walking through a high energy bubble. Without scanning equipment, I have the best chance of being able to stay ahead of any threats."

Nobody spoke for a moment then Alis blurted out what Kasper guessed she'd been thinking all along. "And how do we know we can trust you? It would be easy to slip away and let us get picked off in the darkness."

Rikka rose to that one. She took a step forward and Kasper saw tiny blue flashes in her eyes as she bridled under the accusation. "Ridiculous. Just what are you suggesting?"

Millan stepped between them. "Enough. We stay together. All of us are blind without scanners. We've got a long way to go, and one of our people has already died in here. Safety comes before speed. Four people—" he paused and looked at Prue, "*five* people came in here. Five are going to be leaving."

"I still say it makes more sense to bring this to a quick conclusion," said Rikka.

Millan stared at her. "And I still say that I make the decisions."

Rikka said nothing, but her expression showed her mind was anything but quiet. Oblivious, Millan continued to flex his authority. "Alis, get that sample stored. Newbie, you take watch at the window. We'll need to be ready to move as soon as she's finished," he didn't bother looking directly at Rikka, "and if you could please watch the door, that would help."

Slowly, everyone set about their task. Alis went to the karyack and sifted through the equipment inside. Prue's desperate flailing had done an excellent job of scattering everything, so it took her a few minutes to find and dig out the package she needed.

She carried it over to a table at the back of the landing, removed a hexagonal cylinder from inside it and placed it gently on the tabletop. She took the sample from the dead rodent and slid it carefully into a slot towards the top of the cylinder. Lights flashed beside the slot and the cylinder projected a neat, three-dimensional image of the rodent onto the wall.

"Here we go," said Alis.

She tapped the side of the projector and the rodent flipped onto its back like an obedient puppy. She waved her hand and the stomach opened to reveal colour-coded organs and a brightly-lit nervous system.

Clumps of illuminated characters and numbers sprang out of the stomach and hovered in the air expectantly.

"The mutation matches the pattern found in Irvana's captured tooth," she breathed out and frowned. "But this thing shouldn't be so big. It's more than three times its normal size."

"So, the impact of the excession event is widespread," said Rikka. "We should assume all life in the city is infected in the same way."

Millan sighed. "OK. Agreed. From now on we consider all life is hostile."

He looked at Kasper then jerked his head towards where Prue had made herself comfortable on a nearby couch. "Get her back in the karyack. We're leaving and I don't want her getting eaten."

Chapter
Twenty-seven

J obe held his breath. The rock rushed through the air, climbing high above the buildings like a small, self-propelled ship against the vast purple sky.

It lost pace and arced downwards, heading towards the blank face of the unsuspecting window. A large, dark hole appeared in the window, then a split second later he heard the shatter of breaking glass.

Roddi leapt up and punched the air. "Yes!"

Jobe hopped up and down from his vantage point on an upturned metal trunk. "Yes! Yes!" he said. "Smashed it! You smashed it!"

Wide-eyed, Roddi slowly raised his bare arms and studied them. His right arm was now easily four times the size of his left. Side by side, they looked comical. The left arm was thin and pale, while the right was thick and dark.

One arm had a gentle curve around the bicep and forearm, while the other had a web of pulsing veins, all snaking around a small mountain range of tight, bulging muscle.

Raising his right elbow, he craned his neck to look down his oversized bicep and across the expanse of his shoulder. "This arm makes me invincible. Nobody's got an arm like this. It's total power."

"Yeh, yeh, it is. You're the boss now, Roddi. Go see Laine. Go see Laine," said Jobe.

Roddi dropped his arm and looked up at the purple haze above them. Jobe followed his eyes. It seemed to shift as they looked at it, drawing them in. He blinked to stop it, but it simply started again as soon as his eyelids opened.

The expanding purple cloud had fascinated Jobe since it first coloured the sky. His mother had called it 'The Doom' from day one. She was certain it would suffocate them all, that it was the end of the world and they were to die in its judgement.

The rapid spread of illness had given fuel to her theory, taking his father within a week and causing her to stay indoors with her grief, terrified of the vapours that blurred the edges of everyone's senses.

She cut and bent metal fragments into the shape of stars, then hung them in clusters above the doors and windows. When Jobe asked about them, she said they would return the sky to normal. They would tempt the stars beyond the cloud to push through and reach their family here on the surface. Jobe believed only that she was going mad.

For Jobe, his father was no real loss. Quick-tempered and rarely in the home, the man was better off gone. The Doom had done him a favour, he thought. But the Doom soon stunted Jobe's height, withered his physique and quickened his speech. This brought the need for protection. Luckily, Roddi needed his help with new opportunities, now that people were distracted by The Doom.

As people got sick, others spent their time trying to cope with the failure of basic services. Shops and homes stood deserted while the surviving inhabitants pulled together for the greater good. Ferrying food and medicines, quelling unrest and keeping law and order, or just sitting in tight knots of heated discussion about what to do next, most people had their attention elsewhere.

Roddi was enjoying a petty crime spree of unprecedented success. At least, that was until two days ago when, with his spoils stashed safely away, he had awoken to find his right arm throbbing and swollen.

Other young men might fear the change, frightened that the deformity heralded the sickness that had killed his neighbours. But Jobe knew Roddi was different. Roddi always saw opportunity in change.

"I don't know why people hate this cloud," said Roddi. "Look at me. I'm stronger than ever!" he said.

Jobe skipped excitedly beside him. "Yeah, yeah. See Laine, go see Laine."

Roddi reached over with his left hand and grabbed Jobe by the collar, pulling him off the trunk. "Shut up saying that. I'll see him when I'm ready. Why are you so keen for me to beat Laine, anyhow? Who says I won't beat you first, just for practice?"

Jobe squirmed and wriggled to get away from the grip. Although his shrinking had slowed, he couldn't seem to keep his mouth shut or his weight up, despite eating anything and everything that he and Roddi found or stole between his meals at home.

The result was that after only two months, Jobe had no strength. His own clothes hung off him like hand-me-downs from an older, larger brother. "Ow! Let go! Let go, Rod! It's not funny."

Roddi held out his deformed arm and swung Jobe around towards it. The momentum of the swing made Jobe's head smash into the outstretched limb.

The brief, deep thud made Roddi laugh. Jobe yelled with pain and, losing his balance, flailed for support, then fell on the floor in a mess of scrawny limbs.

Roddi laughed harder, delighting in the sight of Jobe sprawled on the floor. "What are you doing down there, stick-man?"

Jobe propped himself up on one elbow and screwed up his face. He spat on the ground near Roddi's feet. "Get lost!"

Roddi looked down and realised Jobe was genuinely upset. His smile faded. "Get over it, J. Let's go get something to eat. I'm starving."

He turned and walked back towards the apartment block behind them. Jobe got to his feet and ran to catch up. His friend's oversized arm hung between them, puffed up and pulsing with power. That arm had more power than Jobe could muster in his entire body. Jobe looked up at Roddi, but his friend kept his eyes set ahead.

Once inside the block, they headed across the open reception hall and past the bank of useless lifts. All five sets of lift doors had spray paint and dents across their faces, telling a tale of frustrated tenants and bored youths.

It had been weeks since Jobe had seen any light behind the buttons or the blank displays that should plot the rise and fall of each of the lifts.

They walked past rotting sacks of rubbish, holding their breath until they passed through the large doorway and out onto the street on the far side of the building.

"Big Gal's" said Roddi.

"No, she cooks rats," said Jobe.

Roddi shrugged. "Homey's then"

Jobe shook his head. "It stinks in there."

Roddi laughed. "It stinks everywhere."

"How about Mar-Mar's?" said Jobe.

Roddi always seemed to forget about Mar-Mar's. It was a few blocks away, too far for most people who wanted to avoid the worst of The Doom's work. It was a dangerous area if you didn't keep your wits about you, but the tiny café had survived, and seemed to still have large reserves of great food. Jobe knew it was the best option.

"OK," said Roddi. "But try to keep up."

Jobe rushed to keep up with him. He suspected Roddi secretly liked the feeling of being the one setting the pace.

"It's sure got quieter round here," said Jobe. "What is it, only a couple of weeks since we've been this way?"

Roddi didn't answer. It made no difference. Jobe had to continue without waiting for an answer, just to release the words from his head. "Whatever it is, it's not that long since there were still people round here. But there's only a few hanging around now, so where'd they all go? I'd love to know."

"Same reason anyone moves since The Doom came," said Roddi, "they've gone to find a better deal."

"Deal? What do you mean deal?" said Jobe.

"I mean deal, you know, they worked out that staying round here's going to bring trouble. Doesn't matter if it's a fast criminal or the slow purple, they run off before it kills them."

"Yeah, but where to?" said Jobe. "There must be hundreds gone."

Roddi picked a lump of metal off the ground. He examined it in his hand as he walked. "Don't know, don't care. Their loss. If they were tough, they'd have adapted. Instead, they gave up and ran away."

He pulled back his tree trunk of an arm and heaved the object up the street in front of them. It crashed into the wall of a building, taking a chunk of masonry down with it. Roddi gave a short, triumphant laugh and set off again.

Jobe felt his breath getting shorter in his effort to keep up. The Doom was draining his physique, but his mind raced constantly. "I suppose it was clever to run away, right? They'd have known what might happen here. They'd have guessed they might get beaten or robbed, or something worse. They'd have been stupid to stay, right? I mean, if you know it's dangerous, you've got to go, right? Stupid not to, right?"

Roddi slapped Jobe's shoulder with the lightest flick of his giant arm. Wide-eyed, Jobe staggered under the weight of the blow, but stayed on his feet. "Oww!"

"You calling me stupid?" said Roddi. "I stayed, didn't I? My Mum stayed, didn't she? You calling us both stupid?"

Jobe rubbed his shoulder and tried to ignore the shock. He cursed his fading ability to control his mouth. He didn't want to upset Roddi and risk losing his big friend. A big friend with a massive right arm was a considerable asset.

"Of course not! I stayed too, didn't I?" he said, "I just mean, if you're weak, it makes sense to run away, right? We're not, I mean, you're not stupid, but some people can't take it, you know? Some people don't have the..."

"Alright, alright, shut up," said Roddi.

Jobe's mouth slapped shut.

Roddi looked up at the sky, then fixed his eyes on the street ahead. "You know what I heard once?"

"What's that?" said Jobe.

"I heard a soldier say it," said Roddi.

"What? What did he say?" said Jobe.

Roddi paused. "The soldier walked into a diner and ordered his food. The only seat left was on the same table as some civvy. So, he went over and sat down. The civvy started asking stuff, like what regiment the soldier was in, had he seen action, had he killed anyone. All that sort of stuff. The soldier kept quiet mostly, just ate his food and grunted a bit now and then."

Jobe frowned. "So what, he said nothing?"

"Yeah, but not 'til the civvy guy started getting all in his face about not fighting," said Roddi.

"Not fighting?" said Jobe.

Roddi nodded. "He said he didn't believe in killing. Told the soldier, to his face, that he thought the army should be, you know, stopped. Broken up."

"Disbanded?" said Jobe.

Roddi shot him a glance. "Yeah. Disbanded. The civvy guy told a soldier, sitting across from him in full uniform, that he thought what the guy did was wrong and that he ought to leave the army right now. Can you believe that?"

Jobe's eyes went comically wide. "He punched the civvy, right? Knocked him off his chair? Must have done."

Roddi shook his head as he walked. "No, he didn't touch him. But I'll bet he thought about it. The civvy wouldn't have stood a chance. But he just finished his food, pushed his plate to one side and stared at the guy. After a minute or so, he asked him why he thought it was OK to just come out and say what he thought. The civvy didn't even blink, he just said 'It's a free city, I can say what I want.' And you know what the soldier said?"

"What? What did he do?" said Jobe.

"He asked him how he thought the city stayed free. That shut the civvy right up."

Jobe slapped one hand on the other in delight. "Wow! What a great line."

Roddi grinned. "It gets better. He stood up, pointed his finger at the civvy and said, 'you can sit in here, eating what you want, saying what you want, because people like me make it happen. Without us giving you your freedom, you'd get told where to sit, when to eat and when to shit. The people you're bad mouthing are willing to die so you can enjoy your freedom.' Then he walked out."

Jobe's jaw dropped. "No way! That's brilliant."

Roddi's grin faded. "Yeah, I used to think that, too. But now—"

Jobe waited what seemed like a full minute for Roddi to finish. His impatience spilled over. "So what do you think now?"

Roddi looked at him and grinned. "Now I think he should have grabbed that civvy and smashed his stupid face in."

Chapter
Twenty-eight

Alis caught sight of two people leaning out of a window high above them. She pointed them out, but both figures melted away the moment they realised they'd been spotted.

Two streets later, Kasper heard barking and growling coming from a passageway between two buildings up ahead.

Millan called them to a halt. He motioned for Kasper to look. With an image of the dead rodent still fresh in his mind, he walked slowly towards the noise and peered into the purple-tinted gloom. The growling and snarling stopped.

After a few moments, his eyes adjusted and he could pick out one or two shapes shifting around in the darkness. He stepped forwards and heard the growls start up again. The hairs shot up on the back of his neck. "Something's coming this way."

He looked down at his arm and felt the familiar nausea as it hinged, flipped back to his forearm, and moulded into a short barrel.

He swallowed hard and pointed it into the passageway, aiming slightly low, guessing the target had four legs and would be close to the ground.

He was squinting to spot the beasts when a deep voice shouted something inaudible from the other end of the passage. The thudding stopped. More shouting rang through the darkness. The barking dropped to a low, steady snarl. Another distant command silenced the growling, and the shadows fell still. He lowered his weapon.

Rikka sighed. "Just a domestic animal brought to heel by its master."

"Life goes on as normal after all," said Millan.

But Kasper felt his pulse still thudding in his ears. "There was nothing normal about that sound. I've run into nasty guard dogs before. They all sounded like puppies compared to that."

Millan grinned and waved the group forward. "Well then, we're lucky they didn't come out to play."

The sight and sound of people still living their lives became more and more commonplace as they worked their way closer to the centre of the city. Mostly, the figures kept their distance, blurred by the haze and only offering a brief glimpse of themselves before retreating from view. Eventually, as the group pressed ahead, the city's remaining population decided to reveal themselves.

Kasper spotted movement on a balcony of the tenement block looming over them. "There!"

"What is it?" said Millan.

Kasper squinted to see more clearly. "Three people. They're not running."

For the first time, Prue poked her head clear of the karyack's shell to see what they were all discussing.

Millan stopped and focused on where Kasper's finger was pointing. "Are they armed?"

"Hard to tell," said Kasper.

"More spectators. We could be about to run into something nasty," said Millan.

Rikka appeared beside Kasper. "I suspect they are trying to decide whether our arrival is a threat or an opportunity."

"A threat?" said Millan. "There are only four of us. We're not the threat around here. Everything's either desperate, deformed, or deadly in this city. Some things are all three."

Alis shook her head. " Not everyone is out to kill us. For most residents, dark zones just force them to make the best of a tough situation. Those three might be hoping we're here to help them."

Millan grinned. "Irvana found a mutated tooth that had crunched through the bones of people just like them. Of course they're going to hope things improve. Being hopeful doesn't mean you're going to be friendly, though."

Kasper watched the emotion play across Alis's face. She hadn't mentioned Irvana for weeks. Her voice rose as she spoke. "I'm simply pointing out that we shouldn't write them all off as thieves and murderers before we have a chance to study them more closely."

Millan's grin fell. "That's all they are, Alis. Anyway, making friends is not the mission, is it? We agreed to assume all life is hostile. Doing otherwise puts us at risk."

Rikka seemed to ignore the conversation. Instead, she squinted against the haze to get a clear view of the figures on the balcony. "I can only see heads and shoulders, but they look to be deformed. One has a significantly elevated left shoulder. A growth perhaps. Another seems to lack the necessary width in the chest to allow for an adequate respiratory system and the third has a skull that appears to be flattened on one side." She looked at Alis. "I agree with Millan. We cannot be certain of the impact of the changes in these people. It remains prudent to treat them as hostile."

Alis looked unimpressed. Kasper gave her a half smile. He felt more dismayed than he should have when she didn't return it.

They moved on through more long streets, the partly open karyack humming reassuringly as it glided between them. Inside, Prue's face was a pale oval, just visible between the two separated halves of its curved back.

More figures appeared as they pushed deeper towards the city centre. Some lounged against railings, others peered out of windows above. All of them seemed content to linger and watch the small knot of newcomers pass them by.

Rikka twisted her head in all directions. "The neighbourhood we passed through a short while ago had people in it that were simply too scared to be seen. But these people seem far less concerned by us."

Alis nodded. "They're more confident. Looks like they've got life working for them here. They've still got a community."

Alis's words made Kasper think of Charnell and his focus on community and compassion. He focused on the buildings around him, and tried to suppress the image of the old steward's empty, bloody shoulders hanging over his dais.

The street edge to the right dropped away to nothing, and Kasper realised they must have gained height through the past few streets. A wide chasm opened beyond the edge, giving him a foggy view of enormous buildings and broad highways, all running at different heights on the opposite side. Low benches sat along the edge. Sitting here and looking out over the city must have been a popular pastime before the skies turned purple.

The opposite side of the street was a complete contrast. A solid wall of dilapidated shop fronts and businesses stretched away ahead of them. One or two showed signs of recent use, while the rest had doors hanging open, showing ruined interiors plundered of any working or useful components. It looked a miserable trail of economic failure.

Kasper's eyes followed the street to where it met two immensely tall tenement towers up ahead. Both buildings had full width balconies on every floor, sticking out of the walls like rungs on huge ladders. The width of the street separated them, but they looked so close he thought it must be possible to hold a conversation from one side to the other.

As they drew closer, it began to look as though the balconies had cables running between them. He blinked and stared again, trying to focus through the haze hanging around them. "Those towers are joined together. Something's stretched between them."

With each step, the view grew clearer. The balconies on both buildings had long, straight tendrils stretching from one to the other. They hung above the road in a latticework of straight lines.

"Whatever is joining them, it's moving," said Alis, "Look at that one near the bottom. Third floor, I think."

Kasper shifted his gaze to the third floor. Rikka hurried forwards to get a closer look. "It is not the line that is moving. There is something moving along it."

Several of the lines had dark shapes travelling one way or another along them. The road led straight into the utter darkness beneath. Millan called a halt. "We're not travelling underneath that mess. Newbie, get your stolen map out. We need to go back and find a way around this."

Millan started to say something else, but Rikka interrupted him. "I am not certain we have time to go around. Our delay already means we will be in here at night. We must choose the shortest route, whichever direction that takes us."

Millan pointed to the towers, but kept his eyes on Rikka. "With no scanners, we don't know what those things are. Last time, we had a building to hide in. This time we do not. Walking under there is madness. I'd rather we arrived late than not at all."

Rikka was unfazed. "Without scanners, we need the daylight. Taking a longer route means we will be in here deep into the night, when the city is many more times dangerous than these buildings are now."

Alis threw up a hand at Rikka. "We're all aware of what the night means. Let's use the map, rather than our own motives, shall we? Maybe check if the diviner can pick anything up?"

Rikka looked from Millan to Alis, then back to Millan. She looked as though she might speak, but instead she reached inside the hovering karyack. She withdrew the small box and gripped it in both hands. A faint blue glow appeared from within her palms. The light looked alien against the relentless grey and purple around them.

Kasper kept his eyes glued to Rikka's hands as he opened the map. Even Millan stared in silence, captivated by the sight of the diviner at work.

Unblinking, Rikka waited for a moment, then gave a curt nod, as though happy with whatever she'd learned. The glow faded, and she carefully replaced the diviner within the karyack. "There are stronger traces of the infection around us, but they are still peripheral."

Alis raised her eyebrows. "That means we still have a long way to go."

"Alright," said Millan, "but we're still not going between those towers."

Kasper's map finished scribing the nearby streets and buildings, and all eyes turned to study it.

Behind them, Prue put her head out of the karyack. "Kass."

Kasper didn't answer. He held up a hand without looking, motioning for her to wait. She turned her head towards Alis. "Um, Alis."

Alis half-turned her head but kept her eyes on the map. "One minute, Prue."

"HEY!" shouted Prue.

All of them stopped talking and turned to face her.

"Don't shout!" said Millan.

"What's up?" said Kasper.

Prue pointed towards a small shop. "Something's moving on the roof."

They squinted over to where she was pointing.

"Whereabouts?" said Alis. "That roof there?"

"The one with the S and L on the sign," said Prue. "I saw it. Something moving on the roof."

They waited a moment, but nothing moved. Rikka sighed and turned away. "There are plenty of things moving in a dark zone, child. Don't let it worry you."

They turned their backs to look at the map. Kasper had lowered his arm, and the holograph sat perpendicular to his leg.

Millan glared at Kasper. "Lift it back up. We need to get moving."

Kasper heard a loud slap. Millan looked confused for a moment, then gasped and dropped to one knee. He coughed, and his voice dropped to a whisper. "I'm hit."

For the next few seconds, the world seemed to move in slow motion. Kasper and Rikka reached to grab Millan.

Alis shoved Prue's head back inside the karyack. "Stay down," she said.

Kasper helped Rikka pull Millan along the ground. Alis bent to help them just as something hard thumped into the side of the karyack, rocking it violently. Prue screamed and fell backwards, disappearing among the equipment.

More shots whistled past and slammed into the karyack. The three of them pulled Millan behind it. He finished dropping a meditab into his mouth, then cursed at the movement. A loud pop came from where Alis was standing, followed a split second later by an explosion on the far side of the street.

Alis dropped behind the karyack and gave Kasper a broad grin. "Got him." She turned and called out to Prue, "It's all over, Prue. It's OK now."

Rikka sat up on her haunches beside Millan. "He has lost consciousness." She probed at the hole in his suit. "I can see organic tissue damage, but the meditab should already be healing that."

Kasper put his hand under Millan's chin, lifting his head. "He's definitely passed out. We should load him into the karyack and get off this street."

"OK. Let's do it," said Alis.

A barking sound made her freeze. Kasper felt a flash of nerves in his stomach. "I've heard those animals before."

"Sounds like more of them this time," said Alis.

"It's coming from those shop fronts," said Rikka. She stood and peered up and down the street. "We are standing in the open with no cover, only able to move forwards or backwards. We are being ambushed."

Shop doors and windows burst open in clouds of dust and splinters. The barking and snarling reached a deafening level in an instant. Kasper's stomach leapt. Rikka planted her feet, and he watched her hands shimmer as she stared at the busted shop fronts.

Alis shoved him with her foot. "Don't just sit there. Arm up!"

He snapped into gear, blurred his arms and turned to face the din.

She nodded. "Right side, Kass."

The dust parted to their right, and two heavy, flesh-coloured legs appeared from a doorway. The wide, clawed feet were animal, not human. Their immense size reminded him of the junkyard dogs that Leon had seen off years ago. More legs appeared from the broken doorways. Thick, fleshy muzzles pushed through the dust at his own head height. He wished Leon were here now.

Mouths tore at the air. Deep red tongues lashed wildly over rows of sharp yellow teeth. Their legs danced on the spot, giving flashes of curved silver claws, each one tearing at the ground, desperate to lurch forward.

"Canines. Domestic dogs. Massive mutation," shouted Rikka.

Alis turned to Kasper. "Moving targets. Let them get in close before you shoot."

As if on command, the beasts leapt forward from the doorways, a solid wave of scrabbling claws and rippling muscle. They cleared the distance at an alarming speed. Kasper had only a moment to brace himself before aiming at the nearest two and firing.

Two spheres streaked across the street, punching a neat hole through one, then another of the beasts. Howls split the air, and they crashed to the ground. The force of their run sent their bodies rolling forward several times before coming to rest.

Relieved, he picked two more targets and brought those down, too. But these had made more ground than the first, and the next two were closer still.

He fired. One yelped and went down, but the other slammed into him. He lost his balance and staggered backwards under the weight of the impact. Groping claws and searching teeth tore frantically at his suit. His hands came up to protect his head. Hot breath and spit clouded his vision. His legs strained to keep him upright. He could see nothing but teeth, gums, and rolls of pink flesh. He pulled his face away and yelled as he forced the creature's head away from his neck.

The fear of a second beast sinking its unseen jaws into his legs broke the deadlock. He twisted as hard as he could. The hot, heavy body slid to his left side. He let his right arm follow it and brought the barrel level with the beast's head. A single blast blew its throat apart and sent the skull flying backwards.

The weight dropped to the ground, and Kasper staggered forwards. Another snarling ball of muscle and fur filled his vision. He shot without taking aim. The thing howled and dropped away.

Struggling to get his breath, he whipped his head from side to side, his arm moving in a tight arc to blast the next target. To his relief, the sounds of snarling and howling disappeared, and nothing else came.

Breathing hard, he looked across at Alis and Rikka. "Can you see any more?"

"Get down!" said Alis.

Something flashed between them. They dropped to the ground. Alis sent a salvo of loud blasts crashing into one of the shop fronts. "They're dug in," she said. "Bring it down!"

More blasts flashed past them, and Kasper pressed his cheek to the road. He couldn't see anything to shoot at. A loud crackling sound made him look back at Rikka. She stood upright, a bright blue light jumping and sparking between her hands. She shouted once, then flung her hands forward.

The light flew out in a broad arc, smashing through the fronts of the low buildings. An entire section of the row of shops collapsed, the din all but masking the screams of those hidden inside.

She dropped to one knee, breathing hard. Kasper looked from Rikka to the destroyed buildings, then back again.

His mouth hung open. "Why not do that to start with?"

Rikka looked up, her breath still coming hard. "Not that easy."

Alis rushed to the karyack. By the time Kasper and Rikka joined her, she had pulled a spray can from a bag and was tearing at Millan's suit.

"What are you doing?" said Kasper.

She gestured at the spray can. "Covering the wound with that. It'll keep the infection from attacking his flesh."

Rikka picked up the can and studied it. "This contains antibiotic bacteria. There is a high probability that the antibiotic will behave differently in this dark zone."

Alis continued pulling the punctured suit away from Millan's wound. "So what do you suggest, instead? Cut away the flesh to his bone? Give him nothing?"

Kasper frowned. "Didn't he take one of his tablets? The meditab?"

Alis focused on opening Millan's suit. "That will speed up the repair of his organic bone and tissue, but won't help kill the infection. We need to stop the bacteria getting into him through the wound."

Rikka's face hardened. She waved the cylinder at Alis. "We must think. This is a topical biological medicine. It will have direct contact with the infected air in here when applied to the wound. It will react rapidly with mutated bacteria. It might worsen his condition." Alis reached for the can, but Rikka pulled it away. "You are acting on impulse again, Alis. You are putting his life in danger, not saving him."

Alis snatched the cylinder. "We shall see."

She raised the can, clicked it once and ejected a fine spray that coated the wound. For the first time, Kasper saw Rikka truly speechless. The woman slowly shook her head at Alis. "Your presence here puts all of us in danger."

Kasper looked from one woman to the other, then at the corpses of the beasts lying around them. "Do you think there's more of them?"

"Yes," said Rikka. She rummaged through their equipment and produced some dressings. She thrust them at Alis. "So we need to think hard about what to do next."

Alis looked at the dressings. Rikka motioned for her to take them. "These are non-biological."

Kasper turned away and looked at Prue. "You OK?"

She had covered herself in bags and blankets and had both arms wrapped around her head. At least she was well protected, he thought.

He leaned in and rubbed her shoulder. "Here, let's put this on you."

Carefully, he passed a baggage strap over her waist and under her arms, then clipped it into place. Prue looked puzzled, but didn't complain.

He smiled and gave her a wink. "Just in case it gets a bit bumpy when we move off."

Before Prue could reply, Alis waved a hand at Kasper. "Kass, help me get Millan in there."

He shuffled the gear around to make space, then reached down and took hold of Millan's legs while Alis took his upper body. Millan didn't respond, even when Alis knocked him against the side of the karyack on her first attempt at raising him over the edge.

Once he lay flat inside, she strapped him into place and pushed a blanket under his head. As the doors hummed shut, she turned to Kasper. "I might not always agree with that man, but he's still one of us." Kasper nodded. She pointed at his arm. "We'd better have another look at your map."

But as he prepared to display the hologram, the roar of an engine sounded in the distance.

"What now?" he said.

"Just a vehicle somewhere. Come on, open up the map," said Alis.

But the sound got louder, drifting towards them from back the way they'd come. Kasper looked around, searching for the source of the sound. "I hate to say Millan was right, but we should always assume the worst."

The roar of the vehicle came closer. Perhaps only in the next street.

Alis's hands folded back and melted into her forearms. Kasper followed her lead.

She shouted across to Rikka on the other side of the karyack. "Company!"

The sound filled the street and spilled out around them. A low, wide vehicle broke through the haze. The sound rattled through Kasper's bones as it raced directly towards them.

"It's coming straight at us," he said.

Alis raised her arm and two loud pops sent a pair of her Z-13s hurtling towards the vehicle. They struck the front of it, angled away, and exploded against the wall of a nearby building in a brilliant shower of gold and grey.

She cursed and shouted at Kasper and Rikka. "Blast it off the road!"

Kasper looked round, but Rikka wasn't there. "Where *is* Rikka?"

Alis's arms jerked as she blasted the vehicle again. "Just
SHOOT!"

Sprays of gold, blue and white blazed from their weapons,
turning the air warm with smoke and the crackling heat of
electronics. The vehicle wavered, then one blast took out a
wheel, and it slumped onto one side. The metal body hit the
road, screamed, then the whole thing leapt off the ground and
flew towards them.

"Move!" shouted Alis.

They dived to one side. The car hit the ground beside the
karyack and smashed into it, taking it clean over the edge of the
road and falling out of sight.

For a moment, Kasper heard the hungry engine searching for
traction. Then it smashed into the roof of a building on the
street below.

Hi heart leapt. "Oh no. Prue!"

The karyack was gone. In its place were deep furrows in the
ground where the vehicle had bounced across the street and over
the edge.

They ran to the edge and fell onto their chests, desperate to see
any sign of the karyack. The scene below was a mess. The main
body of the vehicle jutted from the roof of a building, spewing
plumes of dark smoke. Parts of it lay in the street, ripped from
the main body by the impact.

Kasper couldn't see the karyack anywhere. "Where is it? I
can't see it."

Alis shook her head and looked up and down the street below.
"We have to get down there." They jumped up, and she pointed
at Kasper's arm, "Map, quick. How do we get down?"

The map finished weaving its precise lines and hovered
proudly before them. Alis jabbed her finger at a steep diagonal
towards the top of the hologram. "There, a ramp or something,
leading down to that street."

Kasper shook his head, "That's the south side of the city.
You're looking in the wrong place." He pointed to where two

long, thin oblongs rose up above a different steep diagonal. "There," he said, "That's the towers beside us. The quickest way down is on the other side."

Alis wagged her finger at the same place on the map, "Those tall structures are these two towers?"

He glanced up at the towers behind them, their upper floors disappearing into the purple gloom of the sky. Dark shapes shifted along the lines stretched between their balconies. He nodded.

"The quickest way to get down is to walk underneath all of that."

Chapter
Twenty-nine

R oddi and Jobe turned the last corner and started down the street towards Mar-Mar's. They walked a few steps before Jobe paused.

"See that? See it? All over those towers. What's that?" he said.

Roddi looked up at the street high above them, and saw the mass of black cables stretched between the two towers. "Don't know, don't care. There's a lot of funny stuff going on around here. Let's get fed."

The faded sign and smeared windows of Mar-Mar's came into view. A too-small-to-cope refuse burner stood near the front entrance, drowning under a pile of empty food cartons. It might be scruffy, but Mar-Mar's was easily the best place with hot food for a few blocks around.

Not only was the food pretty good, despite the leaner times, but the owners were clever. When The Doom had come, they'd realised sick people can't work, so they don't get paid, so they don't spend money. Lots of businesses folded fast, but Mar-Mar's adapted. It started accepting pawned goods in return for meals.

This brought in new customers, but it also meant people came back when they had money. Fairly soon, the little café was doing better than ever before. The food tasted good, too. You just shouldn't look too closely at what you were eating.

"It's open," said Jobe.

"It's always open," said Roddi.

The door had deep scratch marks towards the bottom that looked new. It creaked more than Jobe remembered, but as he cleared the threshold, the familiar smell of warm, spiced sauce hit him. "Wow, smells great. I'm having the goulash. Or maybe the fritters. No, the goulash."

The single room had unmatched tables and chairs set in clusters around a wide, dark floor. Thin trails of steam rose from pots in front of huddled diners. People sat quietly, their conversations just a low murmur from faces held close to their food.

Nobody looked up as Roddi and Jobe strode confidently towards the counter to place their order.

"No fritters," said Roddi, "Only goulash left."

Jobe clapped his hands together. "Goulash it is, then. Knew it. Goulash. Great."

Fumbling through their pockets, they each pulled out items of value. Roddi held a pile of odd-shaped metal fragments in his enormous fist. He tipped them into a wide-mouthed chute set into the top of the counter.

The metal clattered and clanked as it bounced down into the depths. Beside the chute, a panel of buttons lit up, and a small screen displayed a number.

Roddi cursed. "Is that all? Bloody place is getting expensive!"

The fingers on his right hand were too large to press buttons, so he reached across and used his left to tap in his order. Stepping to one side, he waited for his goulash to arrive.

Jobe reached out and dropped a fist-sized metal ball into the chute. A single heavy thud came from the bottom of the chute and a number appeared on the display. Jobe clapped his hands again. He punched in his choice and waited.

Roddi leaned in to try to read the display. "How much did you get?"

"750ml," said Jobe, "Can you believe that ball-bearing was worth so much? I think the machine's got that wrong. There must be something wrong, right? I mean, maybe it needs upgrading, you know? Right?"

Roddi stared at him. In front of them, two sections of the counter slid back and steam billowed in their faces. When it cleared, two pots of hot goulash sat in front of them. Lumps of meat and vegetable poked out at odd angles through the reddish-brown liquid. The smell of the spiced sauce streamed into their nostrils like a spell.

"Aww, wow," said Jobe.

Roddi looked down at his pot. It was smaller than Jobe's. He only had a 500ml serving, while Jobe had scored himself a 750ml feast. He reached over and took the larger pot.

Jobe moved his hands towards the pot, then pulled them back. "Ah, I, er, think-"

Roddi held the pot handle and stared at him. Jobe looked back for a moment, then down at the smaller pot. A familiar weight appeared in his chest. "OK, so you're bigger, so you need more food?"

"That's right," said Roddi. "I'm the one that protects us, so you've got to pay to keep my strength up, right?"

Jobe felt his mouth dry up and had to hold back the torrent of words that pushed up in his throat. "Sure," said Jobe, "It's just—"

"Just what?" said Roddi.

"Well, I wondered if we should share it out, you know, make it so it's one lot of goulash in two pots. I mean, we look out for each other, right? We're a team, aren't we?"

Roddi frowned, then a broad grin spread across his face. "Sure. Let's share it."

Jobe's relief came out in a loud chuckle. "Yeah, we're a team. Take care of the team, right?"

They picked out a table near a window at the back of the restaurant. The combination of dirt on the inside and gloom on the outside meant the window gave little light, but at least they were out of the way of the other tables.

They ate their first mouthfuls fast and in silence. The sauce on the goulash meant they couldn't taste the meat at all. Without saying it, they both understood that was a blessing. Meat was in scarce supply, and you never knew what you were eating, but you could be sure it wasn't too fresh.

"Pretty good," said Jobe. He shoved in another few mouthfuls, then pushed his pot over to Roddi. "Fill her up, teammate!"

Roddi finished pushing a large piece of meat into his mouth. A trickle of sauce ran onto his chin. He looked down at Jobe's depleted goulash, stuck his spoon in, and scooped out the last chunk of meat. "Thanks for sharing."

Roddi laughed and stuffed the meat into his mouth. More sauce spread over his chin. It took Jobe a few moments to realise what had happened. He watched Roddi's laughter and felt the questions surge out of his brain and crash into the back of his clenched teeth.

I thought we were a team? What gives you the right to take my food? You think your stupid arm makes you better than me? It was a titanic effort, but he held his tongue. Roddi's growing strength was protecting them both.

"Sure," Jobe said, pulling his pot back in front of him. "Nice one. That arm needs feeding anyway, so I suppose you should have the most."

Roddi grinned and wiped the sauce from his chin with the back of his enormous hand. "Damn right I should."

Jobe looked down and started on the remains of his food. He felt Roddi's eyes on him, but didn't look up. Fortunately, some more people entered Mar-Mar's, and their loud voices shattered the uneasy silence. All the heads in the place, including Jobe's, turned to look.

A group of three thick-set, scruffy men pushed their way through the tables and up to the front of the cafe. Jobe didn't recognise two of them, but the scar across the face of the third was unmistakable.

"Laine," said Jobe. He ducked his head and tried to sit lower in his chair. He sank down so far that his chin sat just below the edge of the table. His breath thickened in his throat. "This is it! What you going to do? He wants his money, doesn't he? He'll come for it if he sees us, right? He's crazy. What you going to do, Rod?"

Roddi carried on eating. He looked out of the window and up at the strange, black stuff wedged between the tower blocks high up on the roadway above. "Let him come."

"There's three of them!" said Jobe.

Roddi glared at him. "Shut the fuck up. Sit still and try not to shit your pants."

Jobe took a deep breath and bit his lip. A thousand words threatened to come tumbling out. He felt his throat closing in panic. He couldn't see how Roddi could win. They'd been dodging Laine, and he wanted the money. He'd kill them both, for sure.

Jobe sized up the window. Maybe he could smash it and get away before they grabbed him. Too late. A shout came from across the room.

"Ah! There's my friends from the rooftop!" said Laine.

The three of them strode over towards Roddi and Jobe. They drew up level with the table, and Laine burst out laughing.

"What the fuck is this? The small guy's got smaller and the big guy's got bigger! You two been sleeping together? Swapping diseases or something?"

Laine's companions guffawed obediently.

"Bet they have," said one.

"Bet they love it off of each other," said the other.

Jobe tried to sink further in his chair. Both his feet tapped rapidly on the floor with no clear rhythm. Roddi stared up into Laine's scarred face.

Laine's smile dropped. "Hello."

Roddi said nothing. He lowered his spoon and placed it beside his pot.

Laine leaned in towards Roddi. "I said 'hello'. It's rude not to answer, shithead."

Roddi still didn't respond. Jobe calculated the gap between his chair and the table, gathering his courage to dive to the floor if Laine lunged at him instead of Roddi.

"Get him up," said Laine.

The two men moved round the table, and the first one gripped Roddi's left shoulder. Roddi allowed himself to be lifted out of his seat and used the momentum to throw a punch with his mutated right fist. He connected with the first man's chin. A loud, wet crack filled the space around the table, and the man's head flicked backwards, taking the rest of his body with it.

Startled by the sudden violence, Jobe dropped under the table. He saw the man hit the floor nearby and gasped. The man's lower jaw and tongue had disappeared, leaving a bloody hole instead of his mouth.

Laine looked down at his maimed friend, then back at Roddi. "Bad ass now, are we?"

He grabbed Roddi's wrist and held it with both hands. The other man placed his hands around Roddi's throat and squeezed. Gasping for air, Roddi tried to pull his head away, but the man knew what he was doing. The grip tightened.

Roddi flailed at the man with his mutant hand. He missed, but caught Laine with the backswing. The blow lifted Laine off his feet and onto the next table, scattering the diners and sending their pots of goulash crashing to the floor.

Free of Laine, Roddi punched at the face of the man strangling him from behind. It connected, and the man grunted, dropped his hands, and fell to the floor. Roddi rubbed his throat and lashed out at the man with his boot. The man didn't move.

Shouting erupted around them. The diners stood around their broken pots, yelling, and waving their arms at Roddi and Jobe. They lifted Laine to his feet and pushed him towards the door. Kicking it wide, they heaved him through it and onto the street.

Other diners were on their feet, saying the fighting was a disgrace, telling them they should be ashamed and threatening to call the authorities. A man near to them opened one side of his overcoat to reveal the butt of a weapon.

Jobe didn't need the encouragement. He got up and slurped down the last of his goulash. He looked at Roddi standing at the centre of the abuse. "We'd better go Rod, yeah? Now. Let's go."

Roddi stared at the two men lying by the counter. The first would need surgery to get his face back in shape. The second might have a broken nose. Both were unconscious.

Jobe tugged at Roddi's shirt. The words came flying out of his mouth. "We have to go. Come on. We have to move. Get out, OK? Now!"

They moved through the crowd of diners and over to the door. Jobe ignored them all and stared straight ahead, wishing it were over. But before Roddi stepped over the threshold, he raised his mutated arm and shook it at the diners waiting for him to leave.

"YEEEAAAHHHH!!!" he shouted.

Jobe half pulled him out of the door and onto the street. Roddi stepped out onto the pavement and laughed. "Did you see their faces? They've never seen anything like it! They said so, didn't they? Never seen anyone who could do what I just did!"

All Jobe could think of was the police. He was so eager to get away from the door that he literally hopped from one foot to another. "Yes, I heard them, but they weren't happy about it, right? They were angry with you, with us, I mean, with what we did. We hurt people. They didn't like it. They didn't like it at all."

Roddi laughed again. "Yeah, but what if they were in trouble? They wouldn't say that if I'd smashed up a few blokes to help them out, would they? Don't like people getting hurt unless it helps them."

But Jobe didn't listen. In the distance he heard the crack, crack, pop, pop sound of gunfire and held up a hand. "Do you hear that? Laine's gone off and got an army. We're dead now, they're shooting the place up. We're going to get shot now, right? Killed for what we did."

Roddi listened. "Nah, it's coming from up near those towers. He can't get up there so quick." He flexed his arm and spread his thick fingers in front of his own face. "He's run off somewhere to stay out of my way. He knows he's not king rat anymore."

Jobe couldn't stop hopping about. "So what's all the shooting, then? We'd better run, right? Get away from here?"

Roddi shook his head. "Just someone trying to take something from someone else."

"Not with so many guns. That's big noise! It's got to be the Troopers. What are they doing? Why Troopers?" said Jobe.

Roddi grunted. "Not Troopers. Troopers left when the rich folks left. Besides, The Doom's too thick now. Not even the army gets in here. That'll be bandits up there, not government."

"Bandits? This far over?" said Jobe. "Oh no, why? We got nothing for them over here, right? Right?"

"Only one way to find out for sure," said Roddi. "Let's go ask them!"

He stepped away from Jobe and headed off towards the source of the noise. Jobe felt himself try to resist, but faced with either Laine or bandits, he'd rather be with Roddi.

They covered only half the distance before the gunfire stopped and the sound of an engine replaced it. Gunfire started up again, followed by a massive crash, like a building had come down.

Roddi's face lit up, and he beamed at Jobe. "You know what that sound is?"

Jobe nodded. "Vehicle hit a building. Some kind of crash, right? Isn't it?"

"Nope," said Roddi. "That's the sound of pay day. Let's get there before anyone else does."

Chapter Thirty

Two blue flashes split the shadows in the street. Behind a second-floor window in the building opposite, a woman waited. Two more flashes gave life to the darkness. Satisfied, she raised her hand and returned the signal.

She watched a figure spring from the shadows and run towards the ground level entrance to her building. Footsteps sounded in the hall, and she turned to face the open doorway. Like so many others, this building had no power, and the only light came from a dim solar bulb in the ceiling.

The figure entered the room, her slim-fitting green suit touching the floor.

"You're much later than I expected," said the woman. "I'd begun to lose confidence you'd ever arrive."

"We were not fully prepared for the differences in this particular dark zone," said Rikka. "We have no scanning capability. We ran into problems."

"So I heard. I thought you would have tried to move more quietly. Perhaps your group would have tried to avoid the residents completely? Instead, the disturbance will have attracted every living thing for blocks around."

Rikka raised her palms. "That was the plan, but we were ambushed. We had to defend ourselves."

The woman frowned. "Ambushed? You mean a planned attack?"

Rikka nodded. "That is the obvious conclusion."

The woman felt a familiar rush of irritation. Her conversations with Rikka sometimes felt like hard work. "How could they have known which route you would take?"

Rikka shrugged, her face blank. "I am not certain."

The woman cursed. "It's important that we know. You might have been betrayed. Do you have any ideas?"

Small lines creased Rikka's forehead, and she attempted a smile. "I think it is highly likely our attackers had help to arrange the ambush. Our mission was no secret, so I cannot point to a traitor with absolute certainty. Although they must have considerable influence with at least one gang in this dark zone."

The woman nodded. "Thank you. That was a bit more helpful."

Rikka inclined her head. "A pleasure."

The woman smiled, then let it extend to a full grin. Rikka registered the change, and her face softened in response.

A moment passed before the woman sighed. "I think we both know who might have that influence."

"There does now seem little doubt," said Rikka.

The woman looked around the room. "Things are easier in secret. Stepping into full view now is dangerous."

Rikka moved forwards and the dim light flowed over her suit, turning her body from grey to green. She squinted past the woman and into the deep shadow at the corner of the room. "And how is your technology? Have you managed to repair it?"

The woman's face lit up. She turned and reached into the darkness. With both hands, she pulled out a large tripod and set it down gently between her and Rikka.

A long, thick cylinder sat in the centre of the three legs, its base gripped by three large rings. The machine lacked any visible interface, lights, or markings. It looked dumb, like a toy. But the absence of the usual reference points gave it an air of singular importance.

The woman straightened up, her face full of pride. "I've improved it. The parts you provided gave me plenty to work with. It seems even better than before."

Rikka stared at the device. The matt surface bore no sign of the chaos of dents, gouges, and deep scratches that it had picked up from the long fall down the side of the tower. "*Seems* to work better?"

"Well, I obviously can't test it, but I'm confident it's in good working order.," the woman reached out and gently tapped the top of the cylinder, "Just needs dismantling now, ready to be moved."

She squatted beside it, and removed the central column from its circular supports. Her hands worked with the rapid confidence of a skilled engineer.

Rikka watched her for a moment. "And the glowing visitor, the ghost? It still lives?"

The woman let out a short laugh. "Is that what you're all calling them, now? *Ghosts*?"

Rikka shrugged. "I am not responsible for naming them."

The woman shook her head slowly. "They might seem unreal, I suppose. But there's nothing ghostly about them. I've been tracking one for the last few days. This morning, I picked up the first sign of a second. It arrived around the same time as you did. I'm not one for coincidences. I'm guessing they're here for you and your companions."

"That would seem likely," said Rikka. "Are they moving together, or alone?"

The woman tugged at a fixing on her machine. "Alone, as far as I could tell, but I suspect they're communicating."

Rikka rubbed at her chin, "I managed to destroy one alone, so the others might prevail. But if two attack at the same time, the others cannot hope to win."

The woman's hands stopped moving. "You mean you killed one?"

Rikka nodded. "Yes."

The woman stood and peered at Rikka, as though seeing her for the first time. "How did you do that?"

Rikka frowned. "It was weak. I fought it and weakened it further. It got away from me, but I tracked it and shot it."

The woman took a deep breath. She dusted off her hands, then placed them firmly on her hips. "Plenty of people have shot at them, but nobody's managed to kill one. I need to know the specifics."

Rikka caught the note of irritation in the woman's voice and a brief smile flickered on her lips. "We have discussed this before."

The woman's hands left her hips and splayed flat in the air. "Yes, but it is ridiculous to keep it to yourself. We're desperate. You have knowledge we need."

Rikka shook her head slowly. She turned away from the light and walked over to the window, turning into a silhouette as she went. "Millan was injured. He can probably fight, but there are only two of them in full health. They lack the numbers to survive another large attack."

The woman took a step forward. "Don't change the subject. Are you going to help us, or not."

Rikka kept her eyes on the window. "You know I am not permitted to discuss either my technology or my beliefs with you."

"Not permitted," said the woman.

"Not permitted," said Rikka.

The woman sighed. "Are you really so passive? Can't you see the danger we're in and act for yourself?"

At that, Rikka's voice went up an octave. "Of course I see it. Of course I see that I can help you. But if I do—"

"Then we can stop all the death and ruin?" said the woman.

"No!" said Rikka. "If my people knew how to do that, I would not be here now. Even if I could share our knowledge, there is neither the time nor the opportunity to teach the skills correctly. It is too dangerous. I can help by fighting, but I cannot break my vows."

The woman flapped a hand dismissively. "Then go and use them." Rikka's mouth hung for a moment, then closed. The woman continued. "Just go. If you won't share your skills, at least go and put them to use. Fight. Kill as many of the glowing people as you can."

The woman turned her back, and resumed the work on her device.

"We have a plan to see through," said Rikka.

"It just changed," said the woman. "I can still do my part, but we're not leaving people to die. You need to go back and help them. Get them to the tower. I'll meet you there."

Rikka took a step away from the window and back towards the light. "Your chance of survival is lower if we are not together."

The blank face of the device stared back at the woman as she worked.

"I can make it alone," she said. "I want you away from here, using your knowledge. Making a difference. Removing the threat."

Rikka pressed her lips together, and another frown scribed deep furrows in her forehead. She pointed at the device, now disassembled on the floor in front of the woman. "That needs to be back on the tower as quickly as possible, or this zone and everyone in it will die. It makes no sense for you to risk that by trying to get there on your own."

"Well, you can reduce that risk if you get going now," said the woman. "The sooner you go, the sooner you can divert attention. Then I can get moving."

Rikka considered a response but let it drop. Instead, she sighed, then left the room in silence. Alone, the woman crouched, reached down and began packing the device into a harness.

Chapter Thirty-one

"There's nothing moving along those lines now," said Kasper.

He and Alis stood in the street, among the corpses of their attackers. Ahead, the towers stretched up into the purple gloom, the space between them filled by hundreds of dark, criss-crossed lines.

"Whatever it was, it's still in there somewhere," said Alis. "Let's go."

Kasper blurred his arms, took a deep breath, and stepped forward into the shadows.

Inside, nothing moved. He let his eyes adjust. Shafts of dim light found their way through the thick canopy above, but they did little to help him see clearly. He focused on the way ahead, and tried to forget that something could drop on him at any moment from the blackness above.

He walked level with Alis, roughly two metres apart, senses straining for any sign of life in the gloom. In places, the lines sat level with the top of his head and he had to duck as he passed them.

"Try not to touch the lines," said Alis.

She spoke so quietly he had to think twice about what she'd said. He nodded his head wildly, so she could see it clearly in the poor light. She waved back. Something else caught his eye.

He blinked and refocused. His stomach lurched. Something black and bulbous sat silently on her back. Two long, thin stalks moved carefully up past her shoulders and reached over her head.

His throat tightened and his words got stuck before he could shout them. Instead, he shot at it. The blaze of light blinded him, and he brought a hand up to his eyes.

"What the hell are you—" said Alis.

But Kasper didn't hear the rest. He felt a weight press on his back and the bristles pricking at his neck. He threw himself forward, shaking his head and flailing his arms to get free of it. But the weight stayed stuck to his back. Something bobbed twice against his ear.

Desperate, he half-jumped, half-fell backwards onto the ground, bringing his weight down hard to crush whatever was on his back. The second he hit the ground, he rolled away and got to his feet, training his weapon on the spot where he'd fallen. He made out what looked like one large ball and one small ball, stuck together and shifting erratically on long, thin bent legs.

He shouted to Alis. "Run! Get out! Get out!"

Then he squeezed his eyes shut, fired, and ran. The cold sweat of revulsion dripped down his spine. Lines brushed his face as he sprinted back the way they'd come. Something reached down and gripped his shoulder. It pulled at him, but his cyborg legs pulled him forward and tore him free. The shadows fell away, and he was out and running along the open street.

He slowed to a walk, relieved to see the now familiar remnants of their earlier fight lying around him. But Alis didn't appear.

He ran back towards the webbing. "Alis!"

Nothing. Then a light flashed in the darkness, illuminating the criss-crossed lines. A loud cracking sound split the silence. Alis stumbled out onto the street, breathing hard and holding a bundle of greasy fur in her hands.

She dumped it on the ground, and gave it a few kicks to spread it wide. Catching her breath, she placed one hand firmly on her hip and pointed down at the splayed corpse with the other. "More mutation. Arachnid."

Kasper stared at her kill. A fat, round abdomen, bristling with dark hairs, sat on a bundle of long, thin legs. Each one had streaks of oily skin visible beneath clumps of the same dark hair. His throat clogged at the sight. He took a step to the side and leaned in to get a better view of the head.

Lidless, black circles stared at him over yellow fangs. The black circles watched him. He imagined the creature twitching to life and lunging for his face.

He stepped away. "It's huge."

"And aggressive," said Alis. She tilted her head to give Kasper a clear view of her shoulder. Her suit had two deep indents, spaced roughly twenty centimetres apart. "It landed so softly that I didn't feel it. I wouldn't have known it was there until it bit into me."

She raised the spider's head with the toe of her boot. It came up limp, but the fangs stayed solid and sharp. "Good job you saw it. Mutated arachnid venom is not something I want coursing through my body."

Kasper looked from the dead spider to the web, then back again. "That's a lot of webbing for just a few spiders. There must be loads of them in there."

Alis nodded. "Yep. Millan had the right idea. We should find another way down."

Kasper pointed at his empty wrist and cursed. "The map didn't give us another option. We might have to go back miles to work our way down."

The lines nearest to them shifted.

Alis frowned. "Let's just move away from this webbing." She walked to the edge of the street and dropped to her knees to peer down at the wreckage. "We could get down here."

Kasper joined her. The rear of the car stuck up towards them like a finger. "You mean climb down?"

"Yep. Look, there are ledges in the wall, and cables running all the way to the bottom. It's not a bad climb. We can make it," she said.

Kasper's heart sank. He hated heights.

Alis slapped the back of his leg and grinned at him. "No time to hang around worrying, Kass. Let's go!"

She turned on her knees, inched to the edge, and lowered herself down. Kasper leaned over, watching for the handholds she chose. He tried to visualise the route he should take, and to avoid thinking about falling.

He heard Alis's voice float up to him. "Let's go!"

He took a deep breath and followed her lead. He dropped to his knees and turned away from the edge. Movement caught his eye at street level between the towers. The image of the dark pools of the spider's eyes chilled him between his shoulder blades. His heart thudded in his chest.

He inched out over the edge, leant on his elbows, and dangled his legs over the drop. His foot searched and found the first rest. He put his weight on it, moved his hands into position, and dropped below the edge of the street.

As the webbing inched out of sight, he was certain some shadows had moved, stretching out towards him from the foot of the towers.

Alis's voice reached him again. "OK, move your left foot below and to the right. Then your next two handholds are just above that, to your right."

Kasper's body shook, but his new limbs were indifferent to the danger. Clinging to the side of the sheer drop, he moved, grateful not to have to worry about muscle fatigue.

"Stop and look to your right," said Alis from somewhere below him. "See that cable? We're making for that."

He gripped his handholds and looked for the cable. A vast expanse of nothingness surrounded him on three sides, as far as he could see. His face stayed inches from the pitted surface of metal and blockwork, but he made out a cable, dangling thin and listless a few metres away.

Alis's voice reached him again. "We've run out of wall below us. That cable is our only choice. I'll give it a try when I reach it."

Kasper wondered whether he would have tried this without Alis. He decided he would have kept running instead, even though it would have taken longer to find a way down to the karyack. This way, there was more chance of finding the others alive.

Alis's willingness to make the climb had improved their chances of success. *She's the expert, I'm the newbie.* He took a deep breath and felt it shudder in his chest. This needed to be over soon.

Chapter Thirty-two

V ivek narrowed his eyes at the younger technician. Despite his youth, Glym had proven himself a competent analyst, and certainly not the worst on the team. Unfortunately, his obsession with his work brought with it a belief that everybody else would be just as thrilled as he was with highly detailed descriptions of his every thought.

Vivek found it very irritating that the young technician couldn't simply get straight to the point. "Tell me again, Glym. This time just go straight to describing the problem."

Glym's eyes stayed wide with excitement. He barely paused before diving into his third attempt at isolating the problem. "So, I was setting up the mortuary apps, to capture the autopsy data, so we could go over the emulation, just in case we get any casualties and need to be able to—"

A thin limb wafted in front of the young man's face. "Stop," said Vivek. "Just tell me what you have found."

The technician flushed red. "Sorry. Yes, OK. So it's probably better if I show you," he said.

He set off towards a nearby console, and Vivek followed. Above the display, Irvana's decapitated body hung silently in its clear tube. Her damaged suit still bore the story of her death.

"We have a virus," said Glym.

"And?" said Vivek.

"Well, it's brilliant. I only spotted it because I—"

Vivek cleared his throat. Glym looked down at the console. "Sorry. The virus was disguised as one of our own mortuary routines. I've quarantined it, but now I can't seem to destroy it."

Vivek's brow furrowed. "Show me."

Glym's hands danced over the display. Layers of coloured glyphs appeared in rows, running left to right along the screen. He flicked out a finger, and the rows broke up, sending them into wide, random patterns, before they eventually settled back into their original places.

"See? I've tried every security protocol we have, but nothing works."

Vivek leaned in to examine the glyphs on the screen. "And you're sure it's been quarantined?"

"Absolutely," said Glym.

"Well, you're wrong." Vivek pointed to an area on the console. "Here. See that trace suffix? It's a different partner to the tertiary suffix applied in the quarantine zone. This virus is not in quarantine. It has cloned itself and sent a suicide copy to quarantine instead. The true version is still active."

Glym peered at the console, then scratched at the back of his head. "OK. OK. Yes, I see. I really thought I'd got it," he said.

"Apology accepted," said Vivek. "We all meet things smarter than ourselves from time to time. How else would we learn?"

Vivek tried several times to erase the glyphs, but each time he got the same result as the technician. With a sigh, he moved over to the adjacent console. His hands moved swiftly across a myriad of colours, emblems, and glyphs. Glym watched in silence, like a child might wait for an adult.

Vivek paused, frowned briefly, then continued. After a while, he stopped and squinted at the screen. Straightening, he looked up at the headless corpse in front of him and cleared his throat. "This virus is more than just a malicious hack attempt. It is pre-empting our every move to erase it." He turned and looked at Glym. "So, what conclusion should we draw from that?"

The technician squinted at the floor, and thrust his hands into the pockets of his lab coat. After a moment, he raised his head, smiling brightly. "Whoever wrote it must know our protocols!"

Vivek smiled back at him. "Indeed. And what is the most likely explanation for that?"

"Someone from here told them," said Glym.

Vivek's face softened, and his mouth curled into a smile. He raised a paternal finger at the young technician. "Correct. And it is up to us to root them out. So, start by telling me what we already know about this virus."

"Well, we don't know anything at all," said Glym. "To reverse engineer it, we first need to quarantine it. It won't let us do that, so now we're stuck!"

Vivek stayed silent. Glym looked back down at his own feet and furrowed his brow. "OK, OK, what do I know about it already?"

His feet shuffled and his fingers flapped in his pockets, but he said nothing more.

Vivek sighed. "Always start simple. First, why would someone make a virus?"

This was an easy one. Glym quoted directly from his coursebook. "To alter or assume control of systems or entities."

"Correct," said Vivek. "And which of those is the purpose here?"

Glym shrugged. "We have no way of knowing for certain."

Vivek's face hardened. "We're not looking for certainty, we're looking for probability."

The technician tried again. "To alter our systems or entities?"

Vivek sighed. The coursebook still needed a few edits. "The virus knows it has been discovered, but it has still not harmed our systems. The fact that no damage has yet been caused leads us to the probability that our assailant's motive is to use our systems for its own purpose."

The technician shuffled his feet and groaned inwardly at the basic lesson in analytical thinking he should by now have mastered.

Eager to redress the balance, he jumped in. "So, the purpose of the virus is most likely to assume control of our systems."

"Yes. Given the duration of the infection, we should assume that such control has already been established," said Vivek.

Glym pointed at the console. "But we can still control all our systems."

The older technician smiled and shook his head. "The virus would be poorly devised if it made its work obvious. How did the breach occur? What has happened recently that might have allowed it to infect our systems?"

Beside Glym was a small, flat screen on the raised area of a desk. He reached over and flicked it a few times with his finger. "Logs show success in all diagnostics. We're not due an upgrade on the file-stack until late tomorrow. All processors are running at normal load, so—" he stopped and nodded towards Irvana's casket, "she's the only recent event around here."

For a moment, the two scientists looked at Irvana's suspended remains in silence. The younger man felt an uneasiness creep into his thoughts. "You think she might be the problem, don't you?"

Vivek turned and raised a paternal finger once more. "There are no problems remaining. Only several potential solutions. We have deduced that the designer was likely to be one of us. We have also accepted that their virus is highly sophisticated. If it were not for her death, one of the most likely culprits would indeed be the person hanging in this casket."

Glym's jaw dropped and his eyes widened so fast they were in danger of splitting their sockets. "You think she infected us? But why? That can't be possible. If she put it here when she was still alive, she had to know in advance that she would die, be hung here in this casket, and stored at this terminal. We didn't know those variables ourselves, so the odds against her getting them right are, well, really high!"

"Agreed," said Vivek, "which leads us to the impossible conclusion that, for her to be our assailant, she had to place the virus here after her death. Or, put another way, the virus arrived with her body."

The young technician struggled to keep up. "You mean the corpse carried the virus? Like on the body? But how does a dead body load a virus into a computer system?"

Vivek didn't answer. He turned and walked into his office. He returned a moment later with something in his hand. "Open the casket."

Glym's face creased in disbelief. He shook his head. "We're not allowed to do that."

Vivek waved a limb dismissively. "My authority. Open it."

Glym gave an exaggerated 'if-you-say-so' shrug, then ran his hands over a panel beneath Irvana's corpse. A low hum started, joined a few seconds later by a brief hiss as the base of the transparent tube descended to the ground. Irvana's gruesome remains hung exposed and manifest before them.

Vivek pointed at the body. A burst of light leapt from his hand and struck the damaged suit, sending a hail of sparks leaping into the air.

Glym jumped backwards and threw his hands up to shield his face. "What are you doing?!"

Vivek sent another burst from the object in his hand. It smashed into the body.

Glym ducked to avoid the shower of sparks. "What is that thing?"

Vivek let another blast hit the suit, then lowered his hand. Sparks fizzed, crackled, and fell from the corpse, bouncing on the ground like excited children. Glym stared at Irvana's smouldering suit. He wondered when the poor woman's suffering would end.

"Now then," said Vivek.

He leaned towards the console and jabbed a pattern into the screen with his fingers. The last of the smouldering threads fell dark and Glym noticed something unusual.

He looked away, rubbed his eyes, then looked again at the body. It flickered like a hologram. It widened for a moment, then returned to its original shape.

"What was that? Did you see that?" said Glym.

Vivek's fingers continued their work. The corpse shimmered, and the shoulders widened. Each of Irvana's legs and arms extended and thickened. Her feet and fingers stretched, growing dark nails like curved talons.

The corpse hung still. Glym took a few steps backwards. Instead of staring at Irvana's blackened, headless remains, he stared at the corpse of some type of monster.

Vivek rose triumphantly from the console and looked up at the beast. "Ha!"

He turned and smiled at Glym. The younger man fought back the nausea rising in his throat. The blasts and the monster were too much for him.

"Very clever, indeed!" said Vivek. "An encryption transmitting from somewhere within the body. It was preventing us from quarantining its partner, the virus."

Glym rubbed his face and let his hands drop by his sides. "Did you really have to cook a dead body to discover that?"

Vivek's soft smile stayed in place. He held up a small, cone-shaped object. "Simple electro-magnetic pulse. It disrupted the encryption signal long enough for me to spot it."

Glym frowned and gave a slow shake of his head. "But how were you certain that shooting her was the answer?"

Vivek's face darkened. "What did I say about certainty?"

Glym paused. "We're not looking for certainty, we're looking for probability."

Vivek's face relaxed. "Indeed. I did not know my idea would work. It was simply the most probable explanation available at the time. Nothing else has come near our systems since we last checked. The body, therefore, had to hold some part of the answer."

Glym still didn't quite understand. He doubted he would ever really understand anything at all.

Seeing his confusion, Vivek paused and tried again. "Let me put it another way. If the facts don't add up, the facts must be wrong. It's then a simple matter of assuming everything—including a corpse—is not what it seems."

Glym considered that for a moment but then slowly shook his head. "So our Search & Recovery droids pulled this—" he waved a hand at the headless monster standing beside them, "creature, out of the dark zone. It cloaked itself with a hologram and activated the virus. But the virus was here already. So how did it get in?"

Vivek's arm came down with a slap on the technician's shoulder. "Indeed! And what is the answer?"

This time, the technician didn't need a moment to think. There was only one other event related to Irvana's mission. "Her final transmission." He smiled at Vivek like a fellow conspirator. "We couldn't find that message because it wasn't a message at all. It was the virus!"

Vivek's face lit up, and he let out a soft laugh. "Outstanding!"

But another thought occurred to Glym. "How was it that one transmission worked where the others failed?" he said, "She was in the same place, with the same equipment, every time she tried to send it. So what changed to let that last one through?"

Vivek's smile turned to a look of pride. "Outstanding again. What's your conclusion?"

"The field in the dark zone is not consistent across its mass," said Glym. "A transmission might make it out if the field thinned at the right moment."

"Not likely," said Vivek. "It would need a hole in the field. But it does seem likely that Irvana planned this subterfuge."

The technician looked up at the monster hanging beneath the glass tube. "So, what is that thing?"

"That question is not the next question to ask," said Vivek.

Glym thought for a second, then his face lit up. "If the corpse isn't Irvana, where is she?"

Vivek looked at the monster's remains. "Where is she indeed," he said.

Chapter Thirty-three

"Who's that guy? He doesn't look right, does he? Huh?" said Jobe.

The figure on the road ahead paused. It must have seen them, perhaps even sized them up, but decided to move on.

Roddi stared up the street. "Yeah, he's not from round here. That's a skinsuit he's wearing. Anyone with that kind of money is long gone."

Jobe skipped with excitement. "So, what's he doing here? What do you think? Army? No gun. He's on his own, right? Army wouldn't be on his own, would he?"

Roddi kept his eyes ahead. "That was a lot of gunfire. Maybe all his friends got killed."

Jobe cackled. "Maybe. So how'd the army get back in here? The Doom's too strong. Nobody gets in now. Even the army."

Jobe didn't see Roddi's backhand swipe at him. Mercifully, it was his normal-sized arm. The blow thudded into Jobe's shoulder, shocking him more than hurting him. "Ow! Why'd you do that? I'm asking about the man, that's all. What's the prob—"

"Be quiet!" said Roddi. "There might be more of them around. Worse, if the army lost the fight, it'll be the bandits."

Jobe scowled and rubbed at his shoulder. "Sure, ok. I'll try. See if I can do it."

He fleetingly wondered why Roddi kept telling him to shut up all the time. Hadn't Roddi worked out by now that there was a lot of important stuff to talk about, and that it was getting difficult for him to stop talking, even if he wanted to?

Roddi raised his arm again. This time Jobe watched it carefully. But instead of swiping at him, Roddi pointed up the street. "That's Laine."

Jobe followed his finger and squinted at the man. He had stopped on the corner, and now stood in conversation with someone who did indeed look a lot like Laine. "What's he doing? Is Laine jacking him? He's getting jacked! Right?"

But Roddi slowly shook his head. "Doesn't look that way. They're just talking."

As they watched, the man moved round the corner and out of view. Laine followed him. Roddi looked at the large wrecked vehicle on the side of the road. "Looks like he was hanging around that crash."

He headed towards the fallen karyack, while Jobe scampered to stay alongside him. As they drew closer, the hull of the karyack seemed to shine, reflecting the fading light of The Doom, and cutting a bright contrast to the shadows—and to the dark, dead vehicle that pinned it to the ground.

The front of the karyack's hull sat firmly in the dirt, dented and flattened on impact with the ground. It looked like a huge tooth, tearing up through the ground to pierce the front of the vehicle above.

"There's a gap at the bottom," said Roddi, "Go inside and look around."

Jobe looked at the karyack. He had seen nothing like it. Not even before The Doom came. It looked solid, like it had something inside that shouldn't be let out. Whatever it was, it might still be in there. It was a cage. A cage was for something dangerous. An alien beast from far away. He would not go inside. No way. Not him. Something heavy hit his shoulder. He yelped.

"Get IN there!" said Roddi.

Jobe rubbed his shoulder. Roddi was doing that too often. "I don't know, Rod. Could be something inside, right? Someone trapped. I'm going in but then it's still in there, you know?"

Roddi waved his massive arm from Jobe to the karyack and back again. "Does it look like an animal crate? No. It looks like an expensive piece of high-tech kit. Hurry up and get inside."

Jobe looked at the karyack, then back at Roddi. Slowly, he dropped to his knees and crawled through the dirt towards the gap in the hull. He poked his head inside. Bags of equipment spewed their contents around the gap. He reached to move one, and instead felt a tuft of hair.

He pulled his hand back, waiting for something to lunge for him, but nothing moved. He leaned in for a closer look. Lying on the bag like a sack of rags was a small girl. She had her head pushed towards one corner. Staccato sobs spluttered out of her, shaking her shoulders and knocking them weakly against the metal wall. She tried in vain to crawl further into the already tight space. She looked terrified.

Jobe called out to Roddi. "It's a girl, Rod! A girl. She's small, too. Where's she come from? She looks scared. We should help her out, right?"

Roddi didn't answer. Jobe pulled the bag towards him and shuffled backwards into the street. The girl, still clinging to the bag, was dragged closer to the gap in the hull. The moment Jobe's body appeared in the street, Roddi reached past him and pulled the girl out with his huge, gnarled hand.

Lifting her up to his face, he tried to see beneath her hair. But before he could get close, Prue burst into a ragged scream that turned into a cough and finished in more sobbing and shuddering.

Jobe took a deep breath. "Come on, Rod, she's scared." He tried to look into Prue's face. "It's OK, little girl, we're going to find your Momma. Then you'll be OK, right? It'll be OK. We'll get you sorted, OK?"

Roddi pulled at the fabric on her arm. "Look at her clothes."

Jobe noticed them for the first time. "Oh yeah! What's that made of? Looks like plastene, or some metal stuff, maybe? Sure doesn't look like cloth. Maybe it's just coloured funny, or—"

Roddi shook his head. "It's not from here. She's not from here, either. Like that other guy."

Prue squirmed as she hung suspended at the end of Roddi's arm. She flapped her arms, kicked her legs, and cried, like a bird held up by its beak. Roddi watched her, his face blank.

Jobe felt the concern growing in his chest. "Can't take her back home then, can we? Don't know where she lives. What do we do? Huh?"

"She's not from around here, so that means she's worth something," said Roddi.

Jobe looked up at his friend. Roddi's pitted, mutating arm no longer seemed to belong to him. It looked so different from the rest of his body that he could just have been standing beside it, like it was a part of the building, not a part of him.

Jobe remembered when the pair of them had been younger, their fresh, thin bodies developing normally as they spent their evenings sitting around Roddi's house, making fun of people they'd seen that day, then crying with laughter at their own jokes.

Now, standing in a gloomy street, gripping an exhausted, terrified little girl in his alien fist, his friend looked like someone else entirely.

The concern weighed heavier in his chest. "What do you mean, Rod? *Worth something?*"

Roddi lowered Prue to the ground, but kept a firm hold of her shoulder. Too worn out to stay on her feet, she drooped into a sagging mess beneath his hand.

"We can sell her on," said Roddi.

Jobe's mouth stayed open for a moment, then all his words came at once. "You can't sell a girl. Selling's bad. I mean, she's only small. What would you get for her? I just mean, is it worth the law, you know, the police, the people, the army, whoever? Why would you sell her? She's not ours, and anyway you can't sell a girl. It's, it's just wrong, isn't it? I mean it's—really? Sell her?"

Roddi nodded. "Sure, you can't sell a person. But it's not a person. It's an alien. It's an 'it', right? You start thinking of it like a person, and you're lost."

Prue looked as though she might have passed out.

Jobe skipped faster from one foot to another. "You're not serious, Rod? Are you, huh? Where you going to take her though? Really?"

Roddi pulled Prue back up off the floor, and draped her over his shoulder. "There's people looking for girls on the other side of Manson's blockhouse. They'd take this alien for a good price. Its clothes alone are worth a lot, I reckon."

Prue squealed and mumbled, then tried another scream but choked before it got it past her lips. Her shoulders heaved, and she made a low, keening sound before her head fell onto the rough surface of Roddi's shoulder.

Jobe's thoughts came so fast he was almost turning full circles on the spot. "Yeah, but, really? They're animals over there! Selling her? Come on. You, I mean, we can't do that, can we? Right? We should take her to people, if she's from alien, I mean alien person."

Roddi shrugged. "Things aren't like that anymore. We can do what we want now."

Jobe wished he was more like other guys. Other guys wouldn't think too hard about it. They'd just follow the bigger guy, and see where he took the girl. It wasn't wise to question the bigger guy, unless you wanted to spend your life being the last for everything, and the butt of everyone's jokes. Or, worse, get your face smashed in one day for no reason at all.

Roddi started walking swiftly away. Jobe hopped and fidgeted on the spot, watching the girl's hair shifting on his friend's shoulder as he walked further up the street. Before he knew what he was doing, he ran after Roddi and jumped in front of him, hopping and shuffling in his path. Other guys would have known to move out of the way.

Roddi frowned at him. "Shift it. Let's go."

Jobe clamped his mouth shut and stayed fidgeting on the spot.

Roddi stared at him for a moment then his face lightened. "Ok, ok. So you don't like the idea of selling the alien. Sure. I'm doing it anyway, so move, or I'll move you."

But Jobe just hopped faster, like a dancer moving frantically to the finale of his performance. "You can't do it, Rod, she's scared, they'll chew her up over there. We—"

Roddi shoved Jobe aside with two fingers of his huge hand. Jobe flew backwards, cracked his head on the wall, and fell to the ground. He came to rest in a sprawled heap, lying silently in the dirt.

Roddi stepped over him. "I'm doing it."

Chapter
Thirty-four

A lis squeezed her shoulders through the karyack's hull and rummaged through the equipment. Kasper's eyes traced the seam of her suit running down the sides of her legs. He found himself thinking about her skin beneath the fabric.

She shuffled backwards until her shoulders, then her head reappeared. She sat up on her haunches and pulled on a strap with both hands. Whatever was on the other end of the strap bumped against the inside of the karyack and came to a halt.

"There's no one in there," she said. "Give me a hand with this."

They heaved a stubborn pile of clanking equipment out of the karyack and onto the street. Alis stood up and brushed the dust from her suit. "The diviner's not here, either."

She looked up above the karyack, past the fallen vehicle pinning it to the ground, and up to the sharp line of the road's edge. "I don't think it fell out on the road. We'd have seen it. So, somebody must have taken it."

But Kasper wasn't thinking about the diviner. "Where is everyone? Where's Prue?"

Alis looked around. "There's no sign of a fight. Millan and Prue are probably on their way back up to the towers to meet us. But Rikka? " she shrugged. "She could be doing anything."

Kasper looked up and down the street. "I can't see them. The route back up to the top goes right under the webbing. We'd better catch up with Millan before he tries to take Prue through it."

Alis shook her head. She put a hand on each of Kasper's shoulders and looked him in the face. "I know you're worried about Prue, Kass, but she'll be fine with Millan, and we have to find the diviner. Without it, we can't be sure of saving this city. We need to focus on that, OK?"

Kasper looked straight into Alis's eyes. Logically, what she said made sense. Emotionally, he didn't want to go anywhere without her. His thoughts must have played across his face, because Alis grinned, dropped her hands, and moved the pile of kit around with her boot.

The sight of the blankets and straps laid out on the ground reminded Kasper of the dead spider sprawled on the street beside the towers. He couldn't stop himself from stealing a glance upwards to where they'd started their descent to the karyack. No furry, long-legged black bodies came towards them.

Looking back at the kit, he sighed loudly, "So who do you think took the diviner?"

The question was barely out of his mouth before Alis answered. "Rikka. Without a doubt."

The speed of her reply surprised him. "Why her? They both had a chance to take it. Why not Millan?"

"Sure," said Alis, "Millan got shot and knocked over a cliff, then chose to steal the diviner. I don't think so. He's always had access to it. He could have taken it any time he wanted. Why choose to wait until now, when he's in the middle of the worst dark zone we've seen, with no scanning equipment and no droid support. He's an arsehole, Kass, not an idiot." She dropped to her knees and began sorting through the equipment. "Rikka is not to be trusted. She never seems to give us the full story, and the way she kills people is frightening. Plus, she just walked away and left us in the middle of a fight. Doesn't that seem suspicious to you? At best, she didn't care whether we lived or died, at worst she deliberately left so we'd be killed."

Kasper squinted at her, "What makes you so sure?"

She looked up, held his gaze for a moment, then sighed, "She only came here to learn how to save her people, right? You've seen the way she behaves. Stone cold. But it's not a surprise. There's no reason for her to care what happens to us, but every reason to steal our tech to help her people back home."

"I still don't see it," said Kasper. "Yes, she's a bit distant, but she's an alien, so who knows when she's being normal? She could be with the other two, helping to find a way back up to us, right now."

Alis snorted. "Unlikely."

"You still seem pretty sure," said Kasper.

She rolled her eyes. "I am. But it's a waste of time trying to chase her now. We need to find the others and get to the tower."

Kasper dropped it to avoid an argument. It bothered him that Alis was so certain about Rikka. The diviner could just have been thrown clear of the karyack when it hit the ground. He stowed the thought away for later. Kasper briefly considered how else they would find the centre of the cloud without the diviner. The mission was to strike the centre of the infection with the convertor. Only the diviner could pinpoint the right spot. Without it, they would just be guessing. But why would Rikka want them to fail?

Alis stopped rifling through the pile, and picked up a metal tube roughly the size of Kasper's thigh. She turned it over in her hands, then stopped, brought it closer to her face, and traced her finger over a line down the side. She cursed, and threw it back to the karyack. Kasper watched it bounce off the karyack's hull with a loud clang.

The sound in the quiet street made him nervous. "What?"

She waved her hand at the cylinder. "Converter's smashed."

Kasper only needed a moment to process that. No diviner meant they'd have to guess to find their target. That was difficult, but not impossible. No convertor meant that even if they guessed correctly, they couldn't do anything about it.

In that instant, he realised their mission was over. "That's it then. We've failed. Everybody in the city dies."

Alis returned to sorting the pile in front of her. "Maybe. But we can still try not to die with them. Give me a hand here. It's getting dark. We can't hang around."

Together, they graded the equipment by importance and what they could carry. When they finished, they pocketed food, a repair kit, a few power packs, and as much spare ammunition as they could shove into every space in their suits.

They bundled up the rejected kit, and pushed it back inside the karyack. All their monitoring tech was useless in the dark zone, and now nothing more than dead weight, so they tossed all of it as far as it would go inside the hull.

Neither of them said it, but Kasper felt unnerved to be discarding sensors and scopes just as the light was fading around them. If only we had droid support, he thought.

He straightened and peered at the skyline, then jerked a thumb towards his right. "The map said the tower's in that direction, but the route back up to the road goes the other way. Do you really think Millan's going to go backwards? He's more likely to want to push on and expect us to catch up."

Alis squinted past him and nodded up the street. "I don't know for sure. But maybe that little guy saw something."

Kasper followed her gaze to a small figure sitting further up on their side of the street. Alis set off towards him. The figure scrambled to get away from her, but tripped over his feet and fell to his knees. She broke into a sprint, and caught him by the scruff of the neck.

Kasper heard Alis's voice, then a high pitched, scratchy sounding response from the little man. As he approached them, he heard Alis talking. Then she hauled the squirming figure to his feet.

The little man hopped and complained, but Alis had a firm grip on his collar and shook him from side to side like a doll.

He threw his hands up for her to stop. "Ok, ok, I will, ok. You don't have to hold me like that. You can let go, you know, let go? I'm not going to run."

Alis stopped, span him round, and leaned in towards his face. "You do exactly as I tell you, or I will tear off your scrawny little arms and beat your head in with the wet ends."

Jobe took a step back. "Ok, I get it, I get it."

Alis straightened and shot Kasper a wide grin. "This is Jobe. He saw Millan head off in that direction with someone. He is going to tell us where to find Millan. Aren't you, Jobe?"

The little man seemed unable to stand still. He shifted from foot to foot. Kasper wondered what was wrong with him. He looked nervous. People who fidgeted and looked nervous usually had something to hide.

"Yes, yes, well, I think I will. I mean, I think I know where. He's with Laine, you know? They walked off, talking. So Laine must know, you know? Right? All we need is—"

"Ok, you can shut up now," said Alis.

Kasper looked Jobe up and down. "He looks sick. You trust him?"

Alis looked thoughtful. "He described Millan instantly, so knows who he is. Plus, he thinks Millan already knew this Laine person."

"How would Millan know people here?" said Kasper.

Alis smiled, but her eyes stayed cold. Kasper fought the urge to point out that Rikka might not be the villain after all.

She seemed to read his thoughts. "Yes, Kass. It seems Millan knows some people round here that we don't. But we still need to be watching out for Rikka."

Kasper frowned and glared at Jobe. "Did you see a little girl with him?"

Jobe shook his head and pointed back at the karyack. "Not with him, no. She was in there. Roddi took her out and hit me with his big arm. He took her away."

Kasper reached down and gripped the front of Jobe's shirt, pulling it tight under his chin and forcing Jobe onto his tiptoes. "Who's Roddi? Where did he take her?"

Jobe spluttered and coughed in Kasper's grip. "He's my friend. Well, he was, but now he's, well, not. He took her to Madam, south central, she shifts children, you know? Gets them working for people. They get a bed and food. Lots of them. I tried to stop him and he hit me."

Kasper felt the cold rush of horror flood his arms and chest. He tightened his grip on Jobe's throat. "Your friend took her to a sweathouse? A frightened little girl?"

Jobe nodded rapidly again. "Yes, yes, he's gone strange. It's The Doom. He wouldn't listen."

Kasper looked across at Alis, the panic rising in his chest. "Someone's taken her."

Alis nodded. "We'll find her, Kass. Our man Jobe will know where to look, won't you Jobe?"

Jobe repeated his familiar, frantic nodding. "Yep, yes sure. Quite far away, on the other side of where your friend is, so maybe get him first, right? We need more people. The centre's dangerous. Much worse than round here, you know?" he said.

Kasper loosened his grip. "OK. But we have to be quick. Which way do we go? And I mean the shortest route."

With something to focus on, Jobe seemed to calm down. He waved his arm in the direction he'd seen Millan and Laine disappear. "That way. Laine's place is up there, in one of those streets."

"Alright," said Alis. "That's the way we go. You stay close now, little man."

Chapter Thirty-five

"So she could be alive?" said Doron.

Vivek's hand wafted towards the corpse hanging in the tube beside them. The beast's thick, clawed hands looked far too large for the rest of its body. "This body is not proof that she lives. All I can say is that someone wanted us to believe this was her body."

Doron huffed impatiently at his Chief Technician. "Yes, I understand that much, thank you, Vivek. What I need is your theory, not your facts."

Vivek didn't appear to notice either the impatience or the displeasure in his leader's voice. "Someone who knows our protocols designed this subterfuge. Irvana would qualify as that someone."

Doron let the answer hang for a moment then spread his hands. "The encryption key arrived through a gap in the wall of the dark zone. You say it came from her last known location. I'd say all that's left is to understand her motive."

Vivek looked blank.

Doron frowned. "You don't agree?"

Vivek's head bobbed gently. "As a rule, I work mostly with probabilities and avoid conclusions until I have the evidence to substantiate them."

Doron sighed and let his hands drop. Talking to Vivek felt like swimming against the current in the dark. But he respected Vivek's work, so he'd long ago decided not to criticise his methods.

He stared at the corpse while he considered his next question. "If Irvana were to be killed anywhere, it would be on Trage, overwhelmed by this," he waved a hand at the corpse, "new breed of hostiles. But, this attempt to cover her tracks suggests she reached the tower roof as planned. So, can you please work on a hypothesis that she is alive and out there somewhere in the dark zone?"

Vivek nodded slowly. "Very well. Then our first question is indeed her motive."

Doron shrugged. "I can't help you with that. She was always perfectly transparent in her work. What was the last project she worked on?"

"Research. I believe it was related to the structure of the cloud, and an attempt to improve the impact of her instrument. Her convertor."

"What did she find?" said Doron.

Vivek's shoulders gently rose and fell. "She did not share her results."

Doron sighed again. "Presumably she kept records of her work?"

Vivek bobbed his head. "Yes, of course."

He walked over to his office, and Doron followed. They sat at Vivek's large desk, and the Chief Technician began to interrogate his console.

Doron watched him work, marvelling at how someone with such intelligence could at times be so difficult in conversation.

The empty air in front of the console burst into life. Text and images twisted and flashed in front of them. As each one took shape, Vivek replaced it with another, then another, and another; each page of Irvana's work coming to life, then disappearing like brief, controlled explosions.

Vivek stopped. A large, complex design hung above the desk, bristling with angular lines, and ending in neat boxes filled with scrawled, handwritten text.

Doron leaned forward. "This is a diagram of something."

Vivek paused. "It's a cloud particle. The text is annotation added by Irvana." A soft frown wrinkled the skin above his eyes. "Except the annotation refers to biochemistry, not electromagnetism."

Doron arched his eyebrows. "Why biochemistry?"

Vivek lifted his shoulders in what, for him, constituted another shrug. "The text hypothesises that the energy within the cloud originates from chemical reactions."

Doron leaned back. It was his turn to frown, "That is no great breakthrough. The cloud is a gas, so it's obviously come from a chemical reaction. Wasn't she supposed to be focused on working out who created it, not how?"

Vivek looked up at him, "She was studying how energy is transferred inside the cloud. We had considered this the most likely method of energy transfer, but it now appears Irvana thought a chemical reaction was more likely. Much like you and I generate electricity at the cellular level."

Doron flattened both his palms on top of the console, "Cellular level? You mean she thought the cloud might be a living thing? With cells?"

Vivek smiled faintly, "You could put it that way. That would match my conclusion regarding the radiation in the dark zone on Trage, would it not? I could claim she was following my lead, except that she was dead when I presented that theory."

"Presumed dead," said Doron. "So she beat you to the conclusion that the cloud is alive. She also has an explanation for how it can generate its own energy. An impressive feat of intellect. If she was here, I'd honour her work—but she's not, because it seems she faked her own death, and is now up to who knows what."

The image winked out. Another series of bright lines, scrawled text, images, and charts exploded between them. The display stopped on a page holding only a few typed sentences. It hung in front of them like a spectre, its glow lighting the space above the desk.

"This is the most recent document filed in her records. It's the mission prep checklist," said Vivek.

They both leaned in to read it. Doron squinted at the text. "What does *Droids are WFS* mean?"

Vivek leaned back. "It stands for Withheld From Service. It means no droid support was provided on the mission."

Doron nodded slowly. "I see. Well, that much we already know."

"We do," said Vivek, "but there's something else. Look here."

His long fingers danced above the console, and most of the text dropped away to leave just a corner of the document visible. Vivek zoomed in and the fragment rushed up towards them. "There. Do you see those indentations?"

Doron leaned in further, squinted for a moment, frowned, then sat back. "No."

Vivek fiddled again. More of the fragment dropped away. He zoomed in on the remaining sliver.

Doron's face lit up. "Ah, yes, I see them now. What about them?""They are remnants of something removed from the document," said Vivek.

He rose and walked to a cluttered shelf on the other side of the office. His hand settled on something, and he plucked it free of the other objects. Returning to his seat, he clipped a small, round object to the side of the console, then turned his attention to the fragment suspended in front of him.

His hands danced once more over the console and the fragment swelled, as though inflated. The marks sharpened, then blurred, several times. Eventually they took the shape of scrawled writing.

Doron squinted again, then his eyes widened. "Liar. It says liar!"

The word hovered over the desk like a proclamation. Doron sensed progress. His eyes flashed with the chase of the truth. "So, who did she think was a liar? Can we tell?"

"It seems likely to be the author of this document," said Vivek.

Doron opened both his hands toward the fragment. "Right. So, who wrote it?"

Vivek looked down at the console, then back at Doron, his face blank. "The signature is missing."

Doron sighed. His fingers tapped rhythmically on the desk for a few moments, then stopped. "Am I correct that a WFS notice comes from either the service bay or the mission director?"

"Yes," said Vivek.

Doron raised his eyebrows. "And for this mission?"

Vivek looked down at his console. "Mission director."

Doron's face hardened. He inhaled loudly through his nose. The investigation into Irvana's death meant he knew every detail of her last mission. He knew the names of everyone involved, and the role they each played. That included the name of the mission director.

He suddenly thought of Alis. She clearly lacked trust in the people around her. Now it seemed Irvana felt the same way.

He looked down at his robe and smoothed it, without noticing whether it had been wrinkled or flat. "I need to be certain. I'd like you to verify the service logs for all our droids against the timing of this mission schedule. Do it personally. Involve nobody else, and bring your findings directly to me."

Vivek didn't speak.

Doron lowered his voice. "This stays between you and me, Vivek. You are to mention nothing of this to anyone else. Understood?"

The old technician let a thin hand float over the bright face of his console. The ghostly page winked out of view, taking its angry statement with it. "Understood."

Doron nodded slowly, as if confirming his own thoughts. "So, Irvana opened a gap in the dark zone's skin and send the encryption back here, correct?"

Vivek shook his head. "Not entirely. It takes energy to move energy. She would need a significant power source to create even a small gap in the wall of the dark zone. Even then, it would not remain open for long."

Doron looked thoughtful. "She had plenty of power with her, though. Scanners, scopes, data-logging—lots of her equipment was powered."

Vivek's head continued to bob from side to side. "She would need something that could send a substantial amount of energy over distance. We have developed nothing yet to achieve that."

"She could have found something down there to do it?" said Doron.

Vivek paused. "Possible, but it would be alien to Trage."

Doron leaned back and tilted his head. He stared hard at the ceiling, as if trying to study the sky beyond it. He let his words out slowly. "Alien to Trage." He brought his hand up to his brow and let it run down the side of his face. "If Irvana wasn't safe from this liar in that dark zone, then none of them are."

"The zone edge has stabilised. It is solid," said Vivek. "We have no method to reach them."

Doron smiled. "Alien to Trage, you said. Well, we have an alien working with us on this mission. She's an energy expert. In fact, she convinced me she should be a member of the team. Quite a coincidence., in fact." He cocked his head to one side. "Do we believe in coincidences, Vivek?"

Vivek's head bobbed. "We do not."

Doron stood and turned to leave. "You're right. We have no choice but to wait for an outcome. Make sure we're ready for them when they make the jump back here, Vivek."

Chapter Thirty-six

The woman watched Roddi tramping up the gloomy street ahead. She could see Prue clinging onto his massive arm, curled up tight in the crook of his elbow and hiding her face in her hair. His arm rose and fell as he walked. Prue moved with it, like a limpet on a ship's hull.

The woman stepped up her pace and moved closer. Roddi's voice reached her ears.

"At least you're not snivelling," he was saying to Prue. "I couldn't stand it if you were snivelling."

Prue let out a whimper from beneath her mound of scruffy hair.

"There's nothing to worry about, anyway," he said. "They'll make sure you're fed and protected. There'll be others there your age. It'll be better than scavenging around out here."

The woman drew within ten metres of Roddi's back. He wouldn't stand a chance of hearing her until she was almost on top of him.

Ahead, a low light shone in a single, grubby window at street level. Roddi reached it and stopped. The woman darted into the shadows and pressed herself against the nearest wall. He tapped three times on the glass.

After a few moments, the door opened and an elderly woman peered out. Roddi nodded to her. "Hello, Gritten."

From the shadows, the woman watched Gritten looked him up and down. "What is it, Roddi?"

He pushed his arm towards her and let the light from the window splash across Prue's body. Gritten smiled. At least, the action might once have served as a smile, but her mouth didn't stop where a smile should. Instead, as the woman watched, the old woman's lips kept stretching and thinning, turning pale as the blood was forced out of them.

They split her face to her ears, revealing wet, grey-pink gums that glistened at the roots of her ragged teeth. "Very nice," said Gritten.

Roddi pulled his arm out of the light. "She's for selling into work, not for anything else."

"You sure?" said Gritten. "We pay more for *that*."

The words dripped out of her mouth like oil. But Roddi shook his head sharply. "I like my money to come from straight business. You going to let me in, or do I go elsewhere?"

Gritten cocked her head at him. "The money for that kind of" she smacked her lips, *"purpose*, is very good."

Roddi shook his head. Gritten sighed. "In which case, not interested."

She let her lips slide back along her jaws. They made a low, slurping sound, like a drain sucking in the last trickle of water. she said.

"Not interested?" said Roddi. "You're so rich you can pass this up, then?"

She spat on the ground. "We need food, not labour. This little thing would last us a whole week. You'd best get moving, before I decide to take her from you."

The door slammed shut. Still pressed into the shadows nearby, the woman heard Roddi curse.

He brought his arm up to his face and stared into Prue's hair. "We're going to find somewhere else for you, instead."

Prue thrashed and pushed against him, crying and shuddering in a mess of desperation to get free.

But he pinned her against his chest. "Enough! Calm down, you hear?" It'll be over soon, just calm the hell down."

But Prue couldn't calm down. She screamed and shouted, setting the street alive with the noise.

He shook her and raised his voice. "Shut up, now! Just shut up!" he said.

Satisfied that there was no threat from the closed door, the woman stepped out of the shadows. "Children can be a handful."

He spun around. Prue heard the woman's voice and fell still, as if worried that any noise might make something terrible happen.

The woman took a step forward. "Why don't you let me take her? She must be a real headache for you."

Roddi shifted Prue to his weaker side, then flexed and stretched his thickly muscled arm. "Thanks, but I think I'll hang onto her."

The woman paused. "Well, she's a friend of mine. I think she'd rather come with me."

Roddi grinned. "Yeah? Well, forget it. She's going to be someone else's friend very soon."

She flicked her wrist. Roddi caught sight of a thin, dark line as it streaked through the air towards him. Too fast for him to dodge, the tip punctured the front of his shoulder, passed through it, and burst out the other side, taking a chunk of bloody flesh with it.

Before the pain hit him, the line swung under his armpit, then back over the top of his shoulder. It jerked tight, slicing neatly through muscle and bone.

He watched, open-mouthed, as the massive girth of his beautifully powerful arm dropped out of sight. Then he fell to his knees and howled in pain. He toppled onto his back, blood spitting from the stump at his shoulder.

The woman walked towards him, reached down, and scooped up the stricken girl. "Nobody's going to hurt you now."

Ignoring Roddi's screams, she looked once up and down the street and started walking. She shuffled Prue's body into position on her hip, and gripped her waist with one arm. "What's your name?"

Prue's chest heaved, but she didn't reply.

The woman tried again. "How about you tell me yours, and I'll tell you mine."

Prue hid her face in her hair.

The woman smiled. "It could be a while until we find your friends, so why don't I start? I'll tell you mine first. Just to get the ball rolling."

Prue nodded.

"My name is Irvana," said the woman. "What's yours?"

Chapter
Thirty-seven

K asper stared at every window and doorway he passed. The attack at the tower was still fresh in his mind, as was the touch of something furry bumping against his ear.

He and Alis took turns telling Jobe to be quiet as they walked. Their new companion skipped along beside them, jabbering incessantly.

Eventually, Alis gave up telling him to be quiet, and just slapped him on the back of the head each time he became tiresome.

"OW! Sorry, yes, I did it again, didn't I? Sorry, I'll try harder," said Jobe. "Oh wait, that's it there! Over there! You see that big hole under those windows, look!"

Ahead of them, the street ran for fifty metres or so, then turned a sharp left. At the apex of the bend, they could just make out a gaping black space yawning onto the street.

Jobe continued skipping about. "Car hit it months ago. No point fixing it. Everyone just left it. Right? It's Laine's place now. Him and his boys. Violent gang. You're going in to get answers, yeah?"

"Something like that," said Alis.

Kasper looked at the damaged building. Just as Jobe said, he could see a large hole in the wall of the ground floor. Beyond that, everything was dark.

Alis turned to look at him. "Millan has no working tech, just like us. He can't see us or sense us. Follow my lead. We don't know what he's doing in there."

Kasper nodded and was about to speak, but Jobe got there first.

"Could be lots in there, right? You know what you're doing, sure, but you've got to watch out for Laine. He's a crazy guy, you know?"

Alis raised her hand. Jobe flinched and slammed his mouth shut.

"If he's crazy, he makes mistakes," she said. "Let's go."

They reached the building and ducked through the gaping hole. Jobe led the way down the dim corridor beyond. He stayed quiet, except for a brief outburst, which stopped as soon as Alis landed a firm reminder on his shoulder.

The corridor turned a few corners, then ended with an orange glow spilling through a half-open door. Alis held Jobe back and motioned for Kasper to look. He stepped forward to the doorway and let his eyes adjust to the light.

On the other side of the threshold, the floor ended abruptly at the edge of a void. A single rail banister prevented anyone from walking straight off the edge. Craning his neck, Kasper could see that the banister ran straight off to the right for a short distance, then sloped downwards.

He turned away and whispered. "Short balcony. Right-hand staircase. No cover."

Alis nodded once and returned the whisper. "Crawling, then. Recon only."

Kasper sighed inwardly and dropped to his haunches. His scope would have been perfect for this. Instead, he now had to struggle with his own line of sight.

He gently pulled the door towards him, listening carefully for creaks or groans from the metal. It swung open, and the orange glow painted the corridor around him. He dipped his head and pushed out onto his elbows, moving each one in tandem with his knees.

The edge of the landing came up quickly, and he looked down into the abyss beyond. Scrap metal, assorted machinery, and battered technology sat in neat piles on the floor on the level below. Kasper recognised it at once as the looted stock of a gang of scavengers.

A few displays blinked weakly in the piles, but the rest of it looked like junk. It was still an impressive stash, presumably collected—or most likely stolen—by a well-organised gang.

Directly below him, he saw the source of the orange glow. A large brazier crackled and spat, flames licking the air several feet above its rim. Standing beside it, two figures talked, occasionally swatting sparks from their clothes.

Millan had his back to Kasper, but his suit gave him away. It hung in tatters on one shoulder, just above where the bullet had entered his body. A fresh medical dressing bulged through the torn fabric. Kasper recalled that the medkit in the karyack only had four dressings that large, one for each person on the mission. He knew all four were still in the medkit.

The man in conversation with Millan had a ragged pink scar across the full width of his face. Kasper wondered what had happened to him, and imagined the man sprinting face first into the edge of a shelf.

Millan was doing most of the talking. The scarred man spoke only a few words, and spent the rest of the time nodding. Nothing else moved in the warehouse. He decided he'd seen enough.

He slithered back across the threshold, pulled the door gently back into its frame, and spoke quietly and rapidly to Alis. "The entire room drops away into a lower floor. Lots of stuff down there. It would take a big gang to collect and protect that much stuff. Millan's in there talking to someone, a guy with a massive scar across his face."

Jobe sprang into an on-the-spot jig. "That's Laine! That's him. That's him!"

said Alis.

Alis raised her hand. "Be quiet."

Jobe immediately did his best to keep his mouth shut and his feet still.

"I couldn't see anyone else around," said Kasper. "There's a stairway running down the right-hand wall. We could head down it, but they'd see us coming before we reached the ground."

Alis shrugged. "Well, we need to get to him, somehow. We have to know what the hell he's up to."

Kasper sighed. "OK, but we can't just walk in there. He's doing something he shouldn't, so we don't know what he's going to do when he sees us."

Alis nodded. "Fine. So we need a plan." She turned to look at Jobe. "Time for you to be useful. You're going to go down there first."

Jobe froze. "You what? I'm what, why? I can't do any good down there!"

Alis slapped his shoulder and hissed. "Keep quiet! You raise your voice again, and I'll take your squeaky little head off! If they find us, you will be the first to die. You understand me?"

Jobe clamped his mouth shut and nodded furiously. She relaxed her hand. "Good. You're going to go down there and distract them so we can make our move. I don't care how you do it, or what you say, but we'll be watching. If you even think of selling us out—"

She held up her right hand in the glow from the door. Her hand bent to meet her forearm, then blurred into a sharp edge. The tip of her blade came to rest a fraction of an inch from Jobe's eyeball.

He began to shake. "OK, I'll do it. I'm going to do it." He turned and moved towards the door. "I'm doing it."

Kasper stood aside to let the little man pass. He watched him mouth a silent river of words as he crossed the threshold. He wondered what the two men would think when the little figure appeared on the stairs and began to chatter incessantly.

A few moments passed before someone shouted a challenge. Laughter quickly followed, then some loud talking that he couldn't make out. He and Alis crawled onto the landing and watched the scene below. The man with the scar across his face, who Kasper now knew was Laine, had Jobe by the scruff of the neck.

Jobe squirmed in his grip. "Oww."

Laine's gave him a shake. "You want me to believe he's not hiding somewhere here?"

Jobe held up his hands. "It's true, it's true. He hit me and ran."

Laine laughed. "What, so now you want to switch sides? Over a little tap from your mate? You shifty little bastard!"

Jobe shifted and squirmed in the bigger man's grip while Millan looked on in silence. Laine's laugh bounced back from the piles of junk stacked around him. "You know what? I don't think you're of any use to us. What are you good at? You're too weak to lift anything and you're too bloody noisy to have around while we're taking stuff. Besides, you can't be trusted, can you?"

He pulled Jobe closer to the brazier. The fire crackled and sighed, the heat increasing on Jobe's exposed cheeks. Jobe moaned loudly, knowing he had no chance of pulling away. One of his legs shook. He bit his lip and fought back the urge to sob.

Millan motioned for Laine to stop. "Wait."

Laine froze. Jobe whimpered at the reprieve.

Millan took a step forward. "He must have known you'd do something like this to him. So why come here?"

Jobe began to pant with a mixture of smoke and panic.

Laine shrugged. "He's come because he needs my protection. His tough mate with the freaky arm isn't around anymore, so he's come here begging before I get to him first."

Laine shook Jobe so hard that his head bounced from side to side. "That's right, ain't it? Scared shitless!"

Jobe clamped his mouth shut and tried to twist away from the horror of the flames dancing beside his face.

Millan's gaze didn't shift from Jobe. "So, what did you find in the crash?"

Laine shook Jobe again. "Tell the man what he wants to know! Tell him or I'll burn it out of your stupid mouth."

Jobe's mouth couldn't hold back the tide and he blurted out a half sob, half sentence that was completely unintelligible. His throat sucked at the hot air in loud, rapid gasps.

Millan sighed loudly. "Let go of him. I need him calm if he's going to be useful."

Laine's face fell. "You sure about that? Far as I can see, he's just a wimpy little shit trying to talk his way out of a beating."

He let go and Jobe dropped to the floor, coughing and gasping like he'd run a marathon.

Millan crouched and pulled Jobe's head up by the chin. "You found something, didn't you? Your friend took it, and hit you when you complained. I wonder if you also found some friends of mine?" Jobe tried to shake his head, but Millan gripped it in place. "I think I'd like to be certain you'd tell me the truth."

He turned Jobe's head until it faced Laine and the spitting flames. "So, tell me exactly what you found and who you met, or I'm going to let scarface here make you look uglier than he does."

Jobe spoke so fast his words ran into each other. His tongue flapped out of time with his lips, and saliva ran out of the corner of his mouth as he struggled to keep his breath.

Millan listened for a few moments, then let him go and stood up. "OK. Thanks for that."

He turned to Laine and nodded towards the brazier. Laine's smile spread as wide as his scar. He stepped forward and reached for Jobe's collar. Beside him, something clattered along the floor.

Millan grunted and dropped to one knee. Frowning, he raised a hand to his temple and pulled it away. Blood smudged his fingertips. He whirled round, both his hands flipping back onto his forearms.

"Don't do it," said Alis.

Millan stopped. Alis and Kasper appeared slowly from the shadows beneath the staircase. Both had dark, circular muzzles gaping directly at him.

Alis cocked her head and smiled. "When they expect you to be near, be far. When they expect you to be far, be near."

A grin split Millan's face. "Indeed."

Alis nodded. Kasper stared at Millan's head, then down at his chest. His flesh had darkened and swelled up significantly since the fight by the towers. Something thick and slimy stuck out from the wound, like a growth. It stretched up to his shoulder, climbed up his neck, and split into jagged lines that spread across the side of his face. It looked like a giant hand had punched through his chest from behind and was now blindly groping for his eyes.

Alis was staring too. "What the hell happened to you?"

Millan kept his grin fixed in place. "You happened, Alis. You should have listened to Rikka before using that spray on me." He looked down at where the blast had hit him. "That said, a wound like this should still have me on my back, so maybe I should be thanking you."

Alis was silent. Kasper realised Millan still had his hands clamped to his forearms. "Return your hands and put them on your head. Slowly."

Millan glared at him. Kasper glared back until the former leader relaxed his hands and placed them on his head. But something about Millan's eyes seemed different. *Blue*. Millan's eyes were dark, maybe brown or dark grey. But now they were blue.

Behind Millan, Laine looked on, confused. "There's more of you? Why didn't you tell me there was more of you?"

Kasper waved his muzzle at Laine. "You can put your hands on your head, too. Jobe, come over here."

Laine raised his hands, and Jobe got to his feet. As Jobe walked forwards, Laine switched direction with his hands and grabbed Jobe by the throat. His fingers met easily around Jobe's neck, and he squeezed. Jobe's mouth dropped open. The veins along his jaw stood out.

Kasper raised his weapon. "Not a clever idea. Let him go."

Laine crouched, pulled Jobe in front of him, and walked backwards away from the fire. "No thanks. I think I'll be leaving you three to fight each other without me."

Kasper raised his weapon. Jobe's eyes widened, and he tried to shake his head.

Laine grinned. "It's worth getting shot, just to see it if you can hit me without hitting the little guy."

Kasper shrugged. "What makes you think I care about the little guy?"

Jobe's face turned purple and his eyes bulged in their sockets. One hand wagged weakly towards Laine's grip, but Laine didn't move.

"Time's up," said Kasper.

His arm bounced once. A chinking sound came from behind Laine. A moment later he groaned and clutched at the back of his head. He loosened his grip, and Jobe melted from his grasp and dropped to the floor.

Laine rubbed his head, looked from Jobe to Kasper, then fled into the darkness at the back of the room. Light spilled across piles of junk, then disappeared with the slam of a heavy door.

Kasper rushed forward. "I'll get him."

Alis reached out to stop him. "Don't bother. We don't have the time."

She looked back to Millan. "Get on your knees. Wide as they'll go."

Millan obeyed. Alis looked over at Jobe, and jerked her head backwards. "Get behind us."

Jobe didn't bother trying to get to his feet. He crawled—spluttering and coughing and mumbling—over to the metal stairs, and pressed his back to the wall.

Millan looked up at Alis. "So, is this your plan? What are you going to do now, shoot me?"

Alis smirked, "Oh, very good, but you can drop the act. You're the one with the secrets." She waved her muzzle at the surrounding expanse. "Why are you in this place, when you should be focusing on the mission?"

Millan laughed. "Me? With secrets? You're the one who stole the diviner. If it wasn't for Rikka, we might never have got it back." He relaxed his hands and fanned them above his head. "In fact, I'm still not clear on why you ever stole it, or where you'd be now if you hadn't got caught in the act. Pretty suspicious, I'm thinking."

Alis pointed her barrels at his hands. "Put those back on your head, nice and flat, and nice and tight."

Millan did as he was told. Alis shook her head at him. "I went through all of that with Doron. It's old news. What's new, though, is you dragging yourself out of a crashed karyack and coming straight here, instead of coming back to join us."

Millan smiled, his tone casual. "I couldn't see how I'd ever get back up there. Coming here for help was the better move."

Alis's eyebrows shot up. "Help? Help from who? That weird, scarred guy? And where exactly is here, anyway? You've never been on a mission in this zone, so how do you know this criminal shithole exists?"

Millan fanned his hands again, but Alis waved her gun and he clamped them back down. He shrugged. "Alright. Look, it's complicated. After what happened to Irvana, Doron was worried about security. He asked me to work on a clean-up exercise. Like an audit. It covers every person, mission and piece of research we're doing."

Alis narrowed her eyes. A tiny grin curled the corners of her mouth. "So, you're in here with criminals, threatening to burn the locals as part of what? A company audit?"

"No. I'm in here because that guy helped us locate Irvana's body. He helped us again when we investigated her death. I thought he might help us once more. Maybe shelter us overnight, then get us to the tower in the morning."

Alis shook her head. "No. I was the one sent to investigate her death, not you. Remember? When I came out, you tried to take the diviner from me in the taxi."

Millan looked surprised. "Take it from you? Of course, you were supposed to check it in with me. Little did we all know then that you'd already stolen one!"

Alis waved his words away with the barrel of her gun. "Enough. You're here, colluding with criminals in a zone you've supposedly never been assigned to. And your only defence is some secret mission from Doron that we can't confirm?" She paused. "Ratshit."

Millan gave her another shrug. "It must be tough hearing that Doron didn't trust you with the truth."

Alis didn't rise to the jibe. "Give us back the diviner," she snapped.

Millan stared for a moment, then laughed. "You mean this time you really did lose it? Oh, this gets better. So, you've lost the only thing that shows us where we need to be to complete the mission, right?"

"Our mission and your mission don't appear to be the same thing," she said.

Millan didn't seem to hear her. "And you think I took it?" He laughed again. This time his tone was mocking. "You are beyond useless. Where's my motive, Alis? Why would I want to take it?"

Millan's tone irritated Kasper. He should be explaining himself, not wasting time making sarcastic comments. "So why not find us, then bring us all here with you?"

Millan's eyes flicked over to him, all humour leaving them in an instant. "Because, newbie, you two are not so easy to explain. Down here, they think I work alone. I couldn't risk losing their trust."

"But you could risk us getting killed?" said Kasper.

"Keeping you alive is not the mission," said Millan.

Kasper raised his weapon. "Bastard."

Millan grinned. "Maybe. But that doesn't make me a traitor."

Kasper took a step towards him. "That depends on what you did with Prue."

Still grinning, Millan gestured to the wall with his chin. "I gave her the same chance as any other orphan out there."

Anger flared in Kasper's chest. Before he could stop himself, he fired another disc. It bounced loudly off the floor in front of Millan's knees.

The man flinched, but recovered himself at once. "Enjoying your new toys, I see."

"Feel free to find out," said Kasper.

Alis waved Kasper's barrel down. "We're getting off the point, here. The diviner is gone and we know you took it. I don't know why, but I'm guessing you're trying to sabotage the mission."

Millan sighed with elaborate impatience. "I don't have it. Rikka must have it, or it flew clear of the wreckage. We should be tracking it down, not wasting time arguing."

His nonchalance made Kasper want to smash him in the face. He didn't for a moment believe the story about some secret mission sanctioned by Doron.

All their tech had died, and the mission had gone critical after walking only a few streets in this dark zone. If Millan had any official help, he would have used it then. He was hiding something.

Kasper looked at the piles of scavenged loot piled around the warehouse. You didn't get an invitation to a payday like this without a nod from the big guy in charge.

He thought about Laine running away. Strange that he'd run off and left his entire haul in the hands of a few strangers.

His stomach leapt, and he pointed an accusing finger at Millan. "This is your warehouse. You're running that guy with the scar. He left it all behind because it's not his. He's not in charge here, you are!"

Millan's grin widened, but his eyes lost a little of their shine. "Rubbish."

Kasper's mind raced to pull all the strands together. "No. No, I see it now. That's how you knew to come here. I'll bet you're making money off these people. In fact, why just here? You go everywhere! You must have access to gangs on planets all over the galaxy. You could be making a fortune from all of them!"

Kasper knew how rich the scavenger bosses were in his own decaying city. Multiply that by many cities, over many planets? Most people would do anything for that kind of wealth. He had no reason to think Millan was better than most people.

He glared at Millan. "You didn't come alone so you could save face with the people here. You came alone because you thought you'd left us for dead."

Alis took a step forwards. "Sounds credible to me, Kass." She pushed one arm towards Millan's face, filling his vision with the barrels of her gun. Instinct made him pull his head away. "Tell me, traitor, are you so hell bent on gathering wealth, that you'd let countless planets wither and billions of people die?"

The brazier flickered, and the shadows danced on Millan's face. He let his hands slide down his sides. "You're a child, Alis. You lack the maturity to contemplate what you're up against."

She waved the muzzle of her gun at his hands. "Get them back on your head."

He ignored her. He lifted one knee and planted his foot firmly on the ground. "All species need to adapt. Those that do not will always be superseded by those that do."

He got to his feet. Alis took a half pace back, and a low whirring came from somewhere inside the barrel of her gun. "Don't test me, Millan."

He continued to ignore her, and straightened to his full height. "The future is a rising tide. Our morals and preferences will be washed aside as it rushes in to engulf us. I have seen what is coming, Alis. In the end, we have no defence against it." He pointed at the twisting, vascular vines that glistened across one side of his face. "This is our future. Adaptation. Evolution. There are beings in this zone that exceed our understanding of genetic mutation. We both saw the tooth. I have seen more than that. Whatever we think we know, the cloud above us holds something we don't yet understand. It inhabits people, it amplifies their strength. They evolve, they improve."

Alis pushed her weapon towards Millan's chest. "Improve? These people are either dying, or they're eating each other just to survive."

Millan's face hardened. "It's nothing worse than natural selection. The weak die, the rest evolve. At the speed they're changing, who knows what they'll be capable of in just a few months from now? Who knows what they could enable us to do, given the right leadership?"

Anger seeped into Alis's voice. "You want to lead them? You want to keep them in their sick, mutated state because you think it gives you a chance at wealth and power? Is that it?"

He raised his hands wide. "Wealth and power? Sure. But more than that, I want these zones for the knowledge they can bring. We can't turn the tide, so why swim against it? We can learn, adapt, and improve ourselves if we decide to float along with it."

Alis shook her head. "I don't want to strut around like some lord, holding dominion over the fading remains of humanity."

Kasper looked from Millan to Alis, but she gave no sign of wanting him to force Millan back to his knees.

Millan's grin reappeared. "Oh, but you wouldn't. The dark zones already have their lords."

Kasper cut across them. "Gang bosses are not lords. They're just criminals. They can't help you adapt and improve, or whatever it is you think you're doing here."

"I'm not talking about gang bosses," said Millan. "I'm talking about the ghosts. Powerful beings that ride the tide as it washes in around us."

Alis and Kasper fell silent. For a moment, the only sounds came from the whirring of Alis's weapon and the steady spit-crackle of the brazier.

Kasper tried to read between the lines of Millan's rambling, tried to work out if he'd just confessed to sabotaging their mission. But Alis was already making connections of her own.

In one quick movement, she brought the barrel of her gun up hard under Millan's chin. He cried out, staggered, and clutched at his face.

Ignoring his pain, she yelled at him. "You sent Irvana into this zone! You made her stand on a rooftop for hours without droid support. Now she's dead. Murdered! Now we find you're running a criminal network around here. What are we supposed to think about that?"

Millan wiped blood from his chin and groaned as he straightened up. "I'm not running things. I'm trying to tell you. There are others that run things here. I'm not responsible for—"

Alis cracked her weapon across his face. His head shot sideways and he stumbled, falling to his knees. "It was one of your precious ghosts that killed Leon," she said.

She threw a kick at Millan's head, but he lashed out with his leg. She tried to avoid it, but his foot knocked her off her feet and she crashed to the floor. Millan's hand snapped back against his forearm.

Kasper's pulse quickened. He levelled his weapon. "Stop that. Now."

Millan ignored him. A barrel appeared at the end of his arm. He pointed it at Alis. She looked up. Kasper's arm jolted. A flash flared in the darkened space. The blast hit Millan's face, then bounced left, scribing a neat right angle in the air. A quick volley of metal clangs sounded off the stacks of junk behind him.

He roared and jumped to his feet, pointing at the growth on the side of his face. "Ha! You see? Limitless opportunities!"

Kasper's second shot streaked towards him, but he threw himself backwards and it sailed past him.

Alis shouted. "Get down!"

Kasper dropped to the floor. Something blurred past, thudding into the supports of the staircase behind him. A shower of sparks covered the back of his head, stinging his scalp. He flapped them out of his hair. From behind him, he heard the scream of twisting metal. He turned to see the staircase bending and twisting over its severed supports. The free ends swung free beneath it, still glowing orange from Millan's blast.

The whole structure shuddered and roared as he watched. Bolts snapped. Fixings tore free from their anchors in the wall. It wavered for a moment, then toppled. Metal and dust came hurtling towards his face. Instead of moving, Kasper thought of Jobe, trapped—maybe crushed—somewhere beneath the collapsed staircase.

He felt Alis grip his shoulder and pull him upwards. "Move!"

The lower section of the staircase hit the ground, and the entire structure dropped to its knees. A large chunk of wall smashed into his leg, knocking him to the floor. Alis dragged him clear as the rest of the staircase crashed to the ground like a KO'd prize-fighter, coming to rest in a shower of debris a metre or two behind him.

"Hey, newbie," said Millan's voice. Kasper peered through the dust in his eyes. He saw Millan crouched beside a stack of junk, his weapon raised. "Three, two, one."

Kasper froze. He felt a rush of panic. Millan's muzzle began to glow. But before he fired, a bright flash struck his shoulder. The impact knocked him off balance, sending his blast wide. Kasper gasped.

Alis shouted again. "Will you wake up! Get moving!"

Kasper scrambled for cover. A second shot from Millan screamed towards him. It bounced off the wall and skittered harmlessly across the floor. Kasper raised his gun, but Millan sprinted through the aisles of junk towards the back of the room. Alis ran after him, disappearing from Kasper's view down one of the aisles.

Light flared from the back of the room, washing across the heaps of junk. A door banged and the light vanished. Kasper broke into a run towards the sound. He arrived to find Alis pounding the surface with her fist.

"Shit!" she said.

Kasper stared at the door. It took him a few moments to understand that Millan had escaped. His heart sank. "I can't believe we lost him."

Alis blurred her hands back into shape, "We? You mean *you* lost him."

Kasper frowned, "Me?"

"You lost your focus. First the staircase nearly crushed you, then Millan almost killed you. I had to stop and bail you out twice!" She glared at him and tapped the side of her head. The gesture looked aggressive. "I've told you. Focus!"

But he'd tried his best to come to her rescue! The injustice annoyed him. He waved her away with his hand. "There's nothing wrong with my focus. I just didn't see him in time."

Alis looked him up and down. "Nothing wrong with your focus?"

"No, nothing."

"Hold up your hands," she said.

Kasper sighed and raised his hands. The backs were alive with movement. Narrow strips of flesh arced, then dipped, like eels gliding on the surface of a lake.

His stomach lurched at the sight, and he shook his hands, then held them back up to look at them. His skin still rolled and dipped across the backs of his hands. He shook them again, but they continued rippling and shifting with no apparent purpose.

He felt a flicker of panic in his stomach. "What the hell is happening?"

Alis looked irritated and sighed loudly. It pricked Kasper's pride. "I told you," she said, "if you don't focus, you can't control your changes. Now your body's not responding because you're being too emotional. You need to try to calm down."

Kasper shook his hands and stared at them again, but they refused to return to normal. He brushed them together and felt nothing. It was like wearing a pair of thick gloves.

"Calm down? I can't feel my hands!" he said. "Your people's technology doesn't bloody work. They're broken!"

Alis rolled her eyes. "They're not broken. They work fine. They're just not getting a clear steer from you. You need to try to relax. They'll snap back into shape as soon as you stop thinking about them."

She began pressing buttons on the keypad beside the door. Each series of presses ended with two low beeps. She cursed and walked backwards a few paces, studying the door.

Kasper frowned. "Can't you just blast it?"

She shook her head without turning around. Kasper watched her hair float from side to side, a fraction of a second after her head. She pointed down the length of the wall, and he turned to see three large drums with red triangles stamped on their sides.

"I don't know what's inside those, " she said. "But I don't think we want them being hit by a ricochet. Plus, we can't just keep shooting everything. We should conserve power —we don't know what's waiting for us between here and the tower."

Kasper looked at the stubborn keypad. "So, what else is there? The staircase is down, so we still need to use power if we want to get back up and go out the way we came."

She thought for a moment, "It's just a magnetic catch. If we could break the circuit, it'll spring open." She paused. The corners of her mouth pulled back in amusement. Her hand reached down to the communicator sewn into the thigh of her suit. She looked straight at him. Something in her eyes made his blood quicken. "How about you unzip your suit for me?" she said.

His eyes widened, "What?"

That made her laugh, "There's a trick I know with our communicators. Someone showed it to me the last time I got stuck and needed a boost."

Kasper frowned and shook his head. "I don't know *what* you're talking about."

Alis nodded towards the top of his thigh. "Let's just say you're hiding something down there I want to play with."

Kasper felt his cheeks redden. Alis gripped the fastening at the neck of her suit and slid it downwards, exposing her skin down to her navel. Kasper's eyes flicked to the curves holding her suit away from her chest. He felt a flutter in his stomach and looked away.

Alis grinned again and pulled her suit off her shoulders. "Time to get undressed."

Chapter Thirty-eight

The converter sat snug against Irvana's back. She'd designed the harness to move with her body as she travelled through the city. The last thing she wanted was a flapping counterweight throwing her off balance at a critical moment.

Despite the success of the harness, carrying the extra weight over distance had already proven more of an effort than she'd expected. The shoulder straps pressed down hard, like cautionary hands urging her to stop and rethink what she was about to do.

She had good reason to listen. Things had not gone according to plan. She'd heard about the girl and couldn't in all conscience leave her to her fate. But the rescue meant she now had to defend a child if she ran into trouble.

Rapid offensive manoeuvres would no longer be possible. If Irvana found herself cornered on the roof, Rikka would need to arrive a lot sooner than last time.

The end of the next street was as far as they could go before the darkness fully closed in. They needed to hide for the night. She lifted Prue off her hip and placed her on her feet. Prue looked bewildered, but didn't speak.

Irvana mustered her most motherly smile. "I'm looking around for somewhere we can sleep."

Prue blinked several times and rubbed at her eyes. "How long?"

"Not long," said Irvana.

Beside them stood a tall housing block, with neat rows of large windows running like gravestones along its face. On the opposite side, huddled together quietly in the dark, stood several two- and three-storey buildings. These were too small. Too few options once you're inside, she thought.

She looked again at the tall building with all the windows. It had plenty of high viewing positions, each with good visibility.

"You see that building there?" said Irvana.

"Yes," said Prue

"That's where we're going to sleep, OK? Let's go."

Prue paused. "Can you carry me?"

Irvana gave a brief snort of humour and shook her head. "Not while we're on the flat. If there are lots of stairs in the building, I'll carry you then. OK?"

Prue didn't respond. Irvana took it as a sign of agreement and headed to the building.

Beyond the threshold of the smashed entrance doors, a wide reception stood empty, except for a staircase rising from the centre of the floor to a small landing above. Two staircases split from the landing in opposite directions, and disappeared into the walls on either side.

Irvana stooped, and plucked a large piece of fabric from the floor. She rolled it up and tied several knots in the middle, each on top of the last. When she finished, it had a large lump on one side. She passed it around her waist, tied it securely, and shuffled the lump until it sat directly above her left hip.

She scooped Prue up in her arms, sat her on the lump, and put her legs around her middle. "Told you I'd carry you when we got to some stairs."

Irvana pulled Prue close, and climbed the central staircase. At the landing, she took the left arm of the split. It faced in the direction they'd been walking, so it felt like progress. Besides, this side of the building might give her a view of the tower when the light returned in the morning.

The corridor beyond had several doors on either side. She ignored them and walked on until she found herself in a large room, with windows on three sides and a floor littered with desks and overturned chairs.

She decided the corner would give them the most protection, and picked her way around the abandoned furniture. She passed several desks, then froze. Ahead of her, something shifted in the gloom. She stayed perfectly still for a full three minutes before she saw it again. This time something bumped against a desk. Prue stayed mercifully quiet, as though she sensed the need for silence.

The air in the room felt dead. There was no power in the dark zone, so whatever made the noise had to be alive. She gripped Prue hard against her side and dropped into a crouch.

A tufted shape rose from behind an upturned desk in the corner, its outline bristly in the dim light from the windows. She slowly placed Prue on the ground, and whispered into the girl's ear. "I'm right here. Don't make a sound."

Prue nodded. Then Irvana looked back across the room. The head retracted, and another appeared to its left. It quickly withdrew. At least two, she thought. Timid, by the look of it. The corner space wasn't large, giving room enough for perhaps four people in total to hide. She considered her options, and settled upon trying to convince them to leave. It was the quietest and most humane approach. Blasts and shouting could bring unwanted interest.

She rose to her feet and opened her mouth to speak. At the same moment, she heard a sound above her. She looked up and blurred her hands into new shapes. Two bodies fell towards her. She lashed out, and gutted the first to reach her with the new blade that jutted from her left arm. A warm shower of thick liquid sprayed across her face. She bit back the urge to gag, but had no time to avoid her second attacker.

A blow caught her heavily on her right shoulder, sending her spinning away from Prue. She controlled the spin, shifted her weight with her feet, and transferred the momentum into her outstretched right arm. It connected with the head of the second attacker, sending more organic fluid splashing across a desk.

The figure dropped to the ground. They didn't scream when they died. She wondered what living thing didn't cry out when a blade sliced through its flesh. She hopped over the fallen body, and dropped into a crouch beside Prue. Above her, the light-coloured ceiling rippled with long, spindly silhouettes creeping towards them. Around her came the thud, thud, thud of multiple feet hitting the floor. She grabbed Prue and ran for the corridor.

Doors flew open along the corridor as she raced past. Shapes skittered and thumped behind her as she ran. She burst onto the stairs, down to the landing, then onto the last flight of stairs. Gripping Prue hard against her, she cleared the main entrance and skidded to a halt on the dark street. Her skin crawled at the thought of whatever was chasing her, but they hadn't caught up to her yet.

She ran over to the smaller buildings opposite and paused outside, listening carefully for any sounds of movement. Satisfied, she slipped silently through the door. She checked the ceiling. Nothing moved.

Reaching inside a pocket with her free hand, she brought out a small tube and shook it twice. A narrow beam of dull light shone from one end, and she swept the room with it. The light revealed no threats, and just two narrow doors at the back of the room. One of them led to the staircase to the upper floor. She took it, and the short flight of stairs finished at another open room.

The door to this one was heavy, ideal for keeping out unwanted visitors. Inside, rows of empty shelving cut the room into sections, and nothing stood waiting for her, except a few old crates resting against one wall. There was no window, which meant anything that wanted her would have to come through that one heavy door.

She relaxed and headed to the back of the room. Bobbing down on her haunches, she lifted Prue onto the ground and gave her a brief smile. "I'm going to make sure the doors are all blocked up, then I'll be right back. It will only take a moment." Prue gave a quick nod, and Irvana smiled again, "You're a brave girl."

She headed out of the room and back to the door onto the street. It looked as though nothing had followed her out of the other building. She pulled the door closed, then lifted some of the heavier furniture in the room to barricade it. Satisfied, she retreated to the staircase and shut that door, too.

She examined the frame and edges, hoping for metal she could weld together to slow down anyone—or anything—trying to get through. But her light revealed dented, chipped plastic around both the frame and the door. Disappointed, she backed up the stairs and settled for removing the boards from the treads. She returned to the room, closed the door, then pulled a shelving unit across the inside.

She walked back to where Prue lay, and took off the convertor. Her shoulders sang with relief as the straps slid off, and she couldn't resist rolling them to enjoy the feeling. She tucked the waistband under Prue's head. It wasn't much of a pillow, but the girl seemed almost asleep, anyway.

She dropped onto the floor beside her and rested her head on one arm. Silence settled around them both, and she let her eyelids drop. As she drifted into sleep, she recalled the sight of a luminescent man walking slowly towards her across a rooftop. This time, she wouldn't find herself on the tower with nowhere to run.

Chapter Thirty-nine

A lis finished connecting the last wire to the keypad on the door.

"Ready?" she said.

Kasper's eyes traced the wire from the door back to his dismantled comm box. A second cable ran from there across to where Alis's comm box lay on a table.

"This does not look good," he said.

Alis smiled. "It'll be fine."

Kasper's blood pounded, partly out of concern for what Alis was about to do, but mostly because he still held the memory of her bare breasts—revealed to him when she'd unzipped her suit and removed the comms box from its lining.

He looked at her face. She smiled, but her eyes held something back. He looked down at his hands. They still refused to take shape. Even his own fingers wouldn't return.

His mouth felt dry. "OK, then."

She grunted and gripped the first cable. Her hand blurred into a long point, and she poked it carefully into her dismantled comms box. A low hum started from somewhere.

"Look away," she said.

He clamped his eyes shut and turned away. The gentle hum grew louder, stretching and pulsing in his ears like a breeze. It grew louder still, and he moved his hands to cover them, but that only channelled the thump-thump of the sound into his skull.

A loud crack stopped the wind. He heard the clatter of hollow metal hitting the floor. The room fell silent.

He opened his eyes. "Alis?"

Alis didn't respond. She stood beside the burned remains of the two comms boxes, holding the fizzing end of a severed cable in her hand. She stared at the door, her eyes locked on the keypad.

Kasper waited a moment, then said again, "Alis?"

Still, she didn't answer. He followed her gaze to the keypad. It glowed bright green, waiting patiently for the command to open the door. Her plan had worked.

He took a step towards her. "You OK?"

She turned and looked at him. A broad grin split her face. "Let's go!"

Kasper blew out a long breath. It stuttered in his throat as it left him. "You had me worried!"

Alis laughed. "I had it all under control!" Her hands blurred into familiar, short tubes. "Ready?"

He gestured with both hands. They were still just flesh-coloured lumps. "Give me a minute."

He closed his eyes and tried to focus. Alis and Doron had given him relaxation techniques when he first began his training, but he hadn't expected to still need them now. The embarrassment wasn't helping his concentration.

He thought of Alis waiting for him to help find Millan, and how Prue needed him to be calm and capable. They all needed him to pull himself together, now.

He cleared his mind and breathed slowly, focusing on relaxing his shoulders. Something shifted on the backs of his hands.

He opened his eyes and held his hands up in triumph, wagging his fingers at Alis. "All good!"

Alis grinned. "OK. Try to keep it that way."

They stepped through the door and into a broad tunnel. A pair of shiny metal lines ran in both directions along the ground.

The door clicked shut behind them, and Kasper felt a pang of pity for Jobe. There had been nothing bad about the little man. He'd been irritating, but that was all. He hadn't deserved to be crushed to death.

"Which way?" said Alis. "I can't see that bastard in either direction."

"Uphill feels like a good start," he said.

Alis turned and followed the tracks up the tunnel. "It's getting too dark to be out on the street. We should find somewhere to spend the night."

"What about Prue?" said Kasper. "She can't be out on her own."

Alis didn't slow her pace. "We don't even know where to look. Plus, our guide's dead under a staircase and can't help us. She's with people, not on her own. It's unpleasant for her, but it could be worse."

Kasper turned the logic over in his mind. Alis had it right, but they still had to find Prue at some point.

The streets and buildings sat in silence as they walked. All life in the area seemed to have the good sense to get indoors and stay quiet when darkness fell. They came across a building in good condition and chose a solid, deserted room with a single entrance.

They piled up what they could find for bedding and stretched out. Alis lay close, but kept a gap between them. This is a statement, he thought. He resisted the urge to ignore it and move against her, even though he felt his body calling to hers. How's that for focus? He thought. It was the last thought he had before sleep took him.

When Kasper awoke, he felt the warmth of Alis's body pressed against him. The hard ground pushed painfully into his hip and shoulder, but he didn't dare move in case she woke and rolled away.

Instead, he closed his eyes and took a deep breath, delighting in the firm pressure from the curve of her body. He wrestled with the urge to touch her, confused over whether she had moved towards him, or he to her. She had her eyes shut, and the dim light from the window fell across her cheek, making her skin glow in the gloom. He breathed deeply, trying to pick out the scent of her skin.

Gathering his courage, he slowly extended a finger and stroked a wisp of hair from her cheek. He regretted it at once. She woke with a start, rolled to one side and sat up. Her face creased into a frown, and he held up a hand.

She sighed. "Well, you did."

For a few moments, neither of them spoke. Alis stretched her arms and shook her hair. Kasper groped for the right way to explain why he'd been touching her cheek. He opened his mouth to try, but Alis jumped in first. "We agreed we'd try to keep clear heads, Kass. Last night, you couldn't get your hands back. You need to work on your focus, and we both need to prioritise getting out of this dark zone alive." she said.

He looked at the backs of his hands. No ridges, no movements. The skin all looked perfectly normal. "I-I am focused. I just thought that, you know, things had happened to us and we were shut in here and—"

Alis pushed her palms out towards him. "Alright. I'm not saying that I—" she took a deep breath. Her hands dropped. "We've just got bigger things to worry about, right now. Promise me you'll just concentrate on getting to the tower."

He sat up. "OK, I just—"

She shook her head. "No conditions. Promise me."

He looked down at his outstretched legs. They didn't seem like they belonged to him. He looked over at the purple-tinged morning light filtering through the window. They should have beaten back the cloud and been long gone by now. Instead, they were sleeping on floors and wandering blindly around dead streets. Things had indeed got out of control.

"I promise," he said.

"Good," she said. "Now let's get out of here."

He spread his hands. "Where to? No diviner and no convertor, remember?"

"The tower. That's our objective. It's the only reference point for everyone. If you're right that Rikka can be trusted, she should be heading there and can help us find Prue. If not—," she shrugged. "We'll work something out."

Kasper considered the possibility that Millan *and* Rikka might have betrayed them. He didn't think she'd been working with Millan, but he didn't think she'd be too concerned about finding Prue, either. Either way, Alis was right that the tower was the one place they all had in common.

He nodded. "OK."

Alis returned the nod. She walked over and pressed her ear to the door. After a moment, she frowned. "Movement."

They waited while she listened.

"There it is again," she said.

Kasper lifted himself off the floor. The corridor outside was only wide enough for two people abreast, and their room had a window that gave access to the street at the rear of the building. It was a simple room to defend and had a workable escape route.

"People talking. Can't tell how many," said Alis. She crossed to the window. "We should avoid a fight if we can. Let's go this way."

Without glancing back, Alis swung both legs over the sill and dropped through the frame. Kasper followed suit, his legs easily absorbing the shock of the hard landing on the street below.

"The tower should be this way," said Alis.

They set off up the street, but quickly came to a halt at the first junction. A large group of perhaps twenty figures, all different shapes and sizes, loitered ahead of them. Some appeared to be holding long implements, perhaps even weapons. They were too far away to notice Alis and Kasper, but close enough to block the route past them.

"See that?" said Alis, "We're getting closer to the centre. The residents round here are more like the ones I met before."

Kasper nodded. "Let's take a detour."

"OK," said Alis.

They ducked down a side street and made rapid progress, meeting nobody for the full length of two blocks. The small street ended at a T-junction with a much larger road.

Off to the right, away from the tower, another group of figures lurked in the haze. Alis and Kasper headed left to avoid them, but within the length of another street, they spotted a line of vehicles across the road. Roughly ten people hung around it, as though waiting for something to happen.

"That doesn't look good," said Kasper.

Alis murmured agreement from her position beside the wall. "One group behind us and now one in front."

Kasper pointed at the line of vehicles. "Hopefully that's not there because they knew we were coming."

Alis looked at him, her face serious. "Let's find a way around."

They retraced their steps, then turned down a tiny, rubbish-filled alley. This part of the city had suffered the longest under the cloud. Alis was right, that meant more time had passed here for the illness and mutation to develop.

Kasper heard a clatter above them. He looked up and saw a brief flap of movement against a window frame. "Wait."

Alis stopped. Kasper's eyes scanned the windows above. They waited in silence for a few moments, but heard nothing.

"What was it?" she said.

He dropped his voice to just above a whisper. "You didn't see it? There are people moving around up there. Well, one at least."

Alis answered in a similar whisper. "OK, but not so unusual, seeing as it's a residential block?"

"Sure, but doesn't it feel like we've been forced to go this way?" he said.

"Not really. It's pretty standard for gangs to set up barricades. It marks territory, and they can tax anyone trying to get through."

He frowned and looked up at the buildings that hemmed them in on both sides. "So why leave this route open? These alleys mean anyone can get past their roadblock. Shouldn't they have blocked these, too?"

Alis looked thoughtful. "OK. So?"

Kasper waved his hand at the dark windows set into the walls above them. "I think we're being watched. I think when they cut off the roads, a few of them would usually cover these rat runs, too. Today they're not. Instead, they're moving us in a certain direction."

Alis raised her eyebrows. "OK. Or, maybe you've just got yourself panicked and they don't know we're here at all."

Kasper spread his hands. "I only know what I would do if I needed someone to end up right where I wanted them."

Alis sighed then gave him a brief grin. "Alright then. What else would you do?"

"Electronic comms are too easily traced. Scavenger gangs use a network of runners to keep their business going. I'd use them to follow us from Millan's place and report back. I could then decide which routes to close off ahead and lead us wherever I wanted."

Alis thought for a moment. She glanced again at the dark, gaping holes in the walls above them. "I guess it does feel as though we keep being pushed away from the tower."

"That guy Laine was gone a long time before we chased Millan out of there," said Kasper. "Long enough to sort a route for us to follow. It might have been Millan's plan all along, and we're now playing into it."

Alis nodded. "OK, let's assume you're right. We'll see what's waiting for us down here, then maybe double back. They won't be expecting that."

Kasper grinned. Alis returned it. He felt a flash of excitement in his chest. "Agreed."

The alley ended at a larger street and the two of them pushed their heads out to get a view in either direction. Alis gave a satisfied grunt. "Large group, maybe fifteen or twenty. Standing around with nothing to do, right in the middle of the road."

"Same my side, but this lot have a barricade. That's the second one we've seen between us and the tower," said Kasper.

Alis nodded again. "Blocked in both directions this time."

She pointed to the narrow opening on the opposite side of the road. It looked no wider than shoulder width. "So that alley is the only option open to us."

Kasper looked at it and shook his head. The narrow gap didn't look like a proper alley. It looked as though the builders had miscalculated and left a space where the two buildings should have met. "We can't let them force us down there," he said.

"It's either that or pick the fight on our left or right," said Alis.

Kasper looked above them. The buildings at this end of the alley stood two storeys high. "Rooftops. It's dense residential stuff around here. We can work our way across them without meeting anyone at all."

Alis smiled at that. The change in her face gave him another rush in his chest.

"OK then," she said.

They used the last of the power in their boots for a burst of hard air. They grabbed hold of a first-floor window and pulled themselves inside. After a quick glance around the room, they left it and headed for a rough stairway. Taking the steps two at a time, they found their way out onto the roof. At the far end, they came to a halt where a low wall marked the edge of the building.

The rooftop of the next building beckoned to them like an open challenge. Beyond it, a jumble of patios and low-walled edges stretched away from them. Beyond them all, the tall sides of the tower rose sharply towards the purple sky.

Kasper jabbed a finger towards the tower. "There it is! And here's our very own assault course, all the way to the front door."

Alis laughed. "OK, ok. I'll say it. This is an excellent idea, Kass."

Kasper returned her laugh and looked at her. The warmth in her eyes had returned. He felt it filling him up.

They jumped onto the next roof with ease. Running to the far end, they pulled themselves over a wall and dropped onto a patio. They ran less than a hundred metres and came to a sloping roof that hung over the next building.

Kasper felt at home up here. Years spent moving across rooftops made the obstacles fade into pathways. "Watch this," he said.

He sprinted to the end of the patio and dived onto the sloping roof. Keeping his elbows and knees high, he slid down the full length on his stomach. A few feet from the end, he dropped his elbows, rolled to his feet, and cleared the last stretch of the slope in a single jump. Laughing, he turned and beckoned to Alis.

She broke into a sprint and copied his dive onto the roof. But instead of rolling and jumping off the end, she put both hands down, flipped her legs over her head and pushed off the slope, shifting her body into a graceful, feline arc that brought her to a smooth landing beside him. Kasper's jaw fell open.

She grinned and gave him a wink. "Still a lot to learn, newbie."

Within half an hour, they had cleared a dozen deserted roofs, and made it within two blocks of the tower. They could now see its windows and markings clearly, despite the haze that hung around it. Kasper wondered whether Rikka would be there when they arrived, and if she had found Prue.

They crested the next roof. Alis dropped to her stomach, flapping her hand for Kasper to do the same. Beyond the slope in front of them, Kasper saw three figures standing around the edges of the next rooftop, each peering down at the streets below.

Alis cursed. "Great. Just when we were getting somewhere."

"They're on watch," said Kasper, "but looking to street level, not the rooftops. They don't know we're up here."

"Sure, but we can't go around," said Alis. "We either go past them, or down to the street and find another way back up on the other side."

Kasper shook his head. "We'll end up in a fight down there, for sure."

"Then we need to get past them," said Alis.

They retreated to the roof they had just crossed. Alis held up both of her hands. They blurred quickly into one sharp hook and one thick barrel. "So, here's an idea. I'll fire off a round on this side. We wait for them all to run to that edge, then we slide down, drop over the side of the building and use two of these to grapple along it until we can slip onto the next roof. What do you think?"

Kasper examined the hook Alis had made. "You mean we hang off the building and slide these along the roof edge as we go?"

She sighed. "No, that would be too noisy. Just lift and place them. They'll keep their backs to us while they work out what's going on below."

Kasper didn't feel certain, but nodded anyway.

Her face brightened. "Right, let me see you do it."

He held up his hands, and they flipped obediently under his forearms. The blurring followed as expected, and his hands and arms quickly became two hooks, identical to those Alis was holding up.

He wagged them at her. "No problem. Fully focused."

She gave him a half-smile. "OK, good. Stay close. Silence until we reach the other side."

She crawled over to one edge and picked out a large vehicle—stripped of its wheels, seats and roof—sitting silently in the gloom. Taking aim, she shot a single round straight into the engine.

The vehicle blew apart in a roar of screeching metal and flames. The street erupted with shouts and whistles. Kasper watched the three lookouts rush to look down at the commotion.

With one eye on the lookouts, he took a breath and swung his legs onto the sloping roof. Moving quietly, he eased his body down to the other side, then dropped over the edge of the building. The hooks took his weight, and he swung gently for a moment before coming to rest against the wall of the building. Beneath him, a group of figures stood on watch in the street.

A moment later, Alis's boots swung down towards him, narrowly missing his ribs. "Come on, get moving!"

He stretched out his left arm and jammed the hook into the edge of the roof. He freed his right and slammed it firmly into place beside his left. This moved him roughly a metre along the side of the building. It was tough going. He only had to repeat the process twice before his shoulders ached for him to stop.

By the time he reached the edge of the next building, he was drenched with sweat. He hauled himself up, fell over the lip of the next roof and landed on his back, breathing hard and letting the relief flow into his shoulders.

Alis dropped onto the roof beside him. He struggled to catch his breath. "I think we got away with it."

"Maybe," she gasped. "But we'd better stay low until we're out of sight of those lookouts. What are they doing?"

A low wall beside them divided the two roof tops. Kasper eased himself up to peer over the top. A pale face with no nose stared back at him. He paused for a moment, unable to process what was in front of him. Then the face opened its mouth and yelled. Warm, fetid breath blasted into Kasper's face, filling his nostrils and throat.

The creature leapt the wall and drove its weight into Kasper's chest, knocking him onto Alis. Saliva splattered his cheeks, and he fell, cracking his head against the rooftop. Spirals of pain raced across his skull.

Alis wriggled beneath him as the thing raised its head and yelled beyond the wall. Kasper grabbed the thing's arms. It was strong, and he strained to hold it in check. His mind raced. More of these things would be drawn by the noise. He had to end the deadlock, *fast*.

He felt Alis moving beneath him. Her hook flashed up between his arms. A spray of bright red blood erupted from the thing's neck. It fell silent at once. She pulled the hook clear and Kasper felt the pressure on his arms fade. The thing slumped.

Alis banged frantically on his back. "Go! Get off me! Get up, get up!"

Kasper heaved, and the creature slid to one side. Alis scrambled clear of the pile. She gathered her breath. "Run!"

She turned and sprinted towards the end of the roof. Kasper looked at the creature's face. It lay wide-eyed and stupid, staring at the sky. Beyond the low wall, the other two lookouts came rushing towards him. He turned and ran after Alis, her hook still dripping blood on the rooftop.

Chapter Forty

Prue gripped Irvana's shoulder. "Blue man, blue man!"
The man's suit hid his body, but his head, neck, and hands shone like neon in the gloom of the street. He looked full of luminous fluid, each step triggering hundreds of ripples beneath his skin.

Irvana hunched further into the broken doorway. "OK, try to be quiet."

The man took a few steps forwards. His glow faded, and he stumbled. He righted himself and his glow returned, but it looked faint now. He took another few paces forwards then stopped. Slowly, he raised one hand and pointed directly at them. Irvana held her breath.

A flash streaked across the grey street, slicing through the man's body and separating his torso from his hips. He didn't cry out, or even lower his outstretched arm. His upper body slid from above the wound and fell to the ground. His legs stood for a second, then toppled like sticks in the breeze. The glow left his skin and rose towards the cloud like a column of smoke.

Irvana peered around the doorframe to see his killer. There, a short distance away, stood Rikka. She looked hunched, and had two hands pressed to her side. Irvana jumped out of hiding.

Rikka looked up and gave her a weak smile. "I still have not found the others."

Irvana waved the words away with her hand. "Never mind that." She frowned and pointed to Rikka's hands. "What's this you're clutching?"

Rikka pulled her hand away and held it up. A thick, dark liquid covered her palm. Irvana saw that a large patch of the same had soaked her suit. "You're injured."

Rikka inclined her head towards the remains of the man on the ground. "Yes. This one was difficult."

Irvana looked down at the wound. A fresh globule appeared and slid down her suit. Rikka sighed. "He had creatures nearby. Big ones, strong, well armoured. Like the one on the tower that damaged you."

Irvana nodded. "That one was pretty tough, alright."

Irvana helped her inside the building and sat her on a battered chair. Prue looked up, but didn't speak.

"Hello," said Rikka.

Prue didn't answer.

"Is she OK?" said Rikka.

Irvana shrugged and gave Prue a brief smile. "Are any of us OK in here? She's not hurt, but she's seen a lot of things she shouldn't have."

Irvana studied Rikka's wound. "You need to rest for a while."

Rikka shook her head. "I told you. I cannot find the others. The karyack is destroyed. I hope they are in hiding, but if they met a ghost, we must assume the worst."

Irvana heard Prue make a small sound. She flashed her what she hoped was a reassuring look, then turned back to Rikka. "Let's assume you couldn't find them because they're doing a good job of keeping their heads down. They'll still be heading to the tower. They've nowhere else to go."

She pressed Rikka's suit beside the wound. Rikka tensed and turned away. Her eyes fell on the smooth cylinder resting in Irvana's harness.

"Is the convertor intact?" she said.

Irvana nodded. "Yes."

"Then we can still complete the mission. The stronger the infection, the stronger the enemy. If we reach the tower and succeed, we can improve our chance of leaving this dark zone alive."

Irvana stopped her examination and looked up. She frowned at Rikka's enthusiasm. "We should focus on your chance of leaving this building, first. Can you travel?"

Rikka shook her head and sighed. "Not like this. I need you to do something."

"Anything," said Irvana.

"You'll need to seal it for me," she said.

Irvana frowned. She had a fair idea of what that meant. "You think you can stand the pain? I have nothing that will dull it for you."

Rikka nodded. She sat back down on the crate and exposed the wound.

Irvana sighed. "Pain it is then."

Irvana's field surgery skills were strong, but that was on humans. The alien woman's physiology was new. She guessed that sealing a wound was the same all over the galaxy, though You just had to burn it shut.

"Ready?" she said.

Rikka closed her eyes. Irvana's hand snapped back against her forearm and blurred a thin, flat ended pipe. She held the pipe roughly three inches from the torn flesh of Rikka's side.

The air rippled and hissed between the end of the pipe and Rikka's flesh. Rikka gripped the sides of the chair. Her eyes tightened, but she stayed silent.

Irvana worked the beam from top to bottom, moving gently left and right to cover the whole wound. Rikka's legs shook, and her foot kicked the floor. Irvana felt the urge to stop, but fought it. If she allowed the flesh to heat up without burning, Rikka might get an infection. The effect of an infection in this dark zone could be horrifying.

Rikka kicked out again, and uttered a small cry. Irvana continued her work. Eventually, she snapped off the heat, and the room fell quiet. Rikka's body relaxed, but her eyes stayed shut.

Prue crept closer. "Is she OK?"

Irvana nodded. "She's badly hurt, but I think we've helped her. Now she just needs to recover."

Irvana prodded the area around the wound. Nothing leaked. Stepping back, she gave the woman a final look then reached down to her thigh pocket, pulled out the diviner and flipped it open.

The surface of the diviner was dim. She walked to the doorway and held it out towards the tower. It brightened at once. Simple, she thought. She flipped it shut and slid it back into her pocket.

Next, she pulled out a small packet and passed it to Prue. "Eat something. We've got a long day ahead of us."

Prue sat up obediently, tore open the packet and bit into the contents. "How are we getting home?"

Irvana paused. "There's a jump portal in the tower. It's quite simple to use."

Prue took another bite. Irvana unclipped the convertor from its harness and ran her hands over its shell. It felt intact. Her fingers danced briefly over one end of the tube and two small lights appeared on its surface.

She grinned at Prue and pointed to a spot beside the second light. "Press here and... boom!" she said, miming a gun firing into the sky.

Prue didn't seem to notice the convertor. "Where's Kass? Is he coming home with us?"

Irvana shrugged. "Sure. We'll take whoever's at the portal when we get there."

Prue paused her eating. "You have to take Kass home, he's my friend."

Irvana put the convertor down and smiled. "OK, we'll make sure he comes with us, if he's there."

Prue finished another mouthful. "What about Millan, are you taking him, too?"

Irvana felt a familiar rush of anger at the mention of Millan's name. "Same goes for him. If he's there, we'll take him."

Prue shook her head furiously. "You can't take Millan home, he's bad!"

Irvana paused. "What do you mean 'bad'?"

"He went off to meet people and left me on my own," said Prue.

Irvana straightened up. "He separated from the others and went off on his own, did he?"

Prue nodded. Irvana gave her a dramatic frown. "That doesn't sound right, does it? In that case, no. Millan will not be leaving here with us."

Prue smiled. Irvana hadn't seen her smile before. It made her feel like a success.

"That's good," said Prue, "Millan's really nasty."

The sound of shuffling signalled Rikka's return to consciousness. She tried to sit up, then winced, moving her hand to the sealed wound in her side.

Irvana motioned for her to stop. "Be careful with that."

Rikka twisted her head to get a closer look, but there wasn't much to see except blackened flesh and a hole in her suit.

She gave up after a minute and looked over at Irvana. "Thank you," she said.

Irvana dipped her head in recognition of the thanks. "I owed you for the rooftop. Consider it a debt paid," she said.

Chapter Forty-one

A lis fired two shots. Both her pursuers tumbled out of view. The sound bounced around the roofs and walls, echoing down to the streets below.

They ran at full sprint—sailing over boundaries, leaping onto walls, and hopping across gaps. The tower drew closer with every passing minute.

Shots buzzed past them and cracked along the ground. They tumbled up, then down, another sloping roof. Kasper landed face down on a patio, and tried not to cry out with the impact.

Alis beckoned him into cover beneath the eaves. "They're ahead of us. They must have come up from street level."

Another shot whistled off the roof above them. They crawled elbow over elbow across the patio, keeping their heads low to the floor.

Kasper gasped with the effort. "We're too exposed up here. The streets are full of them, too."

Alis grinned. Her chest rose and fell from the effort of the crawl. "Ever tried mouse-holing?"

Kasper shook his head. "I've got no idea what you're talking about."

"If we can't move on the roof and we can't move on the street, we're going to have to move through buildings," she said. She raised her head and snatched a glance over the low wall in front of them. "There's an exit over there. Two shooters beside it, waiting for the shot."

Her arm blurred and slimmed to a single, thick barrel. She shot a section of the boundary wall roughly ten metres to her left. Stonework exploded and she jumped up, fired two shots, then dropped back to a crouch.

The shooters, distracted by the explosion, had their weapons trained on the wrong target. Alis fired twice, and sent them screaming over the roof's edge. "Let's go," she said.

They jumped over the wall and ran to the door. Kasper shot the lock off the handle and pulled it open. They almost fell over each other on the tight staircase, stumbling to a halt in the hallway below.

Alis headed past a flight of stairs leading down to the next floor and stopped a few feet from the end of the hall.

She stared at the wall and waved her hand backwards at Kasper. "Back up a bit."

He stepped back as she clamped her eyes shut and turned her head from her gun. The shot flashed from the end of her arm and slapped hard against the wall. Bricks and steel imploded in a loud crash of dust and grit.

Several small chunks bounced off their suits, leaving a trail of heavy dust swirling around them both. Waving it clear, Alis ducked and crouch-walked through the hole with her weapons drawn.

After a moment, Kasper heard her call out. "Clear!"

He caught up with her and nodded at her arms. "How many of those have you got?"

She glanced down at her weapon. "Three left. So we need to be clever about picking the walls if we want to reach the end of the block."

Kasper looked around at the walls in the room. "We'll have to guess what's on the other side. It's going to attract attention, too."

Alis pointed with her chin to the window on one side of the room. "If we stick to one side of the floor, we can look outside and check for windows in the next building. That will tell us whether there's a room on the other side."

Kasper grinned at her. Despite the dust, her eyes sparkled with life. He felt the excitement. Her bravery was contagious. "Sounds good."

They left the room and ran down a long corridor in the same direction as the tower.

They punched a hole through the next wall and scrambled through to the other side. Without waiting for the dust to clear, they sprinted into the new hallway and past the stairwell.

Alis kicked open the door at the end, then slammed it shut when they were inside. "We're not alone up here. I heard movement on the stairs out there."

Kasper hadn't heard a thing, but Alis looked adamant. "It wasn't going to take them long to work out what we were doing," she said.

He crossed to the window and looked out. A large group of dishevelled residents hung around the main entrance at street level. "There's an army down there."

Alis pointed at the back of the room. A single picture hung in the middle, filthy with dust and age. "Ignore them. Is this the right wall? Check it."

He looked out again. "No windows on the other side. I can't tell."

Alis looked back at the door. "Maybe we go back and head down one level. What's down there?"

He pressed his head to the glass, trying to see the wall below. But all he could see were the hostiles hanging around the door. The group seemed to have grown in just those few seconds.

"I can't see from here," he said.

He didn't catch what Alis said next. Something heavy banged on the door, shaking it in its frame. They looked at each other. The bang came again, this time splitting the door at the hinges.

They both leapt away as the next blow smashed the door into pieces.

Kasper stared at the enormous creature filling the doorway. It could have been a bearded man, except its teeth and nose stuck out too far beneath orange eyes. Torn clothing hung from thick lumps of muscle matted with dark, greasy hair.

The creature leapt at Alis, moving too fast for its size. Alis rolled clear. Kasper raised his weapon and fired. The shot missed. The creature flew past, crashing into the wall. It turned with frightening speed, and this time came straight for Kasper.

He tried to jump clear, but the creature smashed into his trailing leg, sending him spinning across the room. It followed him and lunged. He held his breath, expecting the pain. But the creature fell short of him, landing heavily on the floor.

Alis struggled to hold on to its ankle. She lifted her weapon and pressed the barrel behind its knee. The blast ripped through its leg and it screamed, kicking out with its free foot. It caught Alis above the ear and she fell backwards, grunting and clutching her head.

The creature tried to stand, but its stump flapped uselessly beneath it, and it toppled to one side. It roared, pounded the floor, then fixed its eyes on Alis, lying a few metres away. It dragged its enormous bulk towards her.

Kasper jumped to his feet. He pointed his weapon at the back of the creature's head and fired. Nothing happened: no jolt and no blast.

The creature heaved itself closer to Alis. Kasper willed his weapon to fire again. Still nothing. He lifted it to his face. The surface shifted back and forth across his arm, leaving the edges of the weapon soft and shapeless.

Panic flooded him. Alis tried to pick herself up, but the creature had her boxed into the corner. Kasper aimed again. He tried to picture the shot obliterating the creature's head. Still, nothing happened. Alis groaned from the floor. The creature inched closer.

Panic turned to desperation. Screaming, he leapt across the room and brought his foot down as hard as he could on the back of the creature's skull. The floorboards splintered and, for a moment, its huge head disappeared between them. Jumping again, he brought his full weight down through his legs and onto its neck.

He heard a crack and felt something give way beneath his boots. He pushed off from the floor and brought his heels down again. This time, his boots went through its neck, severing its head from its body.

Alis moaned, and rubbed at her head. She took her hand away, and he saw a wide, dark smear across her palm.

He stepped back from the dead creature and gathered his breath. "Are you OK?"

She nodded and pulled herself to her feet. "I'm alive."

Kasper noted the weakness in her voice.

She gestured towards the splintered doorway. "Cover the door. We're going through this wall, whatever."

He looked at the wall. "We can't. We don't know what's on the other side of that."

Alis stood back and fired. Kasper twisted his head away as the wall disappeared in a massive cloud of dust.

Alis held a hand in front of their face until the worst of it had cleared. "I can't see a floor in there. Might be a warehouse."

Kasper shook his head. "Jumping in there is suicide. We're four storeys up!"

Alis looked more closely, then blew out a sigh. "Ok. So, we've got to fight our way down the stairs and out onto the street."

Kasper pointed at the huge corpse lying on the floor. "We can't beat more than one of those at a time. We might not even beat the next one. And if we get caught on the stairs—"

Alis scowled at him. She splayed her hands. "So, what, Kass? Stay here until they all go away?"

He looked down at the mess he'd made of the creature's neck. Its severed head sat lower than its shoulders, wedged in the broken floorboards as though it had fallen from a great height. Blood leaked into the gap and disappeared.

"Do mice go down, as well as sideways?" he said.

Alis frowned. He raised his eyebrows and pointed at the floor. The frown faded, and she flashed him a smile. "I guess they could, if they wanted to."

The change in her face made his heart soar. He'd made that smile happen, and he loved the way it looked. He squeezed his eyes shut and blasted a hole in the floor.

They knelt and dropped through it, landing heavily on the floor below. They span on the spot, sweeping the room with their weapons. The room had nothing in it but a few scattered chairs and a thick layer of dust.

Kasper blasted another hole, and they dropped to the next level. Again, nobody sat there waiting for them. The door stayed shut, but shouting reached them from somewhere in the building.

Kasper's heart leapt. "They've worked out what we're doing."

Alis pressed her back to the wall and peered at the street below. "They haven't moved yet. Looks like they're waiting around for something."

"OK. Two more floors to go," said Kasper.

They dropped into the room below and held their breath. More shouting and sounds of movement around the building, but nothing banged on the door and nobody dropped on them from above.

Alis nodded towards the window in the room. "Check outside."

Kasper looked down and saw small groups of residents shambling around the hazy street. Every so often, one stopped to look up at the building before moving on once more.

A short distance beyond them, a truck sat idling on the other side of the road. Another group stood next to it. He couldn't tell whether they were arriving or leaving. Like Alis said, they didn't seem to be doing much at all. He thought back to the rodents that had attacked them just after they'd arrived. Perhaps these people were waiting for their leader to direct them.

A picture of Millan's ruined face sprang into his head. It reminded him that Prue was out there somewhere, probably terrified. Millan could have looked after her, but had decided he had better things to do.

Kasper turned back to Alis. "They've got a truck out there. I can't tell if they're arriving or getting ready to go. Either way, that's our only hope of getting out of here."

Alis blinked and shook her head. "I don't feel too good. What about you? How are you feeling now?"

Kasper heard the change in her voice. What she really meant was 'are you focused now?' It was clumsy of her. A short while ago, he'd saved her life by stamping the head clean off some huge beast.

After that, he'd come up with a new way of getting them out of the building without a fight. Now she was asking if he was in control? He wasn't in the slightest bit concerned about his focus. He felt like an utter hero.

"I'm good," he said.

She smiled. He felt the rush in his chest.

"OK. So, let's take the truck," she said.

Kasper glanced back down at the idling vehicle. "Are you sure you're up to it? It's got a gang of killers hanging around it, and you just said you're not feeling good."

"They can't hurt us in a moving truck," said Alis. "We've just got to make it inside that cab."

Kasper heard more sounds filtering down from somewhere on the floors above them. "OK. But we will need to be fast."

Alis clamped her lips tight for a moment. "Sure. You do the floor, I'll fire some loud ones down the street to distract them. When we head out the door, stay this side of the street and keep the wall to your back. We can't let them get behind us."

He nodded. Her bravery buoyed him up. "Right."

Alis leaned back to prepare her shots. He looked at her. "Alis," he said.

She paused and looked back at him, her face only inches from his beside the window. He leaned in and pressed his lips against hers. He felt her draw back a fraction, then she brought her chin up and returned his kiss.

Warmth filled him as her lips softened and moulded to his. She drew back, and something glittered in her eyes. "You're very forward."

He went to speak, but she turned and fired her first shot through the open window. With the feel of her still on his lips, he took aim at the floor.

Chapter Forty-two

Irvana's convertor looked like nothing more than a wide metal tube sitting on two stubby metal wedges. Rikka dropped to her haunches and peered at the single button on the surface of the cylinder. "You said this is the only control?"

Irvana grinned and nodded. "One touch, one shot. That's all."

Rikka widened her large eyes. "One shot?"

Irvana could hardly contain her delight. Her eyes blazed, and she pointed at her creation with both hands. "That's the breakthrough! My old one had to run for hours to roll back the cloud. But now it only needs one shot!"

Rikka's face didn't reflect Irvana's delight. She frowned and shook her head. "It is too small to generate that amount of power."

Still delighted, Irvana shook her head. "No, I've changed the makeup of the payload. I've used a little of the infection to engineer a healing process. One injection at the right spot and it's like the cloud can't help but fade away."

Rikka's face relaxed. "You mean it's like infecting it with itself. Or, precisely, you've created a vaccine so the cloud can cure itself?"

Irvana nodded rapidly, her grin staying fixed in place. "Yes, yes. That's exactly what it is. It learns and multiplies, overwhelming the cloud's metabolism and completely destroying it."

Rikka looked down at the convertor and frowned. "So what happens to the traces of infection within the vaccine?"

"What happens to any infection without a host?" said Irvana.

Rikka didn't skip a beat. "Finds a new one."

Irvana's delight diminished to mere good humour. "OK, so there is an unknown. A residual, perhaps. But my tests show it simply dies off. Burns itself out like fire without fuel. Either way, this convertor is more effective than my last one. That took hours to have any impact on the cloud. It was mostly impossible to defend it for so long."

Irvana bent to dismantle the convertor, but Rikka raised a hand to stop her. She leaned forward and took it apart herself, collapsing it smoothly and then slotting it neatly back into the harness.

Holding the harness up, she stood and faced Irvana. "So, re-infection is a calculated risk."

Irvana nodded and smiled. "Is there any other kind of risk?" She took the convertor and slung it onto her back. She fastened the straps, then paused. "Prue says Millan left her alone and went to meet some people."

"What people?" said Rikka.

Irvana shrugged. "That's all he said. But why does it matter? That removes all doubt about him." said Irvana.

Rikka thought for a moment. Her hand strayed to the wound on her side. "In which case, we'll deal with him if we find him."

She held out a hand towards Prue. The girl hesitated at first, then crept over and let the alien woman guide her towards Irvana.

Irvana picked Prue off the ground and placed her on the knotted waistband. "It might seem quiet, but we still need to keep moving. There is a lot of resistance camped between us and the tower, so we will have to go around them."

Prue shuffled herself into position, then looked at the dark patch on Rikka's dress. "Are you better now?"

Rikka opened her mouth but didn't answer. Prue hadn't spoken to her before, and the choice of question caught her off guard.

She managed a rough nod. "Yes, of course."

Irvana gripped Prue and strode towards the door. "The best route is to the west of here. The streets are narrow, and usually empty. Stay close, though. There's very little light in places."

"Will Kass be there when we get there?" said Prue.

Irvana smiled and brushed a few strands of hair from the girl's face. "Sure he will. He's probably already there waiting for us." From the corner of her eye, she saw Rikka press a hand to her wound once more. "How is it? Are you going to be able to keep up?"

Rikka nodded.

"Ok, then," said Irvana.

Without another word, she led them out of the door, off the main street, and into the lingering gloom of the narrow alleys.

The route seemed to head in the wrong direction. It became so dark at one point that Rikka placed a hand on Irvana's shoulder, just to make sure they didn't lose each other.

Prue tightened her grip around Irvana's middle, but didn't utter a sound. Irvana reached out and felt her way along the wall of the ally—at times catching her foot on the uneven ground, and once almost sending the three of them crashing down together.

Eventually, the alley ended at the edge of the same wide street they'd left a mile or so behind them. Two large piles of rubble blocked the junction, leaving only a short, rough pathway between them and the road.

Irvana eased Prue from her hip, and edged forward to look through the gap in the rubble. Her heart sank. A hundred metres away, the tower stood proud and alone, rising high above the rooftops of its neighbours. But before that, a row of crumpled vehicles jutted out from the far side of the street. Like a great, rusty tooth it curved across the road, leaving only a narrow gap between its tip and the pavement on the opposite side.

The gap it left from the last bonnet to the first building wouldn't allow more than a few people through at a time. Worse, ten or so shabby figures hung around the vehicles like a pack of junkyard dogs.

She pulled back and turned to Rikka. She found the alien woman sitting on the ground, one hand clamped to the wound at her side. Prue sat beside her, leaning against her shoulder.

Rikka looked up. "What did you see out there?"

Irvana ignored the question. Instead, she motioned to Rikka's wound. "How are my medical skills holding up?"

Rikka breathed out heavily. She pulled her palm away from her dress. "The bleed is worsening. It needs sealing again."

Irvana guessed the wound was more serious than Rikka made out. She marvelled at the other woman's attitude. No distress, no complaints. She just sat on the ground, her life leaking onto her dress while she calmly stated the facts.

Out of respect, she didn't probe any further. "They've blocked the road. There's a group of locals standing guard. We could remove them and get past, but I think it will bring others running."

Rikka wiped her hand on her dress. "Then we just need them to be looking the other way."

Prue raised her head and pushed the hair from her eyes. "If we stay here, won't they just go away?"

Irvana dropped to her haunches and smiled. "These people are guards. Their job is to stand there and wait for us to come so they can catch us. They'll stay there all day and all night, I'm afraid."

Prue blinked as the information went in. "How do we make them go away?"

Irvana stood up and sighed. "Good question. We need a distraction. We can't shoot at anything; they'll follow it back to us. Plus, the sound of firing will bring their friends running to help."

Rikka shifted her position on the ground, letting her legs slump to one side. She placed a hand on her thigh and, after a few moments, removed it and held up a flat, box shaped object. "We can use this."

"What is it?" said Irvana.

Rikka turned it around, showing Irvana each side. "It's something we use to help track energy sources. In this state, it's harmless. But, it's very unstable when overcharged."

Prue stared at the object. "What does instable, mean?"

Irvana and Rikka exchanged a glance.

Irvana gave a nod that Prue couldn't see. "Unstable. I think Rikka means we need to be very careful with it."

Rikka looked at the device. "Yes, we should be careful. In fact, I am sure I can make it explode when I choose."

"Maybe we can use it to make those guards look the other way," said Irvana.

Rikka nodded again. "We just need to put it on the other side of the street."

Irvana looked down at Prue. The girl's head shook from side to side as she realised what the two women were thinking. She'd endured a lot on her own: Narrowly avoiding death at the hostel, then being kidnapped in the dark zone. She didn't want to be separated from adults again.

Irvana dropped back onto her haunches and placed a hand on Prue's shoulder. "Here's the idea. Just listen for a moment, OK?"

Prue looked at the floor, trying not to meet Irvana's eyes. "Rikka's badly hurt. We can't walk much further. The quickest way to get to Kass and the others is by going straight past the guards out there. Rikka has a bomb that would make everyone look the other way while we sneak past them. It needs to be put on the ground on the other side of the street. She can't do that herself. If I go, they'll see me and we'll get caught."

Prue shook her head. Irvana smiled and rubbed the top of Prue's arm. "All you have to do is walk to the other side of the street, put it down, and walk back. They're not looking for you, they're looking for us. Just pretend they're not there."

Prue didn't move.

Rikka reached out and held her hand. "You are a strong girl. This will be simple for you."

Prue puffed out a breath and looked up. "Where will you be?"

Irvana held up her hand. It snapped back so the palm sat tight against the inside of her forearm. Her skin blurred and shifted into two, fat pipes.

She grinned. "I will be right here with this. Ready to blast any stupid bad guys that come anywhere near you."

For the first time, Prue grinned.

Irvana rubbed her shoulder. "There's my brave Prue."

Together they went through the plan a few times until Prue stopped looking frightened. Rikka worked on the device and handed it to Prue. The girl took it and pursed her lips.

Irvana put a hand back on Prue's arm and smiled. "Remember to walk slowly and look straight ahead, just like a walk on a sunny day. Turn your back when you put it down, then come back to us. There's plenty of time, so don't rush."

Prue swallowed and nodded. Irvana held up her weapon, and pointed at the entrance to the alley. "I'll be right here watching you, holding this, and protecting you all the way. OK?"

Prue nodded again.

"Great. You're amazing," said Irvana.

She kissed Prue on the head, and lead her to the edge of the alley. "OK. It's going to be easy. Don't worry."

Prue stepped out onto the road and headed for the other side. Two of the scruffy guards nearest to the end of the roadblock turned to watch. Irvana crouched and levelled her weapon. Prue walked exactly like it was a sunny day. Not too fast, not too slow, and completely ignoring everyone.

The guards quickly lost interest and went back to whatever they had been talking about. Irvana relaxed and lowered her barrels. "It's working," she said over her shoulder.

"That's good," came Rikka's voice.

Irvana's free hand strayed to her breast pocket, and she pressed her fingertips against the smooth surface of the Diviner. She would head to the top of the tower, use the Diviner to find the epicentre of the cloud, set up the convertor, and deliver the payload. Just like before, except this time she wouldn't have to hang around and fight off the enemy until the payload did its work. This time, she only needed one injection in the right spot. Like vaccinating a child, she thought.

Prue reached the other side of the street and turned her back to the roadblock. She crouched, and started rummaging in the rubbish. To anyone watching, she was simply scavenging, trying to stay alive in the ruined city. Irvana watched in admiration. Using her for this little job had been the right decision.

From somewhere up near the tower, the sound of an engine started up then grew louder as the vehicle approached. Irvana craned her neck and watched a small truck arrive at the barrier.

A tall man stepped out and barked at the lounging guards. He wore a torn suit, much like her own. The side of his head looked misshapen, as though something had grown across it and attached itself to his face.

The guards stood up straight and pulled themselves together for their superior. He turned his attention to the street beyond the roadblock.

Irvana's chest tightened. "It's Millan."

Rikka shuffled nearer to the alley's entrance. "He knows Prue. He'll recognise her."

Prue turned, and began to walk back towards the alley at an easy pace. Irvana's eyes flicked to the group of killers standing at the barrier.

The guard beside Millan started to speak. He looked like he had his face stitched across the middle. Millan raised a hand to stop him. Irvana tensed. With the same hand, he pointed at Prue and said something to the guard.

Irvana brought up the barrel of her weapon. "Trouble."

Rikka shuffled further up the pile of rubble to get a better view. "The timer still has a minute left."

Two guards walked away from the roadblock and towards Prue. One with a shrivelled arm and pinched face, the other with a mouth and nose shaped like a rat's muzzle.

"Stop there," said Ratface.

Irvana watched the distress spread across Prue's face. To her credit, she stuck to the plan and kept walking. Irvana steadied her weapon and took aim at Ratface's chest.

Ratface shouted. "Stop!"

Prue broke into a run towards the alley. Irvana blasted Ratface, and he flew backwards in a dark spray of blood and bone. The other guard turned to run. Irvana's second blast punched a hole between his shoulders. He dropped to the ground beside his friend.

She caught Prue in her arms and pulled her to the ground. The roadblock came alive with shouting. Millan waved his arms towards the alley, and the rest of the group charged towards them. Irvana blasted two at the front, but the others didn't seem to care. Millan turned and shouted up the street, his arms waving frantically towards the tower.

"Look away," said Rikka.

The explosion cracked once, then boomed around them. A solid wave of heat blew a hurricane of dust and grit down the alley. Irvana's ears rang with the pressure, and she gagged on the dust as the grit clattered and bounced around them. Without realising, she'd thrown her arms around Prue's head. Slowly, she released them and let the girl splutter and shake the dust from her hair. Behind them, dust filled the now silent street.

Irvana reached down to Rikka. "Let's go."

She hooked Rikka's armpit with her weapon and helped her to her feet. With her other hand, she tugged at Prue's shoulder and looked her in the face. "Stay close to me. I need my hands, so you'll have to walk, OK?"

Without waiting for an answer, she hurried them out onto the street.

Chapter Forty-three

The steering wheel bucked in Kasper's grip. He held it tight as the truck smashed aside another rusting vehicle. A violent jolt ran through the steel of the cab and up into his arms.

Air sucked and roared through the cab's broken windows. He yanked the truck to one side, avoiding the next vehicle, but one set of wheels mounted the kerb. Before he could pull the screaming truck back onto the road, the roof hit a balcony and screeched a deafening path along the stone.

Alis's head banged into his shoulder. She flailed an arm to right herself, pushing down on the seat for leverage.

Kasper caught sight of the dark red streaks staining her shoulder like an outstretched hand. The fight to reach the truck had taken its toll on them both, but she now had a blast wound to add to the kick from the creature.

He flicked his eyes to the road, then back to her limp body on the seat beside him. "Alis!"

No response. She had her eyes closed. The truck crashed into another vehicle and her body bounced in the seat.

He shouted as loud as he could, desperate to hear her voice. "Alis!"

She slowly raised a thumb. Another jolt sent her toppling towards the smashed passenger window. She dug and elbow into the back of the seat to stop herself from falling onto the jagged glass. She stayed like that for a few seconds, weaving and bobbing like a drunk.

Kasper reached over, grabbed her shoulder, and pulled hard until she sat up straight. "Hold on to something!"

He yanked the wheel again and surged around a bend. The tower stood ahead of them now, rising high over its neighbours and pushing its tip into the centre of the purple cloud above.

The road widened, and he pushed the screaming engine harder. Movement caught his eye on both sides of the road. Several groups of tall, broad figures were running in the direction of the tower. They moved fast, but they looked ungainly, as though unused to the act of running.

The truck caught up with them, and Kasper watched the nearest group, ready to swerve if they tried to jump on board. But, despite the screaming engine and the obvious size of the vehicle pulling alongside them, none of the runners looked up or changed course.

The blast of hot wind rushing from the wheels pushed aside the hood of the nearest runner. Kasper recognised the distended jaw and mass of glistening teeth. His stomach churned at the memory of stamping through the neck of its kin.

The truck barrelled past. None of them seemed to notice. He passed the next group and the next, but none of them reacted to an enormous truck hurtling down the street. Their heads stayed locked in the direction of the tower. Kasper felt the nerves rising in his stomach.

Alis bumped his shoulder and distracted him. She moved independently now, bracing her feet against the dash and grasping a finger on her opposite hand. She cracked it backwards, so it stood up at a right-angle to the others. A meditab dropped out and into her waiting palm. She shoved it into her mouth.

Kasper shouted over the roar of the engine and the rushing wind. "You OK? Can you move?"

She didn't answer. He gripped the wheel and reached over to shake her. This time, she met his hand with hers. She squeezed it feebly then placed it back on the wheel. Kasper heard her speaking, but couldn't make out the words.

With one eye on the road and one on her, he shouted again. "I can't hear you!"

Alis turned to look at him. A great smear of congealed blood and matted hair sat below her ear. He felt his panic rising. First a kick from a monster, now a blast wound. Skulls shouldn't take that kind of punishment.

Slowly, she blinked, raised a finger, and pointed towards the tower. "Focus," she said, as loudly as she could.

Her head slumped back, rolled to one side, and she vomited, sending light grey fluid splattering over her shoulder and out of the broken passenger window.

Chapter Forty-four

Irvana spat dust from her mouth and pulled Prue closer to her side. Rikka panted heavily, her hand clamped over her leaking wound. Bodies lay at their feet. These were the ones they'd seen coming. They just hadn't seen the rest. Ranks of misfits shuffled, coughed, and murmured in a wide circle around them. On one side lay the roadblock and on the other, the edge of the tower's garden, frustratingly out of reach.

Millan stood inside the circle like some self-appointed messiah —victorious and posturing. "Almost, almost! But not quite. You've done the right thing. I don't want you to die out here on the street. In fact, I'm impressed. You've done very well indeed to get this far. But then I think you, Irvana, have done very well to survive in here for all this time. You had us all fooled," he said.

Irvana kept her weapon trained on him as he moved, but he seemed too busy enjoying the moment to be worried. "You're the one fooling people. Doron, Vivek, Alis, but not me. I knew you were up to something. That's why you tried to have me killed on the tower."

Millan spread his arms, then extended a finger at Rikka. "Yes, and now I see how you escaped that. I'm guessing the explosion back there was you, too?"

Rikka nodded. "You're an idiot. What is happening to this city will kill you, just like the rest of us. You should not believe otherwise."

Millan laughed. "Promises are already made. Deals are already done. The people of light have no wish to get rid of me, nor to ruin my business. They see the benefit of having me prepare the ground for them. There's a trust between us."

Rikka shook her head slowly. "They are not people. They are walking hosts of an enemy we don't understand. There is no reasoning with it. There is no bargain you can make with those who come to spread it. It will destroy you, just as it destroys everything else."

Millan waved towards the ranks of disfigured citizens arranged on both sides of him. "We are loyal. They need us. They want our help to evolve."

Rikka gave a short, mocking snort. "You are not evolving. You are being poisoned. The cloud is sucking the life from your body. It is killing you. Only an idiot would walk through this dark zone and think otherwise."

Millan's face creased into a wide smile. He lowered both hands, and the circle shambled inwards. Rikka slowly shook her head. She dropped one foot back and bent her knees. Dipping her head, she pushed both arms out straight to either side of her, as though bracing two invisible walls.

For a moment, it looked like a mockery of Millan's own messianic posing. Then both her hands glowed bright blue. "Down," she said, quietly.

Irvana dragged Prue to the ground. A solid beam of light sprang from each of Rikka's hands. With a sound like wind through shattered windows, they smashed into the buildings on either side of the street, sending plumes of metal, brickwork, and dust into the air.

The brightness lit up the haggard faces closing in on them. They squinted and scowled at the sudden glare. For a moment, each of them seemed frozen in place, as though time had stopped. Then, spurred on by a shout from Millan, they rushed forwards. Rikka lowered her hands and span on the spot.

The two beams swept around the circle, carving a neat line through the rushing horde. Screams split the air, and Irvana pulled Prue's face closer to her chest.

Heads, necks, and chests split apart, spraying wide fans of blood into the air. The severed bodies danced, then collapsed into piles of blood cloth and stinking meat.

Rikka's beams snapped off, and she dropped to her knees. Open-mouthed, Irvana craned her neck to see Millan. From somewhere in the carnage, a flash of light flickered in front of his face. Rikka hadn't the strength left to avoid the shot. The force spun her round, then dumped her flat on her face.

Irvana blasted Millan's position. A shower of sparks and lumps of fallen corpse erupted from the road. She saw movement under a vehicle in the line. She took aim and poured shots into it, each one hammering through the metal until it slumped lower to the road.

She gripped Prue with her free arm and rushed to Rikka's side. A large gash oozed fluid from the base of Rikka's neck. "Get up! We need to move."

But Rikka gently shook her head. "More are coming. I'll hold them."

Irvana frowned. The tower only stood a short distance away. "We've come too far. You can't—"

"You need to go," said Rikka.

Irvana opened her mouth to protest.

Rikka put up a hand. "Trust me."

Her shoulders slumped, and she let out a sigh. Irvana noticed her eyes. They seemed fogged, as though they were full of smoke.

Irvana put a hand on her shoulder. "You saved my life again, and this time you saved a child's life, too."

She saw the glimmer of a smile appear on Rikka's face. "Perhaps I'm more human than either of us think."

Irvana laughed briefly, uncertain whether Rikka was being sincere or sarcastic. From somewhere in the distance, the sound of shouting and running reached them. Within it was the low drone of another engine.

"Sit me up," said Rikka.

Irvana pulled Rikka to her knees.

Prue tugged at Irvana's arm. "He's still there."

Irvana twisted and saw Millan pulling himself from under the rusty vehicle. She fired, and he ducked out of sight. In the street beyond the roadblock, more groups of his people ran towards them.

"Go," said Rikka. "You'll be surrounded again in a minute." Irvana paused, but Rikka pushed her gently towards the tower. "Help my people next. Please."

Irvana leaned in and kissed the top of her head. Her hair felt rough against Irvana's lips. Then she lifted Prue with her free arm and sprinted towards the tower.

The roar of the distant engine grew louder, and she pushed hard, urging her legs to reach the tower before it arrived. She raced across the withered garden and up the short flight of steps to the doors.

She dropped onto her feet, gripped the handles, and pulled. The doors didn't budge. *Bolted!* She took a step back and blasted a point precisely halfway between the handles. Sparks flashed, and one door buckled. A space opened between them, but it was too small. It took her a moment to weigh up the chances of their both squeezing through before Millan's horde reached them.

She turned back towards the street. "I'm going to force them back. You get down low. If anything happens to me, you go through that gap and hide inside. OK?"

She didn't wait for Prue to answer. Weapons formed below her wrists, and she faced the way they'd come. On the street, bunches of dishevelled figures ran at Rikka as soon as they saw her. Blue blasts ripped through them. She tried to stand, then quickly swung her arm and blasted the legs clean off her nearest foe.

A larger group flanked her, creating a new front on her opposite side. Someone fell to the ground, headless and twitching, but the effort forced Rikka onto her knees. Slowly, she disappeared, obscured by the mass of jostling bodies.

Irvana watched two more flashes light up their ranks. Another figure fell to the ground, its hands clawing at its face. The mob pressed inwards. Towards the centre, she saw heads and arms rising and falling in a frenzy. Helpless, she screamed at them to stop.

After a few moments, the mob fell still. Heads slowly turned towards the tower. Irvana stared at the ranks of ragged figures, a sickness rising in her throat.

Then she was aware of Prue pounding at her leg. "They're coming, they're coming!"

Irvana felt the bump of the girl's fist, and tried to push Rikka's death from her mind. The mob walked towards them and quickly began to pick up speed. Despite their losses, they were still a small army. She knew she couldn't beat them all.

There might be a lot of them, she thought, *but they can't get behind us and they're all bunched up together. They're going to feel a lot of pain before I go down.*

Her eyes picked out targets. A quick burst of sound, and two heads exploded in a cloud of fatty debris. She took aim again and three more bodies crashed to the ground, broken and bleeding. But each time one fell, another one appeared in its place, howling and drawing ever closer.

Behind the throng, Millan urged them forward. The first few reached the edge of the garden. Her weapons shook again. One runner exploded into pieces and the other screamed, its right hand groping at the stump below its left shoulder.

She raised and fired again. Two more fell, but others reached the garden's edge, weaving from side to side, closing the distance and trying to duck her shots.

She felt the tide rising around her and took a single step back, aware Prue still sat behind her knees. In her mind, she plotted an arc around her position. If they crossed that line, Prue would need to squeeze into the tower and fend for herself.

Chapter Forty-five

The truck bucked and roared in Kasper's hands like a tethered animal. He fought to keep it on the road while the wind beat his face and the engine shook him in his seat. Beside him, Alis struggled to stay upright as the truck smashed a path through the dead vehicles lining the street.

Up ahead, a flash shattered the gloom at the base of the tower. For a split second, he saw a crowd of silhouettes surging towards the doors. Another flash—this time he watched it fly from the doors and rip through the crowd.

He gripped Alis's shoulder. "Fighting ahead. Put your feet on the dash and get a weapon up!"

Alis battled against the movement of the truck, but got one leg up. The other leg flailed, and Kasper reached to guide her foot into place. She braced herself, then melted her hands into wide barrels. Through the shuddering gloom, Kasper thought he saw a smile play across her lips.

In the fighting, nobody noticed the speeding truck. Kasper hit the brakes, and all six of its heavy wheels locked. Metal clamps scraped on disks, sending smoke and sparks rushing from beneath its body as it bore down on the garden like a great, eyeless dragon.

It tore into Millan's horde, smashing through flesh and bone, tearing limbs, bursting stomachs, and splitting skulls in a great

wave of carnage. The horde fell back, desperate to scramble clear
of the raging machine crushing a path through their ranks.

Kasper kept his foot pressed hard on the brake, and sent blast
after blast through the broken windows of the cab. Flashes lit up
the interior, strobing Alis's body as she tried to keep her balance.

The truck slowed and hissed, its cab crunching into the base
of the tower before coming to a halt in a chaos of smoke and
groaning steel. The spent engine whirred, coughed twice, and
fell silent.

He let the calm settle for a few moments, then checked on
Alis. She groaned in the seat beside him. He kicked the driver's
door open and dropped onto the street. A woman and child
stared at him from the door of the tower. He turned and reached
into the cab, fumbling for a careful grip on Alis.

Her hand batted his away. "I can do it."

He pulled his hand back a short distance, still doubtful she
could make the drop to the ground without his help. As her feet
neared the street, she gave in and leaned on his shoulder.

"Kass!" said a child's voice.

Prue crashed into them both, gripping their thighs and
pushing her head into Kasper's stomach. Alis steadied herself
against the impact, then reached down and stroked the girl's
hair. Kasper raised Prue's face and smiled, delight and relief
spreading from ear to ear. "Hello, little one. Are you OK?"

Prue smiled back and nodded. "Yes."

But she looked pale and he saw dark patches beneath her
red-rimmed eyes. He smiled again, and her chin quivered. She
quickly buried her head from sight. He gently laid an arm across
her shoulders.

Broken bodies littered the ground. Clothing and chunks of
dark matter stuck out from the deep tread of the truck's tyres.
He covered his nose and mouth with his free hand to block the
coppery stench of warm blood.

The woman by the doors looked familiar, but he was certain they'd never met. She wore a similar suit to Alis and held her hands out as weapons, just as he did. "Is she one of us?"

Alis didn't reply. She looked as pale as Prue from her wound, but her eyes shone beneath a frown that got deeper as Kasper watched.

She nodded, shook her head, then nodded again. "It can't be."

Kasper raised his weapon. "We need to be sure."

Alis reached out and pushed his barrel towards the ground. "It's OK."

As they drew close, Alis gasped. She rushed forward, seeming to forget about her injuries, and threw her arms around the other woman's neck.

Irvana's face lit up, and she returned the hug. The pair of them held the embrace for a few moments, and laughed as they separated.

"How? And, what the hell?" said Alis. "You're a headless corpse, hanging in a tube back on the Salient!"

Irvana laughed again and looked down at her own feet. "It's a long story, Alis. One that started some time ago."

She raised her head and looked from Alis to Kasper, then across at the rear of the truck still blocking a fair width of the street. "There's no time for detail now. We need to get out of the open. Millan's going to regroup and come at us again."

Kasper heard the name. "Millan was leading those...things?"

Alis gestured from Kasper to Irvana. "Irvana, this is Kasper. He's our newest recruit."

Irvana dipped her chin briefly at Kasper. "Welcome. And yes, he was leading them."

Kasper shook his head. "Did you get him?"

Irvana shrugged. "I don't think so."

Alis steadied herself on Irvana's shoulder, and raised her fingers to the gash on the side of her head.

Irvana slipped an arm around her to take her weight. "We're not strong enough to be out here. Let's get behind those doors."

They cut through the metal around the lock and prised the doors apart. The vast entrance hall spread out expansively in front of them. The light was poor, but they could pick out several silent exits in the surrounding walls. Each one had a wide staircase leading up into the darkness.

Kasper thought the place smelled damp, like a tomb. He pulled the doors together behind them and looked around for something to seal them shut.

"I'll do it," said Irvana.

She passed Alis to him and faced the doors. Light fizzed and sparkled as she slowly welded the two steel doors together. Satisfied, she stepped back and looked around the hallway. "OK. We're now stuck in here with whatever else is waiting for us inside."

"What about Rikka?" said Kasper. "She might make it here, too."

Alis let out a hiss. "Rikka? Rikka left us to die while Prue got swept off that road like a bug. She did not know what would happen to us and she couldn't have cared less. Whatever happens now is her own doing."

The last few words came out as a breath and she rubbed at her eyes. She staggered, and Kasper put his hand on her shoulder. She didn't seem to notice.

Irvana fished around in the pockets of her suit. "You're wrong about Rikka, Alis. If it wasn't for her help, I'd be dead now."

Alis scoffed. "I find that hard to believe. She as good as condemned us to death."

Irvana finished rummaging through her pockets, and pulled out the diviner. Flipping it open, she studied the shining, shifting face of the material inside.

Alis's jaw fell open. "How. Where did you get that?"

Irvana didn't look up. "Rikka gave it to me."

Kasper looked at Alis. "She took it!"

Alis threw her hands up. "I told you!"

"Not quite," said Irvana, "I asked her to get it." She looked up at the ceiling, then back down at the glowing surface. "Good, we still have a chance."

Kasper pointed at the diviner in her hand. "So, you asked her to take that from us?"

Irvana snapped the diviner shut and looked at him. "No, I asked her to take it from Millan."

Kasper frowned. "You already knew about Millan?"

She pushed the diviner back into her pocket. "I'd worked it out. He knew I had. That's why he tried to kill me the last time I was here."

Alis waved a weak hand towards Irvana's body. "But he failed. You're alive and well. Your head is still attached to your neck. So why didn't you come back? Why stay in here and leave us thinking you were dead?"

Irvana's face hardened. "I wasn't sure who else was involved."

Alis paused. "You mean me? You thought I was a risk?"

Irvana sighed. "Everyone thinks you're a risk, Alis. I just had to be certain."

Alis threw up another weak gesture. "Really? Everyone? You trusted me enough to get me to hide a diviner in Nasser."

"That's true, but I didn't involve you beyond that, did I?" said Irvana.

"That diviner caused a big problem between Doron and me," said Alis. "He partnered me up with Rikka. She didn't make matters easy. If you hadn't vouched for her, I'd say she was working against us."

Irvana smiled. "You've got Rikka all wrong. Millan tried to have me killed. She saved me," she raised a palm towards Alis. "And don't worry, I obviously think you're completely trustworthy now."

"Well, good!" Alis said. "I'm pretty tired of being suspect number one when things go wrong."

Kasper grinned. Alis was still herself, despite the head wound. "What about Doron?" he said. "Does he know?"

"About Millan?" Irvana shook her head. "Doron can be trusted, but he would want proof. Now that we have it, I can go back and present it to him."

Alis thought back to her own conversation with Doron. He had wanted evidence that Rikka was a traitor. Irvana was right to have her proof ready, but it still didn't explain why she'd trusted Rikka in the first place.

"So, where's Rikka now? Isn't she still supposed to be part of this mission?"

Irvana turned and walked further into the dim entrance hall. "She didn't make it this far."

Kasper's stomach dropped. "She's dead?"

Irvana didn't answer. Kasper realised he'd been thinking of Rikka as invincible. She knew more than he did, held more power than he did. She understood what they were up against. He suddenly felt afraid. If someone like Rikka could die in here, what chance did any of them have?

Irvana pointed into the gloom. "We'll try that one."

She led the way to an open doorway on the north side of the entrance hall. Kasper supported Alis. She half leaned on him, half held herself upright, as though she couldn't decide whether she needed his help. But he couldn't stop himself from helping her. She would have to be a lot more stable if she wanted to walk without him.

Irvana reached the doorway and poked her head over the threshold. "Steps are blocked part way up. Let's try another."

They headed for another doorway, still on the north side of the tower's entrance hall. Irvana stopped after a short distance. "Same with this one. Stay here."

Kasper watched her move down each wall, checking each exit carefully. Every time she peered up a stairwell, he imagined her shouting a warning and running back toward them, chased by a throng of shambling mutants.

He did a quick visual check of Alis's forehead. The blood had dried up, but the wound had dirt all over it. Millan's rampant mutation sprang into his mind. The medical spray had caused that. It should take months inside the dark zone before Alis reached that state.

Irvana finished her inspection. "Two staircases are open, the rest are blocked."

"Blocked?" said Kasper. "Do you mean barricaded, or just covered with rubbish?"

Irvana thought for a moment, then shrugged. "Either way, let's assume it's not an accident. That means both open routes are likely to lead to trouble."

Kasper flexed his fingers, "OK. So we pick one and head for the roof as quickly as we can, right?"

Irvana didn't answer. She walked over to a small recess at the nearest end of the west wall, and began rubbing at it with the sleeve of her suit. Eventually, the dirt disappeared and revealed shards of gloomy light coming in from outside.

She peered out into the street. "I have a different idea."

Chapter Forty-six

Kasper hauled himself onto the window ledge with both hands. He planted his feet, stood on the sill, and tried to ignore the shudder of fear as his breath left his lungs.

Above him, the smooth surface of the tower rose like a blade to pierce the purple cloud. Below, the edges of the tower's garden were invisible in the darkening streets. The urge to slip back through the window threatened to overwhelm him, but he knew that going back would only mean the others would once again convince him they were right. He would still be the right person to make the long climb up to the roof.

He willed his hand into a single short tube, and pointed it at the wall. A beam of light shot from the end, scoring a deep, horizontal furrow as he moved it from left to right.

He squinted against the brightness. The surface melted easily, and he soon realised he could move the cutter faster and still get the depth he needed. He finished and looked around again, studying the garden and gloomy streets for any sign of movement, but the light had attracted no attention.

Pleased with his first cut, he reached up as high as he could and scored a second furrow to match the first. This time, it only took a few seconds. He examined his work. The first two rungs of a ladder grinned back at him from the face of the tower.

He blurred his free hand into a heavy hook, and dropped it onto the lower edge of the higher rung. He tugged at it to lift himself. The hook folded like paper, and his arm fell away from the wall. Panic flared in his stomach. He pushed his feet against the sides of the window frame, and jammed his cutter into the lower rung of his ladder.

The cutter held, and he breathed out. "Shit!"

His back crawled at the thought of the open darkness behind him. He took two deep, deliberate breaths and focused again on the shape he wanted to make. The hook formed in his mind. He reached up and felt for the furrow without looking at his altered hand. This time, the hook locked tightly into position.

Still tense, he tested his weight on it. It held. He lifted himself up, and placed his foot on the lower rung. He straightened up and relaxed as he realised he now stood successfully on the first step of his makeshift ladder. The convertor shifted in its harness between his shoulders, but he barely felt it. It hardly weighed anything at all. *This is going to be fine*, he thought.

The next set of steps went quickly and easily. He found a rhythm in the carve-and-move, carve-and-move pattern, as he cut his ladder and climbed higher and higher.

His confidence grew, leaving his mind free to wander back inside the tower, where Irvana, Alis, and Prue should be well on their way to the jump room.

"Be careful," Alis had said when he climbed out of the window. She'd gripped his arm when she said it. The memory of her touch still excited him. He had every intention of getting back to that warm hand as soon as he could.

The hug from Prue had been nice, too, but Irvana hadn't touched him at all. She'd simply checked his understanding of the convertor, made him repeat every step of their plan, and nodded as he spoke.

Obviously, she wanted to be sure he understood how to work her device, but now he thought about it, she 'hadn't even smiled, let alone wished him luck. In fact, after proposing the plan, she'd been almost downcast. Something troubled him about that, but he couldn't quite put his finger on it.

The scientists he'd met during training had mostly seemed detached, and consumed by their work, so it shouldn't be unusual for Irvana to be the same. She had placed their plan above any personal goodbyes. But that wasn't what bothered him. He replayed their parting in his mind. She had shrugged off the harness, swung it carefully around in front of her, then placed it upright on the ground. She'd beckoned him closer and pointed at the supports, explaining how to remove them from the harness and link them together.

Next, she'd run her hand over the surface and pointed out the pressure pads towards the base. Finally, she had given a rapid, simple explanation of how to align and target the barrel. The business end, as Alis had called it. He remembered Alis's face. Pale, but with a glimmer of humour.

Then it struck him. Irvana had avoided his eyes. She hadn't looked at him once during the entire time she had been talking. She'd even avoided looking at him when they were going over the plan. Like his mother stubbornly rubbing a stain, he couldn't let the thought go.

What makes someone stop looking at you? He scratched around in his memory for times when he'd done the same. He remembered a time at a junkyard with Leon. His heart sank at the memory of his friend.

He heaved himself up onto another rung of his improvised ladder, straightened, and reached for the next cut. He needed to avoid dwelling on his friend's death. If he lost focus at this height, he'd drop off the side of the tower and die in a smashed pile of bone and metal on the cold street below.

But now it was on his mind. He tried to focus on recalling the yard.

There had been two wide steel containers, just beyond the hole he'd cut through the fence. But as he'd climbed between them, the strap on his backpack had hooked the fin of a heating duct. He had taken a step forward and jerked backwards, dropping his light.

The clatter of the aluminium casing filled the silent yard. The guard dogs heard the call of duty and jumped to their feet, barking and snarling as they pounded towards the noise.

Trapped between the containers, Kasper had tugged frantically at the hooked strap. The movement of the dogs triggered the yard's floodlights. He wrestled his pack in a blinding wash of millions of lumens.

The dogs spotted him and howled. Both were over five feet tall and rushed towards him on legs pulsing with muscle. The yard's owner had clearly been worried about security. These animals were the genetically modified kind. Big, expensive and bred for the job of tearing apart intruders.

They closed the distance to within just a few metres. Kasper still couldn't get free. He could see spit flying from their jaws and imagine them clamping onto his shins, tearing through skin and cracking his bones.

He felt the panic rising and gave into it, tearing madly at the strap that still refused to budge. The dogs tensed and leapt, leaving the ground in one smooth, terrifying motion. He shut his eyes and turned away.

As he did so, the snarling stopped, replaced by two yelps and a crash. Something heavy tumbled to the ground on the other side of the yard. He opened his eyes and saw Leon reaching with one hand to unhook the strap from the vent. In his other, he held one end of a thick, metal rod. It sat easily on his shoulder, making him look like an old-time baseball player.

"We should go. I caught them a good one, but they look like they can take a beating."

On the face of the tower, Kasper hauled himself up another few metres and started working on the next cut. He remembered that he'd been unable to look Leon in the face for the rest of the night. They knew that Kasper's mistake could have killed them both.

Worse, he'd needed Leon to save him from being mauled to death. Leon shouldn't have to do that. He'd struck a silent bargain with his friend, then failed to play his part.

He finished his cut and stopped. *Guilt.* He knew why Irvana couldn't look at him. She felt guilty for sending him out here. She didn't expect him to succeed.

Her strength and experience made her the obvious choice to push through the tower with Alis and Prue. After all, she knew the tower. His performance in the city showed she could barely trust him to look after himself, let alone navigate an unfamiliar building, face down a horde, protect a child, and care for his wounded could-be lover.

But thinking he would fail? Her eyes seemed to hide something, he thought. He thought of the three of them reaching the jump room and getting dug in to wait for him. If she didn't expect him to reach the roof and fire the convertor, why send him out here?

The answer crackled through his chest and into his now quivering stomach. *A decoy!* She'd given up on the mission. He was just buying her time to reach the portal and jump to safety without him. It made sense.

He fought to keep his focus on the shape of his hands. His mind swam. The vast emptiness sucked at his back, willing him to relax and fall peacefully into its soft, purple wisps.

He felt fury. Then he felt alone. The structure of his cutter shifted. The bright beam spluttered and died. A cool breeze flowed over his cheeks. He stared at the dark, grey wall just inches from his nose. His heart pounded in his chest and he battled to tear his mind from the long drop beneath him.

He squeezed his eyes tight and focused on the shape of the hook that was holding his weight. He pictured it as a strong, thick, shiny hook, like the type he'd seen lifting vehicles from loading bays, or stacks of scrap metal into junkyards.

The hook stayed still. Relieved, he followed his training. He breathed in a slow, deep rhythm to 'scribe' the image, then moved his mind to recreating the cutter on his other hand.

It occurred to him he didn't need to cut any more rungs. Irvana probably didn't expect him to reach the top, so he could now just climb back down.

But somehow, going back didn't feel right. This damn excession event had killed Leon and now he had a creeping certainty it was trying to kill him, too. He couldn't roll over and die. Decoy or not, if he could see Leon right now, he would want to look him straight in the face. He had to beat it. The cutter sprang into life and he cut another neat foothold.

He soon found himself surrounded by thicker pockets of cloud, hanging like giant drips from the vast purple blot above him. The gloom pressed in, shortening his view of the wall above, as though sensing his determination and willing him to fail.

He reached for another cut and stopped. Something moved a couple of metres to his right. In the gathering darkness, he could just make out a broad shadow. It shifted and turned, its full size more than twice Kasper's height and width.

A triangle of utter darkness stretched like a billowing sail above it. The sail shook once, then sank quietly out of view. *Oilbats*, he thought. *Big ones.*

Kasper marvelled at how high this one had chosen to roost. Perhaps it had something to do with the dark zone, but whatever the reason, he made a mental note to avoid it.

Oilbats were clumsy fliers, and this one had enough weight to knock Kasper clean off the face of the tower. He also knew that they never roosted alone. There would be others hanging around nearby. He set off again slowly, systematically checking in all directions for any more dozing oilbats.

The next three cuts brought no surprises, but on his fourth, he saw a dot of blueish light far below him. It floated towards the base of the tower, then stopped. Oilbats 'didn't reflect light, so it had to be something in the street. He watched it for a moment, but it stayed still. He dismissed it and continued his next cut.

He focused on climbing, but the speck of light nagged at the back of his mind. He took another look. It had moved to one side and now sat directly beneath him at the foot of the tower. He stared at it, willing it to float away from the tower and move on. Instead, it seemed to get bigger. He blinked several times, but the pinhead of light had now grown into a small blob.

Wings flapped to his left and reminded him to keep moving. He tore his eyes from the blob below and cut another groove. But he felt less confident than before. Something sat beneath him, and his legs felt too exposed.

He moved faster. *Cut and move, cut and move.* The naked feeling crept up his spine and he couldn't resist another glance past his feet. The blob had grown larger. He could see movement on both sides of it. Something like pistons pumping around it, moving in a steady rhythm.

His stomach dropped. *It's not getting larger,* he thought, *it's coming closer.* He knew at once it was coming for him. He thought of Leon, sliced to pieces by a man filled with light. A ghost. Those weren't pistons, they were arms and legs, working their way up his ladder. The ladder that finished in front of his face and left him with no escape.

A cold rush of fear surged down his arms and into his stomach, threatening to turn his hands to liquid, and send him plunging to his death. Irvana was right. Without a decoy, whatever came for him now would chase all of them through the building.

He clamped his eyes shut and pictured the distance to the top of the tower. If he moved fast, he could make it. He brought his breath under control and threw himself into cutting and moving.

By shortening the length of the cuts, he could work faster and still fit the toe of his boot into each rung of the ladder. He climbed faster, but his breathing came harder and strained the human parts of his arms and shoulders.

The next twenty metres passed quickly, but then he made a handhold too small and had to stop to make it wider. With a break in his rhythm, he instinctively looked down. The ghost now had definite contours. A head sitting on wide shoulders. Arms moving smoothly as it climbed towards him.

Panic flared again. He almost scrambled up the tower without cutting a rung to stand on. Losing the battle to stay calm, he ripped the wall in a frantic slash-and-scramble, slash-and-scramble action, struggling to stay focused while trying to outpace the ghost below him.

Ahead, the purple haze hid the railings of the tower's rooftop. He guessed at another thirty metres to go, but had no actual way of knowing. His shins crawled at the thought of being grabbed from below.

Without thinking, he looked again. He felt the will drain from his arms and legs. The ghost's body was clear now. Kasper knew he couldn't out-climb it. The cutter spluttered at the start of the next groove. He panicked and lost control of his hands. The skin shifted, and he clamped his eyes shut at the thought of falling to the street below. He breathed hard, groping desperately for the focus he needed to stay alive.

Movement sounded on the wall beside him. The greasy wing of an oilbat struck his left arm, dragging his cutter off track. The bat flapped again and knocked his foot from the lower rung. He fell away from the wall. His stomach lurched. His arm straightened and his shoulder screamed in its socket as it took his weight and swung him into the wall.

He flailed at the surface with his foot, desperate to find a hold and flee from the death that climbed the ladder below him. The bat flapped again. He braced himself for another blow, but a broad shadow beat the wall above him and he felt the wings go past him. He tensed, and tried to focus on keeping the hook in place. It wasn't over yet. The bat's talons could still catch in his suit and tear him from the face of the tower.

He tried again to find a foothold, but his body twisted and pulled hard on the hook. The great, open space at his back begged him to give in and let go. A thick, shiny talon clunked against the wall beside his face. The hardened scales over the bat's knuckles hid the pockets of sucking skin that kept it on the wall. He could almost feel his legs burning away in a blinding blue flame from below.

The idea flashed in his mind for only a second before he blurred his hand and gripped the bat's ankle. He twisted the hook free and swung away from the wall, catching the bat's other ankle with his hook.

Great wings beat the surrounding darkness. Thick curtains of greasy skin flicked in and out of view, each one tinged with the blue light that lit the wall directly beneath him.

He blurred his hook into a hand and tightened his grip. With both feet flat on the wall, he pushed out and arched his back, wrenching the bat free and sending the two of them tumbling into open space.

The bat shrieked like metal blades dragged across glass. It flapped furiously, trying to shake Kasper free. He ignored it and pulled hard on one ankle. The bat banked away from the wall, leaving the glowing figure motionless at the last rung of the ladder.

The sight of the ghost made Kasper furious. It, or another one of its kind, had taken Leon's life. Now it had climbed up here to kill him, too.

The bat moved fast, desperate to throw him off and break free of the weight. He pulled hard on the other ankle and it turned back towards the tower. He waited until the bat almost hit the wall, then pulled hard again, sending it scraping along the face of the tower. It crashed into the glowing figure, and swept it from the wall like dust.

The ghost flapped its arms for a few moments, trying to reach for the wall, then gave up. Kasper watched the bright body spin silently through wisps of cloud, gathering speed towards the dark street below. The silence terrified him. What kind of being falls to its death without making a sound?

He couldn't see the impact, but the light shrank to a tiny dot, then winked out of existence. Relieved, he hauled both the bat's ankles back and felt the lift in his stomach as the creature shifted direction towards the roof.

He let the sensation run through him and laughed out loud, forcing the last of the tension from his body.

Chapter
Forty-seven

A lis watched Irvana push a table into place. She shuffled it about until its steel surface lined up perfectly with its neighbour. Rapping it once with her knuckles, she stepped back to admire her work.

Five heavy steel tables lay on their sides. Their broad tops formed a solid barrier a short distance in front of the jump portal. Alis looked over at the doors. They hung in splinters, opening the room directly onto the corridor. The line of steel tabletops was no substitute for bolted doors, but it gave them some cover to blast whatever rushed out of the darkness.

Alis thought of Kasper, climbing the outside of the tower with the convertor strapped to his back. It looked unremarkable—just a simple tube, strapped into a scruffy, homemade harness.

She turned back to Irvana. "So, you've developed a Convertor Mark 2?"

Irvana smiled. "Actually, it's Mark 3. The first version never left the lab."

"What's different about this one?" said Alis.

Irvana looked pleased with herself. "I've upgraded it. It now works more like an injection."

"What does it inject?" said Alis. "Explosives, I hope."

Irvana shook her head. "A vaccine. It's not a weapon anymore, it's a cure."

Alis cocked her head and let her hands settle on the edge of the tabletop. The dried blood still clung to her hair, but her eyes sparkled with interest. "A cure? What, like it turns everything back to normal?"

Irvana gave a half smile and shook her head. "Not quite. It can't undo the physiological damage to people—or other living things—in the city. It just, well, I suppose the easiest way to explain it is that it makes the cloud attack itself. It's like an autoimmune response. It makes the cloud eat away at itself until there's nothing left."

Alis frowned. A thought occurred to her, and she brightened again. "So, we can kill it with one injection? One shot, then off home? No more standing on rooftops like a buffet for hungry mutants?"

Irvana walked towards the jump portal. "Yes. At least, that's the theory."

Alis took a few steps to follow, but felt faint. She cursed and put a hand to her head. She raised her voice so Irvana could hear. "You know we've only got two passes for that thing?"

Irvana stared at the silent displays on the outer ring of the portal. "It's damaged. The passes would still work, but I can get us all through without them. Surely your plan was never to use them, anyway. There are too many of you."

Alis nodded. The mission kit list hadn't included jump passes. "Whatever the plan was, Millan made it up, so he didn't expect us to get this far." The thought of Millan reminded her of the convertor. "If it's just a theory, how do you know it works?"

Irvana didn't look back at her. "What?"

Alis took a few careful steps forward. "A moment ago, you said killing the cloud with a single injection was just a theory. So, how do you know the convertor works?"

Irvana prodded and patted the face of the portal. "I tested it on samples in other parts of the city. I'm certain it'll kill around eighty-five percent of the cloud."

Alis splayed her hands at Irvana's back. "What about the other fifteen percent?"

"The convertor is a prototype. I need to be in my lab to perfect it. There's only so much I can do alone inside a dark zone."

Alis felt her head clearing, and took a deep breaths to chase the final dizziness away. "So why send Kasper to the roof? All of us could have come straight here, then you could come back later when it was finished. He's out there risking his life for no reason."

Irvana bent and fiddled with something on the lower edge of the jump portal. A loud crack split the air. Sparks flew over her shoulder. Prue, hunkered down behind the tables, gave a sudden start, then settled back behind her mountain of hair.

Irvana continued fiddling with the portal. "He is taking a significant risk, but there's a good reason."

"And that is?" said Alis.

"We needed someone to give us time."

"Time?" said Alis.

Irvana cursed and thumped something Alis couldn't see. The portal answered with a loud rattle of loose metal. "Yes, time."

Alis felt a tingle of nerves in her stomach. "You sent him up there just to draw Millan away?"

Irvana didn't answer. She continued pulling and prodding a clump of cables attached to the edge of the portal. Alis walked carefully towards her. "What's going to happen to him out there?"

Tiny lights flashed, chased each other around the outer rim of the portal, then disappeared. Irvana stood and gave a brief grunt of satisfaction, then rubbed her hands. "He has as much chance as we do, Alis. In fact, being attacked is highly unlikely while he's on the wall. As I recall, I sealed the only access to the roof from the stairs, too, so he shouldn't meet anyone when he gets to the top, either."

Alis continued her unsteady steps. "If the stairs are sealed, why tell him to come down and meet us here?"

Irvana didn't turn from her work. Alis closed the gap between them a little further. "If he's ready to be on a mission, he is ready to do what it takes to make it succeed. Thanks to Millan, I've been stuck down here too long. My research should bring a massive leap forward in the fight. We can't fail again."

Alis stepped to within two paces of Irvana's back. "We need to help him. He's new to this. He doesn't know what he's doing."

"Then, like the rest of us, he will need to learn quickly," said Irvana.

Alis pictured Kasper on the dark rooftop fighting for his life, his face a mask of pain beneath a raging mob of starving mutants. "You can't just leave him up there to die!"

Irvana didn't respond. She fiddled with a set of wedge-shaped plates welded to the portal. They glowed beneath her fingers. She tapped them in a specific sequence. They flickered obediently, sending a stream of pink lines rushing round the circle, painting it with a bright pink halo.

She raised her hands as though praising the portal. "Ah-ha! Excellent." She paused. "Don't worry about him, Alis. I'll look for him when I come back. For now, we need to focus on getting out of here before we're all killed. Millan will soon realise there's no real threat on the roof, and we can't beat another one of those glowing things."

Alis reached out and gripped Irvana's shoulder. She tugged, spinning her around.

"You're not listening to me, I—"

Irvana's hand grabbed Alis's wrist before she could finish her sentence. Irvana pulled and twisted, making Alis yelp at the sudden, spiking pain.

Irvana's voice was hard. "Don't be sentimental. He's one of us; he'll survive until we come back for him. Now pull yourself together. There are far bigger things at play here than your feelings."

Alis felt the rage coursing through her. She aimed a strike at Irvana's face. Irvana moved to block it with ease, committing herself and spotting the feint too late. Alis tore her other hand free, pushed up through her legs and caught Irvana squarely under the jaw with the heel of her hand.

The force snapped Irvana's head back, and she staggered away. The blow didn't knock her over but, on the floor behind her, Prue had pushed out her legs. Irvana's heel caught on Prue's leg and she lost her balance, falling heavily and smashing her head on the steel barrier as she went down.

Alis and Prue watched Irvana hit the floor and lie still. Prue's hands crept up to her mouth, as though stifling a silent scream. Tensing for the worst, Alis knelt and felt Irvana's neck. She flicked away the strands of hair and found a bare patch of skin. She felt a gentle pulse beneath the skin. Relief washed over her.

After a few seconds, she sank back on her haunches. "Shit."

Prue dropped her hands from her mouth, and Alis gave her a reassuring look. "She'll be OK, Prue. She'll be OK."

Prue curled up into a ball and hid her face inside her hair.

Alis checked the doorway. She still felt unsteady, and the adrenaline made her light-headed. If anything comes now, we're dead, she thought. The rim of the portal glowed silently behind her. She didn't know enough about jump portals to know if Irvana had got it working, but it felt comforting, like a life raft in a storm at sea.

She thought of Kasper on his doomed climb to the top of the tower. Maybe he'd worked out that he was a decoy and climbed back down. He might walk through the doorway at any moment. Something quivered in her stomach, and she tried to suppress it.

She hung her head. Kasper used to be annoying. Back at the hostel, he'd irritated her, constantly pushing himself forward as the leader. She'd tried to ignore it. It suited her cover story to let him take charge. But since his injuries, since his 'rebirth', he'd been different.

Of course, it was a shock for him to wake and find he was no longer fully human. He also had to accept that Alis knew more about his planet than he did. So he'd dropped his bravado. She liked that.

He was coping with the change better than others before him, which Doron had quickly put down to her support. He'd coped better because she was there, and because he trusted her, Doron had said.

Mostly, the machine and human integration worked smoothly, but at times he remained distracted. Focus, she'd told him, you must focus. She smiled now at the futility of telling him to focus when he'd first arrived. The change had been too huge for him to ignore.

But later, after he'd pulled it together, he still had minor jitters now and then. On those occasions, she'd get annoyed and tell him to keep things tight. It made little sense that sometimes he lost his concentration, when at other times he was able to focus with ease.

Something softly fell into place in her mind. She finally understood the true cause of his distraction. It was in his eyes when she thought of him now. She felt emotion stir in her chest. Did she feel the same? She couldn't be sure. What she knew for certain was they'd spent too much time together to just leave him behind in an excession-level dark zone.

She looked back at the glowing lights on the portal, then over at the gaping doorway and into the dark corridor beyond. Her eyes returned to Prue, and to the unconscious Irvana, sprawled on the floor.

Her head span. She blew all her thoughts out of her nose in one hard breath.

"Damn," she said.

Chapter Forty-eight

The air at the top of the tower didn't feel right. It sat still and silent, yet somehow it felt awake. It resisted him as he walked through it, as though it wanted him to know he wasn't welcome.

The diviner felt heavy in his hand. He flipped it open, and held it out like an offering to the heavens above. The interior blazed with light. He half expected a bolt of lightning to smash it from his hand in celestial rage, but the cloud hung quietly in place.

He faced the other end of the roof and looked again. The diviner dimmed slightly. He turned ninety degrees, and it dimmed again. Another ninety degrees brought it back to its original lustre, and the next made it blaze like a torch. He headed in that direction.

The comms platform loomed out of the haze, and he climbed its short staircase. The diviner glowed in every direction. He shoved it back in his pocket, slipped the harness off his back, and crouched to unpack the convertor. His back crawled as he took his eyes off the fog. In his mind, it stared at him like an army of ghosts—too intangible to touch him, but wishing him harm, however it came.

He lifted the tube and set it carefully onto its base. Muttering a silent hope, he jabbed at the single button. It sprang into life at once. The tube hummed and its dark mouth blazed, shattering the fog around him and turning night into day.

A thick rod of light shot upwards, piercing the purple cloud. For an instant, the beam connected heaven and earth with a single white tether.

He squinted at the sudden brightness, but found he couldn't turn away. A second later, the beam of light cut itself free from the convertor, flew upwards, and disappeared into the hole it had torn in the heavens. The cloud flinched, as if woken by a sudden shot to the heart. Its vast surface rippled, sending waves in all directions, for as far as Kasper could see. It withdrew from the hole, leaving a small patch of clear sky.

Excitement flooded his veins. He'd done it. The newbie. The decoy. He had climbed a tower, bested the enemy, and delivered a killer blow. His thoughts of failure, of self-doubt, dropped away from his shoulders. He felt success sweep up through his legs and into his chest.

He rose to his feet and stood atop the tower like a hero of old. He looked up at the cloud, clenched his fists, and roared. His throat and lungs felt like they'd tear with the effort, but he held his shout of triumph for a solid twenty seconds before falling quiet.

When he fell silent, so did the top of the tower. The convertor's light went dark at his feet. The shadows of the rooftop crept slowly back towards him. He bent, and started to dismantle the device. His hands worked quickly, and his eyes flicked around the brooding rooftop.

He wondered what the blazing light from the convertor might have brought running towards the tower. He told himself he would easily see any more of the 'blue men' glowing around him, but the quiet rooftop turned threatening at the thought of what else might be coming for him. With a sheer drop on every side of the rooftop, he had no choice but to stand and fight whatever arrived.

He tried to push the thought from his mind as he worked. The first of Irvana's homemade bolts came apart quicker than he expected. It hit the ground with a clatter. He froze, waited a full minute, but heard nothing.

He worked more slowly on the second bolt. It came free easily, and he kept two fingers on one end of it, using his other hand to catch the nut and washer before they fell. He set them down gently and reached for the third bolt. Only one more to go after that.

He twisted it, but it didn't move. He shifted position to get more leverage and twisted harder. His fingers complained at the pressure, but the bolt wouldn't budge. He glanced again at the shadows. Nothing yet, but he couldn't spare the time to hang around.

He flipped his hand back against his wrist and formed the cutter. Irvana would just have to make another bolt, he thought. The laser painted him with a dim circle of light, but the risk of being seen was worth the chance to leave the roof sooner.

He held one end of the bolt, and cut through the head. The laser sliced through it easily. Before he broke through it completely, he heard the loud creak of metal hinges from somewhere on the far side of the roof. Voices broke the silence. His heart leapt in his chest, and he shut off the cutter. Too late, he realised he didn't have enough hands to catch all the pieces. He watched dumbly as the cut end and the mid-section clattered to the floor.

"Over there," said a voice.

"Waste of time, this. Why not put people on the stairs then we go to the jump room?" said another voice.

"The portal's old. It's junk. Been dormant for years. She'll need hours to get it going," said the first.

Kasper's heart raced. He didn't know the second voice, but the first was definitely Millan's.

Footsteps sounded from another part of the roof. Millan had more than one person with him. Kasper willed his hands to form into weapons.

Millan's voice boomed out across the rooftop. "We know you're up here, newbie!"

He sounded confident. He had every right to be. He had numbers on his side, and guarded the only way out. Kasper guessed Millan's squad would fan out in a ragged arc away from the door. He decided his only hope was to stay quiet in the shadows, and ignore his creeping sense of dread.

Staying on the platform suddenly seemed like a bad idea. Irvana had expected him to fail, so she didn't care if the convertor made it back. He decided to leave it. He briefly wondered if Alis also didn't care if he made it back. Pushing the thought from his mind, he set off towards the steps, keeping his body low and his weapons up.

He kept to the edge of the platform, approaching the steps at an angle rather than straight on. He made it a couple of metres before his boot kicked the stray nut from the convertor. It pinged loudly off the metal handrail and clattered down the steps.

Millan pounced on the noise. "There!"

Footsteps came running. Silhouettes appeared from the darkness, rushing towards the steps. He backed away, calculating whether to fire and give away his position, or wait and see if they rushed past him. His luck didn't hold.

Millan's thugs bounded up the stairs and straight towards him. He fired twice, sending bright streaks scything towards them. Both bodies fell back into the gloom.

Millan's voice boomed out again. "I see you!"

Adrenaline pumped in Kasper's veins. He shivered. They knew where he was hiding and soon they would work out that he couldn't get away.

He knew Millan had weapons, but perhaps the others didn't. There had been very few shots fired throughout the fighting in the dark zone. Millan might choose to strafe this end alone, and Kasper had no cover to hide from the blasts.

He retreated a few steps and felt the railings press into his back, stopping him dead. His eyes shifted left and right, trying to penetrate the gloom for anything coming at him.

Millan's voice taunted him from somewhere in the darkness. "There's nothing you can do now, newbie. You could jump over the edge, perhaps. That might be more dignified. At least this time, my target would die. I'd hate to leave you in this place, skulking around causing trouble like that sanctimonious bitch."

Kasper didn't answer him. His chest tightened and his breath finished before it left his mouth. He had to shoot, but he didn't know where to aim. If only he had a flare. Panic lurked in his mind, threatening to turn his weapons into mud. Perhaps he should strafe the rooftop before Millan did the same. It could make him a target, but what choice did he have?

He took a deep breath, pushed himself quietly to his feet, and fired. He forced out everything he had. The blasts split the darkness, setting the roof alight with a torrent of sound and colour. His body shook and his arms jumped with the recoil. He fought to hold them steady, and realised he was screaming with the effort. His shoulders and forearms ached, but he kept firing. Nobody came up the steps, and nothing came streaking towards him out of the shadows.

He stopped firing and threw himself to the floor. Thick silence fell over the roof. He waited for the return of fire. Somewhere in the darkness, he heard moaning. He'd hit one of them, at least. Maybe he'd got Millan.

"You finished?" said Millan. "Feel free to carry on. Take as long as you need."

Cold rushed through Kasper's veins. Millan sounded perfectly healthy. He also sounded closer than before. He shifted as quietly as he could to a new position. The platform was small, and he'd given his position away by shooting, but at least now he wasn't lying where they expected.

More of Millan's jeering floated out of the gloom. "You're sure you don't want to keep shooting? We're all enjoying the light show down here."

Kasper refused to take the bait. They had his last position, and he would not give away his new one.

"You don't want to know what my friends here will do if they get hold of you," said Millan. "All this fighting is hungry work. And they like their meals warm and raw."

Kasper shivered. He told himself it was the adrenalin. But he knew Millan was trying to scare him, push him into losing confidence, so he'd lose grip on his weapons. He blinked to clear his eyes and stared at the edge of the steps, waiting for something—anything—to appear out of the gloom.

Millan's voice sounded again, this time heavy with sarcasm. "I'll tell you what. You're new to this, so I'll count to five, just so you've got a chance to throw yourself over the edge instead of being eaten alive. How's that?"

Kasper ignored him. He focused on the steps, his barrels, and his breathing.

Millan scoffed. "OK, have it your way. One. Two—"

Movement at the top of the steps. Silhouettes rushing towards his last position on the wrong side of the platform. He counted four and opened fire. Each one danced on the spot before dropping to the ground.

He shifted position again, rolling over the hard ground to the centre of the platform. Three bright shots lanced towards him from beyond the steps. They cracked and whistled off the ground where he'd lain a moment ago.

Millan guffawed. "We can play this all night, newbie. I'm not going anywhere!"

Two more shots split the night. Something hot seared down his left calf. He clamped his lips against the pain and rolled again. But this time, he hit a corpse. He couldn't roll any further without lifting himself off the floor. Pain bit into his leg, and panic rose in his chest.

He took a deep breath and turned options over in his mind. Another wild flurry of firing would be a waste. He had the advantage of higher ground, but he couldn't see any targets. He cursed his lack of flares again.

Millan jeered. "Five bodies, plus Irvana's little invention. I'm guessing things are pretty cramped up there, am I right?"

The jeering worked. An image flashed in his mind of the cramped platform surrounded on three sides by a sheer drop. He forced himself to dismiss it before it loosened his hands.

"I'll tell you what, newbie," said Millan. "If you walk to the top of these stairs, I'll shoot you dead. You can die with dignity, instead of screaming in pain and shitting your suit in terror."

Kasper's leg stung. It felt wet somewhere below his knee. He pushed the thought of infection out of his mind. What did Millan say? These stairs. He said these stairs. He must be near them. If he wasn't, surely he'd have said 'those stairs,' or just 'the stairs.'

He rolled once towards the centre, then inched forwards and returned one hand back to normal. He flexed his fingers, reached towards the convertor, and clamped his eyes shut. The convertor leapt into life, shooting its bright beam straight into the heavens.

The sudden burst of light covered the rooftop. He opened his eyes to a squint and leapt to his haunches. His leg screamed, but there stood Millan, one hand over his eyes and lurching for cover at the platform's edge. Kasper fired.

The first shot sailed over Millan's head. The second glanced off the thick veins spiralling around his neck. He watched the third head towards Millan's chest, then something crashed into him, knocking him flat. The weight fell on him, crushing his lungs and trapping his breath. One bloodshot eye and pale, greasy skin blocked out the entire world. Hot breath covered his face and the stench of rotten meat clogged his throat.

He kicked and pushed, frantic to get his gun up against the thing on top of him. Something clamped onto his human shoulder. His suit tore like paper and spikes punctured his flesh. He cried out and thrashed to get free, but the thing pinned him to the floor.

Pain and terror overwhelmed him. His free hand flailed at the back of the creature as it bit harder and found bone. Then something cracked. He screamed and banged the floor. A hard lump jabbed painfully into his palm. He gripped it. The bolt from the convertor. He roared and slammed it towards the face in front of him. The thing roared in reply, and warm liquid spurted onto Kasper's brow.

The grip on his shoulder weakened, and the weight shifted. He pulled his gun hand free, twisted, and fired a burst somewhere into the weight on top of him. The jolt cracked his elbow into the floor. Warmth flowed over his gun arm, choking him with the stench of innards. The thing growled, spluttered, and lay still.

He tried to push it clear, terrified of what might come next, but the pain in his shoulder made his head spin. Gritting his teeth, he hauled himself from under the body and got to his feet. Before he could straighten, his head span again and he fell backwards, landing hard on the ground. He bit back a yell and dragged his weapon across the ground to cover the stairs.

Somewhere within the darkness, Millan wanted to kill him. Either with his own hand, or with his army of beasts. For the first time, Kasper thought it would be easier to throw himself over the edge.

Irvana had sent him up here as a decoy. He'd done more than she thought he could. He'd completed his mission, played his part. It was more than anyone had expected. They'd be long gone by now. Alis and Prue would be safe. He was supposed to die. Let Millan and his beasts come.

But the thought of Alis made him sad. He wanted to see her again. He wanted to ask about her wounds, and hear her tell him to shut up and focus. What would she say about him reaching the top of the tower? And kicking a ghost right off the side of the building! She'd laugh out loud at that.

If he left her now, he'd miss all those good things. He tried to get used to the pain. If he had to die, he would fight until the moment it happened.

He blurred his free hand into a cutter, still fresh in his mind from slicing through the convertor's bolts. He ran the hot blade of the laser swiftly over the beast's body beside him. It moved too fast to cut the clothing, but was hot enough to ignite it.

Flames sprang from the surface, throwing a stuttering orange glow across the platform and chasing shadows away from the steps. He trained his gun on Millan's last hiding place and hauled himself clear of the fire with the elbow of his good arm. Biting back against the pain, he reached the edge and peered down.

Beneath him, Millan's body lay partly hidden by shadow, and completely still. Dull orange light from the fire danced across the shiny sinews of his mutated face. He coughed once, and moaned. Kasper shifted his gun hand and let it hang over the edge.

Millan turned his head to look up at him. His weapon came up slowly, and Kasper pulled back out of sight, leaving his own gun hand hanging over the edge. A shot bounced off the railing beside him, flying harmlessly into the night.

Millan called up to him, his voice weaker now. "You're all dead, newbie. You can't—"

Kasper fired his weapon. He emptied a burst of rapid fire directly into Millan's body. The effort knocked the breath out of him. He waited a moment, then looked back over the edge.

On the ground below, Millan's arms lay straight out on either side of him, his eyes wide and staring at the cloud above. Relief washed over Kasper, and with it came muscle spasms across his chest and shoulders. He moaned and slumped onto his back.

Behind him, the last of the cloth fell away from the beast, and the fire died out. Shadows crept back towards the platform. He blurred his hands back to normal, and gripped his left index finger with his right hand. In one sharp jerk, he snapped it backwards, then held it over his mouth.

The small meditab dropped onto his tongue. It would take more than a single miracle tablet to repair a broken shoulder, but it would help with everything else. He made it to his knees, then used the handrail of the stairs to pull himself to his feet. He took a last look at Millan's shattered body, then staggered back to retrieve the convertor.

Chapter Forty-nine

Kasper held his breath while three enormous figures shambled past him. He relaxed and quietly thanked the tower's architect for the wide niches in the corridor walls. What had once been the latest fashion in interior design now served as a hiding place whenever he heard someone approaching.

The corridor ran through the building in a spiral, placing him on a never-ending left-hand bend as he worked his way further down the inside of the tower. The spiral had its advantages. He hugged the wall to his left, giving his body plenty of cover, while his right hand had two short barrels pointing towards anything that might come at him.

The pain in his shoulder knocked the breath from him every few metres, and he had to stop to let it pass. But it felt less intense each time. Somewhere in his veins, the meditab was doing its work.

He reached the fourth floor and listened for signs of the others in the jump room ahead. No gunfire. No shouting. His stomach dropped. He had expected to hear some hint that they were in position. Maybe they'd jumped without him, or maybe they 'hadn't made it this far.

He reached the smashed doors of the room and peered inside. Alis was kneeling beside someone lying prone on the floor, possibly Irvana. He saw Prue's hair sticking up from behind an upturned table, shifting as she moved her head. A single warm wave of relief filled his veins, and he stepped over the threshold.

Alis brought her weapon up, then let it drop into her lap. He saw her eyes widen, and the delight spread across her face. "Kass!"

He realised he had the same delight spread across his own face. "Hey. Are you OK?"

She jumped to her feet, hurried towards him, and gripped him in a hug that started at her forehead and finished at her toes. Her warm body slotted so neatly against his that she felt like a lost half returning to where it belonged.

He wondered if she would raise her mouth to his, but she pulled her head away and stared into his face. He noticed her eyes looked tired.

"I thought you'd be killed up there," she said. "She just left you. She wasn't going to wait, so I—"

Alis waved a hand towards Irvana, lying limp on the ground. Before Kasper could speak, Prue bashed into his side and gripped him around his waist. "Kass! Guess what? Alis hit Irvana and she fell over my legs. She's hurt her head."

Alis shook her head slowly. "She's ok. She's coming around. It doesn't look serious. She'll have a bastard of a headache, though."

As if on cue, Irvana shifted and raised a hand to her head.

Kasper struggled to make sense of what had happened. "You hit her?"

Alis shrugged. "Only after she nearly broke my arm. Anyway, she lied to us. She used you to buy time. That wasn't what we agreed." She looked up at him and reached for his hand. "I wasn't going to leave you behind, was I?"

Kasper smiled. A warm glow filled his chest. Nearby, Irvana moaned and lifted herself to her knees. She held her head in both hands and rubbed her temples. When her fingers hit the head wound, she cursed and carefully felt the size of it.

Kasper removed the harness and set the convertor down on the floor. He crouched beside Irvana, level with her face. She frowned and rubbed at her eyes. He couldn't tell if that was a response to the pain in her head, or confusion at seeing her decoy alive and well.

He spoke slowly, giving weight to each word. "I did it. I made it to the roof and killed the cloud."

Irvana shook the frown from her face, blinked twice, then grinned at him. "So, the plan worked."

Kasper didn't return her grin. "Was that really your plan?"

Irvana sighed and pushed herself to her feet. She tottered slightly and shot out a hand to steady herself on the upturned tables.

She looked at Alis like a mother might look at a troublesome child. "Thank you for that, Alis. Now there's two of us with head injuries."

Alis didn't reply. Irvana stretched, patted Kasper on the arm, then walked over to the portal. "You're right. There was more than one plan." She focused her attention on a bunch of cables hanging from the metal frame. "There's always more than one answer to any problem."

Kasper felt like he should be angry—outraged at how she'd thrown him to the wolves outside, just to distract them all while she worked. But he didn't feel angry. He felt nothing. They were at war and, if they were all honest, they had come here not knowing whether they'd leave. He'd risen to the challenge and won.

Alis, on the other hand, felt outrage enough for both of them. "What do you mean, two plans? Who did you share them with?!"

Irvana stayed focused on the portal. "Do we need to discuss this again?"

Alis opened her mouth, but a shriek sounded from the corridor and she snapped it shut. Another shriek came, followed by a growl and padding footsteps.

"Get down," she said.

They dived behind the tabletops. Kasper peered over their barrier and watched two heavy-set creatures lope through the broken doorway. Their clothes hung in rags, revealing black fur clumped over sinewed arms.

Both held makeshift clubs, and their heavy jaws wagged as they surveyed the room. As he watched, they spotted the lights on the portal and shambled towards him.

He ducked back down and whispered to the others. "Two of the large ones. They're coming towards us."

Alis blurred a barrel. Irvana shook her head and held a finger to her lips. She raised a long blade where her hand had been a moment ago. Alis smiled. On the other side of the tables, the footsteps drew nearer.

Kasper stared at the blade. The edge of it seemed to glow slightly, as though reflecting a nearby light. He rubbed at his eyes.

Irvana was staring, too. "What—"

The glow travelled down the blade towards her arm, leaving only empty space behind it. Irvana screwed up her face and shook her arm, as if trying to get rid of an insect. But the glow kept the same slow pace up her wrist, leaving nothing but air in its wake.

Irvana screamed.

"Oh no. Oh no," said Alis.

She jumped to her feet. Kasper heard two shots, then the howls that split the air. He jumped up and steadied his weapon on the edge of the table. But the sight in front of him made him stop.

One creature lay still on the ground. The other flapped on the floor, trying to crawl towards the tables. Alis had remembered the weak spots from their last encounter and brought it down easily. But now she was ignoring it. Instead, she poured everything she had into the doorway.

Kasper's eyes followed the bright shots streaming towards her target. A ghost stood on the threshold, dressed in a dark suit and surrounded by a rolling storm of blue flames. Each of Alis's shots disappeared without a trace into the raging blue surface, like rain falling into the sea.

The ghost stared at them with no hint of satisfaction or pain. Kasper wondered if it was actually a man. It looked like the same glowing figure he'd swept off the tower with the oilbat, but he did not know if it was a being, or a machine. Surely a being would have spoken by now.

Irvana screamed and writhed on the floor, flapping her arm to dislodge whatever was eating it. But her arm was shorter now, nothing more than a stump cut off at the elbow. "NO! Get out of my head!" she yelled.

The line of blue light crept past her joint and worked its way up her bicep. With her other hand, she jabbed her finger frantically towards the door. "Kill it, kill it!"

Alis ducked behind the tables to reload. The ghost strode a few paces into the room. The heat hit them like a tide, turning the air dry and forcing them down further behind the tables. A thought pushed its way into Kasper's head. He could almost hear it in his brain.

Leave her.

He stared down at Irvana as she scrambled to get free of the curse creeping higher towards her shoulder. He thought of his long climb up the tower and the glowing attacker drawing closer from below. Without the oilbat, the same bone-eating light could have swept over him on the wall. But Irvana had put him there. She had written him off. Left him to die.

Leave her.

Irvana screamed at him. He could see her mouth forming words, but couldn't hear what she said. Someone gripped his arm and shook it hard.

"Kass! Kass!"

He looked at the hand, realised it belonged to Alis, and snapped his head up to look at her.

"Get a grip!" she said.

He looked at her mouth. Her lips looked soft. He remembered the feel of them on his own. He had a feeling he should do something.

Shooting will not help.

He watched Alis pull her hand back and send it flying towards him. An explosion rocked one side of his face. It thudded deep in his skull and stung sharply across his skin.

"FOCUS!" she yelled.

He raised his hand and rubbed at the warmth of the slap on his cheek. He shook his head. "I-"

She clamped his shoulders and shook him until his head jolted backwards and forwards. "Push back! Push it out of your head."

He felt something like fog moving in his mind. Not fog, more like a cloud. That bastard cloud. He pushed it from his thoughts.

He blurred his hands and grinned at Alis. "OK".

He sprinted to the right, strafing as he went. Flames raged, dominating the shots, turning them to vapour. He gritted his teeth against the heat and kept running, constantly probing and hoping for an opening.

He heard Prue scream above the noise. He was too far away to see her, but he saw the creature Alis had wounded earlier drag itself behind the tabletops. The ghost kept walking towards them. A moment passed, then Alis sprung up and pointed her arm at the floor. Her shoulder jolted once and she paused, her eyes fixed on a spot hidden from view.

The ghost drew closer to the barrier and raised his arm. Kasper shouted. Alis dived for cover. A surge of blue whipped from the hand, smashing into the steel tabletops. They took the blast and held, but the force opened narrow gaps between them. Another blast hit them. This time, they separated completely.

Kasper saw Alis and Prue race into cover, but with the tables sitting wide apart, there wasn't much of a barrier left. Through the gaps, he saw Irvana shaking on the floor, her face contorted in horror.

He reached the broken doorway and stood directly behind the glowing blue ghost. Blurring a wide barrel, he took aim at the centre of its upper back. He breathed out and fired three fast, heavy charges into the same spot.

The first charge disappeared into the flames. The second struck something but faded to nothing. But the third detonated, forcing back the flames and bringing the being to a halt. Kasper had a second to feel a twinge of success before the flames rushed towards him. They hit him hard in the chest, knocking him through the door and out into the corridor.

Pain shot through his chest. The floor smashed into his back, punching the air from his lungs. He struggled to get his breath and yelled at the ceiling above, more in anger than in pain. It took all his strength to lift himself up and find his feet. Inside the jump room, the ghost moved closer to the upturned tables. Beyond the remains of the barrier, the portal shone like a huge birthday gift.

He forced himself back into the room, and raised his weapons. Before he could fire, a bright white light exploded from somewhere behind the tables. It filled the room, searing into his eyes, forcing him to clamp them shut. He shielded his face with his forearm and squinted to see where to shoot.

The ghost stopped. The flames thrashed wildly, growing brighter, and shifting from deep blue to white. Through his half-closed eyes, Kasper watched them grow thin and evaporate.

The ghost turned its back on the light and walked rapidly towards the door. It looked small in the room without its flames—just another person, no bigger or more threatening than anyone else.

Kasper stayed rooted to the spot, his weapons up. He noticed the ghost's face had changed. Its skin sagged over its bones like cloth. The cheeks hung low, narrowing its face, pulling its eyes wide and baring its gums.

Kasper raised his other arm, two short barrels still sitting firmly in place at the end. The ghost was changing now, growing lighter with every step. Its hands and face paled, and the pink outline of the portal behind it shone through its cheeks. Kasper lowered his weapon. The ghost's head collapsed inwards and faded to vapour. Its empty suit dropped to the ground and sent a thin, ghostly trail of pale blue towards the ceiling.

The room fell silent. The air cooled at once, as though the walls had refused to absorb the heat, leaving it with no choice but to vanish. From behind the scattered tables, he heard voices. He walked towards them and heard Alis giggling. "Prue, you're incredible!" she said.

He reached them and saw Prue kneeling on the floor. Her hands still resting on the overturned convertor. Her eyes were wide, and she looked pleased, although perhaps a little confused, too.

Alis shook Prue's shoulder playfully. "How did you know how to do that?"

Prue looked around, shy under Alis's praise. "Irvana told Rikka, and I remembered it."

Kasper looked from the convertor to the empty suit lying on the floor. "You did that, Prue?"

She nodded, shaking her curls. A mighty, fiery demon, impervious to gunfire, reduced to nothing but steam by a small girl. The idea made him laugh. Alis joined in and laughed again.

Prue flushed red and laughed with them. He realised he hadn't seen her laugh since Charnell died. Her life over the last few weeks had been a chain of one terrifying event after another. Seeing her laugh now felt delightful.

A groan came from Irvana, lying a few feet away. Her heels banged against the ground. On one side of her face, her gums and teeth showed through her cheek. Higher up, part of her skull was missing, showing the edge of her eye socket and the melted surface of her modified eyeball.

Alis went to her side. "Talk to me. Can you stand?"

Irvana's body shook, and she moaned again. Her voice came out thin and gravelled. "Bastard. That bastard."

Kasper looked down at her side. It looked as though parts of her had been erased. The light had eaten her arm away completely, moved across her shoulder, then up onto her face. In its wake, it had cauterized the wound, leaving nothing behind, not even blood. Perhaps it was deliberate, the glowing people's way of keeping their victim alive to suffer the horror for as long as possible.

He realised she was too badly hurt to stand. "We'll need to carry her."

Alis nodded. "OK. First let's get this portal online."

They examined the cables and lights on the outer rim of the machine. Kasper knew how to use a portal with a jump pass but did not understand how it did what it did, least of all how to fix it when it didn't do what it should.

He pulled the diviner from his pocket, opened the leather pouch, and pulled out the passes. He found the contact plate and waved a pass slowly in front of it. The portal didn't respond.

"It won't be that easy," said Alis. "Besides, we've got two passes and there are four of us, how's that going to work, anyway?"

He put the passes away and placed the diviner's package on the edge of the nearest table. "OK, fine. So, what's your idea?"

Alis shrugged. "I'm still thinking. I know zero about fixing jump portals. And I'm guessing from that pitiful little wave of the pass that you don't know anything about it either."

Behind them, Irvana mumbled something from the floor. They both turned and saw her pointing an unsteady hand towards the far wall. "Power. Boost the power."

Thick cables snaked across the floor from a hole in the wall, ultimately connecting with the curved edge of the portal.

Alis knelt beside her. "You mean it needs more power? We need to get more power to it?"

Irvana dropped her hand but didn't respond.

Alis looked up at Kasper. "She's passed out. We need to check out where those cables come from."

She stood, paused, and raised one hand to her head. She placed the other on a table's edge. "Ah, too quick," she said.

Kasper moved towards her and gripped the top of her arm, peering into her face. "Are you OK?"

She rolled her eyes. "No, I'm not OK. My head span. I need to sit."

He fumbled an attempt to help her sit down, and she ended up shrugging him clear of her so she could do it herself. She leaned back next to Prue and rested her head on a table leg.

He looked at the three of them, then over at the cables disappearing into the far wall. "I'll go and check them out."

He dragged the tables back into their defensive position around the group. The screeching of metal on the floor could have attracted unwanted attention, but he barely noticed the sound. He just wanted them all to jump out of this place as fast as they could.

Irvana lay unconscious at the feet of Prue and Alis. Prue looked alert, but Alis looked like she, too, might lose consciousness. He shifted the convertor to the end of the tabletops, pointed it at the door and waved for Prue to come and join him. She crawled over and sat beside him like an obedient puppy.

He motioned towards the broken doorway. "I'm going out there for a minute. You keep one eye on the door, OK? If anything comes through it that isn't me, you shoot it with this, just like you did before. Right?"

She nodded and smiled, buoyed up from her last shot with the same weapon. "Sure."

He headed for the door, his hands snapping back against his wrists as he went. Nothing moved in the corridor outside the room. He had half-expected a horde to be lying in wait, but he realised they had no leader. Millan was dead, the glowing man was dead. Unless something came along of its own accord, they were unlikely to have any trouble for a while.

Satisfied with the silence, he moved up the sloping corridor and found the next doorway on the same side of the tower. It was narrow, like a service entrance. It made sense to him that the architects would place power circuits in small rooms. He chose his angle and shot the mechanism. The door slid aside, and he stepped over the threshold.

The room was empty. In the far corner, where the thick portal cables should have appeared through the wall, the surface sat naked and unmarked. Confused, he walked over to it and inspected the wall for the outline of a hatch or a release pad. Nothing. He tapped it with the barrel of his weapon. It sounded no different to walls anywhere else. He cursed and left the room, deciding to examine the cables from the other side of the wall.

As he stepped into the corridor, he heard a loud swoosh from the room ahead. He stopped for a moment, uncertain whether to trust what he'd heard. It sounded again, and his stomach dropped. He broke into a sprint. Shouting reached him and he dashed through the doorway.

Ahead of him, behind the tables, the portal crackled with life. The centre swirled and shone like liquid gold. Within it, a one-armed woman and a small girl faded from view.

He raced across the floor, grabbed Alis, and heaved her off the ground. The portal dimmed, and he bounded towards it, straining everything he had to reach it before it closed.

In front of him, the swirling centre slowed to a halt and turned solid. The pink garland around its edge fell dark. He stared, unable for a moment to grasp how the machine could be an entrance one minute and a wall the next.

He felt the portal's cold denial inches from his face. A mixture of panic and rejection rose in his chest. "She said get power."

"Oh no, no, no," said Alis. She stood, swayed a little, then hammered her fist on the dead machine. "She said to wait until they were through! She said to wait!"

Kasper looked around for the diviner. The pouch lay nearby, as flat and empty as the suit lying near the doorway. "She used both the passes and left."

Alis thrust the flat of her hand at the portal. "She said we wouldn't need them. She said she could get us all through without them."

Kasper shook his head. "She lied."

The room around him felt wide and cold. He pictured the tower from above, a dark shaft thrust into the ground at the centre of miles and miles of decaying buildings and streets. Within that gloom lurked hundreds of desperate, dying people, poisoned by the air and growing into something less human, and more willing to do anything to survive.

He placed his hand on Alis's shoulder. She turned to him and he moved his hand to the base of her neck. He pushed his lips against hers. She returned the kiss, then rested her forehead against his.

He took a deep breath. "We need to focus. Let's get moving."

Continue the story

Follow Kasper and Alis as they try to find their way back to Prue and uncover Irvana's plan, in **Angel Rising** (Book 2 of the Broken Heavens).

Also By Richard Canning

A Message from the Author

Hi – Thank you very much for choosing to read Dark Variant. I hope you enjoyed it. It took me a long time to write and to get it to the point where I could launch it into the world, so I'm delighted it found its way into your hands and onto your bookshelf. It would be great if you could leave me a quick review and tell me what you thought of it.

My own story is very normal compared to the characters in my book. I grew up in the east of England, loving action & adventure stories in films, TV, comics and books. I particularly loved science fiction and their different ideas about existence and ethics led me to study philosophy and politics at university. After that, I worked as a teacher, technology consultant and most recently for a non-profit charitable trust of thousands of people.

Nowadays, I live in England with my wife, five children and four chickens. I write books for the joy of creating new worlds and characters, and to entertain and delight people with fresh stories. If you'd like to say hello, you can always find me at richardjcanning.com.

Printed in Great Britain
by Amazon

83093136R00246